Claudia lives in Dublin where she now works as a full-time writer; the only job, she reckons, where you can wear pyjamas, stare out the window all day and still get paid. Two of her previous books, *Remind Me Again Why I Need a Man* and *I Never Fancied Him Anyway*, have been optioned for a TV series (Fox television) and a film respectively. She is currently hassling producers for a walk-on part and is hoping they might just throw in a free outfit too.

Also by Claudia Carroll

HE LOVES ME NOT . . . HE LOVES ME
THE LAST OF THE GREAT ROMANTICS
REMIND ME AGAIN WHY I NEED A MAN
I NEVER FANCIED HIM ANYWAY
DO YOU WANT TO KNOW A SECRET?

If This Is Paradise, I Want My Money Back

Claudia Carroll

TRANSWORLD IRELAND

TRANSWORLD IRELAND
an imprint of The Random House Group Limited
20 Vauxhall Bridge Road, London SW1V 2SA
www.rbooks.co.uk

IF THIS IS PARADISE, I WANT MY MONEY BACK!
A TRANSWORLD IRELAND BOOK: 9781848270268

First published in Great Britain
in 2009 by Transworld Ireland
Transworld Ireland paperback edition published 2010

Addresses for Random House Group Ltd companies outside the UK
can be found at: www.randomhouse.co.uk
The Random House Group Ltd Reg. No. 954009

The Random House Group Limited supports The Forest Stewardship
Council (FSC), the leading international forest certification organization.
All our titles that are printed on Greenpeace approved FSC certified paper
carry the FSC logo. Our paper procurement policy can be found at
www.rbooks/environment

Typeset in 12½/15½pt Bembo by
Kestrel Data, Exeter, Devon.
Printed in the UK by
CPI Cox & Wyman, Reading, RG1 8EX.

2 4 6 8 10 9 7 5 3

For Pat Kinevane.

With love and thanks for his endless patience, wisdom and humour during late-night phone calls when I'm just about ready to smash the computer up against a wall.

I honestly don't know what I'd do without you.

Chapter One

In relationships, there are two types of women. The ones who bail at the first sign of trouble, and the ones who stick with it, if only just to see exactly how bumpy the road ahead will get.

I belong to the second kind.

Which I suppose, is how I ended up here. Not that I've the first clue where the hell I am, exactly, all I know is that it's very peaceful, muffled, calm and so, so still. Nothing but me and my own thoughts, which is kind of nice. In fact, I *like* it down here. It's almost like being on a spa break, minus the treatments and the annoying pan-pipe music.

There must be countless fathoms of air up above, between me and that other world, the one that I don't think I've actually left; I'm just taking a little commercial break. Just till I get my head together and sort out the mess I'm in, that's all. The thing is, though, the longer

I'm down here, undisturbed and silent, the less I want to go back.

Not that that's stopping them. My mother, sister, VBF Fiona – in fact just about everyone I've ever met in my entire life – seem to be determined to drag me out of this. Someone must have told them that people in my state respond to stimulation, that hearing is the last sense to go, and that, just by chatting to me, or playing music or doing some heavy-duty emotional cheerleading, there's a chance they might be able to haul me back up from the depths.

Between the whole lot of them, they have me demented.

I'm not kidding, it's almost like there's a competition going on: who'll be The One To Bring Me Round? They're at it day and night, telling me all the minutiae of everything that's going on in the outside world; and I really do mean everything, from Mum describing at length the lovely banana soufflé Delia Smith made on TV last night, to Fiona filling me in about this guy she met on Facebook who, honest to God, told her on date one that what he's looking for in a woman is a female John Wayne. Highly unsuitable, but then given what's happened to me, who am I to pass judgement when it comes to useless men? Besides, I think her plan is to try and squeeze a few more dates out of him, like gathering nuts for the winter. Fiona's a bit like a sex camel: she can store up romantic encounters and make them last for months on end.

Mum, I don't care if Delia says it's now OK to cheat, and Fiona, you have to stop thinking you'll find true love on the net, otherwise everyone is going to start calling you Facebook Fi.

I know I must be in a really bad way by how infuriatingly upbeat they're all being around me, particularly Mum, who's starting to sound more relentlessly cheery than a *Blue Peter* presenter trying to put you in a good mood. Then there's the music they keep playing over and over again, stuff they insist is my favourite, but it isn't. It's all stuff *they* like. Mum has clearly decided that I love all these Rat Pack, Vegas-y type songs, and I'm not messing, if I have to listen to 'My Way' once more, I'm staying down here for good.

You're only playing these because they remind you of Dad, that's all. He loved Frank Sinatra, and his party piece was always . . .

'You're nobody till somebody loves you,' I can hear Mum sighing softly, wistfully. But then her voice always shifts gear whenever she talks about Dad. 'I heard it on the car radio when I was driving to the hospital just now, and, do you know, to this day it still chokes me up. I'll never forget your father singing that song to me on our silver wedding anniversary. 'Course you were only about fourteen or so . . .'

I remember, Mum.

'He'd such a beautiful singing voice. Everyone said he could have been a professional, you know, if God hadn't taken him so young. Anyway, love, good news and bad. The bad news is your car is a complete write-off . . .'

Least of my worries. You didn't see the knickers I was wearing when they brought me in here. Up to my collarbone and the colour of wet cement.

'But the good news is that a very helpful girl from the insurance company rang me, and, well, in light of what's happened, she said you're completely covered for a nice new car when you get out of here, and when you're all back to normal again.'

If there's one thing I love about you, Mum, it's your boundless optimism.

'Something a lot safer this time, though, do you hear me now, Charlotte? A Toyota Yaris would be just the thing. Or maybe you could go completely mad and splash out on a lovely, sensible Ford Ka. And if you ever even think about going above fifteen miles an hour, you'll have me to answer to. I am not going through all of this worry again as long as I live.'

Oh, come on, it was an accident; it's not like I did it on purpose.

'Anyway, I got chatting to that very handsome doctor from Ghana yesterday, don't ask me to pronounce his name, but he said the next few days are critical, and all going well, the swelling to the brain should die down a bit. Some long word he used to describe it, I can't remember. So I was asking Sarah, the night nurse who was on duty last night, all about him. Divorced, it seems, with two kids, but definitely not seeing anyone. Now *that's* the kind of fella I'd love to see you with.'

I'm lying here in a coma and you're trying to fix me up?

'The other thing is, love, they did mention something about long-term damage, but don't you worry, I have that all covered. I'm doing three separate novenas, one to Our Lady, because she never lets me down, one to Saint John Licci, who's the patron saint of head injuries apparently . . . did you know they had a separate saint for that? So your Auntie Anne was telling me, although I've a feeling she might have got him mixed up with that saint that's in charge of hangovers. Anyway, I'm doing my magic, fail-safe novena to Saint Jude as well, just so we're really on the safe side . . .'

She chatters on, and God love her, I know she must really be climbing the walls about me, because this is what she does whenever she's worried out of her mind: fills air with words. And there's nothing I can do to reassure her or to let her know that I'm grand really, I'm just taking a bit of time out, that's all. So down I float again, sinking all the way back to the lovely, restful depths. I feel no pain here, not a single thing; I'm just peaceful and warm and completely blissed out. Better

11

than being on a tropical island any day. In fact, throw in a margarita, a spray tan, and a good trashy novel, and I could almost be in heaven.

They must have me on some *really* serious class A drugs.

I don't know how long has passed, but I come back up when I get a sense that Fiona's here. I know it's her because I'd swear I can get a smell of cheese and onion Pringles, and she's the only person I know who always carries an emergency stash of crisps on her person at all times. Fiona's a secondary-school teacher (English and History, Higher Level, if you don't mind), and spends so much of her spare time correcting essays with titles like 'Heathcliff is a man more sinned against than sinning, discuss', that she never gets time to actually sit down to a proper meal eaten off a plate, like anyone normal. So either she just eats on the go, or else plonked at home in front of her computer, usually scouring Facebook looking for fellas.

She sounds so frazzled that my heart goes out to her.

'. . . James has rung loads of times, he's really up the walls with worry about you, Charlotte, I've never seen him this strung out. He's gone up a fair few percentage points in my estimation after this, I can tell you. He mentioned something about the two of you having a bit of a tiff the night of the accident?'

No, honey, we didn't have a bit of a tiff. It would be more accurate to say the bastard ripped my still-beating heart out, flung it against a wall, and then, as cool as a fish's fart, demanded to know exactly how soon I could move out of the house.

Sorry, that's HIS house, lest we forget.

'. . . in fact, he said he'd try to get in to see you this evening . . .'

Great, all I need.

Then I think Mum must be back in the room by the skilled way that Fiona effortlessly switches the subject, putting on her best 'now, pay attention' classroom voice.

'Anyway, as I was saying, I really liked this guy's photo and profile, so we swapped numbers, and at the moment our phone-call frequency is twice a week, which I think is promising. I can definitely tell by his basic level of courtesy that he's interested. And I know you hate me picking up fellas online, Charlotte, but let's face it, I now have cellulite and everyone knows that's God's way of telling you it's time to settle down.'

Mum doesn't even like James's name being mentioned in front of her.

Which should tell you a lot. And believe me, at this stage she'd gladly put up with any aul eejit, just to see me happy and settled. Any eejit barring James Kane, that is. In fact, only the other day she was unsubtly telling me that her organic vegetable delivery man is now newly separated. He's fifty, by the way, and has about three teeth in his head.

Don't get me wrong, my family and friends are all perfectly nice to James – to his face that is – but deep down, I've always suspected they were only tolerating him for my sake. Then, on his side, he doesn't really have *any* pals, only 'second-string friends and interested parties', as he puts it himself. Yet another warning sign I chose to ignore. In fact, with misguided loyalty, I always put this down to a touch of the green-eyed monster, and figured that it must be hard for anyone to be matey with Mr Big Successful Hotshot Producer-Pants with movie deals hanging out of him, and with all his talk about nights on the town with Colin Farrell, then Bono owing him fifty euro for the taxi-fare home. Besides, I used to think, no one gets to the adorable, sweet, private side to him that I do. If you only knew the sheer amount of time I spent going, 'Us, problems? Ha!'

Then, the night of my accident, I find out, in the worst way imaginable, that everyone else was right and I was wrong. Turns out the guy was a horse's arse all along.

And there's something else, too. Something I'm racking my brains to remember, but no matter how hard I try, I can't. It's like I'm grasping through fog from the haziest depths of my poor befuddled brain, desperately trying to unlock something . . . just for the life of me,

I can't think what it is. The more I try to run at it, the more it slips away from me. All I'm certain of is that it's something painful, so painful that I must have locked it away and filed it under, 'To be dealt with at another time, when I am a bit more able to handle sheer, unquantifiable misery.' And now, here I am with nothing else to do but lie in bed all day, and it's gone. Bloody typical. What's worse is that I don't even have the best memory in the world to begin with. I mean, I'm total crap at remembering even little things, and am constantly having to leave Post-its around the house with scribbles on them saying, 'Put out bins. Set Sky Plus to record *Grey's Anatomy*. Buy Cillit Bang.' So trying to remember some major event in my recent life history will be great crack altogether. For God's sake, I could be lying here, racking my brains for months. Might even end up needing hypnosis.

I'm not sure exactly how long I drift off for, but the next thing I know, the room is filled with American accents: two shouty women at first, threatening to rip each other's heads off because one of them has had an affair with the other one's ex-husband, but then some guy starts screaming it from the rooftops that his mother, who he thought was dead, is actually doing a life sentence in prison . . . oh shite, as if I didn't have enough to worry about. *Now* what? Have some lunatic, gatecrashing junkies wandered into the hospital, and are they about to start flinging furniture across the room at each other, over my poor, smashed-up head? Suppose they start ripping up the bedside lockers looking for syringes full of drugs?

My lovely, lovely drugs, the only things that're getting me through all of this.

Then I get a sense that my sister Kate's here. I know it's her by the smell of Estée Lauder Pleasures that always trails obediently around after her.

'Mum, turn off that TV, it could be disturbing her.'

'But it's *Desperate Housewives*! Her favourite programme, love. If that doesn't bring her round I don't know what will.'

'No, I'm putting on some music. Apparently, this song gets a great reaction from unborn babies.'

Next thing I can hear Kate's high heels click-clacking across the floor, followed by a bit of fumbling, then Amy Winehouse's *Back to Black* album, which I love, fills the room.

Thanks, Kate, big improvement on all the Rat Pack stuff Mum had me tortured with. Although I've a strong feeling you're only making that up about foetuses responding to R&B.

I drift off again, but when I come back up, I think it's just me and Kate on our own. I'm fairly sure of that, because she's telling me stuff she'd never in a million years say in front of anyone else, barring that they were in a coma. Kate's very reserved. She's also a bit scary, and right up until she met her husband I don't think she was ever single once in her entire life, something me and Fiona used to look on with awe and envy. Fellas were too terrified of her to break it off, we figured. She's the sensible, slightly bossy older sister that everyone should have in their life, but some of the stuff she's telling me now almost makes me feel like I've turned into a kind of mute confession box.

'. . . so I'm ovulating right now, and, typical, Paul's gone down to the west of Ireland to practise with his bloody atonal band; why he bothers I don't know, all their songs sound equally crappy to me. You know, sometimes I don't think he's taking this seriously at all, I really don't. So I'm giving it another three months and then, that's it, I'm going for IVF, which by the way, only costs about four grand a pop, can you believe it?'

Kate, do you know how lucky you are to have a good man who loves you? Do you know that behind your back, me and Fiona call him Perfect Paul? And all you can do is sit there whingeing about your ovaries.

'. . . and I am so fed up with Mum's heavy hints about how much she's dying to be a grandmother. The other day she asked me was I was putting it off so I could concentrate on "scaling the heights in my career"? I felt like screaming at her, "And what 'career' would that be, exactly?" I'm a part-time receptionist in a health club, for God's sake, and my sole contribution since I started there was to get two new treadmills put in. I only took the bloody gig because I thought I'd easily be pregnant by now, and that it might just suit me to do a doss job. Then on top of everything else, we've to go to a christening next weekend. Which means I get to spend the entire day surrounded by mothers who have at least two perfect kids each, all looking at me with pity, wondering what the hell is wrong with me. Rock bottom, that's where I'm at right now.'

That's your rock bottom? That's my retirement plan. Kate, you're only thirty-three; you've done everything you were supposed to do in life. You've got Perfect Paul and a showroom home. You've a downstairs bathroom that no one's allowed to use because it's so new, and you've a spare room that you probably have the Farrow & Ball nursery-wall colours already picked out for. Of course, when the time's right, you'll be a yummy mummy in a four-wheel-drive jeep, along with the rest of them. Now go away, I want some peace.

But it's not to be. There's a string of visitors tonight, including my boss, Anna, who smells of stale cigarettes and tells me in a voice like aquarium gravel that all our clients keep asking about me, and when I'm coming back? She's an actor's agent, by the way, and I'm her lowly assistant, which basically means she swans off to opening nights and award shows with all her big-name actors, then spends the next day lying in bed with a minging hangover while I hold the fort and spend my time trying to convince her non-A-list clients that things are just really quiet right now, but that their big break is only around the corner.

'. . . and you know, the phone hasn't stopped ringing once since you've been out. It's literally been non-stop.'

It always is, Anna. You're just never there, that's all.

'All these actors I haven't spoken to in months demanding to know why they haven't been seen for that Henry the Eighth series. Quite snippy with me, too, some of them, as if I hadn't enough on my plate . . .'

You have to be nice to them. For some of these people, getting caught on a security camera is not exactly the kind of media coverage they're looking for. Believe it or not.

'. . . then there's that big commercial for some detergent that's casting next week, and I haven't a clue where you keep all the CV shots . . .'

In the CV filing cabinet, in a big drawer with 'CV shots' written in black and white across it. Not brain surgery, Anna.

'. . . I mean, the day-to-day running of the office isn't really my thing. I'm more the face of the business, really . . .'

Allow me to translate. This means that while you take your favoured clients out for afternoon-long, boozy lunches, I actually do all the donkey work for you. For roughly about a third of what you should be paying me.

'So I really need you back, Charlotte. The place is falling apart without you.'

You know what? Not tempting. Go hire yourself a temp and leave me alone. Some of us have real problems, and compared with me, your life is Euro Disney.

God, this coma is making me an awful lot braver than I normally would be.

More noise and chat and kerfuffle, almost like there's a little social gathering going on all around me that I'm the reason for, but not a part of. The noise is getting louder and louder, and I'm hearing a cacophony of voices all chattering over me, then, suddenly, without warning . . . total and utter silence.

I'm just thinking that it's about time some bossy nurse came in and told them all to keep it down to a dull roar, but then I get the strongest whiff of Burberry aftershave and there's only one person I know who wears that . . . oh shit, I do not believe this.

It's him. James.

Has to be. I'd know even by the way the temperature in the room has dropped by about twenty degrees. Here's me in a coma, and I can still sense the tension. There's a rustle of cellophane and a smell of lilies, and I can hear Anna being nice to him and saying something about how divine the flowers are, but then she was always very skilled at arselicking producers. Next thing, for absolutely no reason, I get a flashback to when we first met.

It's all Anna's fault really: she introduced me to him at a film festival and I remember immediately writing him off into the mad, bad and dangerous to know category. Charisma you could surf on, but I just instinctively knew he was the type of fella that, if you were dating him, you'd probably end up on about a hundred milligrams of Valium a day. Back then, he wore a leather jacket, rode a Harley and looked a bit like James Dean, if he'd ever made it to his thirties. Mean, moody and magnificent. A hard dog to keep on the porch, as Hillary Clinton once famously said about Bill. Somehow always managed to look like he'd just been in a fight. There was also a rumour doing the rounds about him that he'd once thrown a sofa over a balcony and into the pool of some five-star hotel in Cannes, the kind of place where no one says a word, just discreetly adds 'replacement sofa' to the bill.

Yes, I fancied the arse off him, as any woman with a working pulse would, but not for one nanosecond did I ever consider him as nice, suitable boyfriend/potential future husband material; I really, honestly, genuinely was *NOT* interested. In fact, I distinctly remember only googling him once after I first met him. To put this in context, I'd have checked out my horoscope plus this fab website I found for designer knock-off handbags far, *far* more; that's how disinterested I was. Anyway, I sometimes think that must have been part of the turn-on for him. So he did all the running.

Producers persuade, that's what they do. They

persuade actors to star in their movies, then they persuade investors to pay for it, then they persuade the public that it's a smash hit; and that's pretty much the tactic he used on me. Persuaded me to go out with him, then to fall in love with him, then, a ridiculously short time later, to move into his house with him. Like the walking cliché that I am, I really, truly believed that I'd be the one to tame the bad boy and turn him into something cuter than a fluffy little kitten sitting on a sofa watching *Love Actually*. And look where it got me. My God, single women the world over should be made to study my dating history as a lesson in what not, under any circumstances, *ever* to do.

He's very close to me now; I can feel his hand gripping mine, icy cold.

'You look so beautiful, Charlotte.'

Clearly, this is too much for Kate, who's very intolerant of bullshit, 'cos I can hear her snapping back at him. 'James, she has a fractured skull, a dislocated shoulder, forty-eight stitches, a broken fibula, and you think she looks well? Trust me, it's the lighting.'

This is what passes for wit in our family.

'I just can't believe that God could let this happen,' he goes on, I'm guessing for Mum's benefit. In fact, I can almost picture him rearranging his face into a look of religious faux-concern, purely on account of her being here.

'Oh really?' Kate snaps back. 'Haven't you read the Old Testament? He's pretty ruthless.'

Another awkward silence, but by now, I'm actually starting to enjoy them. I mean, here's James stuck in the same room with probably the only three women on the planet who are completely immune to his legendary magnetic appeal. His charm assaults, for the record, come in distinct phases: first he focuses on you so intently with his laser gaze that you tend to forget there's anyone else on the planet; second, he asks keen yet insightful questions, somehow managing to cut right to the heart of whatever the conversation subject-matter is; then, the *pièce de résistance*, he'll manage to unearth something from left field, to make you roar laughing about. I've seen him beguile his way out of a thousand tricky situations with this strategy before, but he won't here, not now, and certainly not in front of this audience. In fact, if it wasn't for the coma, I'd probably be lying here having a great aul titter at his discomfort.

Serves him bloody right.

'You know, you look exhausted, Kate,' he says to her, so sincerely that it's actually disarming. 'And you too, Mrs Grey. You must be worn out with worry. Why not go down to the canteen and have a coffee or a bite to eat? I'll stay here with Charlotte. I'd . . . I'd really love a moment alone with her, but only if that's OK with you all.'

NO! Don't, repeat DO NOT go! I don't want to be left on my own with him!

But he gets his way. Like he always does. After much reluctant mumbling and grabbing of handbags, I hear Mum bristling like a Brillo Pad and very distinctly saying all right then, but that she'll be back in ten minutes, her clear implication being, 'So you'd better be gone by then.'

'And FYI,' is Kate's parting shot, 'I don't mind you coming to see her just this once, but from now on, we'd prefer it if just immediate family visited. Immediate family and Fiona, that is. I'll be round to pick up some of her stuff soon.'

'No problem. Any idea when?'

'Whenever it bloody suits me.'

A door slam, then I know we're alone because he immediately lets go of my hand.

'Charlotte . . . Christ, it's so hard for me to see you like this . . .'

Oh please, do we have to do the movie scene?

'You know, I keep replaying that terrible row in my head and . . . well, I can't help but feel partly responsible for what happened to you.'

Did you just say PARTLY?

'You were so upset when you bolted out of the house that night, and I'm kicking myself for letting you drive off into a bloody thunderstorm, the state you were in . . .'

Good. Hope you kick yourself to death.

'I feel so bad about everything . . .'

Serves you right. In fact, that's the best news I think I've heard all day.

'It's not you, you know, it's me.'

Oh, give me a break. In fact, I'm pretty certain I recognize that line from one of your crappy B movies. Unimaginative bastard.

'I know I should have come to you sooner and told you how I was feeling but . . . well, the thing is, I just hated this cosy coupley existence that we'd settled into, doing the crossword together, fighting over the Sunday supplements, all of that . . . I used to sit beside you on the couch watching reruns of *Lost* for about the thousandth time and thinking, this is not who I am.'

No, of course, you wanted to go back to throwing sofas out of hotel room windows.

'And I know I made a right pig's ear of trying to explain myself the other night, but it's just for a while now, I've been feeling a bit detached from you, and that . . . well . . . that I needed a bit of space . . .'

And that's when it happens. Right then, just as he's spewing on and on and on with more of his self-justification shite.

Suddenly, and completely without warning, memories begin to surface. The night of the accident, me driving home, the rumour having reached me in work.

Now I remember.

Heavy traffic, rain pelting, a dark sky, the windscreen wipers going full blast, and my heart rate almost keeping pace with them. I remember hot, angry tears stinging at the back of my eyes. Not being able to catch my breath, mouth dry, gulping – and my hands trembling, like I was having a full-blown anxiety attack. I even remember trying to ring his mobile for about the fortieth time, and him not answering. I remember vomit rising at the back of my throat, and willing myself not to be sick, because the only thing I had in the car I could possibly throw up into was an empty tube of Pringles on the passenger seat beside me.

I knew full well there'd be a confrontation when I got home, and was already doing a mental dress-rehearsal of all my arguments well in advance of it. James is brilliant in arguments, and I'm rubbish because I just get emotional; so, like a good prosecution lawyer, I always had to be two steps ahead of him in any row. I even remember making a list in my head of all the reasons why, if what I'd heard *was* true, and if we did break up over it, it mightn't necessarily be the worse thing that could possibly happen to me. I had it all worked out on that long, miserable drive home, all the pros and all the cons.

Like I said, none of my nearest and dearest ever really liked James. In fact, something Fiona said a long time ago came back to haunt me: she predicted that this would all end in tears. Mine, not his. She used to reckon that James's ideal woman was one with no last name. And that his Jack Nicholsonesque grin would unnerve a shark. Plus, after a few glasses of Pinot Grigio, she'd always be at pains to point out that as long as I continued to live in *his* house, under *his* roof, he held all the aces in the relationship. And what did I do? Forgot the first principle of dating: love is blind, but friendship is clairvoyant. I didn't listen to her, and look where it got me.

Funny, but as I sat in the gridlock that wild, stormy night, thinking that if it was true and if this was it, The End for me and him, I remember, in a surge of positivity, making up my mind that I WOULD move on and I WOULD meet someone else. Furthermore, that somehow along the way, I'd set up as a producer myself, and manage to become very rich and successful, and *then* he'd really be sorry. I'd probably end up on the *Late Late Show* and on the *Sunday Times* Rich List, and that'd completely finish him off, given how important money is to him. And, in my little fantasy world, I'd be famous too, so famous that I'd even have my very own stalker, the hallmark of the true celeb. And every time I'd talk to a journalist, I'd graciously tell them that, yes, although I wasted five precious years of my dating life on a worthless, faithless git, I still managed to turn my whole life around and become a huge success, with an adoring husband and kids, and everything I ever wanted out of life. Even if I can only pass for young, gorgeous and nubile in a power cut. Even if I now have a biological clock that, at this stage, honestly might as well have Roman numerals on it and be carved in stone.

Even if right up until that afternoon, I still loved him so much that it physically hurt, like a stab to the heart. Even if I'd invested so much time and trouble into him being The One that now the sheer climb-down involved was wrecking my head. Yes, all right, so maybe he wasn't perfect, but then what guy is? As Fiona says, at the end of the day, they're all bastards; best you can hope to do is try and find a *nice* bastard. And James was perfect for me, or so I thought. The laughs we had together, the silly, private little in-jokes, the mind-blowing sex, the way we seemed to agree on just about everything, even daft stuff like who should win *X Factor* . . .

Seems to be my destiny to be one of those people that nothing ever, *ever* works out for. Electric doors. Self-tanning lotion. ATMs. And now, I can add relationships to the list. Just look at me: I've officially become a walking cautionary tale about what happens when you pay attention to the little voice inside your head that whispers, 'mate for life, mate for life'. Might as well start a support group while I'm at it.

And there's more. There's something else. Something

I'm trying to haul up from the depths of my mind and can't . . . but, whaddya know, right there and then James saves me all the bother by saying it straight out for me.

'. . . please understand, I tried so hard, but there just never seemed to be a right time to sit you down and tell you. You have to believe me. I never set out to fall for Sophie . . .'

And . . . da daa, ladies and gentlemen . . . there it is. I give you . . . The Missing Key. Sophie bleeding Kelly.

I should fill you in.

OK, here goes. Up until the night of the accident, if you'd asked me anything about Sophie Kelly, I'd probably have looked at you and shrugged. She's one of those people that, although mildly irritating, I really wouldn't have had that much to say about either way. But after what's just come flooding back to me like a tsunami, it's a case of . . . how long have you got?

Right then. For starters, she's a rubbish actress anyway, and now that I come to think about it, I heard James say so plenty of times. Definitely. I'm not messing, the girl has about all the dramatic ability and presence of a cutlery drawer. Then there's the small matter of her high-pitched, squeaky voice. Honestly, I'd rather listen to a roomful of computers dialling up an old-fashioned internet connection. In fact, I distinctly remember saying that to James after we saw her last movie, and he categorically agreed with me.

At least I think he did.

I grudgingly have to admit that she is gorgeous, so good-looking that you'd almost think she travelled around the place with her own personal lighting cameraman in tow. She has corkscrew curly blonde hair, big poppy Bette Davis eyes, and is also thin, thin, thin. 'Look, no carbs!' thin. So thin that every time I see her, all I want to do is ram lard down her bony little throat. However, if there are two types of women in this world, those who are out to help each other and those who aren't, then Sophie Kelly definitely belongs to the second kind. You know, the kind of woman who makes you feel that in life's big VIP aftershow party, she's invited and you're not. She's also Different With Men. And, OK, yes, I have on occasion witnessed first-hand her flinging herself at James like some kind of blow-dried missile in slingbacks, but like the gobshite I am, I used to shrug and write it off. She's an actress, I figured, he's a successful producer, and whether I liked it or not, that's how this business works.

I had no woman's intuition. No sixth sense. No clue as to what was to blindside me. And therein lay my downfall. In the space of one short day in my life, I managed to lose everything. Lover, boyfriend, home, even my career. Because much and all as I enjoy my job, in spite of Anna driving me scatty half the time, our agency represents Sophie helium-voice Kelly, and there's just no way on earth I could handle her ringing the office look-ing for auditions, and me having to pretend to be nice to her. Call me a bad loser, but I'd rather lose a limb. Then there's all the clients at the agency. Word would spread like wildfire, I knew, because let's face it, actors have a grapevine that Ernest & Julio Gallo would be proud of.

Pathetic life CV, isn't it? Twenty-eight years on earth, and I managed to make a complete shagging mess of the whole thing. Honest to God, if there was any justice, I should be hauled up in front of the dating police and have my head impaled on a spike as an example to other single women who put up with crap from men. And what would my defence be? That love makes Andrea Bocellis of us all. Brilliant.

And the laugh is, it took a coma for me to be able to see it clearly.

'You have to believe me,' James is still harping on ad nauseam. 'There just never seemed to be a right time. I never set out to fall for Sophie, but you know how it is. You don't look for love, love looks for you . . .'

Yet another line I recognize from some rubbishy TV show you made. One of those ones that was hardly worth the electricity it took to broadcast it. What are you trying to do, anyway, clear your conscience? Or maybe, like the paragon of selfishness that you are, you really only came here to try and make yourself feel better.

Yep, that sounds by far the more likely option.

31

On and on he goes, remorse itself, apoplexy on a plate, the devil made me do it. Honest to God, if I was to actually listen to the utter crap he's coming out with, he'd have me believing that Sophie Kelly chased him, hounded him, boiled a few bunnies along the way, and basically bludgeoned him into submission, while the whole time he behaved like a perfect model of fidelity and gentlemanly decorum, blameless as a choirboy, every now and then pleading, 'Desist from your advances, you harlot, I have a *girlfriend*, I tell you!' Don't get me wrong, I'd really *love* to believe him, but I know it's total and utter shite, so I tune out and sink back down, down, down, letting him ramble on to an empty house.

Wish I could be like Angelina Jolie. You get the impression from her that if Brad Pitt ever left her for someone else, she'd just shrug her shoulders, shove a cigarette through the overblown bee-stung lips, make a blockbuster movie, then move swiftly on with all two dozen of her kids trailing in her wake. Purely to pass the time, I count all the occasions I distinctly remember Kate telling me to dump him. You don't need to put up with all this crap, she used to say. The guy is pure, liquid man-thrax. But I love him, I'd invariably answer, the ultimate defence of the gobshite. Plus, I happen to like monogamy. For starters, you don't have to wax as much.

By the time I drift back up, James is still there, still stinking of Burberry and remorse, still rabbiting on.

'It just sort of happened on that Venice trip for the film festival and now . . . well, I'm pretty certain that she's the right one for me. I'm so, so sorry, Charlotte, I really am.'

No, actually, I'm the one who's sorry. Sorry that I wasted so many precious years on you. Sorry for loving you so much that it hurt, through thick and thin, because, like the trusting eejit that I was, I truly believed that I'd be the one to change you, and we'd spend the rest of our lives together. I'm sorry I didn't listen to my family and friends and the people who really do love me, and who clearly can't bear even to share the same airspace as you. And you know what? No matter how bad death is, it can't be half as bad as lying here and facing up to the fact that my life has been a complete and utter failure in every way.

'Look at you, lying there so peacefully. I wish I knew what you were thinking.'

Trust me, you don't.

Then his phone rings and, typical, he answers. I'm just wishing that some nurse would burst in, snatch it from him and give him a lecture about how you're not supposed to have mobiles in an intensive-care trauma unit for patients with cracked heads when . . .

I do not believe this. It's her. Sophie bloody Kelly ringing him. Even on the other end of a phone, I can still hear that irritating, high-pitched voice.

'Sweetheart, hi!' he says, and his tone has completely brightened. 'No, you're not interrupting anything, I'm just wrapping up a meeting now, nothing important.'

The lie just trips off his tongue so easily you wouldn't believe it.

'I'm dying to get out of here, actually, and I could do with a drink, so yeah, cool, the Four Seasons for a glass of fizz in half an hour sounds perfect. So . . . hmmm . . . what's your big mad rush to get off the phone? Aren't you going to . . . ehh . . . tell me what you're wearing? Come on, you dirty little tease, you know *exactly* what I mean. Under that sexy little black skirt you'd on this morning? In fact, I've a better idea, why don't we skip the drinks and I'll meet you at my place right now? Yeah? Oh, baby, you're the best . . . hey, I love you, too, come on, you know I do . . .'

I think it was that last sentence that was the final nail in my coffin. Because right after that, I remember the following in one terrifying, panicky blur. A monitor attached to me suddenly going into overdrive, buzzers going off, a nurse barking at James to get the immediate family back up here urgently, then a consultant on duty being paged and told there's an emergency. More doors banging open, more monitors beep-beeping, complete pandemonium, hands all over me, the shock of ice-cold metal paddles on my bare chest. Then a sharp electric jolt so forceful that, for a split second, it makes my eyes open just long enough for me to see Mum standing in the corner crying, with a nurse's arm around her, comforting her . . . right before my numb, inert body crashes back down again.

More beep-beeping from monitors, but far, far, slower this time.

Scarily slow.

I hear a strident, panicky sounding man's voice bellowing for everyone to clear the room while they defibrillate again, then another, softer nurse's voice telling Mum, 'Her heart rate's just slowed right down, that's all. Don't worry about this one, she's a fighter! And we're doing everything we can for her.'

Then nothing. Whiteness.

Chapter Two

'Charlotte?'

My eyes are locked tight. Right now, I'm too afraid to open them. Too afraid of what I might find.

'Charlotte, can you hear me?'

A man's voice. Soft and gentle. One I haven't heard in the longest, longest time.

A shiver shoots down my spine, and suddenly I know exactly who it is.

It's my dad.

Slowly, disbelievingly, I open my eyes and . . . there he is, right here beside me, reaching out to take my hand. My darling dad, looking better than I ever remember, so fit and healthy and wearing the same old corduroy trousers and big baggy jumper he used to wear whenever he was pottering around the house, doing bits of DIY, and puncturing holes in my mother's good furniture with a power drill, when he was always at his happiest.

'Dad?' is all I can manage to stammer weakly. 'Dad? Is it . . . is it really you?'

'Shhhh, come on, pet, it's OK. You've been through a terrible time, but it's OK now, shh.'

'But, if you're here, then . . . then . . . I must be . . .'

'Plenty of time for that later, pet. For now, all you need to know is that you're safe.'

I'm barely able to take it all in, and the next thing I know it's all just too much. Everything comes crashing down on top of me: James and the accident, and the last few awful days, and whatever happened at the hospital just now, and suddenly, out of nowhere, I'm sobbing helplessly like a child. He folds me in his arms, just as he used to do when I was little, his arms tightly wrapped around mine.

'It's OK, Charlotte, I'm here. I've been here with you the whole time. And nothing bad will ever happen to you again, I promise, pet.'

Pet. I forgot the way he always used to call me pet. I forgot so much: the smell of him, his soft, gentle voice, the way he always managed to look a bit like an off-duty golfing priest. (Dad found his style back in 1982 and never saw any reason to change it since.) And how much taller and broader he seems, just like in the photo I have of him, taken in his prime, way back in his rugby-playing days, years before he got ill and wasted away to nothing.

'Dad . . . Dad . . .' I keep sobbing over and over, half-hysterical, half-overjoyed just to see him again. 'But . . . but . . . if I'm here with you, then it must mean that I . . . that I just . . .'

I can't even bring myself to finish that sentence.

But I must be dead, I've got to be.

Dear Jaysus. Like things weren't bad enough?

I think about Mum and Kate and Fiona, and what they must all be going through right now, right at this very moment. And I honestly think the heartbreak and anguish at being wrenched away from them like that will kill me all over again. If I wasn't already dead, that is.

A fresh bout of crying, but this time it's so violent, I think the tears might choke me.

'Shh, shh, pet, you've had a shock, that's all.'

'Oh, Dad . . .'

'I'm here now, Charlotte. Just remember everything's going to be fine.'

'But . . . I don't understand, where am I?'

I can't even see properly, everything around us is just all blurry and blindingly white.

He grips my hand tight.

'The easiest way for me to describe it to you, is that you're in a sort of, well . . . assessment area, really, would be the best way of looking at it, pet. Just till it's decided where's the best place for you to go, that's all. The main thing is not to be frightened.'

My mind starts to race. Mainly because whenever anyone tells me not to be frightened, then that's when I panic. An assessment area? Like . . . like purgatory or something? Suppose they assess my miserable little life, decide I was a crap human being, stamp me with a big F for failure, then send me straight to hell?

'Oh, come on now, pet, look at you, all worried.' Dad smiles gently at me, gripping my hand tight. 'I faithfully promise you, there's nothing at all to be scared of.' Then he puts his arm around me reassuringly, which does calm me down a bit. 'Have a look around for yourself, if you don't believe me.'

For the first time since I came to . . . whatever this place is, the glaring whiteness that's all around us starts to dim a bit; slowly, barely perceptibly, things begin to come into focus as my poor, bewildered brain takes in our surroundings. I'm not even a hundred per cent certain where I'll find myself, either. Maybe, I dunno, standing outside pearly gates with a bearded Saint Peter keeping guard like a bouncer at a nightclub, checking the VIP list to see if I'm on it? Or maybe it'll be a giant concourse with escalators to all floors, like in a shopping centre, except that some of them will lead up to heaven, while others will go down to the lower depths, where it's all smoky, with flames shooting out and little red-horned devils with spears running around the place cackling.

And a plaque outside saying, 'Abandon Hope All Ye Who Enter Here.'

Tell you what I didn't expect. To find myself in a sort of . . . well . . . old folks' home, really. Minus the smell of wee and boiled cabbage, that is. I'm not kidding, as my eyes gradually adjust to the light and I get up and stagger around the place, it's like Dad and I are in some sort of day-care room. He stays sitting on a sofa at the very back, eyes watching me protectively, while the afternoon racing from Cheltenham blares away on the TV. There's about four or five people here, all glued to the screen, and nobody gives me as much as a second glance. I'm slowly wandering around, totally confused, desperately trying to make eye contact with someone, but they're all too engrossed in the race, and every now and then one of them goes, 'Come on, Northern Dancer!'

Plus, apart from Dad, there is no one here under the age of about eighty.

I stumble back to Dad and slump on to the sofa beside him, numb.

'Did you think it would be fluffy clouds and angels, pet?' he asks gently, correctly reading my thoughts. 'Just remember that this is purely temporary, that's all. You came to us . . . well, let's just say you came to us before your time.'

'And I'm . . . I'm just here till they . . . like, *assess* me?'

'Which, as I say, is nothing for you to worry about.'

'And . . . well . . . when will that happen?'

He doesn't answer immediately, just looks at me keenly.

'All in good time.'

'But suppose they send me away from you? I mean, you've got to belong up in heaven, you never did anything wrong in your entire life. But I did plenty of wrong things and . . . well, suppose they separate us? Suppose you're sent back up above, and I'm flung down below to fry out the rest of eternity in hell?'

He smiles at my blind panic, and at the teary wobble in my voice, which, oddly, comforts me.

'It doesn't work like that, pet. Don't you trust your old dad?'

"Course I do.' I sob weakly. God, I must sound like I'm about five.

'Then come and sit down here beside me. We have an awful lot to catch up on, pet.'

I'm not sure how much time passes; it's bizarre, everything really does seem to stand still here, wherever we are. All I know is that it's ages later, and Dad and I are still together, totally engrossed in each other's company, with me a bit calmer now, but still clinging to his hand, terrified I'm going to lose him all over again. And I can't, just can't. I am *not* going through that unbearable pain for a second time. I just feel so safe and minded here, with him beside me. Like as long as he's here, wherever we are, I never have to worry ever again.

For as long as I'm here, that is.

The more we talk, the more gobsmacked I get. It's incredible. There's absolutely nothing that Dad doesn't know about any of our lives since he died, and that was, like, nearly ten years ago. I was eighteen, and I remember thinking that the void he left in my life would never be filled, and that I'd never meet a man who could hold a candle to him. Correct on both counts; it never was and I never did. Wherever we are, you'd nearly swear there was CCTV footage with twenty-four-hour live coverage of what's going on in all our little lives below, a bit like the command centre at Cape Canaveral.

He's just extraordinary. He knows all about Kate's marriage to Perfect Paul, and that she's desperately trying for a baby; he knows tiny, inconsequential little things like that Mum's joined a book club, and how she pretends to have read all these literary books, but if they bore her, she cheats by reading the reviews on Amazon, then throws in the odd knowledgeable quote to impress her pals, and just blags the rest. He even knows stuff about Fiona, and I only met her when I went to college, not long after he died.

'Dad,' is all I can keep saying over and over again, alternately through sobs then smiles, rubbing his big, rough, red, shovelly hands, terrified that he'll disappear or beam up or something in a minute. 'I love you and I missed you so, so much. There's not a single day I don't think about you.'

Funny that. I was never able to tell him that I loved him when he was alive, but now that I've passed over, there's no shutting me up.

'But I'm right here, pet. Even when you don't realize it, I'm never too far away,' he smiles softly. 'Like in that beautiful poem that you read out at my funeral. I've never left you, just stepped into the next room, that's all. I'm always close by. I've never stopped watching out for you, and I'm certainly not going to stop now.'

'And Mum and Kate, too?'

'Come on, pet, do you honestly think I'd let my three best girls out of my sight even for a moment?'

No, no, of course he wouldn't. He adored us all so much, and was always happiest when it was just 'we four' as he used to say, all together. Suddenly I remember being eight years old and nagging him incessantly to let me get the bus to school, so I could be a proper, grown-up 'big' girl. He eventually gave in, but I'll never forget him driving behind the bus in his car, just to make sure that I was OK. Then there was the time, aged fourteen, I begged to be allowed to go to Wesley, the local disco, with the rest of my pals. Oh, the teenage mortification; not only did he drive me there, he walked up to the DJ and politely asked if he'd mind keeping an eye on me for the night.

Always minding, always protecting, never letting go.

'I often send you little signs.' He smiles, giving my hand a gentle squeeze. 'Just to let you know that I'm right here. Your mum's by far the most open to that, though.'

'How do you manage that?' I ask, thinking . . . *signs*? Isn't that just a bit . . . *Close Encounters of the Third Kind*?

'Lots of ways, you'd be surprised. Sometimes I can suggest things to her, random thoughts, like hypnotism. The easiest thing, though, is to wait till she's asleep, and then have a proper chat with her while she thinks she's dreaming. She's got so open to that now; all I need do is give her a wee nudge every now and then to remind her to put out the bins, or to lock that back door which she's always forgetting about. "Is there oil in your lamp?" I'm always asking her.'

I'm all lumpy-throated now. That was a phrase he often used; his worried way of asking us if we were prepared for all eventualities and emergencies when outside the front door and away from his watchful gaze. You know, stuff like: have you enough petrol in the car/cash in your purse/a first-aid kit if travelling/have you allowed time for TWO punctures if you're going to the airport? (Because once, back in the seventies, honest to

God, this actually did happen to him, and decades later he still never let any of us forget it. Or did you allow for an extra hour if you're on the way in to do a big exam? The list was endless.

'Or sometimes, if your mum's a bit low, I get her to turn on the radio so she can hear . . .'

'. . . "You're Nobody Till Somebody Loves You",' I sob, smiling at the same time. 'I know, she's always hearing that song, and she says it reminds her most of you.'

My eyes are welling up again, just thinking about how much he idolized Mum. The way he'd light up whenever she'd walk into a room, even after they'd been married for nearly thirty years. I don't think I ever once heard them having a row. Dad would never argue with her. He'd just roll his eyes to heaven and let her have her own way; at the end of the day, anything that made her happy, made him happy. Gas to think that they met back in the days when your relationship compatibility test went along these lines: 'You mean you like *soup*? That's incredible, I like soup too!' And yet, it worked out for them. In every relationship, there is the lover and the loved, and that's pretty much the way it was for them. Mum's outgoing and sociable, whereas he was always more ponderous and thoughtful, the supporting player to her star turn. Visitors would call to the house, and he'd sit quietly, as happy to be entertained by all her funny stories and anecdotes as guests were. If you didn't know him well, you'd almost think he was a bit stand-offish, as often happens with people who are just more comfortable with silence than with talking shite the whole time. Which, believe me, frequently happens in a family with three women.

Then, when he got really sick and had to have round-the-clock care, I remember how he'd cling to Mum's hand and tell her over and over that marrying her was the best thing he ever did in his life. Bloody throat cancer. How could a man who never looked at a cigarette in his whole life get throat cancer? And what made it worse was the way he bore it with such dignity and humour. I was the one who was angry, so angry that I even took up smoking for a bit, just to piss off God.

Mum almost fell apart after he died; he'd protected her so much. None of us knew just how much till he was gone. All her happily married life, he'd done everything for her: she'd never had to drive herself anywhere or pay a bill, or deal with the banks, or even think about practical little things like changing plugs or applying for passports, or any of that malarkey. In the years since he's gone, though, little by little she's begun to do so much better. Egged on by me and Kate, she's slowly grown independent. She has her own little circle of rock-solid friends now, a lot of whom are widows too. The Merry Widows Kate calls them, and they all take trips abroad together: weekends to London for a bit of shopping, and then a pilgrimage every summer, to Lourdes or Knock, or basically anywhere that Our Lady ever appeared. She goes to plays and Mass and meets her pals regularly in each other's houses for sherry and long, cosy chats.

But I know that a day doesn't go by where she doesn't miss him and pray for him and ache for him.

'Mind you, it could be a fair wee while before she's ready to come over here,' Dad says, softly. 'She's not exactly tearing through that list of hers, now is she?'

I do not *believe* he knows about that. Mum's list, I should tell you, is a big catalogue she made of all the things she wants to do before she's ready to rejoin him in the afterlife. Stuff like:

1. Get to shake hands with George Clooney.
2. Walk Great Wall of China. (NB, buy comfy shoes first.)
3. Finish crossword without cheating, and once and for all learn how to work Sky Plus while I'm at it.
4. Tell George Clooney have single daughter. (See point 1, above.)
5. Go on that submersible thingy to seabed where wreck of *Titanic* is, but find out toilet arrangements first, as apparently it takes three hours to get there, the very same as a drive from Dublin to Galway, and I know I'd never last that long without a loo.

'But, Charlotte, it's you I've been most worried about. Particularly in the last while.'

'You mean with the accident and then me being in hospital . . .'

'No, since well before that,' he says, looking keenly at me. 'You see, I don't think you've been really happy with your life for a very long while. Have you now, pet? Be honest.'

It's like turning a knob on the radio a degree to the right and suddenly everything clicks in. Like stepping outside of myself and taking a third-person audit of my twenty-eight years of life. Suddenly I remember back to what it was like to be eighteen again, and to have actual, proper, *dreams*. Mine were vague at first; I knew I wanted to work in the creative field, but wasn't quite sure what as. Next thing, I got the job with Anna's agency, which was initially to be only for a few weeks, but somehow I ended up staying for six years. And I enjoyed it and thought that I might even set up on my own someday. Maybe even as a producer.

Then James Kane tornadoed into the calm waters of my life, and that was pretty much that. It makes my feminist hair stand on end even to admit it, but somehow he managed to make himself my number one priority, taking up, ooh, I dunno . . . only about a thousand per cent of my time. Once he and I are permanently together, was my warped reasoning, then

I'll tackle the rest of my life and career and everything will all fit beautifully into place. And I'd no doubt in my mind that it would eventually happen; just a question of when and not if. 'You're so good for James,' anyone who knew him used to say. Like I was the broccoli of dating.

In the meantime, my dreams of being a producer pretty much went out the window; one look at the way James went on, and I just knew I'd never have the steel-lined stomach needed for it.

'If you want to know whether you've got what it takes to be a producer,' he used to say to me, 'then go to the bank, borrow two hundred grand, set fire to it and walk away without a backward glance. If you've the nerve for that, then you can produce. Gotta be a risk-taker, baby.'

Now my idea of taking a risk is to eat a carton of Muller Light yoghurt from the fridge that's more than a day past its sell-by date, so no, I figured on second thoughts, maybe I'll just stick with the nice, safe job I have. Although, in the first couple of years we were together, I often used to pitch James ideas I had for movies and TV shows. And he went with a lot of them, and they worked, and I was so proud, except, now that I think back, I never really got credited. Example: the sitcom he made, *My Trophy Husband*? My idea. Likewise the documentary he made about this new dating craze where women go dog-walking in order to meet fellas. *Leashes and Lovers* it was called, and it got a huge response. Also my idea. Not tooting my own trumpet or anything, but it got to the stage where if ever he needed projects aimed at a female audience, then I was his first port of call. But somehow in all the hoo-ha after broadcast and reviews and press stuff, James always seemed to forget where the germ of the idea had originally come from. I'm not whingeing, just saying it wouldn't have killed him to say thanks, that's all.

Then all sorts of other flashbacks come reeling back to me, a speeded-up montage of signs which, at the time, I should have been able to read, but chose to ignore. All the countless red flags that when we love, we rationalize away. The time Kate's Labrador had puppies and I wanted to take one. 'But think about how it would compromise our lifestyle,' said James. 'We wouldn't be as free as we are now,' he said. 'We wouldn't be able to just hop on a flight to Rome or Paris for the weekend if we felt like it.'

'But we never *do* fly off to Rome or Paris for weekends,' I said. 'Do we?' One heated row later, I backed down; secretly hoping he might have had such a romantic weekend planned and wanted to surprise me. But he didn't. Not then and not ever.

Then there was the time we were at my cousin's wedding, and someone innocently asked him whether he and I would be next. Perfectly reasonable question to a couple who've lived together for five years.

'We don't believe in marriage,' James smugly replied for both of us. 'It's just a conspiracy to deny the dark and confirm the light.'

I think he meant to be smart-arsed and funny, but I just remember turning away, absolutely mortified, and then spending the rest of the day in a temper with myself for not confronting him there and then, telling him that he didn't speak for me, and that actually I did believe in marriage, thanks very much. Plus, there's nothing like going to a wedding to put a magnifying glass on problems you're having in your own relationship. Something to do with being surrounded by all that love and happiness and hope for the future. Anyway, like the complete eejit I am, I convinced myself that James just wasn't ready *right now*, but would eventually come round in time, when he realized how much he loved/needed/couldn't live without me.

Funny how every ill in my life can be traced back to him. Like he's the square root of all evil. To my shame, I just can't justify why I stayed with him for as long as I did, nor can I even begin to describe the magnetic appeal he held over me. The only defence I have is this. It's like at birth, the magi gave James three gifts: good looks, intelligence and an uncanny ability to charm his way out of any situation, no matter how hopeless. A bit like James Bond, as played by Sean Connery. So, after every row we'd have, and believe me, there were many, he'd somehow get around me, find something to make me laugh at, and wham! I'd be right back to square one: the adoring girlfriend, completely blinkered by love and utterly prepared to put up with just about any old shite.

Amazing how you can be madly in love with someone and, at the same time, not particularly like them.

It's so weird; the last boyfriend I talked to Dad about was a guy who took me to his school graduation do, aged seventeen. (Who subsequently turned out to be gay, but I can hardly be blamed for that, now can I?) Right now, though, it just feels so natural for me to spill out my guts about James. How all along I thought I was with the love of my life, but now I know he was just passing time with me, until he met the love of his. Dad just sits there, patiently listening while I rant on and on about how completely daft and blind and pathetic I must have been to a) have fallen for the bastard, and worse, b) stuck with him for so long and allowed him to become the focal point of my entire existence. My theme seems to be: 'Picture the perfect relationship. Right, now forget about it and let me tell you all about mine.' Like there's rock bottom, then two hundred feet of crap, then me. I don't even mean to blather on and on; it just all comes tumbling out and I don't even know why, apart from the fact that it's lovely to have a new audience that hasn't heard my tale of woe before.

'I hope I'm not driving you mental?' I ask Dad, and he just smiles back.

'Charlotte, the unexamined life isn't worth living.'

Oh my God, I'd completely forgotten that: how he was always throwing little inspirational quotes at me and Kate when we were small. I think in the misguided hope that it would expand our minds.

'Keep going, pet. It'll eventually get better, I promise. Remember, you're one that loved not wisely but too well.' His face is completely impassive and blank, he just lets me talk on and on again, till the pain that's searing inside me whenever I even think about the unholy mess I'm in starts to ease a bit. For the time being, at least.

And there's something else that's really, seriously bothering me. The fact that I'm here to be assessed. Even the word assessment is enough to terrify me, mainly because in school I failed just about every assessment I ever had to take. Time and again, I keep bringing it up, but Dad keeps waving all my fears away, telling me not to worry, that it's nothing to be afraid of. But, biblical and all as it sounds . . . supposing whoever's sitting in judgement on me decides I was a complete waste of space when I was alive, and I get sent . . . well, sent to hell?

I don't want to go to hell. Neither would you if you

knew what heat and sulphur do to my hair. But suppose I don't make it up to heaven? What then? I mean, I have to be honest, the last time I was inside a church was for Kate's wedding. Three years ago.

Shit.

I could really be screwed here, couldn't I? Unless maybe there's some kind of 'hell on earth' trade-off scheme, where you get time off for all the crap you had to put up with on earth, such as being a freckly ginger like me. Or burning to a crisp after more than five seconds exposure to strong sun. Or putting up with non-committal, cheating boyfriends.

Then again, on the other hand, maybe damnation isn't quite as terrible as it's made out to be. Maybe there's a chance that heaven is for people who enjoy . . . heavenly pursuits. You know, things like daily Mass and Sunday afternoon garden fetes and watching *Songs of Praise* while nursing a nice cup of cocoa. Maybe hell just gets a bad press, that's all. It could be for people more into vodka and cigarettes and sleeping with the wrong men. (Guilty on all three charges.)

Kind of like a twenty-four-hour nightclub.

Then something else strikes me. Suppose I get to meet God. Actual . . . *God*. But for some reason, whenever I try to get a mental image of what God looks like, I don't picture a kindly but firm bearded old man in robes and sandals; the only thing I can see is Morgan

Freeman, from the *Bruce Almighty* movie. He could even be a woman for all I know, although it's doubtful that any woman would ever have created an unimaginable bastard in the likeness of James Kane. I wouldn't mind having a good, stiff word with him or her, though. I mean, let's be honest, fair's fair, God has been messing me around for years and years. So much so that you'd nearly think he was having a laugh at my expense; maybe to entertain himself and all his saintly pals. Like I'm the leading lady in a long-running soap opera who everything keeps going arseways for. Get a load of this, lads, I can imagine him saying, here's Charlotte now, telling her mum and sister that they're wrong about her boyfriend, and that underneath it all, he's actually a kind, caring human being who always empties out his pockets for homeless people on the streets, and never looks twice at other women. Isn't it hysterical just how deluded these mortals can be? Tune in tomorrow, when she'll be at home wrestling with a Nigella recipe for a cosy dinner, just the two of them, while he's in Lillie's Bordello for the night, partying like a brain-damaged test monkey and accessorized by blondes, the way Donald Trump always is. Best part is he doesn't even bother texting her to let her know. Hilarious!

I put my worries to the side for now, and decide to enjoy and appreciate just being with Dad again. We've more majorly big long chats, then, after a time, the racing on TV comes to an end and people begin to drift in and out of the room. A sweet-faced elderly lady wanders over to us, smiles at me kindly, then asks Dad to introduce us. It's odd, because she's reminding me of someone but I can't think who. Then it hits me. She looks like me, right down to the freckles and the ginger hair. At eighty, that is. She's me with a side-parting and support tights.

'This is your great-aunt Martha,' Dad says, as we politely shake hands, like we're suddenly at a cocktail party for the deceased.

'Charlotte, love, I first came here when you were only a baby.' She twinkles at me. 'But I've always kept an eye on you, you know. You're so very welcome here. And if you ever fancy a little flutter on the horses, just come straight to me. I'll give you good odds.'

God knows how long has passed, but I'm still here, Dad's still beside me, we've talked and talked and talked for what feels like days – about anything and everything – and I've absolutely no regrets about dying at all.

Well, not really.

Don't get me wrong, I'm not ungrateful or anything, but . . . the thing is, it kind of gets just the *teeniest* little bit monotonous here after a while. Now, everyone's very sweet, and I've met so many relatives I never even knew I had, all of whom passed away decades ago, but who've come back to this assessment area, or wherever the hell it is I am, just to stick their heads in, say hi and to introduce themselves. Some I vaguely recognize from old family photos, like Dad's grandfather who died in the Civil War. (Nothing dramatic, though, he wasn't shot at dawn in front of a firing squad or anything, the big eejit just went out without his scarf and got a chest infection.) Then there's some I never heard of, I just figure they're ancestors because of the wiry red hair and the freckles. You should see us all gathered together. We're like five generations of the Weasleys. In fact, I'm spending so much time with family it's a bit like permanent Christmas Day here, minus the selection boxes and the vicious rows over whether to watch *The Sound of Music* or *Pirates of the Caribbean*.

They're all so lovely and they all have such great stories to tell, but it's just that . . . you see, they're all so much, well, *older*. Not that I'm complaining, far from it, but . . . they do all spend most of the day watching TV, then later on there's bingo and sometimes, to add to all the unbearable excitement, bridge. Which is terrific. It's just that, now that I've been here for a while, I'm starting to wonder how well I fit in, that's all. I'm not exactly sure what I thought the afterlife would be like, but I sure as hell didn't expect stair lifts, and Thora

57

Hird, and an elderly lady in a Paddington Bear hat wandering around with a corgi trailing after her and a gin and tonic in one hand, who I'd only swear is the Queen Mother.

I suppose I expected death to mean that you might get to hang out with Princess Diana or Elvis. Or Kurt Cobain or even John Lennon, but I guess they must have all passed their assessments years ago and are now partying away in wherever it is that all the cool, hip, young dead people go, while I'm somehow stuck in the Florida of the afterlife.

At this stage, Dad's getting expert at reading my thoughts.

'Not really your cup of Bacardi Breezer here, is it, pet? I know it's hard because you're so young, but you have to understand that to everyone else here, this is the equivalent of partying like it's 1899.'

Shit. He's sussed me out. I'm frantically racking my brains trying to think of a polite way of saying . . . what, exactly? That I made a pig's ear of my time on earth, and now it turns out that the afterlife isn't exactly a barrel of laughs, either?

'There is something else you might consider, you know,' he goes on, his face giving absolutely nothing away, but then Mum always reckoned there were times when you'd need to be Sigmund Freud to figure him out. 'Just to pass the time.'

'Yeah?' I say, wondering what he means. Give hell a try, maybe?

'It's not for everyone now, but there is an opening, and I think I could possibly pull a few strings for you . . .'

He looks at me, and there's just the tiniest giveaway glint in his eye, like he's had this up his sleeve for a long time.

'Charlotte, pet, maybe you'd consider putting in a bit of emmm . . . well, work experience, I suppose you'd call it, really?'

Sounds OK, I think. I mean, no one seems to know how long this assessment lark actually takes. I've all this time on my hands, so I might as well do something useful with it. Plus, we used to do this in school as part of detention. Saturday work experience in old folks' homes, that is. You know, make tea and sandwiches, help people in and out of wheelchairs, make sure everyone got the right medication, referee any rows about what everyone watched on TV, that kind of thing. Never thought I'd end up doing it in the afterlife, but there you go. If you think life's full of surprises, you should try giving death a whirl.

'Absolutely,' I smile up at Dad, delighted that there's some way to relieve the boring, tedious monotony and make myself useful for a change. Plus, if some higher power is, as we speak, busy evaluating my sad, dismal little life, then, maybe, just maybe, if I show a willingness to muck in here, they might go that bit easier on me. Give me a kind of posthumous effort cup, if you will.

'I'd love to.'

Chapter Three

Don't ask me how it happened, but the next thing Dad and I are both sitting in what looks a bit like a bank-manager's office. Tiny and a bit gloomy, with leather swivel chairs, a load of corporate-looking files lying on the desk opposite, and phones ringing in the background non-stop. I'm not joking, half of me feels like I should start filling out a mortgage application form. Across from us, there's an older, smiley-faced lady sitting behind a computer who's having a conversation with . . . well, with no one, actually, at least no one that I can see. She's bubbly and warm, and would nearly put you in mind of an Aer Lingus hostess that's about to slip you a little bottle of Chardonnay from off the drinks trolley with a discreet wink and not charge you. She's also dressed head to toe in pink, with plump pink cheeks; Jaysus, even her glasses have a pinky rim. For a second, it flashes through my poor befuddled brain that she kind of looks a bit like a human marshmallow. Every now and then, she relays the other side of the conversation back to me and Dad, a bit like they do on the *Eurovision Song Contest*, when the Ukrainian vote is coming in.

'Sorry about this.' She smiles at us apologetically. 'Bit of an urgent situation I just need to troubleshoot, then I'll be right with you!' And back she goes, talking to thin air again. 'Gabriel, before this escalates, I think you may need to step in. Number 742 is at his wits' end here, this really is a code red . . .'

I throw a 'huh?' glance at Dad, who just looks ahead, as impassive and expressionless as ever.

'Did she just say Gabriel?' I whisper at him, unable to shut myself up. 'Like, as in THE Gabriel?'

No response.

'Dad! Is she talking to the Archangel Gabriel?' I hiss at him. 'I mean, I doubt very much if she's having a chat with Gabriel Byrne . . .'

He makes a tiny, 'shhhh' frowny gesture, but otherwise just stays focused straight ahead. Bloody hell, he'd have cleaned up as a poker player.

'. . . no, no, his charge is now sitting in his car at the end of a pier contemplating, well, let's just say, he's at his lowest ebb and I think we may need urgent backup . . .' Then smiley lady flashes a big 'don't worry, all under control' professional smile at me and Dad.

'Oh yes, I have all the files here in front of me, his charge is going through a very acrimonious divorce at

the moment, in fact that's exactly what started all this
. . . no, go ahead. I'll hold,' she says, top of her voice,
before whispering back to us, 'So, so sad. Lovely man.
His wife went to work part-time in a garden centre and
ran off with someone else she met there. The fella in
charge of the water features. She worked in aquariums,
and one fine day their eyes met across the faux rocks and
the lily pads. Like something you'd see in one of those
Sunday evening sitcoms with Robert Lindsay, isn't it?
Tragic. But sure, what can you do? That's what comes of
giving mortals free will. Don't blame me, I didn't vote
for it. Anyway, what the poor deserted husband doesn't
know is that his whole life is about to take a turn for the
better in ways he can't even begin to imagine . . . hello?
Yes, Gabriel, I'm still here . . . yes, that's lovely. Fine,
well, let's hope that does the trick, and I'll call you again
shortly with an update. Copy that. Over and out.'

Copy that, over and out? I think. I'm half-wondering
if I've wandered on to the set of a cop show when smiley
lady stretches out her hand to introduce herself.

'Regina Angelorum is my full title, but everyone
around here just calls me Regina,' she says warmly,
whipping off the pink glasses, which manages to make
her look slightly less marshmallow-like.

'Lovely to meet you, I'm Charlotte Grey . . .'

'Oh, yes, we know all about you, love. In fact I've a
full dossier here somewhere on you,' she says, waving

vaguely at the big mound of files on the desk in front of her. 'Now, wait till I see, where did I put it? Oh yes, here we go. Be a good girl and fill in that for me, will you?' she says, passing me over a biro and a very official-looking form.

'Car crash, wasn't it, love?' she asks sympathetically, and I nod. 'Don't bother with page one, we have all that information already. Just fill out page three and that'll be grand. Oh, if you only knew the amount of road fatalities I've seen in my time, and do you know it's getting worse every single year? I'm hoarse saying it . . .'

Regina chatters on to Dad about speed-limits and the general uselessness of penalty points and drink-driving laws while I wade my way through the paperwork trying to find page three. God Almighty, it's like applying for a passport. The form is headed AWE and it's only when I look closely that I see what that stands for.

Angelic Work Experience.

OK, now I'm starting to feel like I'm stuck in a Harry Potter movie, and am almost half-expecting to see flying owls and kids playing Quiddich fluttering past the window any minute.

'Excuse me, emmmm . . . Regina?' I interrupt her in full flow about road-death statistics. 'Am I seeing things? Or does this really, honestly say angelic work experience? Like . . . for real?'

'Ye-eeeeessssss, dear.' She smiles, looking at me as much as to say, 'What the hell else did you expect?'

'So, I'm going to be . . . like . . . an angel?'

'Just fill out question three, paragraph two, dear and we'll see how you get on.'

I flick ahead to the right page, my hands trembling, half with excitement and half with total disbelief. No, I definitely am not seeing things. There it is in bold type.

Q3. TAKE TIME TO OUTLINE, IN YOUR OWN WORDS, YOUR REASONS FOR WISHING TO PARTAKE IN THE AWE PROGRAMME. ANY UNFINISHED EARTHLY BUSINESS SHOULD BE CLEARLY SUMMARIZED BELOW.

Oh my God, this is unreal. If I wasn't actually sitting here, I'd never believe it in a sugar rush. Here I am, about to become a bona fide actual angel. Me, that made such an almighty mess of my time on earth, and now look at me! Suddenly, I think about Mum, Kate and Fiona. What they must be going through. But then I think of how much more I can do for them from where I am now. I mean, I'm sure I'll get to look in on them and work all sorts of miracles for them all. 'Cos everyone knows angels have, like . . . powers, don't they?

Ooh, I just thought of something. Bet I could help

Kate to get pregnant. And Fiona to get her face out of that computer, start spending time among the three-dimensional people and then maybe find a gorgeous man who'll treat her like a queen. I'll help her to make her life *work*. The way that mine didn't. And I could get Mum through that list of hers, although how I'll arrange for her to meet George Clooney is another thing. Then there's all the actors at the agency. Bet I could make all kinds of fabulous things happen for them, too. Apart from Miss Helium Voice, that is. But otherwise I'll be a perfect model of angelic behaviour.

I will completely reinvent myself, just like Madonna. Or Carla Bruni.

For the first time in ages, I've got the biggest beam spread across my face. I grab the biro and, honest to God, once I start writing, there's no stopping me. Under 'reasons for wishing to partake in the AWE programme' I write two full pages about how, although my own life didn't exactly work out the way I'd imagined, now I want to devote myself entirely to helping others. I must sound gushier than a contestant on *Miss Universe*, and am only short of writing 'have deep, burning desire to promote world peace'.

Anyway, I must have done something right, because after Regina reads over my answer she smiles, winks at Dad, and tells me I'm clear to go.

To a classroom, to be exact. As if things couldn't get

any more bizarre. The old-fashioned type, with wooden floors, and an actual blackboard, and an overwhelming smell of chalk dust. Kind of reminds me of the time myself and Fiona signed up for a night class called 'Screenwriting for Beginners' in the local adult education centre. I was all up for it because I thought it would help me in work; Fiona thought it would be a good way to meet fellas. Anyway, we were both disappointed: the course was total rubbish, and the one and only guy in the class happened to be gay. But I digress.

There's two other people here: an elderly man with a goatee beard wearing what looks like an ancient Victorian frock coat, and a middle-aged woman, very attractive in a pale, hollow-eyed, Mary Pickford way, with shingled hair and bright red nail-varnish.

'You're Miss Charlotte, aren't you?' says goatee man politely, not even a raised eyebrow about how I just managed to . . . I dunno, beam into, or somehow get landed wherever it is that I am now. Just like in a dream; I haven't a clue how I physically got from A to B, all I'm sure of is that I'm here now.

'Emm . . . yes, but the thing is . . . emm . . . I don't mean to be rude or anything, but emm . . . I don't suppose you know exactly what's going on here, by any chance?'

'Motoring accident, wasn't it?' says shingle-haired woman, mildly curious.

'Emm . . . yeah . . . but . . .'

'Yeah,' goatee man repeats after me, pondering. Honestly, the more I look at him, the more he'd put you in mind of Gladstone or Disraeli or some other Victorian frock-coated, elder statesman type.

'I could never get used to that abbreviation. A little like "OK". One hears it so often nowadays, and it never fails to amuse me. Well, I do hope your accident wasn't too painful, my dear?'

'Ehh . . . no, actually, never even felt a thing, really, it was all over so fast. I think the shock must have numbed me. There was a storm and I was, well, I was . . . I was . . . emm . . . really upset about . . . something. One minute I was trying to overtake a car in front of me, but I didn't see that there was a truck coming towards me on the opposite side of the road, till it was way too late, then, next thing I was in hospital . . .'

Funny, though, the little things that, bizarrely, do stick in my mind about the accident: Watching the bonnet of my little car crumple like an accordian in slow motion as the truck struck it full-on. Remembering too late that I forgot to put my seat belt on. Feeling my head crash forward through the windscreen at full force, shattering it as easily as if it were made of icing sugar. Then opening my eyes and seeing the panicked truck driver, standing on the road beside me in the pelting rain, screaming hysterically down his mobile phone for the ambulance to hurry the f*ck up, that this could be a fatality.

But I'm grand, I thought looking over at him. Just can't move, that's all. Then I remember feeling a hot, oozy slime dripping down my face and into my open mouth. It was only when a bit of it dropped on to my tongue that I realized it was blood.

Then nothing. Blackness. Peace.

'What was it that happened to you, Charles?' asks shingle-haired woman in an English accent so cut-glass you'd swear she just stepped out of an Agatha Christie whodunnit.

'Typhoid.'

'Typhoid?' I can't help repeating after him, stunned. In fact, I couldn't be more stunned if he'd just said 'the Black Death'.

'Yes, dear. Perfectly common in 1849. How about you?' he asks shingle-head.

'Influenza.'

'Flu?' I blurt out. Sorry, couldn't help that, either, I'm too busy thinking, do people really *die* of flu?

'They certainly did in 1919,' she replies curtly, reading my thoughts. 'More people died of influenza than did in the whole of the Great War, you know . . . ah, here's Minnie now.' She breaks off as a little girl of about ten or eleven comes in, with long brown hair tied in a ribbon, wearing hobnail boots and a kind of smock dress. She's adorable and looks a bit like one of the Railway Children, and I'm just about to ask her to come and sit beside me when she strides up to the top of the class and, in her sweet little-girl voice, tells us that today we're going to be learning about giving signs, communication through dreams, and guiding without interfering with free will.

'But she's only a kid!' I whisper to shingle-head on my left.

'Oh, don't make that mistake, dear. Minnie's an older soul than any of us. She's had over two hundred earthly charges to date you know.'

Bloody hell.

We learn so much I can barely take it all in. And let's remember that up till this intensive crash course, my knowledge of the spirit world was pretty much derived from movies like *The Sixth Sense* and *Ghost*. Then something that Dad said comes back to me, about how he sends little signs to Mum all the time. And now I've learned how to do exactly that. At least, I think I have.

My head is swimming, and all I really want to do is rush back to Dad and fill him in on everything. But things don't seem to happen like that here. No sooner has Minnie wrapped up, than I'm whooshed back to Regina in her bank-manager's office, where she looks like she's been sitting alone, just waiting for me.

'All right then, love? Minnie is really something, isn't

she? I remember when she first came here, oh, must have been in Queen Victoria's day, but she really is a wonderful spirit, and a very gifted teacher . . . now, my dear, I've got quite a challenging assignment for you. I haven't just been pulling strings for you, I've been pulling *ropes*. Wait till I see, where on earth did I put that file? One of these days I am determined to clear this desk, once and for all . . .'

I'm on the edge of my seat, all excited now. This is just like in a Bond movie, when Judi Dench tells 007 what his mission will be. Minus the gadgets of course, but . . . hmmm . . . wonder if I get issued with a set of wings?

'Oh yes, here we are,' she goes on. 'Hmmm. Interesting. This charge's last angel only left a few days ago. Wrote it off as a hopeless case. So why don't we see if you can do any better, dear?'

'Bring it on,' I beam brightly, half-wondering if there's any more training to come before I'm dispatched. Maybe some kind of angelic boot camp. Where they give lessons in, I dunno, flying and general miracle-working techniques.

'Now, you do know that if the going gets too rough, you can come back here at any time?' Regina asks, peering at me over the pink glasses, the big marshmallow face looking a bit worried. 'No one would blame you a bit. It's not everyone who's cut out for angelic work experience.'

Not likely, I think, a bit smugly. I was a total failure on earth, but by God, for once in my miserable life, I am going be a success. I'm going to put my mind to this task, totally apply myself and really impress everyone, myself included, at just how well I can do. I'll whole-heartedly devote myself to spreading joy and happiness, a bit like an Irish version of *Amélie*, minus the subtitles.

I'm going to spend my time here doing good on earth. People down there will probably light candles to me, and whoever this hopeless case is, I'll completely turn them into an honest, upstanding, kind to stray dogs/ doing meals on wheels at weekends/volunteering at soup kitchens/charity-giving-type person . . .

'Just remember the golden rule, dear. We never, ever interfere with free will. Keep that to the front of your mind, and you'll be just grand. Yes . . . here we are, I have the charge's name here. You know, we generally assign to people that you already knew in the mortal plane, makes things so much simpler, really.'

How fab is this? I'm thinking . . . Mum? Kate? Fiona? Someone I don't know all that well, but whose whole life I'm now about to transform for the better?

'Right then. I see you know this person intimately, so that should help you a lot. It's a Mr James Kane.'

Oh F★★★★★★★★★★★★★★★★★★★★★★★★★★★★★★★★★★CK . . .

Chapter Four

JAMES

I have never been so totally and utterly shocked in my entire life. Sorry, death. What's worse is, I can't even do what I'd normally do, or what any normal person would: i.e., go straight to the nearest pub, order a double vodkatini, then knock it back in a single wrist flick. Because before I've even had a chance to a) splutter or b) hurl myself out the nearest window (sure, what the hell, I'm dead anyway) . . . I'm back at home. Bloody hell, I'll tell you one thing. There is absolutely no arsing around on the angelic plane, that's for sure.

Sorry, did I say I was back home? I meant back in James's house, she sez through gritted teeth. In our bedroom, to be exact. I mean *his* bedroom. In my defence, though, can I just point out that, in the five years since I first moved in here, I've poured a lot of my own blood, sweat and tears into the place, so you'll excuse me for sounding a bit territorial. So would you if you knew the sheer amount of man-hours I spent decorating/scrubbing Dulux's Himalayan Blush off my clothes/waiting in for hours on plumbers whose entire work-schedule seemed to revolve around the FA Cup Premiership/guarding a ten-tonne skip at the front gate from kids setting fire to it.

You name it, I was that soldier.

I know, I know, technically it is James's house; he'd bought it not long before we met, mortgaged up to the back teeth, but I was project manager on it because he asked me to be, both of us swept up in the romance of transforming what was then a semi-derelict shithole into a gorgeous period house, close to town, close to the sea, yadda, yadda yadda. Phase one in the taming of James Kane, was my reasoning. OK, so his sole contribution was to put in a Bang & Olufsen TV then leave the rest up to me, but I was more than happy to do it. I mean, everyone knows the direct mathematical correlation between buying a house and spending less time in nightclubs and more in Woodies DIY looking at outdoor decking, don't they? We'll be like a couple in a Homebase ad, I blissfully thought.

'You and me could be so happy here,' he used to say. 'We'll get engaged/exchange vows on a beach some-where/try for a baby really, really soon,' he'd say.

'Any idea how soon?' I'd say, not really caring about which particular order these wondrous miracles would happen in, but understandably anxious to put some kind of time frame on it, without sounding too impatient.

'Just as soon as this movie gets off the ground/right after I get the green light for this TV series/once I get investors on board/when the LA trip is out of the way,' he'd say.

Always the dangled carrot, always the magical 'when', but there was absolutely no doubt in my mind what he really meant. That as soon as things settled down for him, at some unforeseen date, this would be our permanent home. So, I happily figured, no harm to put my own stamp on the place while I'm at it, sure, it's an investment in the future, isn't it? I can't even explain my rationale: maybe that by picking out soft furnishings, curtain poles and tablecloths that matched the napkins, I'd somehow seal the deal for him and me. That the Cath Kidston catalogue was all it would take for him to commit to me.

And now I'm back.

I catch my breath and nervously look around the bedroom, not having the first clue what to expect. Nope, everything looks just the way I left it when I was last here, God knows how long ago. The last time I remember everything being normal. Which, given what's happened in the meantime, is beyond weird. So funny to think that I would have hauled myself out of bed that morning as usual, hopped into the shower, got dressed, gone out the door, worried about a contract that should have arrived at the office the previous day but hadn't, wondered if I'd be home that night in time for *The Apprentice*, debated about whether or not I'd cook that night or else leave it to James, who fancies himself as a bit of a Gordon Ramsay in the kitchen, right down to all the effing and blinding. All the normal thoughts and cares and worries that go through our minds every day. And then in the space of one short afternoon, I managed to lose everything. Boyfriend, lover, home, job . . . life. Unbelievable.

I must be alone because the house is so quiet. Whenever James is around, it's always like a three-ring circus: mobiles going off (he has one for LA and one for Europe, for absolutely no reason that I can see, other than to show off with), people banging at the front door, and him always searching for something he's lost, demanding to know where it is at the top of his voice. A misplaced script/passport/car keys/a Pop Tart he was eating that's now vanished into thin air. Honest to God, there are five-year-olds out there who are probably able to take better care of themselves. And the sad thing is that up until my whole life turned upside down, I used to find that carry-on sweet and endearing.

Absolutely nothing has changed. There's still a squeezed-out tube of cleanser belonging to me lying on the dressing table. An old *Hello!* magazine with Kate

Middleton on the cover that I bought weeks ago is strewn across the bedside table, even some underwear is exactly where I left it: shoved down the back of a radiator. And it's not the good, sexy La Perla stuff either, it's a knackered old bra and knickers, gone grey from several thousand washes. (Not my fault, I mean it's not like I went into Marks & Spencer and said, 'Do you have anything faded and droopy with hooks missing at the back?')

Suppose somebody was here and they saw that? is the completely irrational thought that goes through my addled brain, like I'd nothing else to be worried about. Instinctively, I go to whip the offending articles from behind the radiator, but nothing happens.

Shit.

I try again.

Nothing.

I try it slower. Still nothing. I have to do it in slow motion a few times before I finally cop on.

My hand is going clean through them. Definitely. I'm not imagining it.

Anxiously, I look around for something else to experiment with, and my eyes immediately light on a photo of me and Kate taken on her wedding day that's plonked on the dressing table, beside my GHD hair straighteners. She looks like a young, glamorous Fergie, with the red hair piled elegantly up on her head, all tall, thin and gorgeous; whereas I'm like a shorter, more freckly version of her, stuck in a lime-green bridesmaid's dress (not a good colour if you're a ginger, trust me), made out of what looks like the same fabric they use to prevent the space shuttle burning up on re-entry.

I try to pick up the picture frame and nothing happens. Same thing. My hands just glide clean through it. And I don't even feel a thing, there's no sensation whatsoever. Tentatively, I move towards the mirror on the dressing table and look in. There's nothing there, no reflection, even though I know I'm standing right in front of it. I wave, then jump up and down, then stick my face right up close to it, the way presenters do directly to camera on kids' TV shows.

Big fat nada.

So this is it, then, I think.

I'm really dead.

I mean, it's not like I didn't already know, it's just that somehow, being back here, in this dimension, if that doesn't sound too *Star Trek*-ky, is really hammering it home. Half of me just wants to pull whatever emergency cord there is and yank myself out of here, or else find a tardis and make a run for it, like they do on *Doctor Who*, but the other half is, well . . . a bit curious, if I'm being honest. I mean, it's not like I just moved out of this house in a huff or something, I actually *died*.

All the things I wanted to do and never got to. Like

having a baby. Taking a train ride through India. Paying off my credit card. Finally getting around to writing my novella. Meeting Johnny Depp. Telling every-one my Oscar picks for next year. Then I think about the sheer amount of time I wasted worrying about crap. Not fitting into my skinny jeans any more. Will Amy Winehouse get her act together? Is Prince William losing his hair? Would Ikea ever open in Dublin?

Oh my God, I wonder what my funeral was like? Who am I kidding? By that I really mean one thing: was James there, and did he cry embarrassingly copious amounts? Or maybe give a big graveside oration? Make a holy show of himself telling everyone now that I was gone, his life might as well be over, too? After five years together he must have felt something or . . . was the bastard back here that night with his new girlfriend cracking open a bottle of Châteauneuf-du-Pape?

Then I think about Mum, and suddenly all I want is to be with her. What must she be going through? I mean, she gets unbelievably, irrationally distraught when her satellite dish goes on the blink and she has to miss an episode of Agatha Christie's *Marple*, her favourite TV show, so I dread to think how she's dealing with this. Then there's poor old Kate who had to take a full week off work when her Labrador was put down . . . how is she coping? And Fiona, too . . . oh shit, you know what? I have to get out of here. Right now. I have to find them all, and let them know that I'm OK and that Dad's OK, and that there's nothing for anyone to be worried or upset about, and that I'm going to do everything I can to help them and work all sorts of little miracles for them.

Just from this side of the fence, that's all.

I stride over to the door, grab the handle and . . . my hand just swipes clean through it. I try again and again, but no joy. Honestly, it's like slicing a knife through butter.

Oh, for f*ck's sake, does this mean I'm going to be trapped here until James decides to show up and let me out?

As if on cue, there's a deep, rumbling, oh-shit-is-it-morning-already moan from under a big mound of duvet, and I nearly leap into the air with the fright.

I don't believe it, he's here. Actually in the room with me. My heart's having palpitations, and then I remember . . . he can't see me. To all intents and purposes, I might as well be the invisible woman.

I stand there, completely frozen as, first, his fist comes out from under the mound of bedclothes, and then his head appears, with the hair standing up on end, like he's just stuck two fingers into a plug socket. You should see the state of him: right now, Russell Brand is probably better groomed. He's looking dog-rough and dishevelled, with the eyes completely bloodshot.

Good.

He looks around, disorientated, then picks up the clock on the bedside table. Just gone eleven a.m. Which is about the normal time he'd be getting out of bed at. He shoves the clock back and slumps back on to the pillows, rubbing his eyelids with the palms of his hands. It's a gesture I've seen him do a thousand times, but right now, it's making the breath physically catch at the back of my throat. I feel like an intruder in my own home, watching a live theatre show being played out in front of me. Watching, and yet distant from it. Then, I'm not joking, James looks directly at me. Right over to where I'm rooted to the spot, standing at the edge of the bed. My side of the bed.

'Fuck,' he half-whispers.

He sees me.

'I am so fucking late,' he mutters under his breath, hauling himself out of bed and pulling himself into a pair of the underpants strewn across the floor, right beside where I am.

He doesn't see me.

Next thing he's out the door and stumbling down the narrow, uneven stairs, dodging the overhead beams because he's tall. He heads into our, sorry *his*, gorgeous living room, with its amazing view right out over Sandymount Strand, providing the traffic's not too heavy, and you don't end up looking out at ten-tonne

81

haulage trucks, backed up along the road for miles. Except staring out at gridlock isn't what's bothering me right now, it's the state of the place. I only wish I was joking, it's messier than Jackson Pollock's studio. Even worse than a nightclub the morning after the night before, with empty bottles of wine and Jack Daniel's strewn all over the floor; I'm numbly staring at the mess thinking, who exactly did James have over last night? Metallica?

The coffee table is piled high with piles of scripts, more scripts, and an empty pizza box, but somehow he manages to unearth a half-empty box of Marlboro and lights up.

James, outside! You know it's a non-smoking house!

Oh, would you listen to me. Trying to nag from the other side of the grave.

Then his mobile rings, and it almost makes me laugh watching him delving through the mound of crap on his desk trying to find it.

On top of the fireplace, gobshite.

He eventually finds it and answers. It's his business partner, Declan, and although I can only hear one side of the call, I'm guessing it involves a finance meeting which James has just slept it out for. He slumps down on the couch, pulling on the cigarette right down to his feet, nodding mutely as poor old Declan rants on and on.

Couple of things you should know about James in business.

1. His production company is called Meridius Movies, named after the lead character, Maximus Meridius, in the movie *Gladiator*. (Russell Crowe is James's big role model in life.)

   Couldn't make it up, could you?

2. Actually, he's not at all bad at what he does, and, in the past, has had a good few hits, mainly because he applies the Madonna principle: i.e., surround yourself at all times with the most talented people working in your industry, and you're laughing. Declan, for instance, who's brilliant, and who has quite highbrow taste, always wanting to produce the kind of TV series you nearly feel you deserve a graduation cert after watching. He's also such a sweetie, I once tried to match him up with Fiona. She rejected him out of hand on account of the following: she thought his skin resembled a topographic map of the Alps, that his man-breasts were bigger than hers, and that she had twice his upper-body strength. Very choosy girl, but fear not, fixing her up is high priority on my list of miracles to perform.

3. James always reckons that being a producer is a bit like being a plumber. Do your job right and no one

notices. Do it wrong and everyone ends up covered in shite.

4. When filming, his motto is, 'If less is more, then think of how much more that more would be.' No, really. When *not* filming, his motto is, 'Live fast, live hard, die young.' Whereas there I'd be in my furry slippers and PJs, sipping a marshmallow hot chocolate in front of *Desperate Housewives*, nice and early on a Thursday night; ever the stabilizing influence. And yet I'm the one who dies first. Now do you call that fair?

'Dec, just listen to me,' he's growling down the phone, spewing out cigarette smoke, then sitting forward and tipping ash into the empty pizza box.

That is disgusting!

'It's been a rough few days, what with Charlotte and everything . . .'

Suddenly I catch my breath. That weird, intriguing feeling of eavesdropping on a conversation about yourself.

Declan says something I can't hear, but it must be sympathetic.

'. . . thanks, yeah, thanks, man, I appreciate it. It's so hard for me, being here without her . . . I'm still in shock, I suppose . . . yeah, you're right . . . time will heal but, man, I really hope you never have to go through this. Wouldn't wish it on my worst enemy. You really don't know how much someone means to you, until you see them lying in a hospital bed and know there's damn all you can do for them . . .'

Oh my good God.

'. . . yeah, I know, she's one gal in a million. Can't believe how much I'm missing her . . .'

I'm sitting right beside him now and I'd almost swear I can see his eyes glistening.

'. . . no, I haven't the first clue what I'm going to do, I mean, how do you even begin to get through something like this . . . hey, man, thanks for being so understanding.'

No, there's no mistake. He's actually *crying*, he really is. Definite tear action going on. Half of me is so overwhelmingly touched, and the other half wants to hug him and let him know I'm actually right beside him, with my bum wedged on top of the remote control, to be exact. I move in close and gently put my arm around his shoulders. He shudders like a wet dog, then gets up and staggers to the kitchen, also like a pigsty, but right now I don't care.

I did not come back from the afterlife to load dish-washers.

'Sorry, man,' he mumbles to Declan down the phone, 'gotta switch on the heating. It's like a fucking fridge in here.' Then he stumbles back to the living room and

85

slumps back on to the sofa, pulling a throw I got in Avoca around his shoulders.

You should see him. Dark circles under the eyes that Jack Sparrow would be proud of, stinking of stale booze, with nesty hair and days of stubble covering his pasty, knackered-looking face. Right now, there are hobos sleeping rough out there in better nick. He keeps grunting down the phone at whatever Declan's saying, and all I can do is stare open-mouthed.

I had no idea. None. Only that I've seen it with my own two eyes, I'd never have thought he'd be this . . . *lost* without me. He's even still talking about me in the present tense, like he just can't accept that I'm gone. There's only one logical conclusion. The whole Sophie Kelly thing was just a blip, temporary bewitchment, no more, and now that I'm not around any more, James is officially falling apart.

Which means that all this time, he really, truly loved me. Without question.

Next thing, there's a knock on the door and he goes to answer it.

'Someone here, Dec, probably FedEx with a delivery, yeah . . . great . . . call over and pick me up now if you can . . . oh, thanks for offering, man, yeah . . . ehh . . . some Marlboro Lights and maybe an Americano . . . great, see you shortly. And . . . hey . . . thanks,' he says, hanging up as I follow him to the front door.

I do not bloody well believe this.

Sophie bleeding Kelly. Wearing her usual dressed-down faux-hemian gear that tries its best to say, 'Look at me, classically trained, ready to play Chekhov at a minute's notice, and yet still finding the time to dress like a bargain-basement Sienna Miller.' Her Mini Cooper with the top down in *my* parking space, and the blonde hair in stupid-looking curly pigtails.

Wish I had the power of my hands; right now I'd love to rip the beret off her poodley head and pour extra-strength Domestos all over the car seats.

And by the way, Sophie, on Carla Bruni, berets look chic and sophisticated, on you, more like you're trying to channel Frank Spencer.

'What are you doing here?' James almost hisses at her, grabbing her by the arm and dragging her into the hall. 'Declan's on his way over, suppose he sees you?'

'Well, excuse me for being worried!' she snaps back, and I'm not messing, anger makes the screechy voice sound, if possible, worse. Thank God we don't have a dog, is all I can think, the poor creature would be persecuted listening to her. Then a horrible thought hits me right in the solar plexus: he must really be in love with her. Because, let's face it, you'd have to be; there's no other way you could put up with that decibel level otherwise.

The bastard. Bad, bloody bastard.

'Your phone's been off all last night and all this morning, I've been out of my mind. And what's more, I was right to be worried: it's a Monday morning and look at the state of you!'

'Sophie,' says James, folding his arms and sucking in his lips, something he only ever does when he's at boiling point. He also tends to talk reeeeeeallllllly reaaaaaallllllly slooooooowly when majorly pissed off, the way FBI counter-terrorists do in films. You know, 'Step awaaaaaay from the veeeeeehicle.'

'I thiiiiiink I made it cleeeeeear,' he says, 'that this is a veeeeeery sensitive time right now, and that it's an unbelieeeeeevably bad idea for you to be seeeeeen here.'

'I know, I know, you already spelt it out to me. Suppose Charlotte's elderly, interfering bag of a mother, or that poker-faced sister of hers, who's more tightly coiled than a walnut whip, called to pick up her things, seeing as how they both feel they've carte blanche to barge in here at any hour of the day or night. Suppose that happened, and suppose they found me here? Believe me, I know all the risks; I just wanted to see you.'

WHAT did she just say?

I'm looking at Screechy Sophie now, shocked. I mean, how bloody dare she? I just stand there speechless, trembling with rage, giving her the evil eye and wanting nothing more than to bitch-slap the stupid, poodley head off her. If I wasn't dead, that is.

'They're still Charlotte's faaaaaamily, and right noooooow, we neeeeeed to respect that, OK?'

Next thing, completely ignoring his hung-over narkiness, not to mention the stink of stale booze, Sophie's right in on top of him, rubbing his arms suggestively and pulling down the throw he has around his shoulders. *My* throw.

'Oh, now come on, babe, don't be annoyed with me just because I was worried,' she half-whispers with studied sexiness, moving in to nuzzle against his earlobe, which I happen to know is a major turn-on for him.

'I missed you, that's all, Jamie,' she murmurs slowly, sensually.

Jamie?

'I was lonely without you. We haven't been together since before, well . . . what happened to Charlotte . . .'

Oh PLEASE, it's eleven in the morning!

'Mmmm,' he mumbles thickly, letting her play with his lank hair, then letting her kiss his neck. With the eyes darting guiltily around the front drive in case Declan arrives, I notice.

OK, if it's possible for angels to barf, then I think I'm going to throw up. Right now.

'You still feel the same about me, don't you?' she murmurs, moving up to kiss his face now, the voice so saccharine, it would nearly give you diabetes.

'Mmmm,' he half-groans, kissing her back and feeling up her thigh at the same time. 'And I'm sorry for snapping at you, baby.' He's breathing heavily now, murmuring into her ear.

'It's OK. I understand.'

'Still love me? Even though I'm a cruel bastard?'

'Still love you. And you're not cruel, you just like people to think you are. Underneath, you're really a pussycat.'

'Even though I'm narky? And I haven't been treating you right?'

'Still love you.'

'Even though, at the moment, I'm sure I stink like Calcutta at low tide?'

Vintage James Kane: get around a woman by giving her the little-boy-lost look, then cracking a gag. Albeit a rubbish one.

'Still love you,' she giggles. 'Now stop talking and take me upstairs.'

OK, now . . . actual vomit is beginning to rise at the back of my throat.

'RIGHT, THAT'S IT, THAT'S ENOUGH! You can bloody well STOP that carry-on this instant!' I find myself yelling at the top of my voice, starting to feel like a voyeur and hating it, and not able to take any more of this crapology.

'What?' says James, pulling back.

'Nothing, darling,' says Sophie, puzzled.

'You just told me to stop.'

'Did not.'

'Did, too.'

'OH, WOULD YOU HAVE A LITTLE BIT OF RESPECT FOR THE DEAD,' I snarl at the pair of them, furious. With myself as well, for being dozy enough to think that the bastard actually loved me and was in tatters without me.

Blinded to reality in life, and now in bloody death too.

'Sophie, did you just say something about respect for the dead . . . ?' says James. But there's no shutting me up now.

'SOME OF US ARE STILL WARM IN OUR GRAVES, I'LL HAVE YOU KNOW, AND HERE'S YOU PAIR ACTING LIKE . . .'

'Can you hear that?' he says, looking all around him, like there's a burglar loose in the house.

'Hear what?' says Sophie.

'Stuff about . . . graves?'

I do not believe this. Can he actually hear me?

'James?' I say, tentatively.

'Who is saying that?' he shouts, half-terrified. 'Is someone in here?'

'Would you please mind telling me what's going on?' says Sophie, the voice getting back to its usual screechiness. A big improvement, by the way, on her sexy voice.

'Tell me you just heard that,' he shouts at her, panicky now.

'Heard what?'

'James Kane?' I say again, slowly and distinctly, and I might as well have added 'testing, testing, one two three', on at the end. This can't be true . . . can it? Can he really hear me but no one else can?

'My name, someone just said my name, Jesus Christ, Sophie, you must have heard that.'

'Heard what? You know, I think you're still a bit drunk from last night.'

'Who is *there*?' James shouts now, heading up-stairs, as if he's about to take on an intruder. In his underpants, armed with a mobile phone, the cack-head.

My head's swimming. I mean, no one in angel school even mentioned that this might happen. But now that it *has* . . . suddenly I get the strongest urge to start messing.

'THIS,' I say, following him and talking in a deep, slow booming voice, like a scary Vincent Price, 'IS THE VOICE OF YOUR CONSCIENCE.'

It's hysterical. He nearly falls over with fright, then runs back downstairs and starts checking out the living room and kitchen, panicking, looking behind the curtains, then under the coffee table, racing around the place like a lab rat on amphetamines. I'm right beside him, desperately trying not to laugh, hands to my mouth like a megaphone.

'RESISTANCE IS FUTILE, YOU ARE DOOMED, JAMES KANE, DOOOOOOMED I TELL YOU!'

'Sophie, will you for God's sake tell me that you can hear that!'

'James, I really think that you need to lie down . . .' she screeches back at him.

'Can you tell her to shut up?' I say in my normal voice now. 'Otherwise half-deaf Mrs Brady from next door will be able to hear her.'

'Charlotte?' he asks to thin air, the picture of terror. 'Is that you? Are you there?'

'No,' shrieks Sophie. 'Charlotte is NOT here, how can she be? It's ME. Sophie. Your girlfriend. What has happened to the not-insane part of you?'

James waves at her impatiently to shush, and if you saw the sight of him wandering around in his underpants, ashen-faced and shaking, like he's waiting on the walls to suddenly start talking to him, you'd crack up.

'James, I'm speaking to you,' says Miss Screechy Voice.

'Shhhhhh!'

'Don't shush me! Oh, for God's sake, is there a brick wall here that I can talk to instead?'

'Will you shuuuuuut uuuuuup!' he snaps at her.

'You know, if you think it's OK to speak to me like that, you're very much mistaken,' she yells back, adjusting the beret.

Bloody hell, she's an awful lot tougher on him than I ever was. A zero-tolerance policy on putting up with all his rudeness. Which, come to think of it, is possibly where I went wrong.

'Charlotte,' he says, slowly, very slowly. 'If you're there, will you say something?'

'All right then, if you insist,' I say, really starting to enjoy myself. 'Tell Sophie I'm standing right beside her, and can see for myself that all the rumours are true and that she definitely had a botch Botox job. You can tell by the way the eyelids look droopier than a cocker spaniel's. Dead giveaway.'

'Sophie has not had a botch Botox job,' he shouts back, facing the TV, with his back to me, which sets me off in peals of laughter again.

'And ask her is she still breaking in the new nose?'

'That is NOT a new nose!'

'What did you say about me?' says Miss Screechy. 'Something about Botox?'

Oh God, this is turning into a sitcom.

'Furthermore,' I say, sitting comfortably on the sofa

and stretching myself out. 'At the agency we have rude nicknames for all the clients who annoy us. And hers is Screechy Sophie.'

'Nor does Sophie have a screechy voice!'

'Plus, out of all the actors I know, she is by a mile the single biggest drama queen.'

'That is so unfair . . .'

'You know what they say, "If the tiara fits . . ."'

'EXCUSE ME!' yells Sophie from the door, with the Bette Davis eyes nearly popping out of her head, looking like the flesh is about to melt off her face at any second. 'If you think I'm going to stay here watching you screaming at thin air about Botox and insulting my voice then you've another thing coming, James Kane. Why don't you sleep off all the booze, then call me when you're feeling a little bit more like yourself? You have my number.'

'Still six six six then, is it?' I call innocently after her.

'Sophie,' he says, following her to the door, running his hands through his hair and making it even messier. 'Please, baby, just hear me out. I don't know what's going on, I could have sworn I heard . . . look, I dunno what's happening, but I'm sure there's a perfectly rational explanation.'

'Of course there is. You're still pissed,' she snaps, flouncing back to her Mini Cooper and banging the car door so hard, the windows rattle.

'And another thing,' I call out from where I'm stretched out on the sofa, unable to resist a parting shot. 'Tell her that car will for ever more be associated with Mr Bean.'

Hee, hee, hee.

Might as well have a bit of fun with this.

Chapter Five
FIONA

Incredible. Unbelievable. In fact, I'm really starting to get into the swing of this whole angelic-realm lark. Declan arrives, and immediately starts briefing James about the meeting he missed this morning, filling him in about some other big investor they have to try and schmooze later on this week. I'm lying on the sofa, bored out of my head and idly wondering how Fiona is . . . and the next thing is . . . I'm with her. It's that easy. Like I've suddenly got this free pass into everyone else's life. I'm not showing off or anything, honestly; I just thought about her, and somehow, now I'm right here beside her, in the empty staff room at the secondary school where she works, to be exact. Definitely. I've been here with her a few times before and I instantly recognize it by the horrible flowery lino on the floor, which you'd only ever find inside a school run by nuns, not to mention all the statues of the Sacred Heart tastefully dotted around the walls. Not.

And there's my girl, sitting in this little individual cubicle all the teachers use whenever they've a free period and they're supposed to be correcting homework but are actually online, or in Fiona's case at the moment, half-heartedly checking out fellas on one of her favourite websites: www.maybemorethanfriends.com. There's an unopened, untouched packet of Tayto cheese and onion beside her, which is odd as I happen to know they're her favourites. Also, even more bizarrely, there's a photo of the two of us sellotaped to her wall, and just at the exact moment I plonk down beside her, she turns to stare at it. Dear God, just the sight of that slightly bewildered, teary look on her pale, drawn face is making me feel winded, like I've physically been punched in the chest. What makes it worse is that this isn't a girl who ordinarily does emotions; she's not a high/low person like me, so to see her now, looking all red-eyed and wistful, is breaking my heart.

'Fiona?'

I'm perched on the desk, only inches from her, but she can't hear me.

Shit.

'Honey, I'll give you good money if you throw out that photo. You know perfectly well all evidence of me

98

with the fringe is banned,' I say cheerily, trying to lighten the mood.

Still nothing.

Bugger.

The one time I actually really do have loads of urgent news to tell her. I mean, Fiona and I have been known to have two-hour-long phone chats slagging off some of the more lunatic ideas that end up on *Dragons' Den*, so you can imagine the length of time we'd need to get through this latest twist.

What's doubly weird, though, is that I'd swear she's getting some kind of sense of me, because she hasn't taken her eyes off that bloody photo. Not once. Oh, this is so frustrating. I know by looking at her that she's missing me, and I miss her so much it aches, and there she is, thinking I'm the dear departed, and if she only knew that I'm actually right here, at her shoulder, just waiting to work a wondrous miracle on her behalf.

She picks up the photo now, and props it up beside the computer screen, chin cupped in her hands, just staring blankly at it. A highly offensive snap I might add, taken on an InterRail holiday, the summer we left college. One of those studenty, let's-rough-it-around-Europe trips that to this day, whenever I'm away, still makes me childishly, pathetically grateful to have an en suite bathroom with a working loo and actual toilet roll.

We ran out of money in the first week, and basically

ended up living off baguettes, bananas and beer while grabbing showers wherever we could in train stations. Believe me, in the photo it shows; I look manky and greasy-haired, Fiona looks exactly the same as she always does, only skinnier and with a peeling red nose. Otherwise, apart from wearing contact lenses instead of jam-jar glasses now, she hasn't changed a bit: the same big hopeful eyes, same neat blonde, bobbed Victoria Wood haircut, same free-flowing clothes and frilly blouses, and so teeny tiny that all the sixth-years tower over her and look miles older than she does. We often laugh and tell her that the Queen has reinvented her look more often, but Fiona's very much of the 'if it ain't broke don't fix it' school. Plus, when it comes to clothes, she was always a great one for preferring comfort over high fashion any day. Plus there's another reason why I remember that InterRail holiday as clearly as I do, but more of that anon.

Anyway, to look at Fiona, and when you factor in that she's a schoolteacher, you might fall into the trap of thinking that she's a bit conservative in a nice-old-fashioned-girl kind of way. To quote Julia Roberts in *Pretty Woman*, big mistake. Huge. When I first met Fiona, not only was she the wildest person I knew, she was the wildest person that anyone I *knew* knew. If we'd known James back then, I bet she'd even have given him a run for his money when it came to hard-core partying.

You just would never have thought it at first glance, that's all. Sort of like a Batman/Bruce Wayne thing she had going on. By day, she led a normal, ordinary existence; by night she'd drink you under the table, then pour you into a taxi, get you home, then ask you if you fancied a nightcap before you crashed out on the floor.

Lesson: never judge books by their covers, particularly if they happen to be flowery Laura Ashley covers.

But, somewhere along the way, everything changed. As soon as we graduated, she started working part-time in Loreto College as a HDip, but still managed to maintain a respectable degree of her old wildness: i.e., she'd never let a Friday or Saturday night pass without a decent binge, usually ending up in Renards, and on one famous occasion even getting a lift home at seven a.m. from the poor, bleary eyed fella that owns it, who was swaying with tiredness and probably figured this was the quickest way to get her out of there and him safely home to his own bed. Then, not long after, she was made a full-time member of staff and, all of a sudden, just never had any free time any more. A classic example of someone who's cash rich, time poor. I was forever blagging her tickets to movies or premieres that James had, and she'd always skite off home as early as she could, pleading that she had a pile of essays to correct for the next day or some school-related time-consuming project that she just *had* to work on. Not long after, she stopped coming out at all, claiming that it was a total waste of time, time that she didn't have and that, what's more, she made far more progress scouring for fellas online than she ever did in clubs, pubs and bars. A huge source of endless rows between us, with me constantly telling her that she's only one hundred tins of beans and a knitted jumper away from being a survivalist. That's when I wasn't worrying myself sick, thinking that the main reason for this massive social about-turn could all be laid firmly at the door of a certain Mr Tim Keating.

OK, I probably should explain.

Tim was Fiona's BIG love, her first boyfriend, who she dated from second year in college onwards, and you just never met a more suited pair. It's not that often you come across true soulmates, but honestly, these two were the real deal. He was every bit as wild as she was, with Barack Obama/JFK levels of charisma, and even being around the pair of them was the best fun you could imagine. Just like our Fiona, Tim had all the outward appearance of normality, but all you needed to do was scratch the surface to see the latent headcase that lurked beneath his oh-so-conservative exterior. Mad into the Clash, the Cure and the Sex Pistols; back in college he was something of a legend, and was always pulling off wild, mental pranks for the sheer hell of it. Like the time he raided the drama society's costume department, then went out on the piss with his friends dressed as a very convincing nun. Or, after a night on the tear, when he'd ended up crashing out on some friend's sofa, the way you'd see him strolling into lectures the next day with two pint glasses full of water in his hands, one for each of his contact lenses. My God, even sitting on top of a bus with him and Fiona was an adventure.

Then, after he graduated, Tim landed a big, important, flashy job in some pharmaceutical company in London, and off he went. They tried doing the long-distance relationship thing for a while, and thanks to cheapie Ryanair flights and mobiles, did manage to keep things going for a bit. But the long-distance thing eventually took its toll, and, although they stayed friends, they eventually parted company, mutually agreeing it was best if they both went their separate ways.

In fact, that InterRail holiday is for ever etched in my mind because it was just after the big break-up and I remember being astonished at how incredibly upbeat Fiona was about the whole thing. 'What was I going to do anyway, marry him?' she used to shrug at me, when I'd ever-so-gingerly pluck up the courage to ask her how she was doing, usually after a few cheapie East German beers, all we could afford. 'For fuck's sake, Charlotte, I'm twenty-one years of age. Who gets married at twenty-one? Cousins and internet brides, that's who.'

Anyway, a disgracefully short time after they split up, next thing news filtered back that Tim had got engaged to an Irish girl called Ayesha who he'd met in London, and who was doing some kind of course in TV presenting so she could achieve her ultimate goal of reading the six o'clock news on Sky, or, failing that, doing the same thing, except back home on RTE. When we all eventually did meet this famous Ayesha, I think myself and Fi half-expected her to be like a young Kay Burley: you know, a ferociously intelligent, hard-hitting journalist type. Like a female Jeremy Paxman. But she wasn't. Not at all. Instead she turned out to be this perma-tanned blonde who'd been to Mount Anville, spent all her summers at Ring learning Irish, and now fancied herself as the next Gráinne Seoige. Nor did she take too kindly to her fella being as pally with his ex as Tim was with our Fiona. More sweet-natured people than me all reckoned this was perfectly understandable, but the rest of us all figured you could practically hear the boooiiinnnggg of his bungee rope rebounding. Fiona and I were invited to the wedding, and Fi was so cool with it that she even got up and sang 'Evergreen' by Barbra Streisand at the reception. Now, take it from me, if you can do that with your ex's new bride looking daggers at you, that's all the world needs as proof that you're totally, one hundred per cent over him.

And therein lies the source of my worry. I often think that, at the time Tim and Fiona broke up, she and I were both just too young to realize what a rare diamond she'd let slip through her fingers. And who knows? Maybe that's the reason why she hasn't found anyone else since: he was just such an impossibly hard act to follow. That's the trouble with being twenty-one. You think the Tim Keatings of this world grow on trees. Anyhoo, not long after his wedding, they sort of lost touch, the way you do. To be brutally honest, we both always suspected Tim's brand-new wife wasn't a big fan of having his ex-girlfriend around, and gradually demoted Fiona to a second-, then a third-string friend, and then, within an alarmingly short amount of time, to someone they only ever exchanged Christmas cards with, scribbling across them, 'Must meet up soon, it's been ages!' But never really meant it.

Occasionally, bits and pieces of news about them would flitter back to us on the grapevine: they've relocated back to Ireland/he's changed jobs and is now working for Repak calculating people's carbon footprints/something about them having twin girls. But, as I'm always saying to Fiona, you never hear the news you really *want* to: i.e., he's realized that, actually, Fiona was the one true love of his life, and is now going around telling anyone who'll listen what a colossal mistake his rebound marriage was/that Ayesha's now in love with a Guatemalan professional poker player, so splitting up would suit her down to the ground as well/that, in the interim, she's also put on three stone.

Ho hum.

Anyway, back to the awful photo which Fiona's still staring at, and the more misty-eyed she's getting, the worse it's making me feel, so if only just to prevent me from coming over all sniffily, let me tell you a couple of things you should know about her in work.

1. She teaches English and history, and gets majorly pissed off whenever people tell her she has a jammy job, finished at four, long holidays, etc. The actual classroom stuff, she reckons, is the doddley part; fifty per cent crowd-control, and fifty per cent cattle-prodding. The real work is when she has to sit down every night and correct pile upon pile of essays with titles like, 'Analyse the part played by Bismarck in the history of the German empire, 1871–1890' or else, 'In what way might Wordsworth's "Surprised by Joy" be termed a typical Romantic poem?' Deserves every red cent she makes, if you ask me.

2. It's a posh, all-girls, fee-paying convent school, which effectively means Fiona's chances of meeting a guy through work are slim to none. Apart from Mr Byrne, the art teacher, who's late sixties and very likely gay (he went to Vegas last summer to see Céline Dion . . . go figure), all other staff members are female, married or else nuns. Also, a disproportionate amount of them are, for some reason, called Mary, but I digress.

3. Don't get me wrong, the rest of the staff are all lovely, but Fiona is the youngest by a good ten years and is always saying that the collective age of the others is about two thousand. So you can understand her feeling a bit out of it when they're all sitting around eating lunch and talking about Communions/Confirmations/worrying about leaving their kids in the hands of Filipino housekeepers while they're all mad busy at work/stressing about selling up their holiday homes for far less than they paid for them because of the recession, etc.

   Hence Fiona spending most of her free-period time with her face stuck in a laptop. And half the time, I don't really blame her.

4. Because she's the only staff member without kids, she always ends up getting roped into running the school's summer camps every year. Now Fiona always says she's perfectly happy to do it, and that the extra cash comes in handy in paying off the mortgage on her new house, but if you ask me, it's just another excuse for her not to come out at night when she's supposed to be on her holidays. The pattern would be: I'd suggest dinner or a movie, or that she come over to me and James for a barbecue, and she'd faff on about the fact that, come the summer months, she actually ends up working harder than she ever does during the academic year.

And that no one realizes, blah, blah, blah. At first, I figured she didn't fancy spending time around James, as, to put it mildly, they never really got on. Took me a while to realize that these days, the main relationship in her life was with her computer. Hence the constant push/pull battle between us, with me constantly trying to drag her out, even if only for an early bite, and her wanting nothing more than a night at home with a glass of Sauvignon Blanc in front of the bloody internet. To summarize our respective viewpoints: her attitude is that online dating is the way of the future, whereas mine is that you only end up meeting fellas with profiles like, 'bachelor, early sixties, experimental, seeks nubile early twenty-something lass for good times. Must have own chicken.'

She gives a deep, heartfelt sigh then drifts back to the computer, and my eyes follow hers. There's about ten guys' profiles onscreen and she's going through them at speed, finger hovering at the delete button. She discreetly checks over her shoulder, making sure the staff room's still empty, then turns back to mutter at my photo.

'I know what you'd say if you were here, Charlotte.'

'I am here, babe,' I say, but she doesn't react. So strange.

'You'd tell me, in no uncertain terms that I'm wasting my time . . .'

'It's a no-brainer, but then I'm a great advocate of getting a date *without* the use of a modem.'

'. . . and I'm beginning to think you might have a point.'

I nearly fall off the desk in shock.

'Hallelujah, the girl has seen the light. Almost worth dying, just to hear you say that.'

'But you're not here and I miss you so much it hurts.'

I can't answer. But I'll tell you this much. Whoever said that angels can't feel pain was talking through their arse.

'Charlotte, if it's one thing I've learned from what happened to you, it's that life's short. I have to get out there and *carpe* that *diem*.'

Another quick check over her shoulder to make sure the staff room's still empty, which luckily it is, or else they'd have poor Fiona locked up for talking to inanimate Polaroids.

'And I know you don't approve of the whole internet dating notion . . .' she mutters.

'It's not that I don't approve, hon, it's just I don't happen to believe that anyone can download love. It's such a waste of time, and if it's one thing I've learned recently, it's that we have NO time to waste. None.'

'. . . but I can't think of any other way to fill this void that you've left in my life. So if you think about it, indirectly, this is all your fault.'

'Oh, come on, it's not like I set out to die at twenty-eight.'

'You know where I'm coming from, Charlotte. I'm just too knackered these days to get out there and do the whole clubbing, pubbing scene, so therefore this is the only avenue of meeting potential partners that's open to me. Whether you like it or not, internet dating sites are the latter-day equivalent of fifties dance halls.'

Honest to God, she might as well add 'discuss' on to the end of that sentence. Like she's doling out English assignments.

'So,' she says, turning back to her laptop, in her schoolmarm voice, only not nearly as shouty, given that she's talking to herself. 'Allow me to demonstrate what's out there, and I'll also provide a brief translation from guy-speak into English for you.'

'I'm right here, babe, trying my level best to be non-judgemental, but just so you know? You're completely wasting your time. Besides, isn't wading through all these profiles like some kind of misery tourism?'

'When a guy, such as this one here, describes himself as "fun", that means annoying. Similarly "wild" means gets drunk easily. For "new age" read smelly and hairy, and for "headstrong" read argumentative. "Enjoys pubbing and clubbing" means he's an alcoholic, and this one here,' she says, tapping her biro on the screen, 'says he's "cuddly" which is a well-known euphemism for grossly overweight.'

'Listen to you, when it comes to fellas, you've more ridiculous rules than Blockbuster Video.'

'Honestly, when you read how these guys describe themselves, then you meet them in the flesh . . . some of them could give lessons in self-delusion to Heather Mills. But, on the plus side, what I do have going for me is that my expectations are very low. If you ask me, all relationships are one per cent romance, forty per cent being pissed off when they let you down . . .'

'And fifty-nine per cent picking socks off radiators,' I finish the sentence for her.

Weird, not getting any reaction.

'However . . .' she scrolls down a bit, then clicks on another guy's profile.

'. . . hello there . . . this one shows promise.'

'Shows promise? Isn't that teacher-code for what you write on school reports for kids who are rubbish at a subject but try hard, and you know their parents will kill them if they go home with any less than a C minus?'

'A dog owner,' she muses hopefully. 'This means that he's capable of emotional attachment to another living being, and can therefore be interpreted as a Very Good Sign.'

She clicks on his profile and starts filling in personal details about herself. Except that under 'age' she knocks three years off, and under 'occupation' she puts 'personal trainer'.

'You dirty big liar!'

'You needn't sit there judging me,' she mumbles back at my photo, almost making me think that the girl's been a bit psychic all this time, and none of us noticed.

She definitely senses I'm close by, she *must*.

'This is just to hook him in, that's all. When they think I'm hanging around gyms all day in a spandex leotard, I get an average of fifty per cent more hits than I do when they visualize me sitting in a staff room correcting essays. Besides, everyone sexes up their life online. It's not like this is a Stasi report, now is it?'

'Fiona, I don't know where your soulmate is but I can tell you one thing, he most definitely is NOT on a website. Besides, I bet his profile photo is airbrushed or Photoshopped and that in real life he's BOBFOC.'

Body off *Baywatch*, face off *Crimewatch*.

'OK, then, Mr Loves German Shepherds,' says Fiona, turning her full focus back on to the screen. 'Maybe it'll turn out you look like someone saving up for a sex-change operation, but there sure as hell is only one way to find out.' She immediately starts clickety clacking in her reply, and I'm not joking, the girl is faster than a travel agent at the keyboard. I peep over her shoulder and see what she's written:

> *Hey there, you sound interesting, WLTM. Free tonight for drinks at Dunne & Crescenzi?*

'Fiona, don't tell me you're actually going out at night? Like, without me having to physically put a gun to your head?'

She keeps typing, though.

> *Let me know soonest so we can fix a time, Lexie Hart.*

'Lexie Hart? What's going on, hon, are you leading some kind of secret cyber life?'

Then a bell rings in the distance, and suddenly the place goes from total silence to complete chaos, with the unmerciful thunder of classes changing and kids rushing anywhere and everywhere, screeching at each other. In the space of a few seconds, the staff room fast fills up with teachers all dying for teas/coffees/bitching sessions about the students. Sister Teresa, the principal, strides over, giving Fiona just enough time to snap her laptop shut and look like she's SO engrossed in a pile of history essays about Bismarck that she couldn't possibly have noticed anyone come in. I know by how practised she is that this is a very regular occurrence.

You can do a lot of things, Fi, but you can't fool the dead.

'Miss Wilson?' Sister Teresa says to her, at her shoulder now. 'A word?'

'Yes, Sister?'

Sister Teresa is standing right beside us now, and my God, you should see her: not one single wrinkle, and the skin all dewy and glowing, like she'd just stepped out of a salon having had a La Prairie facial. And I wouldn't mind, but she has to be at least my mum's age . . . what is it about being in a convent that halts the ageing process? If it's some enzyme that you only produce when in a non-male environment then scientists should bottle it and sell it quick.

Mark my words, this is how vast fortunes are made.

'I just wanted to say how very sorry I was to hear about your friend's awful accident. Such a trial of faith when these horrific things happen.'

'Thanks, Sister.'

Fiona's eyes have welled up again.

Come on, hon, whatever you do, don't cry, because if you start, I'll start and there'll be no stopping me.

'Just so you know, we're all praying for her in the community.'

'That's very kind. I'll be sure to let Charlotte's family know, too.'

'And you know what I always say: trials keep you

strong, sorrow keeps you human, failures keep you humble, but only *you* keeps you going.'

So, so nice. And Fiona's always giving out about her, and the way she constantly talks in religious euphemisms. She also claims that the minute school's out for the day, the nuns crack open the martinis, and that half of them smoke and watch porn. But if you ask me, it's exactly like in *The Sound of Music*, minus the Alps and the Nazis. Anyway, she and Sister Teresa chat on about the mock Leaving exams and my thoughts go back to Fiona.

I have to communicate with her, or I'll never be able to help her. I have to use everything I learned on my angelic crash course, except without frightening the living daylights out of her and giving her a heart attack. That pleasure I will save for James Kane, thanks very much.

Because, let's face it, my work here is clear. I have to find the perfect guy for Fiona. Or should I say Lexie.

Chapter Six

KATE

'I was so very sorry to hear about your sister.'

'Yes.'

'We all were.'

'I know.'

'How is your mother taking it?'

'Not so good.'

Next stop Kate. Don't ask me how I managed to do it; honestly, it's as if time and space have absolutely no meaning on whatever plane I'm on right now. Totally mental, I know, and if I was a nuclear physicist working at CERN in Switzerland, I might have some outside chance of giving an explanation, but I'm not and I don't. All I know is that one minute I'm focusing intently on someone, the next minute I'm with them. What can I say? I'm starting to feel like *Alice in Weirdland*. And I wouldn't mind, but this beaming in and out of situations lark would have come in particularly handy when I was alive. Like when Anna at the agency where I worked had a minging hangover and was in a fouler, for instance. Or whenever Mum was nagging me yet again about finding a less rubbish boyfriend. Or when I was alone at night for hours on end miserably wondering where the hell said rubbish boyfriend was.

I could go on for hours.

Anyway, the bad news is Kate's not on her own. Shit. I was dying to test out whether or not she can hear me, but now I'm afraid of mortifying her/making her jump six feet out of her skin in front of someone else. Like I said, hilarious with James but, believe me, Kate's just not the type you mess around with.

'Such a pretty girl,' says Chidi, the gorgeous Zimbabwean therapist who works with Kate at the health club. 'Always so funny . . . always joking.'

As ever, I get a lump in my throat when I hear people talking about me in the present tense. And saying nice things somehow makes it worse. Not that I ever expected them to say, 'Oh isn't it great Charlotte's dead and buried? God, I hated that stupid cow, and I'm so glad she finally got her comeuppance in life, there's the law of karma for you.' It just would have made me far less teary and emotional, that's all I'm saying.

'I know,' Kate answers, curtly. Briskly. Like she's trying to get rid of a telemarketer off the phone.

'It's heartbreaking when these things happen.'

'Mmmm.'

'This must be a very hard time for you.'

'Yes. It is.'

Monosyllabic answers, Kate? That the best you can do? Come on, she's only trying to be nice.

An awkward silence as Kate fumbles herself into a big towelling dressing gown while trying to hide all her girly bits from Chidi. Hang on, except Kate's normally at the front desk and Chidi's a therapist. Then, looking around, I slowly realize we're in the changing area of The Sanctuary, the spa that's a part of the health club where the pair of them work, and now it's all starting to make sense. Jammy cow must be getting some kind of treatment done. Kate, I should tell you, has a lot of time on her hands. I mean, she's the type of person who could tell you to the nearest euro the price differences in organic potatoes between Tesco, Lidl and Aldi. *That's* the kind of free time we're talking about. Whereas for me there are just never enough hours in the day, and I always seem to be chasing my tail around the place like some kind of demented puppy.

Sorry, I should put that in the past tense. I keep forgetting.

'But you know we're all here for you. And if there's ever anything I can do . . .'

'Right then. Fine. Thank you.'

Not even the merest trace of a wobble on Kate's lower lip, nothing. But then, I mentally remind myself, she has a tendency to react with anger and not anguish to things. Example: when Dad died, she was just furious with everyone and everything for about two years afterwards, which is about how long they say grief takes to heal to a bearable level. I went for bereavement counselling, which incidentally was a total waste of money. The only pearls of wisdom I got were that there are apparently five stages you go through: numbness, disbelief, anger, all of which are a sort of dress rehearsal for the depression which follows, then finally one happy day you arrive at acceptance, or at least that's the theory.

It took six grossly overpriced therapy sessions even to be told that much, and the dull, gnawing pain I was going through didn't lessen a jot. All I could do was sit there thinking that for the exact same money I could have had a lovely new Fendi handbag. I had all the grief to deal with anyway, might as well have had a decent accessory to go with it. I really *am* that shallow. Kate, on the other hand, absolutely refused point blank to talk to anyone about Dad's death; she just went into a very bad mood for years, and didn't really come out of it until she met Perfect Paul.

In her defence, though, I do have to point out that you'll go a long, long way to meet someone with a heart of gold quite like hers. Always worrying about Mum, always minding her, calling her every day, doing all her grocery shopping for her, generally taking care of her in an older, responsible, big-sistery type manner. Then there's the way she's forever giving me little lectures about how she'd basically rather see me dating an Ebola-ridden test monkey than a messer as non-committal as James Kane. Not her exact words, and certainly not what I ever wanted to hear, but that was her general drift. She only says these things because she cares, I'd have to remind myself through gritted teeth. And there really, genuinely, isn't anyone as caring, generous or concerned as our Kate. Honestly. It's just that sometimes you have to mine quite deep to find that thread of gold that runs through her, that's all. Besides, she only ever gets *really* thorny when a) stressed, b) pre-menstrual, or c) grieving.

Which might go some way towards explaining her behaviour right now.

'If you'd like to come this way?'

Kate says nothing, just mutely follows Chidi down a narrow corridor and into a dimly lit treatment room, with aromatherapy candles burning and a lovely smell of rose oil. Up she hops on the bed and whips off the dressing gown as Chidi gently covers her with a load of towels.

'OK then, let's go through your questionnaire, will we?'

Kate doesn't even answer, just clicks her tongue in this really impatient way she has.

'Let's see, now,' Chidi says, speed-reading her way down the clipboard in front of her.

'Thirty-three years old, no allergies and no previous health problems, is that right?'

'No, I just thought it would be fun to lie on the form. Yes, that's right.'

'Ooooookaaaaaay.' Chidi's clearly good at picking up narky vibes. 'There's just a few more questions I need to ask before we can start the treatment. So, how many hours' sleep have you been averaging per night?'

'I don't know. Six or seven. A normal amount.'

'That's good, considering, well . . . considering what's happened recently.'

'Well, that's Valium for you.'

'Oh, right, I see. And how's your diet been?'

'Fine. Perfectly balanced. Still a size ten, aren't I?'

Chidi just smiles politely, and at this moment I'm thinking the girl could probably give lessons in patience and forbearance to the Dalai Lama.

'And no muscular problems to speak of?'

'None.'

'Do you smoke?'

'Eughhh, no.'

Too bloody true. On the rare occasions she'd invite

me and James over to her pristine show house (or Ajax Towers, as he nicknamed it), she'd make him smoke on the street outside. Not even in the privacy of her front garden, as it annoys her when smokers tip ash all over her geraniums. And if you think that's bad, you should see her in action when serving cold drinks on warm days, where the cast-iron house rule is 'under ten degrees, use a coaster'.

Poor old Perfect Paul, there are times when you'd really have to feel sorry for him. James and I would often speculate on how he put up with Kate and her worse excesses, such as the 'no shoes to be worn at any time indoors' policy, when she got the wooden floors done, or the fact that she sends out her tea towels to be ironed. Or (honestly) the fact that she can't even put the bins out without her lipstick on. Through romantic goggles, I would put it down to Perfect Paul loving and adoring the ground she walked on so much he'd put up with just about anything, which was always inwardly followed by the tacked-on worry . . . so why doesn't my boyfriend feel the same way about me? James just reckoned that behind the steel magnolia exterior, Kate was a tiger in bed, and that's what made it work for them as a couple, but then sex is pretty much always his answer to everything.

'Do you drink alcohol?'

'No.'

Oh, you dirty big liar, Kate. You can sink a half-bottle of Merlot quicker than anyone I've ever seen.

'Do you have a regular exercise regime?'

'Yes.'

Yet more lies. Strolling around the Dundrum town centre does *not* count as a workout. And don't get me started on the time Mum and I clubbed together to buy her a course of Pilates classes one Christmas. She managed one, then decided that the floor in the dance studio where classes were held was far too dusty and splintery to lie on for a full hour, and packed it in. If there was an award for the greatest gym dodger alive, it would go to Kate, hands down.

'Would you describe your lifestyle as stressful?'

'Most definitely not. For God's sake, look at the form, I ticked the box that said I was relaxed, didn't I?'

Even though she's lying down Kate's arms are tensely folded and I can see poor Chidi discreetly rolling her eyes, probably being made to feel a bit like an interrogator at Guantánamo Bay by now.

'Do we really need the preamble?' Kate eventually says, sitting up now, face like a wasp. 'Can't we just get started? Please? I have a list the length of my arm of things I need to do today.'

'Kate, I really need to ask you these questions before we can begin the course of treatments. You know this. You work here. Be patient.'

Silence. You can nearly physically see the penny dropping with Kate that she's gone a bit far.

'Fine,' she says, moodily lying back down again. 'Sorry.'

'So,' says Chidi, softly, softly. 'Would I be right in saying you're here for help with . . . well, with what you must be going through at the moment.'

A long, long pause.

Oh, Kate. If you knew that I'm only inches away, watching over you.

Mind you, knowing her, if she did know I was right by her side, chances are she'd order me out of here, then rip my head off for daring to invade her 'me' time. Prickly gal, our Kate, at the best of times.

'Yes,' she eventually answers.

'I completely understand,' Chidi nods sympathetically.

'And . . . no,' Kate continues, propping herself up on her elbows and eyeballing her. 'There's something else. But if you breathe a word to Heather at reception I'll come after you. You know what a big mouth she is.'

As I said, Kate's unbelievably private. About her own stuff, that is. Like me and Mum, however, she's perfectly happy to gossip away about other people.

'I want to get pregnant.'

Chidi just nods.

'OK. And how long have you been trying?'

'I don't know. Three years. Too long. Since we got married, and by the way, up until then, my principal method of contraception was prayer. And before you ask, yes, I've tried everything and nothing works. I'm on just about every vitamin known to man that's supposed to help you conceive, and absolutely no joy. B6, B12, zinc, folic acid. I even have Paul on them as well, I'm not taking any chances. Honestly Chidi, shake me and I'll probably rattle.'

'Have you spoken to your GP about this?'

'She says I just need to chill out a bit, and that there's no reason why it shouldn't happen naturally. She's the one who suggested I give this a try. If it was up to me, I'd just get hard-core fertility drugs and lots of them, followed by a good blast of IVF. Which is my next stop, by the way. But apparently relaxation is the key. Everyone is constantly telling me to relax, relax, relax. Which is why I fail to understand why I haven't got pregnant by now. I'm one of the most laid-back people I know. If I was any more laid-back, I'd be dead. Come on, you know how little work I put in: when I am here I spend most of my time gossiping with you, or else reading trashy magazines, or else on the phone. Who, I'd like to know, is more relaxed than I am?'

I'm not kidding, her knuckles are actually white as she says, or rather snaps, this.

Chidi just looks on, worried.

'Kate, love, it's been a terrible time for you and your mum. Your body needs time to recover from what you're going through emotionally.'

'No, it bloody doesn't. I want to get pregnant and I want it to happen asap. Over the age of thirty-five it's far, far harder to conceive, everyone knows that. Which only gives me two years. TWO YEARS. Bloody hell, I barely have time to have this conversation with you.'

'Reiki can help with your reproductive health, Kate . . .'

'Good, then let's get going.'

'But stress is very often linked to fertility problems and, you'll forgive me for saying it, but you do seem a little strung-out.'

Understatement of the millennium. You should just see Kate, lying there drumming her fingers off the edge of the bed, so tightly strung you could tune a guitar by her.

'Which is only natural, Kate, given what you're going through right now. What I'm trying to say is, reiki can help to restore balance to your body and realign your chakras, but are you really sure that right now is the best time for you to conceive?'

'Never been more certain. If I've learned anything from . . . recent events . . . I mean . . . from what's happened . . . with Charlotte and everything . . .'

The voice is starting to wobble a bit now, and I'm

willing her not to cry, if only because it'll start me off and I won't be able to stop.

'. . . it's that we have to get on with life. Simple as that. I want babies and lots of them, and I want them now. I have NO TIME TO WASTE. So can we get going? Can you start rearranging my chakras or whatever it is you do to help me chill out, now, please?'

Chidi sighs, and I wish I had the power to read thoughts, because right now she's probably thinking this is the single most hopeless case she's ever had.

'OK, then. I'll be back in one moment,' she eventually says to Kate. 'I just need to get some more rose oil. So, I'll leave you here to relax.'

'Fine.'

'Kate, you heard me. RELAX.'

'OK, OK.'

She dims the lights, and no sooner has she slipped out the door than I'm over to Kate, sitting on the edge of the bed now, like we used to as kids, when I was pleading for some unwanted, no-longer-loved toy of hers to play with. Usually a doll that she'd have flung away anyway without blinking. She just enjoyed seeing me beg.

'Kate?'

She turns her head sharply.

'Kate? It's me. Don't get a fright.'

Now she's up on her elbows, looking puzzled. Oh my God, this is amazing, she hears me, she must. YES!

This makes the task ahead SO much easier in every way.

'I'm here, Kate. Right here.'

I touch her hand, but she doesn't react. Not a shiver, nothing.

'Kate? Katy Katy Kate!! Do you read me? It's Charlotte, I'm here!! Beside you!! Hello, hello helloooooo? Earth to Kate!!'

She's still looking around her, confused. Then, out of nowhere, I start to hear what she's hearing, or at least I think I do. It's a very faint buzzing noise coming from inside the pocket of her dressing gown, hanging on the back of the door. In one bound, Kate's out of bed and over to the door, towel draped over her. Then she fishes her mobile out of the pocket, buzzing away like a vibrator.

Bugger. That's what she heard. Not me at all. Which means James is the only one who can hear me. Which, now that I think about it, means I've *seriously* got my work cut out for me.

'Hello?' she snaps at whatever poor unfortunate just rang her. 'Oh, for God's sake, did you have to ring right now?'

I can't tell you it is, but I'm guessing it's Perfect Paul, because you could really only cut the snot off your nearest and dearest like that and still live to tell the tale.

'No, I'm not at home,' she answers to some unheard

question, sitting up beside me on the bed, arms folded, all ears. 'Why, where are you?'

More mumbling down the other end of the phone.

'OK . . . well then, you could run into Marks & Spencer and pick up dinner for tonight . . . no, Mum is coming over . . . we've already had this conversation, remember? Because it's not good for her to be on her own. We need to support each other now, more than ever, Paul. You know how upset she is . . . because I *worry* about her, that's why. Oh for God's sake, how many times do I have to repeat myself? Yes, I DID tell you about the dinner, several times in fact. Is it my fault you were watching the bloody Premiership at the time?'

A deep, put-upon sigh here, and more mutterings from the other side of the call, while Kate starts massaging her temples, like she's a migraine coming on.

'. . . right then, here's what we need. Chicken fillets . . . the ORGANIC kind, not the cheapie ones, the ones that are oven-ready . . . Paul, are you writing this down? Because I don't particularly feel like having to traipse back into town for all the stuff you forgot, that's why. Because that's what *always* happens on the rare occasions that I ask you to do something for me . . . Fine, thank you. Courgettes. Lemons. Parmesan cheese, pre-grated. Dauphinoise potatoes . . .' She's ticking things off her fingers as she works through her mental list.

'. . . Oh, and something for dessert. Anything . . .

no, no, except that. Because cheesecake gives Mum an upset stomach, as you well know . . . there's no need to get snappy with me, I'm just telling you . . . I am NOT nagging, and you better take that back . . . Because, for bloody ONCE, I'm taking a little bit of time out today, and supermarket shopping doesn't happen to be part of my agenda, that's why . . . (*Another big shuddery sigh here.*) . . . having reiki, if you must know . . . because . . . because . . . because it might help, that's why. Because I'm prepared to try anything. But most of all because I need to try to . . . you know . . . get pregnant . . . to help me feel anything other than what I'm feeling right now. Because I can't cope with it, with . . . what's happened . . . and . . . just missing my little sister so much that it's killing me . . .'

Oh, good God. It's like the floodgates have opened, and now that they have, the tears won't stop. She's sobbing uncontrollably, and I've got my arm around her and am cradling her to me, but she doesn't even realize. I knew it. Knew she was misdirecting anger when she's actually grieving, and using poor old Perfect Paul as some kind of human punch bag. This is just what she does. I mean come on, no one gets that worked up about organic chickens and cheesecakes from M & S, now, do they?

Oh, Kate, Kate, Kate, I think, hugging her tight.

I know you want a child so much that it's eating you up, and I know that'll help you heal. And you'll be a wonderful mum, too. OK, maybe a zero-tolerance one, but there's no doubt about it, you'll be great.

I just haven't the first clue what I can do this end to help. Apart from going in there and magically fertilizing an egg for you.

I am not the bleeding Little Flower.

So what AM I going to do?

Chapter Seven

JAMES

I don't even know how it happened, but now I'm suddenly back with James again. In the meeting room of Meridius Movies, as it happens, which is in one of those old Georgian houses in the centre of town, except recently it's been converted inside out. Well, for 'converted', read 'tarted up a bit', so now it's all restored pine floors with every spare surface painted white. Lovely, or at least it would be only James insisted on putting a snooker table into the bay window, for no other reason I can think of than to impress boys. Women, myself included, tend to just roll their eyes heavenward at such a shameless display of boy-toyism. Kind of like walking into an elegant, fabulous town house, then, once you're inside, discovering you're actually in the Playboy mansion.

James is sitting here with Declan, looking a hell of a lot more sparky than he did first thing this morning. I mean, OK, so he mightn't exactly look like he was carved by Michelangelo, but you get the picture; in the interim, somehow he's managed to have a shower and clean himself up a bit. Anyway, from what I gather they're going through their pitch for some big investors' meeting they have coming up. Really boring idea too, called *Let He Without Sin*, about an elderly priest with Alzheimer's who breaks the seal of the confession box and starts telling anyone and everyone who'll listen about all the sins he heard down through all the decades. Woman in the thirties goes to bed without nightgown shock, and lonesome farmer terrorizes sheep, that kind of thing. I know, yawn, yawn, my, won't that pack them in at the multiplex. Believe it or not, it's actually based on a bestselling novel of the same name, written by an ex-priest, who launched the book to great acclaim, then spent what felt like the next two years permanently on the telly plugging it. In fact, when James first optioned the book, I used to get him to read chunks of it out loud in bed to help me fall asleep. Better than half a Mogadon any night for knocking me out for the count.

Back to the meeting, and honestly, it's like James and Declan are stuck in first gear: they're crunching out boring, boring budget costings in advance of said investors' meeting, and it's the same boring figures that are being bashed out over and over again, till I'm so brain-fried I'd nearly hurl myself out of the window just to get away. What the hell, I'm already dead.

I'm just picking my moment to start a conversation with James, mainly to double-check that he can still hear me, seeing as how no one else seems to be able to, when out of nowhere, in bounces Hannah, Meridius's TV development executive. A very posh and important title, I know, but basically her job involves wading through the mountainous slush pile of scripts they get sent daily from hopeful screenwriters, sifting the filmable ones away from the dross, then developing the ideas from there to something that we end up watching on TV on a Sunday night and saying, 'Jaysus, how in the name of God did that crap ever get made?'

Hannah's worked here for ever, and aged about forty or forty-one, she's that bit older than everyone else. She's attractive in a Teri Hatcher sort of way, you know: wears barely-there make-up with tight denims, high heels and Zara tops all the time. She's also unbelievably discreet about her own personal life. Which, let me tell you, is kind of unheard of in the independent production business: a tiny, close-knit community, where everyone's private stuff is kind of like a soap opera for everybody else to enjoy. I mean, God alone knows the sheer hours of entertainment James and I must have provided over the years with our many flaring rows and public bust-ups, and you name it. Then there's Declan, who tries his damnedest to cultivate this hard man 'rock and roll' exterior, right down to the leather jackets; always going to gigs of bands you never heard of, with names like the Ting Tongs, and always out late-night carousing, probably as much to keep up with James as anything else. But within the business, everyone knows right well that he still lives with his mammy, and each evening goes home to his dinner on the table, all his washing and ironing done, plus cable telly. Bloody hell, I'd move back in with my own mum tomorrow if I could look forward to that kind of red-carpet treatment.

Sorry. I should have put that in the past tense.

It keeps slipping my mind.

Hannah's not like the rest of us, though. I don't know how she manages to do it – keep the lines clearly delineated between work and private life, that is – but the fact is, I know as little about her now as I did the day she first came to work here, years ago. James and I often used to try to fill in the gaps as we'd lie awake in bed at night. We'd have great crack working out all these elaborate fantasy speculations: the best one was that she'd actually been married, but the husband was a huge drug baron and she didn't realize it till it was too late, then when he died in a gangland shootout in West Tallaght, his multitudinous enemies came after her, so she went on the witness-protection programme and was issued with a whole new identity and sent to work in Meridius Movies, but one fine day, they'd come after her and it would all end up in a bloodbath. A bit like *Goodfellas*, except set in South Dublin. James would then throw in his tuppence-worth: that she was secretly working as a high-class escort girl for extra cash, to keep her in the lifestyle she was accustomed to, and that she's not at all averse to threesomes. Typical him, always having to introduce sex into the mix.

'A real mystery woman,' he'd say admiringly, rounding off the conversation, before we turned out the lights. He fancies her, I'd then think, lying awake in the dark staring unblinkingly at the ceiling. Inevitably, then, I'd slowly fill up with a totally irrational jealousy, followed by a bout of self-hatred for being so possessive over him. I mean, why did he have to have this effect on me? And what was I supposed to do, anyway, follow him into work every day to keep an eye on him? Funny, exactly what I had to go through just to see what a dysfunctional and ridiculous relationship I was in.

'Dec, just popping out for a latte, want anything . . . ?' Hannah breaks off, spotting James for the first time. 'Oh my GOD, I didn't expect to see you back at the office for . . . well . . . for a good while yet,' she says, stunned. For a split second I wonder if she's about to hug him, then I remember . . . she's just not the demonstrative type. And I'm right, she doesn't.

'Thanks, Hannah, that's really sweet of you,' says James, looking up from a spreadsheet and smiling at her appreciatively. Not quite his usual full-on, charm-fest grin, given the circumstances, but not too far off it, either.

'So . . . how are you doing?' Hannah asks, genuinely concerned.

'Holding up, you know yourself.'

'I understand. I really am so, so sorry about what's happened. And just so you know, we're all here for you.'

'Thanks.' He smiles. 'That's good to know.' I'm not joking, he even manages to eye her up and down while delivering this perfectly innocuous speech, like his uncontrollable flirt-gene just takes over. When you're James Kane, women are there to have the pants charmed off them, regardless of what might be going on in your private life. Not even bereavement can stop him. Which, quite frankly, is starting to make me so, so angry.

Anyway, Hannah disappears off to do a coffee round, Declan moves on to the even more boring topic of location scouting for the TV series, and now I'm sat right beside James, bum on the big mahogany desk, inches from him, waiting to pick my moment.

He starts to shiver after a bit, so I know he's sensing something's up.

Good.

'Can we get the heating on?' he interrupts Dec. 'I mean, is it just me or is it bloody freezing in here?'

'Ehh . . . it's just you,' says Dec, looking worried. 'It's the middle of May, it's not cold.'

Then James's phone beep-beeps as a text comes through. Declan just looks up from across the table, clearly not impressed by another interruption, but too polite to say so. I'm right beside James, though, and can read the text over his shoulder.

JAMES, I WANT TO SEE YOU. TONIGHT? MY APARTMENT, SAY 8 PM? NEED TO TALK, SXXXXXX

Oh for f*ck's sake, I do not *believe* this. If I hadn't already copped who it was from, there it is right in front of me. I look up into the address bar and see one name. Sophie.

'Anything urgent?' Dec asks.

'Eh, no, just Charlotte's mum wondering if she can call over later to pick up some of her stuff,' he answers, cool as chilled steel.

And that's what starts me off. Not that he can lie so easily, without it costing him a single thought, but at his having the brazen bloody neck to drag my mother into it.

Right then. War.

'Oh Jaaaaaames?' I'm almost shouting into his ear, like an Avon lady, and the reaction is hysterical: I swear I can nearly see the blood draining from his face.

He ignores me, though, and lets Dec drone on and on about the feasibility of a night shoot in some shopping centre, made to look like it's daytime, to avoid gangloads of kids running up to the camera and sticking their tongues into it.

'I know you can hear me, James, and FYI, I've no intention of shutting up,' I bellow at him, right into his face.

No reaction, just the merest eyelid flicker. Take more than that to put me off my mission, though.

'No, dearest James, you weren't imagining things this morning, either. Yes. It's me. Your beloved Charlotte. Who you're so, so SO upset about that you're still taking texts from your new girlfriend.'

He coughs, and stays so unnaturally focused on Declan that now I'm half-wondering if what happened in the house this morning was just some kind of blip and . . . well, maybe he can't hear me at all any more. Just like Fiona and Kate can't.

Which effectively means I'm f*cked.

I mean, how am I supposed to wreak vengeance on the bastard, now?

'Does Declan know about you and Screechy Sophie, by the way?' I ask, probing, wondering how in hell I can provoke some kind of a reaction out of him. I try to pick up the glass of water in front of him, but nothing, my hand just glides straight through it. Shit. 'Because I'm sure I can figure out some way of telling him,' I bluff, pretty certain that if James suddenly can't hear me any more, then it's highly unlikely Dec can.

Still nothing. He's still giving Dec his most laser-like, concentrated look, as if night shoots and budget costings are suddenly the be all and end all of his very existence.

One last try and I know exactly what's guaranteed to drive him mental. My singing. No false modesty here, but I have, without doubt, one of the worst voices known to man, so bad that whenever we were having a row (i.e., often) all I'd have to do was break into a couple of verses of 'Let It Be' by the Beatles, and he'd either lock himself into the bathroom to escape the caterwauling or else concede defeat in whatever argument was blazing. Anything, just to get me to shut up.

I clear my throat, like a Covent Garden soprano about to launch into warm-up.

Right then, at the top of my horrific voice, I start belting out 'Cabaret' by Liza Minelli, the only song I know most of the words to. Now, I'm no Simon Cowell, but if by some miracle James *can* hear me, I'd say he'd rather listen to human nails being dragged down a blackboard than what I'm coming out with now.

I'm just at the bit, 'When I go, I'm going like Elsie', and am giving it an ear-shattering, diva belt, full throttle, the whole works, when out of nowhere James, white-faced, interrupts Declan.

'Man, are you . . . ehh . . . hearing something . . . by any chance?' he asks tentatively.

Yes, yes, yes, yes, yes, yes yes!

'Hearing what?' says Dec.

'That. That noise. That horrible noise. It sounds a bit like . . . emmmm . . . singing, actually.'

I'm happily caterwauling right into James's face the bit about admitting from cradle to tomb not being that long a stay, and it's hysterical, the louder I get, the paler he gets.

'Maybe there's . . . a radio or something on upstairs? Yeah, that's it . . . a radio,' he says, hopefully. 'That . . . emm . . . Hannah might have left on?'

'Ehh, no,' says Declan, looking really worried now. 'There's no radio anywhere. Are you absolutely sure you're OK, man?'

'Never better,' he lies stoutly. 'Go on, you were saying about the . . . emmm . . . oh yeah, the costings?'

Right then. I take a big, dramatic pause to refill my lungs so I can really do justice to screech-ing out the very last bit about coming to the CABAAAAAARRRRREEEEEET!!' Bingo. Success.

James is up on his feet, green in the face and making an immediate beeline for the door, which he flings open, then listens intently, with his hand to his ear. A bit like a gesture you'd see someone doing in a bad play, only funnier. For the laugh, I stay totally silent now, just to play a little mind-game with the aul bastard.

'Hello?' he calls out, from the foot of the windy Georgian staircase right up to the top of the building. 'Anyone up there?'

Silence.

Declan's at his shoulder now, really concerned.

'There's no one else here, man,' he says, gently leading him back into the conference room. 'Hannah went out to get coffees, remember? Don't you remember her asking you if you wanted anything? You chatted to her, just now. Do you remember? Tell me that you remember.'

Hysterical, he's actually talking to him like a mental health professional.

Hee hee heee.

'I could have sworn I heard . . .' says James, looking bewildered.

'Totally understandable,' says Declan firmly.

'No, you don't understand . . .'

'Yes. Yes, I do. I think you've been through a terrible time, and maybe you should think about going home for a lie-down. I can take things from here. Listen to me. Go HOME. Sleep. Rest. Chill. Relax. Everything is under control.'

'Not a chance, man,' says James, shoving past him back into the conference room. 'I wouldn't leave you high and dry, especially after me letting you down like I did this morning. It's not fair on you. I'm telling you, I'm OK. Just . . . thought I heard a voice, that's all.'

Poor Declan's anxious-looking face says it all. 'You heard a *voice*?'

James looks at him, as if weighing up whether to confess all or not.

'Charlotte's voice,' he eventually says, sheepishly.

'I see.' Declan sighs worriedly.

'Not for the first time, either. Happened earlier today, too.'

'You know, I can't begin to imagine what you're going through, man, but I do think you might have come back to work too soon. Why not take a bit more time off, maybe even talk to someone about this?'

Just the merest hint of a suggestion that he consider talking to a therapist is too much for macho-man James, who reacts as if it was suggested he join a church choir.

'I don't NEED to see anyone, I just could have sworn I heard . . .'

Oh, to hell, I'm perched on a swivelly chair, and I can't keep shtoom any longer.

'You weren't imagining it, James. It *is* me. Charlotte. And I'm right here, as it happens. Don't ask me how come you can hear me and no one else can, but there you go. Great unanswered mysteries of the universe and all that.'

Honestly, for a split second, I actually think he's going to throw up.

'Declan, please, for the love of God, will you tell me you heard that?'

'Heard what? There's nothing to hear.'

'Charlotte, I swear, I can hear her. She says she's here, in the room with us. Oh for fuck's sake, what is going on?' He's getting hysterical now, and the more his voice rises the giddier I get. Well, could you blame me? He is single-handedly responsible for bringing about my demise, after all. I mean, I'm *entitled* to want his whole life to go up in smoke, aren't I?

'Tra la la la la, Tra la la la la,' I hum loudly, the music from the Vodafone ad, just to annoy him.

'She's singing now.'

'Singing?' says Declan flatly.

'Yeah. The song from the Vodafone ad, I think. Can't be too sure, she has a minging voice.'

Just for that, I start singing even louder, as Declan moves into him, grabbing him by both shoulders like the Mafia do in films.

'James, I want you to listen to me very carefully. You know that it's not possible you're hearing Charlotte right now. Don't you?'

'Yeah, but . . .'

'It's just impossible.'

'I know.'

'And you also know that there's no way on earth she can be singing you the theme from the Vodafone ad, or any other commercial for that matter. I think what's happening here is that you've been fraught for the last while, you've been strung-out, and now you're just a bit over-emotional . . .'

'I am not over-emotional, I am hearing her sing, will you *listen* to me?'

'Let me finish,' says Declan, gently but firmly. 'This pitch tomorrow is too important to us. We only get one shot at hitting William Eames for finance . . .'

'You think I'm not aware of that?'

'Come on, you know what I'm getting at. We need a hit or we're down the Swanee. We've had two consecutive flops, and we're not going to survive a third one.'

'I know, I know . . .'

Bloody hell.

I, on the other hand, did *not* know.

That the company was in trouble, that is. I mean, I knew his last two projects lost money, but then James is always so brimming over with confidence and gusto and showmanship, I figured, sure his next film will make him back everything and more, won't it?

For a second, I feel a tiny bud of sympathy.

Then I remember Sophie and it instantly withers and dies.

'. . . You, of all people, know how it is in this game,' Declan is saying. 'You're a bit like a footballer, only as good as your last match. Which leaves Meridius Movies with a helluva lot to prove. So I strongly suggest you take a bit of time off and let me take the meeting. I'll handle it. William Eames will understand, what with everything that's happened in your private life.'

You should just see the pair of them squaring up to each other, like in a Western. James looking so pale, you'd swear he'd just donated a few litres of blood to a passing vampire. Declan, gripping his shoulders, designer scruffy sleeves rolled up on a shirt I know right well his mammy probably ironed for him on his way out to work this morning.

'Dec,' James eventually says. 'This project is my baby, and it has been from day one. There is just no way I won't be there tomorrow. I'm not going to let you down. Come on, I can do this in my sleep, you know that.'

'I'm just saying that a bit of time out might do you some good . . .'

'Forget it,' James bellows, so forcefully that it shuts me up singing. Then he must realize that he's being overly brusque with Dec, because he immediately back-pedals.

'Sorry, man, I didn't mean to bite your head off.'

'It's OK. You're stressed out. I understand.'

'I'll be there, and we'll raise the eight hundred grand we need, and that's all there is to it.'

'And no more talk about hearing voices in your head?'

'Whatever's going on with me, I can control it.'

'You know, Betty Ford set up a clinic in the desert based on that very statement,' says Dec, doubtfully.

'I guarantee you.' James smiles, a bit more confidently, a bit more like himself. 'I'll be in better form for this meeting than you've ever seen me in your whole life, and that's a promise.'

Oh really, James dearest? You think so?

Chapter Eight

I'm still with James. Sorry, but it's all got that bit too interesting and, what can I say? My inner nosiness just took over. A lot I didn't know, and a lot to find out. Declan's taken him off to Toner's pub on Baggot Street, round the corner from the Meridius office. So now the two of them are sitting at a table in the snug, looking for all the world like a pair of old geezers, whingeing about the youth of today/price of a pint/ state of the country being run into the ground by politicians and bankers/having to go outside and stand in the street to pull on a Sweet Afton cigarette because of the smoking ban, etc., etc. Well, that is to say, a pair of old geezers who both happen to be wearing denim jackets with one single stud earring each. You get the picture. Not for this pair one of those *über-cool* bars only down the road, with Armani-suited bouncers on the door looking like the secret service, packed to the gills with accountants trying to pick up models, and lawyers trying to pick up anyone who'll speak to them. No, James and particularly Declan, who never lets the hardman persona drop, not even for a millisecond, will only ever drink in a proper pub with sawdust on the floor and a smell of stale beer, where the average age is about ninety-seven and there's no women. Probably scared off by the horribleness of the toilets, no doubt.

They've been talking for well over an hour now, and I'm sitting across the table from them with, I'm sure, a face like a slapped mullet. And I haven't even opened my mouth once since we got here to torment James, but then that's the effect that total shock tends to have on me.

There's so much I didn't know.

That Meridius is on its last legs, for instance. I mean, OK, I knew they hadn't had a big hit in a while, but I'd no idea just how critical things had become. It seems the last project they produced that actually made a profit was *Liberator*, a four-part documentary about Daniel O'Connell. Made three full years ago, which in production terms is a lifetime *not* to have had a hit in. And that was only because the DVD sales to schoolkids who had to study him for their Leaving Cert were so high. An in-built captive audience, so to speak. Declan's project, too, I hasten to add, but then anything highbrow produced by Meridius always is. James is more

149

of the 'bread and circuses' school of thought. Sorry, make that bread, circuses and sex.

I hadn't the first clue how bad things actually were, and in my defence, would you blame me? James was always so full of swagger and big talk, it never crossed my mind that the company was in trouble. When something he produced got slated in the press he'd just riff on about what a bunch of mindless morons TV critics are, and that if they had the slightest modicum of talent, they'd be out making TV shows, not sitting with their arses stuck to couches criticizing them. Likewise, if investors bailed on him, he'd put it down to them not being real risk-takers, and that they'd be sorry when whatever they'd passed on then went on to make millions and get showered with awards, IFTAs, BAFTAs, you name it. What can I say? I got so swept up in all his confidence and bravado that, like him, I always believed that the next big thing was only around the corner, and that would set him up for life.

But it looks like that was all front. All showmanship and hot air, and now the good years are over and they're in trouble. *Real* trouble.

It must be coming up to about seven in the evening and the state of play is thus. Declan is still trying to persuade James to retreat to a nice padded room with no sharp implements lying around, and recover from the nervous breakdown he appears to be having. James, on the other hand, is not only insisting that he'll be there for the big-money meeting with their number-one investor tomorrow, but that they need to have back-up, emergency, contingency plans in case the unthinkable happens and they're flung out the door, cashless.

'OK, we do a reality TV show, because they're so cheap to make . . .' he pitches to Declan.

'Done to death, man,' says Declan, shaking his head sadly. 'Reality TV has had its day, and it's over.'

'Hear me out. A reality TV show meets a chat show, except with only one guest, who has to live for twenty-four hours in a single room with the host.'

'Crap.'

'Three cameras max. *Big Brother*, except there's only two of them in there. In their underwear.'

'I hate it.'

'And the guest is a celebrity.'

'I hate it more.'

'And we get the guest plastered drunk before they go on, so there might be a fight. You know me, Dec, I don't suffer fools gladly, but I'll gladly let fools suffer.'

Poor old Declan doesn't even answer, just stares morosely into his pint. Wish I could read thoughts, but from the look on his face I'll bet he's wondering whether or not he should desert the ship before it sinks, or else stay where he is: on the *Titanic* rearranging deckchairs. He used to be a journalist for *Hot Press* before he went to work for Meridius, and I'd say half of him is wondering whether it would be worth his while asking for his old job back. Sorry, make that crawling over broken glass on his hands and knees, *begging* for his old job back.

'OK then, property TV,' says James, undeterred.

'Hadn't you noticed? We're in a recession. The property market is dead on its feet.'

'You haven't heard me out. Pimp my house, except it's done by the two sexiest-looking presenters we can find: that leggy blonde one from *Xpose* on TV3 . . .'

'I have to stop you right there,' says Declan, firmly.

'What's up? Why are you being so unenthusiastic? Sure, we've had a few knocks, but this business is cyclical, everyone knows that . . .'

'James, really, please just drop it.'

'OK, I have it. We shoot a low-budget chick-flick. 'Cos everyone knows they make a fortune at the box office. One of those ones with a cheesy tag-line like, "Sometimes you have to lose yourself to find yourself."'

'Please shut up. Now.'

'Or no, I've a better one. "Lose your heart and come to your senses." Every thirty-something that queued up to see the *Sex and the City* movie would pay good money to see this. Guaranteed blockbuster. I can *feel* it.'

'Either you can shut up with your crap pitches or I can leave and go home. Take your choice.'

'What's up with you?'

'Nothing.'

'Spit it out.'

Declan takes a big gulpful of his pint, then wearily sinks back. You should see the hopeless look on his face: it's like he's ageing ten years for every minute spent sitting here.

'It's just that . . . you and me, man, we used to be like . . . the David Bowies of the production world. Whatever everyone else was at, we were two years ahead of them. And now look at us. Fighting for survival. Barely enough cash in the bank to pay the rent on the office. I don't know about you, man, but I'm starting to feel like . . . like we're analogue players in a digital world. Know what I mean?'

'Temporary setback. Nothing more,' says James firmly. But then this is where he excels himself and really comes into his own. When all hope is lost, he's the guy at the back going, 'This? This is nothing!' The type of fella that in a tsunami would be saying, 'Yeah, all right, so it's a big wave, but to be honest with you, I've seen worse.' If he'd been around for the San Francisco earthquake, he'd have come out with, 'Bit of a tremor, that's all.' Or at the Charge of the Light Brigade, he'd have said, 'Yeah, OK, so maybe there's a *few* canons, nothing to worry about. Promise.'

'But this is the baby that'll turn it all around for us,'

he's insisting now, refusing to let any negativity get next to or near him. '*Let He Without Sin* will be huge, we'll syndicate it, sell rights all over the world; believe me, man, I know a hit when I smell one.'

The classic James Kane motivational catchphrase. Except this time it's falling on deaf ears. Poor old Declan is still staring into the middle distance, twiddling with his earring so intently that I'm half-wondering if he whips it out before going home to dinner, lovingly cooked by his mammy. After a long, long silence, he simply says that they'll just have to give it their best shot tomorrow, and see how it goes.

'And if that doesn't work out,' he adds sadly, 'I'll have to look into bringing in the BBC and seeing if they'd be interested in doing it as a co-production. Unlikely that they will – most of their drama budget is already allocated by this time of year – but might be worth a shot.'

Now, ordinarily James would have a mild coronary at the very suggestion that any TV channel would be coaxed in to co-produce anything, his main reason being that 'they interfere with his vision'. Honest to God, you'd swear he was Cecil B. DeMille. The actual reason, I happen to know, is that if a show is a hit, he just hates sharing the glory with anyone else. Always has to be Gladys Knight and not a Pip, if you're with me. And it's a terrifying measure of just how up against it the lads are, that James just nods and lets it pass.

And that's when I begin to feel sorry for the pair of them. All their hard work, all their years of grafting, of blood, sweat and tears. Getting productions off the ground, commissioning writers, doing the endless round of investors, desperately trying to get them to stump up cash so a project can be 'green lit', and then, after all that, the real work starts. Hiring a decent director (harder than you'd think; James always reckons the majority of directors are just traffic wardens for actors, and that half of them don't know their arse from their elbow), a stellar cast, a production crew prepared to put in regular sixteen-hour days, and that's all before day one principal photography, when the director calls 'action'.

What's totally knocked me for six, though, is that the person my heart's really going out to is James. After everything that's happened, all I feel for him right now is sympathy. Meridius Movies was his from the word go, his creative baby, and unless by some miracle this magical investor comes up trumps for him tomorrow and all's well that end's well, then . . . I can't imagine what he'll do with the rest of his life. Declan, I'm certain, will be fine, his stock is high and he could stroll back into his old job tomorrow. But James has made his fair share of enemies along the way, and as for his future prospects . . .

No, no, no, this is mental! I cannot allow myself to start feeling sorry for the man who ruined my life and played an indirect part in my death . . . NO!! My God, do I have to remind myself that there's such a thing as Schadenfreude?

My hand had been on the table, right beside his, and I instinctively pull it away.

I know he must feel something because he shivers, then shoves both his own hands under his armpits, suddenly trying to warm up.

And that's when Sophie bleeding Kelly comes bouncing in.

OK, then.

So much for that mini bout of empathy, now we're back to full-scale, de luxe, out-and-out war.

'Oh HI!!' she shrieks in fake surprise, like we were the last people she expected to bump into.

Sorry, make that like Declan and James were the last people she expected to bump into.

I keep forgetting.

'Ehh . . . hi there,' says James, after he's finished sputtering on his pint. 'Sophie, yeah, hi, good to see you. You remember Declan?'

'Yeah, hi, Declan,' she says, breezily, swishing back one of the stupid-looking girlie pigtails and standing right on top of the stool I'm perched on, with her bum practically in my face.

'Eughhh, get off me,' I shout, springing up to my feet. James reacts with a jolt, but no one seems to notice. Screechy Sophie is too busy doing her, 'Oh my Gawd, like, imagine bumping into you guys here, of all places, like what a coincidence!' act, with the poppy eyes bulging out of her stupid-looking head. And fooling no one, well, certainly not me.

'I met you at the premiere of *Nine Lives, and I Picked This One?*' she smirks at Declan, hand outstretched.

'Oh right, yeah, I remember,' says Declan, although I know by him he's only lying to be polite. 'So, eh, are you meeting friends here or what?' It's unspoken, but there's the merest hint of suspicion there, all the same. This spit-on-the-floor dive bar is most definitely not the kind of place girls come into, particularly girlie girls with their boobs on display like her, wearing more bronzer than you'd normally see on the whole of Girls Aloud. Already the half-dozen or so scruffy aul fellas at the bar are reacting like a gang of freemasons whose secret handshaky meeting has just been interrupted by some bird in a Wonderbra.

'Ehh, noooooo, not exactly,' she lies back at him. Then digs a deeper hole for herself by adding, 'Just came in to use the loo, actually, ha ha ha.'

'Right,' Declan nods, letting his suspicions pass, but then I suppose he has other things on his mind. Interesting, I note, though, feeling very Miss Marple altogether; either he's the best actor this side of Daniel Day-Lewis, or he genuinely doesn't have concrete proof that there's actually anything going on between James and Poodle Head. In fairness, it would be hard for a gentleman like Dec to believe how any man could do that with his ex-girlfriend still warm in the ground.

I can barely believe it myself.

'So, like, how ARE you?' she shrieks at James, 'I haven't seen you in like, for *ever*.'

'Yeah, yeah, it's ehh . . . been a while, all right.'

Oh, for f★ck's sake, now it's like I'm watching a play being acted solely for Declan's benefit. Badly acted, at that.

'So . . . emm . . . OK if I join you for a sec?' she says, plonking herself down right where I was sitting, without waiting for an answer. Neither of them say a word, Declan just drains back the dregs of his pint and says he's going to take off. No doubt code for: 'Or else mammy will murder me for being home late for the meat, spuds and two veg dinner.'

No sooner has he left than Sophie ups and moves right in beside James.

Ohh, this'll be good.

'I called to the office and Hannah said you'd probably be here,' is her opener.

James says nothing, just does his moody staring off into the middle distance thing.

'I've been out of my mind with worry ever since this morning,' Sophie goes on, dropping the voice decibel level a bit, always a relief. 'Are you aware of how weird you were acting? At one point, you actually claimed you could hear someone talking to you. I mean, I was there, like, not having a clue what to do with you. Whether to call an ambulance or just drag you upstairs and force you to sleep off whatever it was you'd been drinking the night before.' Then she does this really irritating tinkly laugh thing as if she's trying to lighten the whole situation and write it off as a big joke.

Some hope.

'You can tell her from me that you weren't imagining it,' I chip in, cool as you like. James jumps and looks around a bit, but otherwise keeps up this whole brooding, intense silence thing he has going on.

So on and on Miss Screechy Voice goes, how she's fully aware of what a difficult time this is for him (plus she manages to do this without actually mentioning my name, no mean feat), but that it's been tough on her too, and that all she really wants is to be there for James. But it's difficult when he's a) behaving like a mentalist, and b) not answering any of her calls/persistent texts, etc., etc., blah di blah di blah.

'Do you mind if I just hum through her monologue?' I ask. Good and loud so he can definitely hear me.

James reacts as if he's just been given a short, sharp electric shock. Hilarious.

'You know,' I say, right into Sophie's face as she's yakking on about how she's used to guys chasing all over town after her, and how it's never, *ever* the other way around. 'If I'd wanted to listen to mindless droning, I could have just stayed home and switched on the air conditioner.'

With that, James is up on his feet, right in the middle of her ramble about how neglected and unloved she's been feeling of late.

'I need to go,' he says abruptly. 'I mean, leave. Now. Alone.'

'*What* did you say?' God, it's so funny how the screechiness rises in direct proportion to how pissed off she is.

'Long day, very tired, emotional, stressed, need to go. Goodbye.'

'I'm coming with you,' she says, instantly on her feet, and following him out the door where he stands squinting into the traffic, trying to pick out a taxi with its light on.

'A quick word to the wise,' I say right into his ear. 'If she as much as sets foot in our house, I'll sit beside you all night singing the entire Andrew Lloyd Webber canon. Not an idle threat, my darling. Remember, I've all the time in the world.'

'NO! Please, no!' he shouts, leaping away from me and nearly colliding with an old lady passing by, laden down with Tesco's bags.

'Well, there's no need to shout,' screeches Sophie. 'I only wanted to make sure you were OK.'

'Oh yeah, and another thing. Any chance of getting her to bring the voice down to foghorn level?' I ask, innocently.

'How the fuck is it possible that I can hear this?' James demands to thin air.

'Hear what?'

'Oh, forget it, nothing,' he trails off, knowing she'd never believe him.

Just then a taxi pulls up, and he hops in. Sophie tries her best to jump in after him, but he's too quick for her. Like a bolt, he's off, leaving her screeching after the car, 'James Kane, do not think for one second it's OK to treat me like this . . .' She's clearly not the brightest bulb on the tree, though, as it takes a second or two for her to cop on that she's shouting after a car that's just skidded off, so instead she whips out her pink mobile, punches in his mobile number, continues screeching down the phone at him, realizes that she's hurling abuse at his voicemail, then hangs up and starts furiously texting him instead.

Clearly, a last-word freak. And a text maniac to boot. Who knew?

Times like this, I'd really love to hang around, if only because she's like a walking master class in how *not* to treat men, and God knows, I have a lot to learn. Guys like James, for instance, respond well to being treated like crap, but run a mile when you hound them and chase them all over town, viz.: precisely how Sophie's behaving right now. If my downfall was that I was always too nice to him, then hers is that she's too available/obsessive/downright scary.

Believe me, I'd love to stay for more of the sideshow.

But there's somewhere far more important I need to be.

Chapter Nine

FIONA

I'd almost forgotten. Her date. With Mr Loves German Shepherds. The charm continues: all I need do is really focus on her, and next thing here we are. In an underground car park, to be exact, where Fiona's sitting on the driver's side with me plonked down on the passenger seat beside her, watching her shove her face into the rear-view mirror and lash a gooey layer of lip-plumping gloss over yet another gooey layer of lip-plumping gloss.

'You look gorgeous,' I can't help saying out loud. No reaction, of course, but then I didn't expect one. Plus, it's only the truth; she's dazzling tonight, she really is, except, there's something different about her that I can't quite put my finger on. Then I look down at what she's wearing, and it all starts to make sense. She's out of all the sensible school gear and is now wearing a tight-fitting pair of Diesel jeans, a gorgeous flowery top that I've never seen before but looks like it cost a small mortgage, and actual high heels, unheard of for her. Not unlike what the old Fiona used to strut around in, back in her drink-you-under-the-table-in-Renards days, oh so long ago. As if her online alter-ego, Lexie, comes with a completely different wardrobe to F. Wilson, mild-mannered schoolteacher.

'I look like shite,' she mutters to herself, and I just know by her that she's not even getting the slightest sense of me. 'Mutton dressed as lamb.'

Then she does this thing of staring at herself in the mirror while simultaneously pulling the skin back from her eyes and up from her forehead. She's always at it; the idea is to see what she'd look like with a facelift.

'You're beautiful just as you are,' I say gently. 'Any man's fantasy.'

'I'm old, haggard and looking down the barrel at a lonely middle age,' she half-whispers under her breath.

'You're twenty-eight, for Jaysus' sake.'

Then she whips out her Mac bronzer and lashes on even more of it, concentrating on her boobs particularly, I can't help noticing. Next thing, and I'm not making this up, she starts giving herself a kind of pre-blind-date pep talk. Honest to God, it's a bit like watching an actor doing a warm-up before a show.

'Hi, it's so great to meet you,' she practises, flinging the make-up back into her bag and putting on a miles more seductive and breathier voice than her usual 'quiet at the back!' classroom strict-teacher tones. 'I'm Lexie, I'm twenty-three . . .' Then she breaks off and double-checks herself in the mirror again, tilting her eyes to the light to inspect the crow's feet under the fluorescent light. 'Shite. No, make that, I'm twenty-*five* and yes, I work in Westwood as a fitness instructor. My favourite aerobics class is bums, tums and thighs . . .'

I know she can't hear me, so what the hell, I might as well take advantage and say what I bloody well like.

'Honey, no rudeness intended, but is this really how you want to start off a potential relationship? By lying through your teeth?'

She's ahead of me, though.

'. . . I do teach in a regular school, too. Only part-time, though.'

Right, then. Clearly, not the first time she's done this, then.

'My name is Lexie, Lexie, Lexie, Lexie, Lexie,' she repeats over and over like a mantra, hopping out of the car and slamming the door behind her. This must be it, then, the transformation from Fiona Wilson, Higher Level schoolteacher, to Lexie Hart, expert on bums, tums and thighs. Kind of like watching Clark

Kent twirl around the phone box a few times until he transforms himself into Superman. Then, only a few steps away, she smacks her hand off her forehead in frustration, does a twirl in her high heels that's worthy of Baryshnikov, and dives back into the car. Forgotten something, obviously. Next thing, she whips a Listerine mouth spray out of the glove compartment and squirts so much of it into her mouth that my larynx nearly shuts down from the triple-X strength of the minty fumes alone. Another furtive rummage around the back seat, crammed high with textbooks and a pile of essays about Charles Dickens's *A Christmas Carol*, and she produces a chemist's bag from under her laptop, lying on the floor. Then she whips out a packet of condoms, looks at them, pauses, thinks for a second . . . and shoves them into her handbag.

Oh dear God. My plan was not to leave her side tonight, not for a moment, but if she's planning on hopping into bed with Mr Loves German Shepherds, I am so outta here. Honestly, you'd think they'd issue us angels with blindfolds or something to censor some of the more X-rated stuff we're expected to watch over. Then Fiona clutches her chest, does a burp that would do a breakfast-roll-eating builder proud, pulls a wedgie out of the bum of her jeans and jumps out, banging the door behind her.

The things people do when they think there's no one

watching. In fact, I'm only waiting on someone to start picking their nose.

I'll *never* get used to it.

7.55 p.m.

Typical Fi, always a few minutes early for everything. Must come from years of handing out detention, and being the poor gobshite that's for ever in charge of ringing the nine o'clock school bell every morning. Anyway, she walks into Dunne & Crescenzi, a gorgeous Italian restaurant with the best wine list in town, and does a lightning quick scan of the place. For a horrible second her eyes light on an elderly man, sitting all alone in the corner. Nothing wrong with him, except he's about sixty-five, with a beard so long it's actually streeling into the bowl of spaghetti Bolognese that's in front of him. Eughhh. But just then, the restaurant door opens from behind us and a silver-haired woman with a sprightly walk and a reusable Marks & Spencer's bag hanging off each arm heads over to join him, giving out to him for starting without her, and asking him to order her a large glass of the house red.

Phew.

8.00 p.m.

OK. Fiona's now sitting at a table for two, strategically positioned so she can see all the comings and goings through the door, and yet still be unobtrusive and discreet. I'm sat right opposite her, and although my disapproval of her picking up fellas online has been well documented, now I'm actually wishing, hoping and praying that Mr Loves German Shepherds will turn up on time, and be handsome and gorgeous and wealthy and kind to his mum, and not any kind of mentalist weirdo who rips heads off chickens or dances naked at the full moon *at all*.

8.05 p.m.

Fiona's studying the menu, but every time the door opens, she nearly gives herself whiplash looking over, the eyes dart up and the look of hope in them would nearly break your heart.

Please, please, please let him sweep her off her feet. And be kind, caring and considerate. And not into weird internet stuff like threesomes or swingers' parties, or have a basement in his house stuffed full of iron maidens and whips and bondage gear.

And that last one is no idle worry, by the way. May I be struck down this minute if this is a word of a lie, but one time Fiona struck up a relationship with a guy she met online, who turned out to be a university professor of history at Trinity College. That bit older, divorced with grown-up kids, and a dead ringer for Michael Palin, according to her. Match made in heaven, you might think. Except that life isn't like that, is it? They'd a few perfectly civilized dates, dinner, the theatre, long walks in Powerscourt Gardens, all very respectable and above board, and all Fiona could think was, when the hell is this fella going to make a move on me? After a month, he still had yet to lay a finger on her, not even a chaste peck, nothing.

Until one fateful night, he invited her over to his bachelor pad for supper. It was exactly how she imagined a history professor lived: in a crumbling old early Victorian townhouse, most likely held up by the wallpaper, with dusty first-edition books lying around the place in piles everywhere. 'Would you like a tour?' he politely asked.

'Love one,' she simpered, wondering was this just a clumsy ruse to snog her once they got to his bedroom? Which would have been absolutely fine by her, I mean, after four weeks of being courted like a Brontë heroine, her hormones were hopping all over the place. So far so good, until they got to his basement. Which was one huge, big open-plan space covered in trellis tables, wait for it, with hundreds upon thousands of tiny toy soldiers all re-enacting scenes on an hour-by-hour basis from the Battle of Waterloo. Stunned, Fiona then made the fatal error of shoving her handbag down on top of a cluster of tin soldiers, and knocking the 'eight a.m. till eight-thirty, Mont-Saint-Jean', tableau all to the ground, which made history professor guy so apoplectic with fury she actually thought he was having an anxiety stroke.

Needless to say, she never heard a word from him again, but I did have great crack slagging her about what his intentions were. The two of them dressing up as Napoleon and Josephine, maybe; him chasing her round his basement with one arm shoved into his breast pocket shouting, 'I'm coming for you, do not wash,' and her squealing, 'No, not tonight!'

8.10 p.m.

You know what, God? I changed my prayer. Please let this German Shepherd guy just turn up. I'll settle for that.

8.15 p.m.

Still no sign and now poor Fiona's starting to get antsy. I know by the way she keeps flicking the menu over and over again. She orders a cappuccino, then whips out her BlackBerry and starts clicking away at it, pretending to be checking it for messages, I'd guess.

'God bless the mobile,' I say to her, 'the ultimate sitting-alone armour'. Then I look over her shoulder and I realize.

She's emailing me.

8.20 p.m.

From: fiwilson@hotmail.com
To: charlottegrey@gmail.com

Dearest Charlotte
Me. Yet again. I know, I know, I know you can't read this. Of course I know, and please don't think I'm going mental by emailing you all the time and forwarding you on all those YouTube links. I suppose half of me thinks that someday, somewhere you'll eventually get to read these, and who knows? Maybe even end up having a laugh over them. Plus, it's just about keeping me sane; this way, I feel that in spite of what's happened, at least I can keep in contact with you. Although I do stress that I only sent you the Rick Astley link of him singing 'Never Going To Give You Up' for the sheer post-modern irony of it.

Sometimes Fiona's that bit too clever for me and I'm left scratching my head and going 'huh?'.

But I read on, right over her shoulder.

. . . I'm missing you so much, it hurts. And what's weird is that I keep forgetting you're not at the other end of the phone. If you only knew the number of times something funny happens in work and I've thought, oh I must tell Charlotte . . . and then I remember. The other day, for instance. The Junior Certs are allowed to bring calculators into their maths exams, and one of them forgot hers. So Mary Bell, their year head, called the kid's mother and said find the calculator and get it back to the school asap. But, in her mad dash, the poor frazzled mother brought the remote control for the DVD instead. We were all falling around the staff room laughing, and I thought, wait till Charlotte hears, she'll howl, and then I remembered. Anyway, keeping in touch with you is just making all of this bearable. That and going to see you as often as I can.

She looks at her watch for about the two hundredth time.

8.25 p.m.
On she types, and on I read.

    . . . OK, the thing is, there could be a perfectly valid
    explanation why he's late.

Come on, Fi, like what? Some German Shepherd-related emergency? His dog bit a small child that had to be rushed to the A & E? The dog ran away with no muzzle on, and this guy is now combing the greater Dublin area with the ISPCA trying to find the mutt before it starts snarling and taking lumps out of innocent strangers?

... lots of reasons why he's delayed. Traffic for one. Or maybe he got the date wrong. Or maybe he was in a car accident on his way here. Or, better yet, got mugged in town this afternoon and they took his mobile, which is why he hasn't called to say that he's delayed. Then when he went to report it to the police, they somehow got it all wrong and arrested him by accident, and now he's sitting in a police station somewhere, protesting his innocence and saying, 'But I can't possibly take part in a police line-up, I have a date, a date, I tell you!' This to be accompanied by much banging and thumping of his fists on the table, like in all those miscarriage-of-justice movies.

Poor old Fi. She was always great at spinning yarns; with her love of fiction, she really is a natural English teacher. I think, though, she must be reading my thoughts and slowly starting to face up to the unfaceupable. The poor girl has just been stood up, in public, without him even having the manners to call, text, or email and cancel.

Bastard. Unimaginable, rude, bloody bastard.

Inwardly she admits defeat. And although she must feel like overturning a table, she manages to ask for the bill in a slightly-too-bright voice, leaves a way-too-generous tip, and is still able to leave with her head held high, bless her brave little soul. I walk her back to the car and she clambers in, looking numb and disappointed and silently mortified all at the same time. It's only when

I spot the pile of essays on *A Christmas Carol* lying on the back seat, waiting to be corrected, that the brainwave comes to me.

Suddenly, with astonishing clarity, a lightning bolt of inspiration strikes. And in a split second, I know *exactly* how to help Fiona. There's just something else I need to check out first. Something important. Something so obvious, I can't believe I never thought of it before.

It doesn't even take me all that long. That's how confident and secure I'm getting here in the angelic realm. In fact, I'm so completely and utterly blown away by what I've just discovered, and also what I'm about to do for her, that, to be honest, I'll be very surprised if I don't get promoted to, like . . . archangel or something after this, I think, smug as you like. Best part is, all I have to do is wait till Fiona's asleep, so I can get to work.

She goes back to her gorgeous little house, kicks off her shoes, switches on the telly and pours herself a large glass of Pinot Grigio, her tipple of choice. By now, she seems . . . actually quite OK after what's just happened, but then, as I say, Fiona's not a high/low type person like me or Kate. She's not given to whingeing or sniffling or flinging stuff around the place in a temper, as we are. She tends to deal with knocks quietly, silently, inwardly, too proud to let any chinks in the armour show. Anyway, she slumps back on the sofa, looks wearily around her and takes a big, lovely, nerve-calming gulp of wine.

Then she picks up a pile of essays she's lugged in from the car, and after correcting only two of them, with much flourishing of her red biro and mutterings of 'that is NOT an answer', she's just about done draining off the glass of wine. It does the trick. In no time at all, she stretches her feet out on the sofa and starts to doze off, knackered from a long day's work and a night's being stood up, God love her.

Right then. That'd be my cue.

Don't get me wrong, what I'm about to do is extremely tricky, this is my first go at attempting it, and I *really* have to concentrate. Every little detail has to be right or I'll blow it. I remember back to everything I learned on my angelic crash course, really focus hard on what I'm trying to achieve, then, with a snore from Fiona that you'd nearly confuse with a Zeppelin passing overhead . . . I'm on.

Next thing I know, her eyes are wide open and she sees me. And what's completely weird is that I know she's fast asleep because the cushion she was lying on is now looking a bit like the Shroud of Turin, there's that much make-up mashed into it. She sits up, looks right at me, blinks her eyes exaggeratedly, shakes her head, then slowly, in total and utter disbelief, she gingerly reaches out to touch me, patting me up and down my arms and shoulders.

Honest to God, it's like something out of a cartoon.

'Sweet Baby Jesus and the orphans,' she eventually says, with her jaw somewhere around her collarbone. 'Am I seeing things?'

'No, babe, and apologies in advance if I gave you a heart attack. You're not hallucinating, it's me. Really.'

'OK,' Fiona says slowly, propping herself up on one elbow then rubbing her eyes incredulously. 'The part of my brain that's still functioning is telling me that this is a dream. I know it's only a dream, I know right well this isn't happening, but I'll say this for my subconscious mind: bloody hell, it's certainly done its revision. You look . . . well, just like you. You sound like you. You even *smell* like you. Clinique Happy, your favourite.'

'Oh, Fi, do you know how good it is to be able to talk to you? I've so much to tell you, but we don't have much time . . .'

'I can't believe this,' is all she keeps saying, over and over. 'This is so incredible! I just can't take it in . . .'

'Now, don't get alarmed, hon, but there's somewhere I need to take you, and we really need to go right now . . .'

She's too dying for a catch-up chat though. 'No, no, no, you're not dragging me off anywhere till I talk to you. What the hell, if this is a dream it's certainly the nicest one I've had in a long time, and it certainly replaces the horse's head at the foot of the bed I'd probably be hallucinating about otherwise, given the nightmare of an evening I've just had.'

'I know, babe. I was with you the whole time. And I hate to say "I told you so" about all those nutters you meet online, but wait for it, here it comes, no one can download love . . .'

OK, now she and I are doing this thing we do, whenever we haven't had a chat for a good while (more than twelve hours, usually), of talking over each other excitedly, both of us tripping over ourselves to get our stories out. Honestly, you should see the pair of us in action, we're capable of keeping three or four totally separate conversations on the go simultaneously, and still keeping perfect track of exactly what the other one is saying.

'That's so weird, I was thinking about you in the restaurant, God, I even emailed you . . .'

'I know. Sure, I was standing reading it right over your shoulder . . .'

'I do that a lot, you know. Email you, I mean, and sometimes I even phone your mobile, just to hear your voicemail message, it makes me feel like you're OK . . .'

'I *am* OK, I really am . . .'

'Then I got back here, and I was just so stunned at being stood up like that. Was tonight boring? My God, I nearly spiked my *own* drink with Rohypnol. Then I got back here and kept thinking, I was just on a date; I should have a tongue stuck in my ear right now. Thing is, he sounded nice online, he really came across like one of the good ones, and you know me, Charlotte, I've pretty low expectations of men in general, but I just couldn't believe that he'd go and do that . . .'

'Mr Loves German Shepherds is clearly a rude bastard, and you'd a lucky escape if you ask me. He's probably into threesomes and bondage, and all sorts of kinky shite.'

Then something strikes me.

'Fi, can I ask you something?'

'Anything you like. God, it's just so good to see you.'

'Do you go out on your own to meet fellas you pick up online a lot?'

'Go on, love, rub it in, why don't you? Yes, is the answer. You know me: if he's straight, single and not in prison, then hey! He passes the Fiona Wilson test.'

'But . . . what about all those times that I badgered you to come out with me and James, and you'd cry off? There was I thinking you were home alone, face stuck in the computer, and all the time you were out dating.'

Fi blushes a bit, but says nothing.

'So, how come you never wanted to come out with me, instead?'

An embarrassed silence, but I can guess the answer before she even says it.

'Because of James,' we say together.

'Oh, Charlotte, don't be annoyed with me, it's just, well, you know I've always found him . . . a tad challenging to get on with.'

'But then, how come you never wanted to come out with me on our own? You know, on a girls' night?'

She sighs. 'Christ Alive, Charlotte, I could never in a million years say this to you, only that I know I'm dreaming, so none of this is real. It's just that, even when he wasn't around, you . . . well . . . you either talked about him all the time, or else you were constantly phoning and texting him to see where he was. I'm sorry, but I just hated seeing you in such a bad relationship. So besotted with a messer who clearly didn't feel the same about you. Worse part was, the way you'd always stick up for him and make excuses for his crap behaviour, time after time. It's like, you weren't madly in love, you were *badly* in love . . .'

'OK, get the picture, enough already,' I cut her off, a bit brusquely.

Mainly because I feel just like I've been punched in the solar plexus. Was I that bad? That obsessed with James that I even drove my best friend away? And was it so obvious to everyone around me that I was wasting my time with a complete and utter fuckwit?

179

Everyone except me, that is.

Right, then. Let this be my epitaph. Let the word go forth from this time and place that I didn't die in vain, because at least now I've come back to spread The Word. The gospel for single women the whole world over. I've said it before and I'll say it again:

Love is blind, but friendship is clairvoyant.

'Oh, I'm sorry. That hurt, didn't it?' says Fi. A deep breath, a big smile and a mental note that this isn't about me. I'm on the other side of the fence now, and my job is to help my best pal find a loving, warm, gorgeous man who'll make her happy, just like she deserves. Just like I never got.

'Back to you, hon,' I manage to say, sounding an awful lot more upbeat than I feel. 'And that gobshite who just stood you up.'

'Don't talk to me. I couldn't get my head around it, Charlotte, I really couldn't. I mean, for God's sake, look at me. I live in a flat where the curtains match the duvet covers, how can I be getting stood up in a restaurant? Surely that's someone else's life, not mine?'

'You've just been romantically challenged, that's all, but that's what I'm here to fix, with a bit of luck . . .'

'A lot of luck, more like. Might as well face it, love: up till now, my sad pathetic love life might as well have been sponsored by the people who make Kleenex . . .'

'Honey, you need to take my hand,' I interrupt firmly.

Rude, I know, but I've no choice. If Fi and I get stuck into a major chat about her recent dating history, we'll end up sitting here for the night and then my cunning plan is shot. 'You could wake up at any second, and we've bugger all time to lose.'

'I mean, I just don't get it. I'm a nice, normal, reasonably OK-looking woman, living in a society where plenty of other nice, normal, reasonably OK-looking women have all been snapped up. So why is there something fundamentally un-marriable about me?'

'Fiona . . .'

'And I wouldn't mind, but I don't exactly have exacting standards when it comes to men in the first place. I mean, once they're single, straight and can use a knife and fork without difficulty, then, hey, they're in with a shot.'

'Jesus, you don't half talk a lot when you're dreaming. Now would you ever shut up and take my hand?'

She does what I ask and, magically, it works, just like they taught me it would. Next thing, we're both sitting side by side at the back of a packed church where there's a wedding in full swing. The sun is beating in through stained-glass windows, an invisible choir is trilling away 'Panus Angelicus' and there's the strongest smell of flowers . . . oh no, wait a minute, that's just the Clinique Happy wafting up from me. Fiona looks around, a bit dazed, then looks down in horror at what the pair of us are wearing. She's back in the jam-jar glasses and I'm in a horrible, purple flowery suit with big hair and waaaaaayyyyyy too much blusher. Hard to believe that the crap I'm kitted out in was all the fashion only six short years ago.

'What are you trying to do to me?' she hisses. 'I was really enjoying this dream, and now you're turning it into a nightmare . . . look at my glasses, for God's sake. Deirdre Barlow from *Coronation Street* would be mortified to be seen in these.' She whips them off and waves them in front of me. 'This is a deeply humbling experience and I don't know why you're putting me through it. Can't believe you even remember I used to wear these.'

'God gave us memories that we might have roses in December.' I smile back at her serenely, quoting Dad. 'Besides, if you want to feel a bit better, look at the dress I'm in. It could double up as a cover for a Hummer, no problem.'

She sniggers, and I nudge her to shut up, as the besuited old geezer in front of us turns around to give us a filthy glare.

'Hey, Charlotte, seeing as how this is all just a dream, any chance you could rustle up Brad Pitt to stroll by? Or one of the Wilson brothers: Luke or Owen, either one of them would do. You know me, I'm not fussy.'

'Just shut up and put your glasses back on, will you?' I hiss at her. 'Then take a good, long look at the altar.'

She does as she's told, and I swear I can physically see the blood draining from her face.

'Oh shit, and double shit,' she says so loud that the old man in front has another good glower at us. 'Tim Keating's wedding? You decide to take us back to Tim Keating's wedding? Why would you do that? Did you maybe think it wasn't icky enough for us the first time around?'

'Just be thankful I didn't take you back to the reception part, where you'll recall that you decided it would be a great idea to get up and sing "Evergreen". After your fifth vodka and tonic, that is. I just didn't want to inflict that memory on you out of the goodness of my heart, not that I'll get any bloody gratitude for it.'

'Oh, for God's sake, get us out of here, Charlotte, quick! Before he sees us!'

But I've brought her here for a very good reason, and there's no way I'm letting her off any hooks yet.

'Look, I know this may seem a bit weird . . .'

'A BIT weird? Please, I'm redefining weird on a minute-by-minute basis.'

'But if you ask me,' I whisper, 'that doesn't look like a groom that's deliriously happy to be taking his vows. And you needn't tell me I've been watching too many soaps, either. I haven't seen any telly at all since . . . well, you know . . .'

We both focus on the priest and, more importantly, on the bride and groom standing in front of him. The groom, in particular.

'Do you, Tim, take this Ayesha to be your lawful wedded wife, to have and to hold, in sickness and in health, till death do you part?'

There's a long, long pause and I shoot a significant look at Fiona.

'I do,' Tim eventually says, with a resigned half-smile.

'I'll bet he's thinking about you,' I whisper to her. 'The woman he really wanted to marry, that is.'

Fiona looks at me like she's been winded.

'What are you trying to do to me?' she asks, gobsmacked.

'Bring soulmates together, that's all.'

'But he's *married*! Or hadn't you noticed? With kids and everything; twins, if memory serves.'

'Like I told you on the wedding day, I give it six years, max,' I say. 'And it turns out it was one of the few things in my life that I was actually right about. So, when you wake up from this dream, just remember my words: those six years are now up.'

I could have added that no one knows her better than me, and no one else remembers how, whenever she was with Tim, it was like she was lit from within. I could have told her that I know he's the only guy she ever dated who she still looks for in crowds, even after all this time. But I don't want to push my luck, so I leave it there. No point in letting her see my grand plan for her just yet, no point in revealing the wizard behind the curtain. Tonight's just about planting little seeds in her head, that's all.

Or should I say, that's all for now.

I wait till she's settled back into another dream, then off I go, on with my angelic work, she sez, feeling fierce smug altogether. It's gas; by now, I've finally accepted that time and space just don't seem to exist on whatever plane I'm on, but the really amazing part is that I don't seem to need any sleep, either. Or food. Or to keep running to the loo. All earthly and bodily functions seem to have been completely suspended for the time being. Which would have come in really handy when I was actually alive, but there you go.

Right then, my final port of call for the night. To visit someone I've been wanting to see for just the longest time, but well . . . other more pressing matters somehow got in the way. It takes a few goes for me to really focus hard on her, because every time I think about her, I start welling up. Or getting wobbly. Or else just bawling. Third time's the charm, though, and there she is. And it's just my luck that she's fast asleep on the sofa, a half-drunk mug of cocoa on the table beside her, and the crossword from today's paper lying on her knee, with only about three clues left to answer. The cryptic one, not the halfwit one that's more targeted at eejits like me.

But then, that's my mum for you. She's always been brilliant at crosswords, and claims they're better than half a sleeping tablet for knocking her out at night. Crosswords, sudoku and solving murder mysteries on telly. (Jane Marple, Hercule Poirot and Inspector Morse are her great role models in life.) In fact, Kate and I often reckon that Mum's idea of a perfect, blissfully happy retirement is to live in a small cottage in the country, and go round the place solving mysteries before the local police do, eventually gaining the trust and respect of the station sergeant, who'll start coming to her for advice first, the minute any major crime is committed. Which she'll solve effortlessly, before anyone has time to start talking about forensics or DNA tests. Just like in an Agatha Christie.

And that's when the tears really start. I don't think I can do this. I love her too much and I miss her too much. She looks so peaceful and serene, dozing away; God knows what the sight of me howling and wailing into her face would do to her. I want to visit her when I'm more in control, when I can talk to her calmly without this block of unbearable pain that's surging up inside me, just at the sight of her beautiful, pale face. The sobs are choking me now and I know that if she were to see me in this state, I'd only end up upsetting her more.

I want her to have a happy, comforting dream about me, one where she knows I'm OK, not a shagging nightmare.

So, instead, I look down at the crossword and my eye falls on 3 Across.

Verbal expression of strong affection for another, arising out of kinship or personal ties.

Three words; one with one letter, one with four, one with three, and by a miracle, I think I can guess the clue.

I try to pick up her biro from where it rolled out of her hand and on to the sofa, before she conked out, but I can't pick it up. I try again, nothing. My hand's just gliding clean through it.

Shit.

The one time I actually know what the answer is, too; and I want nothing more than for her to sleep soundly, then wake up in the morning with the clue done and somehow just know that it's a little sign from me.

The answer, by the way, is 'I love you'.

Chapter Ten
KATE

Bright and early the following morning, I find her at home, in her pristine bedroom, that's been interior designed, and feng shuied, and scrubbed and decluttered to within an inch of its life. Kate's room, in fact Kate's entire house, always reminds me a bit of the Barbie house she used to play with as a kid: everything you look at is either cream or white, or else comes with a ruffle on it, and I always feel like I'm dirtying the place just by being there. Sullying it by my mere presence. Her 'no shoes policy' is actually making me feel guilty for sitting on the bed beside her, fully shod.

I'd never, in a million years, get away with it if I was alive.

In fact, I remember one famous occasion, when the house was all newly built and Kate and Paul had first moved in. Anyhoo, she went through about a six-month-long phase of dying to show it off to just about anyone she could. Neighbours, family, friends she hadn't seen for decades; all you had to do was innocently stroll by her front door and glance in the general direction of the house, only to be dragged in, kicking and screaming, and made to admire the Waterford chandeliers/the kitchen that was carried flat-pack by flat-pack all the way down from Ikea in Belfast/the cashmere rug that no one's allowed to stand on, not even in bare feet/ the Villeroy & Boch kitchen sink that all dishes have to be washed in first before they're deemed clean enough to be loaded into the dishwasher. And by the way, I am *not* making that last one up. I only wish to God I was.

So Kate had Mum and I over for our inspection trip, and the two of us were sitting nervously in her immaculate, snow-white drawing room, terrified that we might mess something up, and listening nervously to the tick, tick, tick of the reproduction grandmother clock, a wedding present from Perfect Paul's family, while Kate stuck the kettle on in the kitchen. Eventually, just like in a prisoner-of-war movie, Mum cracked, her will to chat was just too much, so she dragged her repro Georgian high-backed chair over the thick cashmere carpet to where I was sitting in the bay window, too afraid to park my bum on the cream silk furniture, in case I might leave a mark.

'So, like I was saying, love,' she said, continuing a conversation we'd been having in the car on the way there. 'Nuala wants the whole gang of us to go to Medjugorje this summer, after the disaster of Lourdes last year, you know, when she had a list the length of your arm of stuff to pray for, and not one single thing was cured, not even her ingrown toenail, and you know how painful they can be . . .'

'MUM!' Kate screeched, interrupting us with the tea tray. 'What are you doing, moving furniture around? That chair does NOT belong there. We already have four imprints on the good new carpet, we do NOT want eight!'

'Can't wait for her and Paul to have kids,' Mum muttered darkly to me, much later, on our way home. 'All I'll say is, I hope she has five, one after the other, like the steps of stairs, and I hope they're all boys, really, really messy boys who never wash themselves without being threatened first, and what's more, I hope each one of them plays either rugby or soccer, and that they come home from practice every day, filthy from rolling around in the dirt and mud. That'd sort madam out quick enough, with her imprints on the carpet.'

Honestly, there are times when even Mum is a bit intimidated by her.

Right now, though, Kate's sitting on the bed, still in her nightie, but with the red hair tied in a neat bun, leaving me looking at her in awe, wondering whether she even sleeps with her hair tied up, so it doesn't get messy. Probably, I wouldn't be a bit surprised. She's also having a conversation with Perfect Paul through the door of their en suite bathroom. Well, to be more accurate, a conversation that's bordering on a row, if you're with me. The gist of it seems to be that Paul's just told her he won't be around for the next day or two, as he's promised to go to Galway, where all his family live, which is a good three-and-a-half-hour drive away. One of those half-work, half-business trips: he's supposed to have a business dinner down there with a few work contacts, then meet with banks and solicitors the next morning, so there's hardly any point in him coming all the way back home, only to face into the long drive down yet again the next day, blah di blah di blah. Paul's a property developer, by the way, and this would be all in a normal day's work for him. And he loves what he does, and he loves being busy, and he loves making money, but never in a 'ram it down your throat' kind of way, like, 'Oh come here till I show you the new Jackson Pollock etching I just *had* to have.' Or, 'Don't talk to me about the traffic jams in Marbella these days, sure a second home on the Costa is hardly worth the hassle.' No, conspicuous consumption wouldn't be his thing at all, that'd be more Kate's department.

In fact, Paul's one of those naturally street-smart

guys who left school at sixteen and went to work on building sites, first as a brickie, then gradually worked his way up and started buying plots of land, taking out bank loans to finance houses he'd then build on them. He has three brothers, who all came in on the act, and pretty soon, at the height of Ireland's property boom, they were flying. One of the brothers is an electrician, one's a carpenter, and the youngest is a plumber. So between the lot of them, they're a kind of building one-stop shop. 'If you stand still in this country for long enough,' Paul said to me once, 'sooner or later, somebody's going to get planning permission to put an apartment block on your head.' It was at the time when the whole entire country seemed to be one big building site and, as Mum said, you'd nearly be afraid to leave the garden shed door open at night in case you came down in the morning and someone had opened up a Starbucks.

Oh, and, for the record, yes, all of Paul's brothers are as handsome, lovely and down-to-earth as he is, real meat, spuds and two veg kind of guys, but sadly, all are married and long since spoken for, and all happily settled in the west of Ireland with their large and ever increasing hordes of kids. When he and Kate first got engaged after a whirlwind romance, I did of course dutifully check out all his brothers and their romantic availability, natch. Just in case one of them would have been a lovely fella for Fiona. When matchmaking, you always have to have your eyes open. But no joy, not a singleton among them.

On top of that, each one of the brothers are really into their big and blooming families, and all of the wives always seem to be forever pregnant. At the last count, there were something like twelve nieces and nephews, including twins, and I think Paul himself must have about four godchildren. It's like they're the most fertile family in Ireland, and according to Kate, the women they marry all have ovaries like Sten guns.

Anyway, lately in Paul's line of work, things have started to shift. And not in a good way, either. The construction industry in Ireland, after years of being stretched to capacity, suddenly took a huge downturn. Polish workers, who almost single-handedly kept the building boom going, started going back home in their droves, as work here slowly began to dry up. Paul's development company, thankfully, didn't suffer too much, as he'd made most of his money by then, but for a workaholic like him, it's hard to only have one or two building jobs in the pipeline *per year*, when not so long ago, they were beating his door down, and he could pretty much pick and choose what he wanted to do. So, tuning in to his side of the argument that's blazing in front of me, it's easy to see where he's coming from. We're in recession, work is scarce and he needs to be over in Galway with

193

all the brothers for the next few days, and that's all there is to it. Fair enough.

Then Kate gets going, and the gist of her counterargument, all conducted through the bathroom door by the way, is that, while she has no problem with him going to Galway to meet with a gang of other businessmen, can't he just come straight back home to her afterwards? Does he really have to stay down for the extra night so he can practise with this band that he plays in?

This, by the way, would be the 'pleasure' part of Paul's trip to the west. The band (a four-piece outfit with him on lead guitar) is a big part of Perfect Paul's life, and they're not half-bad either, in a traditional, ballady kind of way. Cover versions of Beatles classics, that kind of thing, all very easy listening and no one gets paid; whenever they play, it's purely for the laugh, and people tend to show their appreciation by buying them drinks for the night. Either that or shouting out, 'Ah, come on lads, do youse not know anything by The Dubliners?' Anyway, apart from Paul, his brother Sean is the bass guitarist, his cousin Tommy is the drummer, and a local girl, who sounds a bit like a younger, huskier Dusty Springfield, is lead singer. Her name is Julie and although tipped for great things (there was even a rumour doing the rounds that Louis Walsh was interested in her), she seems perfectly happy to sing with the band at night and work in her dad's pharmacy by day. Anyway,

Paul loves playing with them, and is forever zipping off down to Galway just to work on new songs or play at neighbours' birthdays/knees-ups/first Communions/ whatever you're having yourself.

Back to the row, where Kate's thrust is that, after what's happened to me, she and Mum are under huge stress right now, and instead of sitting in some pub belting out 'Yesterday' for about the two-hundredth time, she needs him here, at home, where he belongs, taking care of her.

I keep forgetting. Thing is, I've probably spent more time around Mum and Kate in the last few days than I ever would normally, so I constantly have to remind myself that they haven't a clue that I'm actually grand. Never been better. And right here. And just waiting for the chance to perform wondrous miracles for them. Although, mind you, I think Kate could prove to be my toughest case yet.

Just then, Perfect Paul emerges from the bathroom, with a cloud of steam from the shower behind him, and a lovely whiff of some musky, very male aftershave. He's only wearing a towel around his waist, and in all the time I've known him, I never realized what a hot bod he was packing under all those Hugo Boss suits, which only adds to his general, all-round picture-perfectness. He's one of those chunky, solid, rugby-playing guys who look more at home on a football pitch than in the

Barbie palace Kate's created. He's not what you might call conventionally handsome, and he doesn't have that WOW factor the minute you look at him either; no, he'd be more of a slow burner, looks-wise. Light brown hair, blue eyes, fair skin, and, like Kate, he doesn't have a freckle in sight, the jammy bastard. So big, he's roughly about the size of a barge, with a neck the approximate width of a small tree trunk. The human equivalent of a pint of Guinness, Fiona always says about him. After the first sip you wonder what the big deal is, it's only when you acquire the taste for it that you realize what you've been missing out on all this time.

Fiona's very fond of her tortured metaphors. Typical English teacher.

'Look, it's only for a night or two, that's all,' Paul says, reasonably. 'If you don't want to be here on your own, then come with me.'

'No,' she says, sulkily. 'And don't stand on the carpet in your bare feet, you'll leave water marks.'

'I don't get it. Why not?' he asks, but gently, usually the best way to handle Kate.

'Because . . . you know perfectly well why. Besides, I can't leave Mum.'

'Your mum is going to be fine for forty-eight hours . . .'

'Suppose she isn't? Suppose something happens and I'm not around? You know how she worries. She was bad enough before, well . . . before what happened, but now it's like every time I'm driving, her new worry is that I'll end up in a car crash, too.'

Oh Kate. If you could only see me, lying on the bed beside you, absolutely nothing wrong with me. Well, nothing apart from being dead, that is.

Mind you, if she saw me sprawled out on her good Frette sheets, she'd probably drag me off to be dipped in a bathtub of disinfectant, like they do on veterinary programmes with animals who have fleas.

'Kate, we've been over and over this. You know I have to go, it's as simple as that,' Perfect Paul insists, pulling open a shirt drawer, with all his shirts perfectly ironed, starched, folded and . . . I'm not kidding . . . actually arranged in descending colour order, darker ones at the bottom, white ones at the top, like in Benetton.

'We need this contract too badly,' he goes on, as I stare at him, mesmerized, half-willing him to whip off the towel that's covering his modesty so I can get a proper look at him in all his glory, if you're with me. Christ Alive, Kate must be made of marble to be able to look at him and not want to drag him on to the bed beside her and shag him senseless.

'If we land this deal in the bag, it could set us up for another year, at least. You know that.'

'Of course I know that, but why can't you just come straight home after your meetings? Why do you have to stay on for bloody band practice? Isn't what Mum and I are going through more important?'

'It's not just band practice, we're playing at a fortieth-birthday do in Sheehan's pub.'

'First I've heard of it.'

'I told you the other day.'

'Well, excuse me for being a bit distracted. I've other things going through my mind at the moment, in case you hadn't noticed.'

'Well, if you don't want to be here on your own, why don't you just pack your bag and come too? What's wrong with that? Jesus knows, Kate, you've earned the break.'

'I just . . . don't really feel that . . .'

Suddenly I get the feeling that she's faffing, searching around for another excuse, and I don't quite know why. Paul cops it, too.

'I don't get it,' he says. 'I mean, of course I know what you and your mum are dealing with right now, after . . . well, you know . . . poor old Charlotte . . .'

I gulp. Still not used to being talked about, when they don't know I'm here. Beyond weird.

'. . . but sometimes it's like you never want to spend any time with my family, Kate. Ever.'

'Stop bringing Charlotte into it. Are you aware of how insensitive you're being right now?'

'Now you're just being unfair. Christ, it's like treading

on eggshells around you these days. I can't seem to say or do the right thing . . .'

'That is not true . . .'

'So how come every time I suggest we go down to the west, you come up with some excuse?'

'If you're suggesting that my not wanting to leave Mum at a time like this to swan off down the country with you is some kind of excuse to get out of seeing your family, then you'd better apologize for that remark right now.'

'So what about last Christmas, then? And the Christmas before that? And my niece's Communion? And Connor's housewarming? And my godson's first soccer match? You always manage to get out of coming, and then the lads at home want to know why, and I'm left standing there like an eejit not knowing what to tell them any more. You're starting to run out of excuses, Kate.'

'Can't you stop thinking about yourself for one minute?'

'Actually, you're the one who needs to stop thinking about herself, for a change. I know what's happening now is rough, but what you're going through is ongoing, and you can't expect everyone around you to put their lives on hold for you. Life goes on, Kate. All I'm asking for is two days of your time. If you don't want to come with me, fine, but don't make me feel guilty for going, because I've made promises that I don't intend to break.'

'I don't want to be around your family right now because it's very difficult for me . . .'

'There you go again. You before everyone. Why don't you just say what this is really about?'

'PAUL!' She's really shrieking at him now, and it's getting uncomfortable to watch. To put it mildly. Kate's a great one for keeping up a perfect shopfront, so to see her now, screaming her head off and tearing lumps out of Paul, is really disconcerting. Kind of like seeing the Queen suddenly losing her temper and flinging a Dresden china plate across a room at a corgi.

'Do you really want to know what this is about?' she hollers, scarlet in the face, while he just blanks her and keeps on getting dressed, with his back to her. 'Fine, I'll tell you. Have you the first clue what it's like for me to spend time with your brothers and all their wives and ALL their two bloody dozen kids, or whatever it was at the last count? It's OK for you – the boys drag you off to look at a site, or to the pub to play with the band, or to some match that one of their kids is in – but I'm left sitting with all the women, while they eye me up and down and wonder what the hell is *wrong* with me. All they can ask me is, now that we have the big house, when will I have news for them all? And then they prattle on about how I can inherit all their buggies and Babygros and strollers. And don't get me started on your father, who actually said to me that after we start a family, we should consider moving back to the west so that our child can grow up among all his or her cousins. That it's totally ridiculous you and I living in Dublin, so far away from them all . . .'

'Well, now that you've said it, it is a bit crazy my having to drive up and down every time there's the sniff of a building job. If you ask me, it would make a lot more sense for us to at least have a base in Galway . . .'

'And leave Mum here on her own?'

'Don't jump down my throat. I wasn't suggesting we move lock, stock and barrel, all I said was that maybe, just maybe, we should consider getting some kind of bolt-hole down there, that's all. So I wouldn't have to crash out in my brother's spare room whenever I need to be there.'

'For God's sake, Paul, there are times I think you're like some kind of Mafia family who all have to live on top of each other, and you're Tony Soprano. Honestly, could you blame me for feeling like I'm married to the bloody mob . . . ?'

Kate, you need to shut up right now, while you still can. And did you really have to compare his family to the Sopranos? I mean, wouldn't the Waltons have done just as well?

'I'm going to stop you right there, Kate,' Paul eventually says, with an expression in his eyes I've never seen before. Icy fury. Very frightening. 'Before you really start crossing lines. My family are just trying to

201

include you in their lives, and I apologize if we're not good enough for you.'

'Now you're deliberately twisting it. I never said they weren't good enough, you're completely missing the point . . .'

'You know, I think it's probably best if I just leave now, before you say anything else you mightn't be able to take back later on. I'll be back in two days, and I'll see you then. Tell your mum I'm thinking of her.' And with that, he's out the door and gone.

'Kate,' I blurt out loud, unable to sit here and see two people I love so much tearing shreds out of each other. 'Go after him. Just get up off your arse and chase him to his car, and hug him and tell him it's all a big misunderstanding. Tell him it's not that you think you're too good for his family; it's that you think they're all too good for you, because they have big boisterous families and you don't. At least, not yet you don't. And that's what's making you insecure and petty and wanting to snipe at him all the time. What's tragic here isn't that you don't have kids, because you will in time, I'm sure of it; it's that you're letting it drive a wedge between you and the loveliest, gentlest, kindest husband any woman could ask for. Why can't you just appreciate how lucky you are to have a decent bloke who'd do anything for you? Now go, Kate, go after him. Right now, just do it.'

Great speech, I think, pausing for breath. Shame she never heard a single word of it.

'OK then, suppose he was in a car crash and ended up like me? Bet you'd be sorry then.'

A wasted guilt trip. She just lies on the bed, staring at the ceiling, looking about as bleak as it's possible for any person to look. A loud thud as Paul bangs the front door behind him, and she still doesn't flinch. She just lies mutely on the bed for a sec, then, rubbing her tummy like she's suddenly got a sharp cramp, she hauls herself up and heads for the bathroom. I don't follow her, because even angels have to respect other people's boundaries and, let's face it, she could be doing more than just a wee in there. A minute later, I hear the loo flushing, then the bathroom door opens as she comes back into the bedroom, opens up a locker drawer, rummages around and produces a big box of Tampax.

Ahhhhh, now I see. So that's what's really up with her. She's just got her period.

And suddenly, in a flash, I know *exactly* what to do.

She makes it so, so easy for me. Like shooting fish. Still rubbing her tummy, she goes back to the bathroom and bangs the door shut. A minute later, she comes back, opens a drawer in her bedside table, takes out a couple of paracetamol, then hops into bed, knocking back the pills with a glass of water. Minutes later, she's dozing fitfully.

Right. That'd be my cue then.

Next thing, I'm back at home. In Mum's house that is, except it's her house as it was about eleven or so years ago. The giveaway being the revolting sludge-brown carpet that's long since gone, and the woodchip wallpaper and actual stippling on the ceiling. Eughhh. Throw in the revolting sheepskin rug in front of the fire and you'll get the picture: this is the house that taste forgot. Pride of place, though, just above the telly, is a 3D Sacred Heart lamp with a blood-red flame flickering in front of it, a souvenir of Mum's trip to Rome, years ago, on the famous occasion when she and her parish church group managed to get an actual audience with the Pope. Mum, of course, bragged to the entire road before she went, thinking that this meant they all sat down with John Paul the Second in his living room and had a lovely chat while he poured them all tea, handed out Jaffa cakes and asked them how they were enjoying their holidays. The reality was they were shoved into a conference hall with about three thousand other pilgrims, and got a blessing from this tiny white dot on the horizon who they presumed was the Pope, but turned out to be just some aide. Then her pal Nuala got pinched in the bum by person or persons unknown, so every time Mum looks at the offensive lamp with the Sacred Heart glowering down at her, she sighs and says, ''Course I bought that the day poor Nuala was goosed up in St Peter's Square. Terrible randy race, the Italians.'

Anyway, I'm in my school uniform trying to watch an episode of *Sex and the City*, and Mum is wrestling the remote control from me, because it clashes with *Midsomer Murders*, her favourite programme.

'Ah go on, you'd all day to watch telly,' I'm pleading my case with her. 'I've my Irish oral exam in the morning, and this'll help me switch off. Don't you want me to do well in the exam so you can bask in reflected glory? Don't you at least want me to do better than Nuala's daughter, she of the straight As in her mocks?'

When I was living at home, this slightly below-the-belt tactic never failed to work, mainly because Nuala is Mum's most competitive friend, and her daughter is my age and a right cow.

'No, Charlotte. I refuse to watch four women sitting around talking about their unmentionables. Suppose your father walks in and they're all using the c word? He'd be mortified, and I wouldn't blame the poor man, either.'

The door bursts open, but it's not Dad, it's Kate, at least the younger version of her, fresh from a first date with some fella she met in college. She marches in, flings her handbag on to the coffee table, hurls her little pump shoes as far away from her as she can, and slumps into her favourite seat on the sofa beside me. All this done wordlessly and furiously, with Mum and I looking on, both of us dying for the full juice.

'Well then, love,' Mum eventually says, after a lot of 'oh dear God, it mustn't have gone well' loaded looks thrown in my direction. 'How did it go with . . . emm . . . Luke, wasn't it?'

'Don't want to talk about it.' Kate's standard answer for when she's so pissed off she can barely restrain herself from flinging things around the place.

'Well then . . .' says Mum, fishing, and honestly, you can nearly see curiosity getting the better of her. 'Just say he rings here looking for you, love, what'll I tell him?'

'That I've emigrated.'

'Oh, OK then.'

'Suppose we tell him you've emigrated, then he spots you out and about somewhere?' I ask, giving a surreptitious half-wink to Mum. 'What then?'

'You're worse than the bloody Gestapo, you pair,' Kate snaps at us, realizing that she won't get a minute's peace till she comes clean and omits no detail, however trivial.

'Go on, love, give us the full nine one one,' says Mum, who watches far too many cop dramas for her own good.

'If you must know, the stupid bastard arrived half an hour late for our date, then said he'd come out without his wallet, and would I buy him pints? Then he had the gall to tell me that he was the best offer that I was ever going to get, just because he happens to be studying law at Trinity, and I'm only doing a computer course. Oh, and just to add insult to injury, then he goes and asks me for the lend of a fiver so he could shoot a few frames of snooker with his friends, who all look either like goths or else drug addicts. Bloody shower of losers. So I marched out of there and got the bus straight home so I'd be back in time for *Sex and the City*. So why aren't we watching it?'

Back to the present, and Kate turns over in her sleep, tossing off the duvet cover.

Right then, time for round two.

It's exactly the same scenario, except time's moved on. Same living room, same woodchip on the walls, same sludgy carpets, except now there's photos of Dad dotted all round the place and Fiona is sitting on the sofa with me and Mum, all three of us glued to *Friends* on TV.

'Oh, I've seen this one before,' says Mum, absent-mindedly thinking out loud. 'Rachel flies to London for Ross's wedding, but then he says her name in his vows instead of Emily's, and there's murder.'

'SHHHHHH, don't tell us, you'll ruin it!' Fiona

and I chorus, when Kate bursts in, fresh from another date.

'Ah, there you are, love, how'd it go, with . . . ehh . . . Simon . . . something, oh yes, Walker, wasn't it?'

'Shut up and no one move,' Kate snaps, switching off all the lights and pulling the curtains over, just like in an Alfred Hitchcock thriller.

'What in the name of God is going on?' I ask, afraid she'll make us all lie flat out on the floor in a minute. She's over by the window, though, intermittently peeping out through the curtains and waving at us all to shut up.

'Kate, tell me the truth, did that Simon fella turn out to be a drug baron?' says Mum, alarmed. After some documentary she saw on *Prime Time*, her greatest fear in life is that one of us will end up marrying a crime lord. 'Because your poor father, God be good to him, will spin in his grave if some eejit you pick up in a bar thinks he can start dealing heroin from outside the front gate. If Nuala gets wind of that, I'll never hear the end of it.'

'He is not a heroin dealer,' Kate hisses, still peering out into the street. 'Oh for God's sake! Will you all keep your heads down, please?'

'Are we going to be in a drive-by shooting?' Fiona asks nervously. 'Because, if no one minds, I really need the loo first.'

'He's a bloody obsessive weirdo,' says Kate in a stage whisper. 'I told him I was an asthmatic and . . .'

'You forgot your inhaler . . .' Mum and I finish the sentence for her. It's Kate's standard, failsafe excuse for getting out of a rubbish date.

'. . . But the headcase insisted on driving me home, so I thought I'd wait until his car drove off and he was well out of the way. Then the plan was, I could slip out and head back into town, to Café en Seine so I could meet up with my gang, but would you look at the bloody lunatic? He's still sitting in the car, parked outside. I mean what's he planning on doing? Keeping a stakeout going all night to check I don't go back out again? Honest to God, is there a sign over my head that says "will happily tolerate fixated headcases?"'

'Define fixated,' Fiona pipes up, all ears.

'Oh, you know, after one date, practically mapping out our whole future. Ordered the meal for me. Nearly went off his head when I took a call on my mobile from another guy in my class. Invited me to his brother's wedding. In eight months' time. And now he's camped outside my front door checking up on me. Stalker Walker, I should call him.'

'Sounds perfectly all right to me,' says Fiona, as we all turn to look at her. 'Well, what's wrong with a fella being attentive?' This, I should point out, was in the days when we were humble freshers in college, not long before she met the lovely Tim Keating.

'Fiona, the guy practically has me under surveillance,' snaps Kate.

'Well, I'm just saying. If you're not interested, maybe you'd set me up. One man's meat and all that.'

Kate rolls over again in her sleep, and now I instinctively know it's time for the *pièce de résistance*.

God, if I say so myself, I am really getting good at this.

Right, then. We're back in Mum's living room yet again, except now a few more years have passed, and Mum and I are plonked on the snot-green sofa flicking through interior design magazines, with me trying to talk her into ripping up the sludgy carpet and sanding the wooden floors underneath. Then stripping off the bloody woodchip that's been there since I was a baby, and setting fire to the corduroy curtains. Or getting a TV makeover show to film the kip, so it can be the 'before' on one of those 'pimp my crib' shows. Or, as a last resort, just putting a bomb under the place, claiming on the insurance, then heading off to the Bahamas for a fortnight.

Just then, we hear a key in the front door, and Mum immediately flings the magazines away and throws herself back on the sofa, knuckles clenched and staring rigidly ahead, like she's strapped into a 747 that's about to take off.

'That's them!' she stage whispers. 'Her with the new fella! Now I don't want to jinx it by saying that this could be The One, but I really do have high hopes this time round. So act natural, for God's sake, will you!'

Then Kate breezes in, all smiles, and looking even prettier and more relaxed than I ever remember, in tight boot-cut jeans that she never wears any more, with her hair all loose and windswept and casual.

'OK, guys, here he is,' she beams at us, glowing, then goes back out to the hall outside. 'Come on in,' we can hear her coaxing. 'It's OK, they won't bite.'

'This,' she introduces proudly, dragging a very familiar face in by the hand, 'is Paul.'

So far, so good. There's even a little half-smile on Kate's face as she turns over, happily settling down into a deeper slumber. I'm just about to take her back to her first few magical dates with Perfect Paul, having cleverly reminded her of the string of morons she dated in the lead-up to meeting him. All those years that she spent spinning like a hamster on the dating wheel until that happy day, not so long ago, when she was at the races with a gang of her friends, and he sidled up to her and gave her a tip for the three-thirty. If the horse loses, he promised, I'll make it up to you by taking you out to afternoon tea.

Now Kate has the worst luck with horses of anyone I know, and is always joking that bookies have to write up tickets especially for her and whatever poor unfortunate nag she backs, who invariably is still limping towards the finishing post at ten o'clock that night. However, as fate would have it . . . that one time, she actually won. And then was silently raging, as it meant the afternoon tea offer with her big hunky beefcake stranger was off. But Perfect Paul, true to his name, still insisted he'd bring her out for tea the following day, leaving Kate like a basket case back at home, trying on at least fifteen different outfits before hitting on something suitably chaste for a daytime date, but yet that still hinted at underlying sexiness beneath. Oh, and making me walk around her taking Polaroids, as she doesn't fully trust mirrors for three-hundred-and-sixty-degree accuracy. All this bother just to meet a fella for a bloody pot of tea, I remember thinking at the time, thinking how old ladyish it all sounded, and half-wondering if this mystery man would turn out to be gayer than Christmas in Bloomingdales.

But, as usual, when it comes to judging guys, my radar was one hundred per cent wide of the mark. He picked her up on the dot, and . . . wait for it . . . took her to Ashford Castle for the tea . . . In County Mayo. Oh, and did I mention that he flew her there in a helicopter belonging to one of his rich developer friends? Hard to top a first date like that, particularly as, for me and Fiona, first dates usually involved a few warm glasses of white wine in a pub while whoever we were with drank himself into a stupor. Then whoever was the last man standing had to somehow figure out where the nearest Eddie Rockets was on the way home. And that's only if we were lucky, and he happened to be one of the romantic ones.

'He's just such a nice guy,' Kate kept saying over and over again, when she first started seeing Paul. Now, in my experience, whenever a woman describes a fella as 'nice' it basically means she'll break up with him after a week, then spend the next seven years dating alcoholics in leather trousers. But, in this case, I couldn't have been more wrong if I'd tried. Within two months, they were engaged, and before the year was out, they were married. A real whirlwind if ever there was one, but somehow the speed at which it all happened didn't matter. Why would it? They were *perfect* for each other.

Anyway, I'm just about to take Kate back to that happy, loved-up glow she first had after meeting Paul: how she couldn't eat or sleep or do anything really, except talk about him and leap six feet into the air whenever he called her mobile, which was an average of about sixteen times a day, when . . . oh shit, I do NOT believe it. The phone on her bedside table starts pealing, and suddenly Kate's wide awake and hauling herself up on one elbow to answer it.

'Hello? Oh hi, Mum,' she says sleepily, rubbing her eyes. 'No . . . just dozing. Yeah . . . that's fine . . . whatever time suits you . . . no, I'll just hop in the shower, and I'll be right there . . . I'm glad you rang, I was having the strangest dreams, actually.'

Here we go, I think smugly. About her nightmare exes which were all a warm-up act to the happy day when she met Perfect Paul, and how, for the first time, she fully appreciates what a wonderful, loving guy she has, and how bloody lucky she is.

I am SO going to earn angelic brownie points for this one. In fact I wouldn't be a bit surprised if Kate races after him, pausing only to pack a little overnight bag, then puts up with all the brood mares in his family gaping at her, just so she can spend time with her perfect man, all loved-up. Now that she's been gently reminded of exactly how miserable life was without him, that is. In fact, if I can keep up this campaign of post-hypnotic suggestion for the next few nights, it'll be candlelit suppers for two for the next month at least, and then, who knows what great joyous news that might soon lead to?

'. . . no, Mum, more like a nightmare,' she's saying. 'I kept dreaming about the time you had that horrific sludgy brown carpet with the woodchip wallpaper and the manky curtains. Eughhh, I need a shower just thinking about it. In fact, scrap that; I need a Silkwood scrubdown.'

Oh bugger, bugger, bugger.

Honest to God, I'd have more luck getting a message through to Alcatraz.

So *now* what?

Chapter Eleven

JAMES

Big day. Big, big, big, big, day, and to think, I'd almost forgotten. The scary pitch meeting later on this morning to try and cajole money out of their number-one investor, so James can inject it into his rubbishy idea for a TV series. Please don't get me wrong, after hearing just how badly Meridius Movies is doing, my intentions are nothing more than to sit innocently on the sidelines, witnessing exactly how James and Declan get on. I'll be an impassive observer and nothing more. Perhaps throwing in the odd insightful comment if I think things aren't going too well for them. Because, let's be honest here, their project is complete and utter shite. Anyway, cross my heart, the plan is to help and do good, benevolently imparting wisdom and sage advice from the side of the hedge I now find myself on. Hopefully without giving James a heart attack in the process. He doesn't deserve it, but there you go. That's just the kind of considerate and compassionate angel that I am. So, as usual, all I have to do is really concentrate, focus on him and no one else, and next thing I find myself right by his side.

Oh bugger. And immediately I wish I didn't. Mainly because he's on the loo, and now I'm plonked on the side of the bath beside him. With no visible means of escape.

Feck it, anyway.

'Sorry, sorry, didn't mean to interrupt, sure I'll drop back later . . .' I say. Then he does that hilarious thing of looking sharply around, like there's a tape recorder hidden behind the cistern or something. I try to get out, but of course, can't open the door.

'James? It's me again. Now don't panic, I'm not here to cause trouble today, I know how important this meeting is for you. Just think of me as a casual observer, that's all. A bit like a UN weapons inspector. Damn all use to anyone, yet comforting just to know they're there. But if you wouldn't mind just getting the door for me, it's just that I'm not great with physical stuff like door handles . . .'

His eyes shoot around, all panicky, and getting bulgier by the second. Then he starts doing deep soothing breaths, like in a yoga class. In for two, out for four, in for two, out for four.

'I am having hallucinations caused by stress,' he mumbles slowly, slowly, slowly, closing his eyes and gently rubbing his face, like the skin's about to physically melt off it. 'Exhaustion, strain and overwork, that's all that's wrong here . . .'

It's actually funny. Him on the loo convinced he's losing his reason, and me only trying to get out the door and away from him asap.

'James, really it's OK, I'm here to help, really. Now if you can just let me out . . .'

'A long, long holiday,' he murmurs, and I'm not messing, he's actually rocking back and forth as he says it. Like an extra in *One Flew Over the Cuckoo's Nest*. 'That's what I need. Way too much has been going on, and no one needs a break like I do. Beach, sun, no phones, no emails, no pressure, no stress, no money worries, no meetings, and most of all NO Charlotte's voice inside my head, telling me that she's here, now, in the bathroom with me . . .'

Suddenly, out of nowhere, there's a dull thumpety thump on the bathroom door, and now it's my turn to nearly get a heart attack. Then . . . I do NOT believe this . . . an all-too-familiar screechy, breathy voice.

'Jamie, sweetheart? Are you OK in there? You're doing that thing of talking to yourself again, and you're worrying me.'

More door thumping, getting insistent now.

'Am I *hearing* things?' I say, completely and utterly gobsmacked. 'Or are you telling me that . . .'

'Pressure can manifest in many strange and unusual ways,' says James, eyes closed, still swaying. 'But remember, I'm a tiger. I'm a tiger, I'm a tiger. I thrive on pressure. I eat nerves and shit success.'

'Jamie?' says Little Miss Screechy from outside. 'Answer me, will you? You're starting to give me a fright. This is like a repeat of yesterday evening all over again. And what are you going on about tigers for?'

I turn to look at him, and I'm only raging the bastard can't see the expression of horror and disgust that must be carved in stone on my stunned face.

'Are you honestly telling me that Sophie *stayed* here? She actually slept the night here? In our bed? In our room?'

I can barely stammer the words out, but, if I needed actual proof, James then hops off the loo, pulls up his trousers, flings open the bathroom door, and there she is, Screechy Voice herself. She's wearing one of his white shirts and nothing else, bare legs immaculately fake-tanned and waxed, and toenails freshly pedicured, with all the blond confidence you'd normally only see in a Tommy Hilfiger ad. Bed sheets in total disarray and the T-shirt and jeans she had on yesterday strewn carelessly across the floor. Just in case I really needed it hammered home to my poor, disbelieving eyes.

Oh, for f*ck's sake.

For a split second I actually think I'm going to be

sick. Instead, I slump back down against the bathroom door, in total and utter shock. I mean, yes, I knew James was a complete cackhead, but I at least thought, out of respect for my memory, he'd cooled things off with his girlfriend. For form's sake, if nothing else. But what happens? I take my watchful gaze off him for one bloody night and he moves Miss Screechy Voice in. After the row I witnessed between the two of them on the street last night. After seeing, with my own two eyes, him practically leaping into a taxi just to get away from her. She must have trailed after him, landed on the front doorstep, somehow inveigled her way around him and, true to form, he bloody well let her. Unbelievable, just unbelievable.

Did I say that I was going to try to help him at this big meeting? Because, I'm terribly sorry to disappoint and all that, but there's just been a major change of plan.

About half an hour later, James is behind the wheel of his flashy little black Porsche. (Well, what else would you expect him to drive? Honest to God, their ad might as well say, 'Buy a Porsche. The Choice of Wankers.') I'm right beside him, in the passenger seat, not a word out of me, just staring furiously ahead, tight-lipped and still in shock. I never would have thought that ghosts could behave snottily, but there you go; it seems you never stop learning, even beyond the grave. James and Screechy Voice parted company back at the house, *our* house, in *our* front garden, with her waving him off, like she already lives there, insisting she'll see him later on and that she's so sure the meeting will go well that they can really celebrate in style tonight.

I just stood there looking at the two of them, still stunned, thinking that, after this, I honestly won't be happy until I see James's whole life go up in smoke.

It's at times like this I really wish I had the use of my limbs, if only just to give her car tyres a right good kicking, and then to knee him in the goolies. And don't tell me the pair of them haven't asked for it.

Anyway, at ten fifty-nine on the dot (this, believe me, is not a meeting you'd want to be late for) we finally arrive, after about a forty-minute drive all the way to County Kildare, via countless twisty turny lanes. Pretty soon, the houses gradually turn into mansions and their gardens, sorry, their *grounds*, seem to be so vast that each one is about eight miles away from the nearest neighbours, separated by high fences with granite walls all around the perimeter. I know rich people are different to the rest of us, but it does make me wonder the lengths you'd have to go to if you were unfortunate enough to run out of milk late at night, and had to drive five miles to your nearest Spar, or else brave security gates, CCTV cameras and probably a horde of ravenous guard dogs at a neighbour's house, just so you could borrow a carton of Avonmore from them.

221

Declan's here ahead of us, and has pulled over beside a high electronic security gate with a very scary looking sign on it, threatening that this is private property and that trespassers WILL be prosecuted. As if that wasn't intimidating enough, there's also a drawing of a security guard with a Dobermann on a lead, enough to make me want to run for the hills.

I should explain. My relations with Dobermanns are thus: I am terrified of them, and they somehow smell the fear and manage to make it all so, so much worse. Like the way a cat will always make a beeline for the one person in the room who's allergic to them, Dobermanns somehow instinctively sense that I'm terrified, and I'm therefore, naturally, their first target. Our neighbour has one; a particularly scary looking monster with the highly inappropriate name of Mrs Fluffles, and every time the mutt is out in the front garden, cue hysterical, mortified phone calls from me to said neighbour pleading with her to bring in the savage, salivating beast just long enough for me to run to my car without being mauled and scarred for life. James, of course, finds my fear hilarious, and often goes over the fence purposely to pet Mrs Fluffles and make me feel like a total scaredy-cat/roaring eejit/pathetic coward in the process.

Charming, sensitive man, isn't he?

Anyway, there's a wall around the property about fifteen feet high, with the name of the place discreetly written on a brass plaque embedded into the security gate.

Four Knots Stud.

Yeah, right. Fort Knox, more like.

A second after spotting us, Declan hops out of his car and indicates to James that he'll press the intercom to buzz both of them in. Stressing just how important this meeting is to them, Declan has for once ditched the rock daddy gear and is wearing an actual suit. James just waves imperiously at him, shades pushed up into his hair, looking like an Eastern European pimp. And I still haven't opened my gob, on the principle that revenge is a dish best eaten cold, and I really, *really* want to pick my moment here. A minute later, the steel gates slowly swing open and we're away . . . down a gravelled driveway so long that you can't even see the house from it. Honestly, there are five-star country hotels that pale in comparison, and at one stage I even spot someone driving around in a golf buggy. On and on we go, past rolling, manicured meadows on each side of us, and eventually, after what feels like about three-quarters of an hour, we eventually pull up at a house that looks just like Scarlett O'Hara's in *Gone With the Wind*. There's even an actual peacock on the lawn outside, strutting around for pure show and nothing else. All I can think is, my mother, who loves nothing more than having a good nose around other people's gardens, would have

Claudia Carroll

a field day gawping around here. Particularly as there's not a garden gnome or a boxed hedge in sight, her two personal pet peeves.

We park behind Declan, hop out, and clamber up the dozen or so stone steps that lead up to what has to be the most imposing front door this side of the pearly gates. And believe me, I know what I'm talking about. First-hand experience and all that. Poor old Declan is laden down with files and folders and a briefcase, and you can practically feel the nerves hopping off him, while my gobshite ex-boyfriend actually has the bare-faced cheek to look relaxed and cool. Like he's a guest arriving for a few rounds of golf before drinks and a cosy dinner with the host. After a discreet length of time, the door is opened by a real live butler, a dead ringer for Michael Caine in *Batman*. He's far too polite and posh to ask for names, he just does a little half-bow and says, 'Good morning, gentlemen. Sir William is expecting you. If you'd care to come this way, please.'

And we're off again, trailing through a marble-floored hall the approximate size of the Natural History Museum, completely covered in paintings that I know by looking at them must be old masters. One I even recognize from the cover of a history book I had in third year. To the left is what looks like a giant library, and I'm half-expecting us to be led in there and for the famous Sir William to swirl around in a big leather armchair, like the baddie in a James Bond movie, stroking a white Persian cat and coming out with lines like, 'Not so fast, Mr Bond.'

But we're not. Instead we're ushered through some frighteningly chic French double doors and out on to a beautiful sun-soaked terrace, with a water feature that would put the one in Versailles to shame tinkling elegantly away in the background. In the far distance, I can just about make out someone galloping on a horse that looks about ready for the Grand National and that's probably won countless other major races already, given how vastly, bottomlessly wealthy our host is. And da-daaaaaa, there he is, the man himself, the mighty Sir William, wearing a dressing gown and with a pair of binoculars around his neck, studying the horse that's just a tiny speck on the horizon. Small, red-faced and portly with it; out of shape, even for an Irish person.

'Ah, there's the lads now,' he says, spotting us and shaking hands warmly. One of those big firm, knuckle-cracking handshakes. 'How are you all, great to see you, yeah, lovely day for it. If I'd known youse were going to be on time, I'd have put clothes on, ha ha.'

OK, I should probably fill you in a bit.

The oligarch we now see before us, he with a finger in just about every pie going in the world of Irish business, was actually born into far humbler surroundings than the palazzo we're in now. Sir William actually started out life as plain old Billy Eames, and grew up selling fruit and vegetables from a barrow on Moore Street with his granny, supporting about sixteen younger brothers and sisters along the way, all of whom had either scurvy, typhoid or polio. They lived in a two-up, two-down corporation house in the inner city, and had to sleep seven to a bed under piles of coats to keep warm in the winter. Oh yeah, and hide behind the few meagre sticks of furniture they had whenever the landlord called to collect the rent money. I'm sure it wasn't a bit like that in reality, but you know how urban myths are: once they sprout wings, it's as good as biography. In fact, to listen to the stories of Billy's . . . sorry, I mean Sir William's, early life, you'd nearly confuse his formative years with that *Monty Python* sketch about the Yorkshire men who compete with each other to see who actually grew up in the harshest poverty. It's all documented, and I'm sure exaggerated way out of all proportion, in his self-mythologizing autobiography *It's A Long Way From Robbing Penny Apples*.

Anyway, aged sixteen he got a job as a messenger boy for a tiny domestic airline out at Dublin airport and so, legend has it, the seeds of his entrepreneurial zeal were first sown. In those dark days, air travel was only for the super-rich, and a week on the Costa del Sol meant you were either a drug baron or a multi-millionaire. Or both. Anyway, the myth goes that young Billy spotted a gap in the market, and quickly realized that the future lay in low-cost travel to airports about forty miles from where you actually wanted to go, on flights that left at five in the morning and that charged you extra for everything: from checking in, to carrying baggage, to having the temerity to breathe their oxygen while on board and to using their steps to get on and off the aircraft. The rest, as they say, is history. Within a decade, Billy rose to managing director of the airline, and is now one of Ireland's most successful exports, with all the trappings which that entails: VIP magazine shoots, appearances on the *Late Late Show*, the works. A self-made billionaire who came from nothing and hauled himself up by his bootstraps? It's a wonder he hasn't been stripped and sold for parts.

Then, only about three years ago, he was knighted for all the commendable work which the charity he set up to help underprivileged children had done, and in a blaze of publicity, plain man-of-the-people Billy morphed into Sir William. I can still remember all the photos and TV coverage he got outside Buckingham Palace; he was dressed like he was off for a day at the races, and came out to meet the press florid-faced and beaming, claiming that the Queen was, 'A lovely bird, great crack altogether, but I wouldn't like to see the amount of cash herself and Philip must fork out on heating bills to keep that gaff warm in December, wah ha ha.'

A great supporter of the arts, he kind of fancies himself as a latter-day Renaissance man, and has invested in everything from Impressionist exhibitions to fledgling theatre companies. And, needless to say, over the years, has been more than generous in funding Meridius Movies. In production circles, they refer to rich investors like Sir William as angels. Which, given that I'm sitting in on this meeting right now, is kind of ironic.

Anyway, Billy, sorry . . . Sir William invites the boys to sit down, the butler from *Batman* brings out a silver tray laden down with tea and coffee pots and we're away.

Disaster Number One

'Lovely horse,' James says, pulling out a wrought-iron chair and plonking himself down, one leg crossed over the other, owning the space all around him, confidence personified. As if this is the style he's accustomed to.

'Ehh . . . yeah, yeah, lovely!' Declan agrees, over-chirpily, on the edge of his seat with nervousness.

'Ah, do you like her, lads?' says Sir William, training the binoculars on the horizon. 'I'll give you a tip, so. She's called Sinead O'Connor Ruined My Life and I'm running her in the Gelding Stakes at the Curragh, Saturday fortnight. Worth a few quid each way, boys, do you know what I'm saying? Ha ha!'

James and Declan both do dutiful man-laughs and

that's when it happens. Gobshite James, who always has to push the boat out that bit too far, then pipes up, 'Who's that riding the horse now? Is that your jockey?'

'Ahh, you're gas, so you are,' guffaws Sir William doing his big rawl rawl rawl laugh. 'No, sure, that's Eloise up there. She's a natural, isn't she? Poetry in motion, what, lads?'

The penny instantly drops with me, but not James. Mainly because he's not as well-up on the gossip pages as I would be. So, I'm half-willing him to say it, and yet half-dreading the response. In the distance, Eloise comes galloping closer and closer, then pulls up at the fountain and dismounts, striding towards us and waving to Sir William. She has a fantastic figure and is gorgeous-looking in a Judi Dench, silver-haired kind of way; looks a fair bit older than anyone else here, but with cheekbones you could grate cheese on, all her own teeth, and a forehead that's never been within six feet of a Botox jab.

'Eloise . . .' says James, as if he's heard the name somewhere before, and is racking his brains to make the association. Then he sees her coming closer to us, and in his own, inimitable dimwit way, you can practically see him weighing up her connection to Sir William and how he should address her.

'Ahh, yes, Eloise! Your mother, isn't she? So how are you doing, Mrs Eames, it's lovely to meet you.' He even stands up to greet her, flashing her his cutest, most charming smile, with his hand outstretched, which she completely blanks.

There's a stony silence all around. A horrified look from Declan, a red flush from Sir William and an icy glare from Eloise herself.

'I'm not his mother, I'm his wife, actually,' she snaps. 'And for your information, it's Lady Eames, not Mrs.' And with that withering put-down, she clips back up the stone steps and strides inside the house, not even pausing to be introduced. And, in fairness, would you blame her? She and Sir William have been married for about six months now, and are probably the highest-profile couple in the country, even more familiar to most people than the President and her husband, and they're, like, on the fifty-five cent *stamp* and everything.

The only thing that's slightly unusual about them as a couple is that Sir William is younger than his new wife, by about fifteen years. It shouldn't have, but at the time, the wedding caused a ripple of shock waves throughout posh Irish society, as I suppose people expected a man like him to go the Hugh Hefner stereotypical route and run off with someone a) young enough to be his granddaughter, never mind his daughter, b) a former pop star/topless model/presenter of a magazine show on TV3, and most of all c) a pneumatic blonde. Eloise is gorgeous and classy, but is most definitely none of the above. In the meantime, Sir William's ex-wife, who he married aged eighteen, and who he has about seven children with, then went on a publicity rampage, including a now-infamous appearance on the *Late Late Show*, where she savaged her ex's brand-new title and brand-new wife. 'And I wouldn't mind,' I can still hear her sniffling, 'but the bastard didn't even have the decency to leave me for someone younger.'

It's a sore, sensitive spot with both Sir William and his new lady, which James just ripped the scab off and poured carbolic acid all over. Round one to me.

And I never even had to open my mouth.

Not yet.

Disaster Number Two

Red-faced, Sir William eventually sits down, and after waving away the two dozen or so mortified apologies from James, and particularly Declan, whose face is hardwired into a grin so wide I think he might pull a muscle, the meeting eventually gets started.

'So,' says Sir W in this 'cut straight to the chase' way he has. 'What have you lads got for me, then? Gimme your pitch in one sound bite. I've to be in the helicopter and on my way to Dublin in forty-five minutes flat. So you'd want to be quick.'

An encouraging look from James to Declan that might as well say, 'You be the warm-up act, then I'll step in with the killer blow at the appropriate moment.' So off poor old Dec goes, talking up just how much of a blockbusting bestseller *Let He Without Sin* was, how many languages it was translated into, how many weeks it spent in the *Sunday Times* top ten list, and how lucky Meridius were to secure the rights at all, when there was practically a bidding war over them.

'I'll stop you there, son,' Sir William interrupts. 'I only ever read books I wrote meself. Did you read *The Twenty-Fifth Hour*? Me latest bestseller, about how to squeeze more time out of the day. Read it and weep, lads, wah, ha ha.'

Declan pauses for a millisecond, realizes he's getting nowhere by talking up the source material, so he then produces budget costings for the TV show which will be based on the book, spreadsheets and projections of investors' earnings, market demographics; in fact just about everything bar Sir William's internet horoscope comes in neat folders out of his briefcase. Meanwhile the man himself just looks on, in a Don Corleone way; blank, impassive, patiently waiting to have the socks knocked off him.

And waiting. And waiting.

Eventually, in the middle of Declan's big spiel about tax incentives for investors, he interrupts. 'So, lads, let me get this straight. What have we got here? What I mean is, what are we actually dealing with? What's the heart of the story? Because story, lads, is what it all comes back to. Sure I remember a few years back, a producer coming to me, without an arse in his trousers, looking for cash for a film . . .'

Declan, I notice, politely sits forward, all ears to hear whatever anecdote is coming. Which kind of makes me think that this must be a regular occurrence: Sir William taking these wandering meanders down memory lane, that is. And clearly, if you're looking for money from him, you're expected to sit back and put on your 'enthralled' face. It's hard to tell what James's game plan is; he's just sitting there, watching, waiting, listening, drinking it all in, cool as you like. Honestly, I wouldn't be a bit surprised if he clicks his fingers and orders more coffee from the *Batman* butler. Arrogance, thy name is James Kane.

'. . . so I says to them, "Tell me what the film's about, lads," Sir William goes on. "It's about a ballerina," they said. "Not really my thing," I said. "For starters, it's a chick flick." "Just hear us out," they said. "It's a twelve-year-old boy who wants to do ballet." "So it's about a kid who's gay?" I said. "No," they said, "at least not to start with, but his dad is a coal miner." "Ballet and coal mining?" I said. "Doesn't really mix, does it?" "Not only that," they said, "but it's set during the miners' strike in the eighties. In Thatcher's Britain." Then they told me the story, they took me on that kid's journey.

Not a word of a lie, there were tears streaming down my face, and do you want to know why?'

'Eh . . . no, why was that, Sir William?' Good old Declan, always so polite. So well brought up by his mammy.

'Because it got me here,' Sir William goes on, thumping at his heart dramatically. 'Pulled me by the aul heartstrings. A film about a kid who comes from nothing and has dreams to make something of himself in the world, now *that* is a story I can relate to. And do you want to know the name of that film?'

'I'm guessing *Billy Elliot*,' James pipes up, kind of stealing Sir William's thunder a bit.

'The very one. And do you know how much I made out of it? A two hundred and fifty per cent return on my investment, that's how much. Because I trusted my instincts, lads, that's why. Then Elton John goes and makes it into a musical, and I make the same amount of cash all over again. And I said to Elton, on his yacht at the Cannes Film Festival, I said, "Elton, my lad, this money is a reward for listening to my inner voice." And he agreed with me, too. Very nice fella, considering he's gay.'

'Oh yeah, he's a terrific guy,' says James. 'I met him at a premiere at the Odeon, Leicester Square, once.'

Oh, to hell with this, I've stayed quiet long enough.

'James Kane, you're a filthy name-dropper. Spotting

Elton John from the far end of a packed cinema and waving at him does NOT constitute meeting the man.'

I'll never get over the funny colours James's face goes when he hears me but is pretending that he can't. Right now, he looks as though he just walked into a buzz saw, and it serves him bloody right.

'Back to your pitch then, lads,' says Sir William. 'You're telling me you've an elderly priest with Alzheimer's and a young one doing a transition-year project for school. So, the old priest starts rambling on and on and on . . .'

'Absolutely correct,' says Declan, taking up the baton. 'But, critically, without realizing that he's inadvertently breaking the seal of the confessional.'

'Speak English, will you, son?'

'Ehh . . . sorry. Well, the thrust of the story arc is that this is a ten-part drama series, and in each episode, our lead character, the elderly priest, tells a tale he's heard in confession decades ago, not even realizing what he's doing.'

A look over to James, who steps in.

'Over ten weeks, we get to look at each of the Ten Commandments which have been broken, so each episode, if you like, is a mini short story.'

And then he starts off on what I can only describe as a vicious circle of lies. So and so is interested, he says, naming a well-known international actor. And X, the hottest director in town, is mad about the script. All utter shite, I happen to know, but that's the way producers seem to have to work. No one ever wants to be the first person to commit to a project, so cue James and his candy floss of spin. Fortunately for James, though, talking crap happens to be his one big strength in life.

'Talk me through one episode,' says Sir William.

'A pleasure,' James beams confidently. 'For example, off the top of my head, we have one hot episode called "Thou Shalt Not Commit Adultery". So then we get a story about this guy who's cheating on his wife with another woman, who he eventually leaves her for and subsequently marries. He's been married to the first wife for decades, they've a big family, and of course she isn't even remotely suspicious, because he's always away on business trips anyway, until she comes across his credit-card statement and discovers . . .'

Sorry, but I can't keep my mouth shut any longer. My will to talk is just too overwhelming.

'You do realize,' I say right into James's face, 'that you might as well subtitle that episode, "The True Life Story of William Eames"? Or maybe, "Billy Eames: E! True Hollywood Story!" Don't you ever read gossip pages in the papers? Or maybe you're trying to write his biography for him, you unimaginable moron. Oh, and just so you know? There's a false laugh coming out of me right now with your name on it.'

He rubs his temples, and I can see him starting to break a sweat. Good.

A panicky look back at Declan, who takes over and shuts him up.

'. . . of course, that's just one episode, there are nine other stories to come. For example, in the episode entitled "Thou Shalt Not Kill", we tell the story of two middle-aged brothers sharing an old, derelict Georgian house, which has been left to them equally, but they hate each other and each spends the entire show trying to drive the other one away. They even share a bed-room, divided down the centre by a stack of old newspapers . . .'

'Take a look at Billy Boy's face, will you?' I say to James. I'm right at his shoulder now, so there's just no way that he's not hearing me. 'The picture of boredom. He's actually making the same face that kids do when they're being force-fed spinach. No offence, but your idea is a pile of shite, and if you want my advice, you'd want to come up with some better ideas . . . like . . . *now*.'

'Emmm . . . I'm so sorry to interrupt,' says James, looking grey now, 'but could I possibly get some water?'

'Sure,' says Sir William, looking at him a bit oddly, and waving for the *Batman* butler to come back in.

'Thanks.'

'Are you OK, son? You've gone very pale, if you don't mind me saying.'

'Fine thanks, just emm . . .'

'Imagining things, dearest?' I finish the sentence for him. 'Just like you did this morning? Oh, now this would be after you slept with your screechy-voiced girl-friend in *our* house, in *our* bed.'

I know he's hearing me. I know by the way that he clears his throat, then sits intently forward, really, *really* focusing on everything Declan's saying, as if by just ignoring me, I'll eventually disappear. Some hope, babe.

Sir William eases himself back into his chair, con-templating the pile of documents in front of him. 'You see, lads,' he eventually says, 'I have to ask myself, is this show the kind of thing that myself and Eloise would want to sit down in front of the telly on a Sunday night and watch? And, no offence or anything, but the answer is no.'

'See?' I say to James, right into his left ear to be exact. 'Told you it was a rubbish idea. I'm hoarse saying it, in fact. I don't get it, why didn't you just listen to me in the first place? It's got nothing going for it. Plus you're trying to cut corners in all the wrong places so it'll end up like . . . like *La Bohème* performed by finger puppets. The pilot episode is total crap, too. In fact, the only thing that connects the characters is that their names follow each other on the script. A cat could have coughed a better script out of its bum.'

'The pilot isn't crap, it's a gem,' James says out loud. I don't think he meant to, that was just the effect of my taunting him; it just slipped out, probably without him even realizing it.

Both Sir William and Declan turn to look at him in shock.

'Ah now, son,' says Sir William, completely taken aback. 'I never said it was crap, I just said it didn't grab me by the short and curlies, that's all.'

'Sorry, sorry about that, yes, I totally understand, that isn't what I meant at all . . .' James says, or rather stammers.

I take a moment and look around the table. Sir William, deeply unimpressed and beginning to suspect that James is losing it, Declan frantically searching through all his spreadsheets and folders trying to whip a last-minute rabbit out of a hat, and James, ghostly pale, on the verge of a nervous breakdown.

A kinder, more humane person than me would shut up now, would recognize that these guys are fighting for their professional lives, and would maybe even try to help out. I've loads of suggestions that I could have prompted James with, too. Maybe not arty-farty ideas like this one that they're in mid-pitch for, but other stuff that might have . . . shall we say, broader, mass-market appeal. Declan, I know right well, has nothing else up his sleeve, but then he's the money man, whereas James is the one in charge of concepts and 'the company vision'. (His gobshite phrase, not mine.) Anyway, the bastard is always laughing at anything I come up with, dismissing it as 'lowest common denominator' TV, although, when it suits him, he's perfectly happy to filch my ideas and rebrand them as his own, particularly stuff that could be targeted at a female audience.

So I've two clear choices here. I could do a Cyrano de Bergerac and prompt James about another pitch, one that's been at the back of my mind for a long time, and is titled, *God Created Man, But I'd Have Done a Better Job Myself*.

I could, but I don't.

Because just then, the haunting, ugly image of Screechy Sophie standing in my bedroom, wearing my boyfriend's shirt, with me barely cold in the ground, comes back to me . . . and that's all it takes.

'You should have listened to me about that rubbishy old priest pitch but you didn't,' I say to James, and I'm not messing, but now, the beads of sweat are actually rolling down his face and neck. I'm shouting at him now, and I don't even care. I'm getting so upset that I'm sure the freckles must be hopping off my face, just remembering this morning and the awful shock I got. OK, so this mightn't be the ideal time or place to have this out with him, but then, do I really care?

'Too busy lying to me, cheating on me, then moving that over-painted trollop into our house. And what really makes me sick is there you are in public, acting the part of the broken-hearted boyfriend. But here's the one thing that I just don't get . . . did I mean that little to you, James? Did I really?'

'No, no, no . . .' he says, massaging his temples, like he has the world's largest brain tumour, and it's about to kill him.

'Son, are you sure you're all right?' Sir William asks, concerned.

'He's . . . been under a lot of stress lately, personal stuff,' says Declan, trying to salvage the situation. But there's no shutting me up now.

'I mean, I was so good to you,' I continue ranting. 'I put up with all of your moodiness and your arrogance, and it's only now that I can see things clearly. No one really likes you, you know. Not my friends or my family, and it turns out they were right about you, all this time. They were right and I was wrong. You're nothing but a self-centred, over-confident, egotistical gobshite. My God, Napoleon probably had a James Kane complex.'

'This isn't happening,' he mutters, swaying in his seat, 'not now, not here.'

'Sorry to disappoint you, dearest, but yes, this is

your worst nightmare. I *am* your worst nightmare. And I don't even feel remotely guilty for telling you right here and now, because you know what? After the way you've behaved, you don't deserve Sir William and his money. And you don't deserve a partner like Declan either, who, by the way, will go on to do so much better without you.'

'I do deserve it,' he's half-moaning now, like he's lost all grip on reality.

'Oh, and one last thing? Copernicus called. It turns out you're not the centre of the universe after all.'

I had scarcely realized it, but James is practically gibbering, repeating everything I say over and over. Like Rain Man.

'I think maybe we should call a doctor,' says Sir William, who's standing up now, really concerned. 'That fella's not well. Look at him, rambling on about Copernicus and Napoleon. I don't get it, you pair are normally on top of things, what's the deal here?'

It's left to poor Declan to try and do damage limitation, but it's waaaaaayyyyyy too late.

Because that's when disaster number three strikes.

Disaster Number Three
With impeccable timing, two particularly vicious-looking Dobermanns come around out of the house, sniffing for trouble.

'Ah, here's the lads,' says Sir William, probably delighted with the distraction, as he takes a fistful of posh finger biscuits and waves them at the dogs. 'Who's been my good little fellas, then? Who wants a little treat?'

With that, the pair of mutts are over to him, licking his hand and gobbling down the biscuits.

'Jesus Christ,' I half-scream, 'James, get rid of them!'

I'm actually standing on a chair now, terrified. And, true to form, they smell the fear.

Honestly, if it wasn't so frightening it would be funny. Me on a chair, screaming for all I'm worth to get them away from me, James rocking back and forth, massaging his temples with the sweat pumping out of him, and the two Dobermanns at my feet, snapping and growling, completely sensing that I'm there.

The rest is a blur. I remember the following in no particular order. Sir William trying to coax the mutts away, unable to understand why they're barking at thin air. James gulping back water, trembling and shaking and generally acting like he should be in an intensive-care unit and not the garden of a county mansion. Declan frantically gathering up all his files and folders and telling Sir William that they have lots of other ideas they could discuss in the future? Down the line? Maybe? If he's still interested? Please and pretty please with knobs attached? 'Yeah, yeah, yeah,' Sir William says non-committally. 'We'll all have dinner sometime,' I remember him saying, dismissing them off-handedly. But you'd need to be a right thicko not to pick up on the clear, underlying implication.

Dinner for you and a CAT scan for your mate.

Next thing, I'm back in the car, safe from dogs and with James at the wheel beside me, clasping on to it for dear life. Trembling, shaking, breathing deeply, in for two, out for four.

'Are you sure you're going to be OK?' asks Declan through the passenger window beside me. James just nods. He can't even answer him, he's that shell-shocked. Like he's going to turn around at any minute and ask, 'When, oh when, will the lambs be silent?'

'Well, I'll drive behind you, just in case.' Poor old Declan, always so concerned.

Just then his phone beep-beeps as a text comes through.

'Oh, it's from Sir William,' says Declan, holding out his phone, so I'm conveniently able to see it but James can't.

It reads thus:

HOPE YOUR MATE IS OK. I CAN GET YOU NAME OF TOP HEAD SHRINK IN COUNTRY IF YOU WANT. SUGGEST HE SEES SOMEONE ASAP.

NOT NORMAL BEHAVIOUR.

Declan scrolls down and my eyes follow the rest of the message.

GOOD LUCK WITH YOUR TV SHOW. INTERESTING IDEA . . .

He keeps scrolling right down to the very last, killer line.

JUST DON'T EXPECT ME TO INVEST.

Chapter Twelve

FIONA

'Sarah Casey, will you kindly stand up and tell the class what is so funny? If it's that amusing, maybe you'll be good enough to share it with the rest of us?'

Fiona is *soooooo* scary in class. I should know, I'm right at the back, *quelle surprise*, having left James to stew in his own juice for a bit, after the unmitigated disaster of this morning. And oh my God, but it's boring. It's also stifling hot, sticky, and for some reason, there's an over-powering smell of cheap perfume mixed with gone-off egg sandwiches and cheese and onion crisps, which immediately brings me back to my own miserable and wasted schooldays. Written on the board is today's topic: 'How successful were Stalin in Russia and/or Mussolini in Italy in using the personality cult as an instrument of propaganda?'

My oh my, won't knowing the answer to that particular conundrum come in handy later on in life.

'Sarah Casey, I'm waiting. In your own time, please.'

Poor old Sarah, the chief messer herself, is actually doing something completely innocuous: reading this week's *Heat* magazine under her desk, and filling out a questionnaire entitled 'What's Your Sex Number?' Nothing Fiona herself didn't do in her day. In fact, she got up to an awful lot worse back in college: she was forever being kicked out of lectures for acting the eejit, and on one famous occasion, even turning up pissed out of her head.

There you go, beware of the poacher turned game-keeper, and all that.

Sarah's *Heat* magazine is duly confiscated, Fiona shoves it into her briefcase, and I know right well she'll spend her lunchbreak probably filling out the sex number quiz herself. Anyhoo, she tells the class that they've got from now till the bell rings to answer the question on the board, and that they'll all be subsequently graded on their answers. Honest to God, you'd need a heart of stone not to melt at the sight of the pale, drawn faces scribbling their little hearts out about Mussolini and Stalin, the rise of fascism in the early twentieth century and yawn, yawn, yawn.

'Such a total waste of time,' I can't help saying out loud, but no one reacts to me.

No one psychic in the class, then, which I suppose is kind of a relief.

'Sorry, everyone, but where I'm coming from, there's nothing more maddening than seeing people wasting time.' I turn to the poor unfortunate next to me, who has train-track braces on her teeth, smells of Dove deodorant, and is tearing across the page with a biro like her life depends on it. Her name is written at the top of her copybook . . . Oonagh, spelt like that, with two 'o's.

'Come on, Oonagh, do you honestly think it's going to matter in ten, twenty years' time that you know all about Mussolini and Stalin and on what exact dates they came to power? Do you think you'll even remember it the day after you finish your exams? Look out the window, it's a beautiful sunny day! You should be out meeting boys, hanging out with your friends, having fun and . . . you know, actually *enjoying* the few precious years we're all given on this earth, instead of stuck in here learning boring crap that you'll forget all about the minute you get out of the exam hall and set fire to your history books. And that goes for the lot of you, too. Take it from the dead girl: you'll leave school, and one day you'll all look back and only regret the things you didn't do when you were young and gorgeous and free and you had the chance.'

I look around, feeling like I deserve a round of applause, and half-wondering whether or not I should leap up on to a desk and start shouting out '*carpe diem*', like Robin Williams does in *Dead Poets Society*, but, as usual, all my best speeches fall on dead ears. I head up to the front of the class, then something strikes me, and I turn back to talk to the top of all their frantically scribbling heads.

'Ohh, here's some unasked-for advice, though, something that no one ever tells you. Much as we all hate the misery and torture of having Irish rammed down our throats, it comes in very handy for when you're abroad and need to communicate with one of your pals in such a way that no one will understand. Like having a secret code, almost. Mark my words, you'll all be travelling on the Metro in Paris one day, and you'll urgently need to tell whoever you're with to check out the cute fella sitting opposite. If you ask me, that's really the only Irish vocabulary you need bother your heads with. How to talk freely about foreign guys abroad, in public, at the top of your voice, so they'll never understand. Trust me on this: get your Irish teacher to teach you phrases like, "Would you say your man opposite is married/gay/seeing anyone?" Or here's another one, "Please can we get the hell out of this dump of a hellhole, the guy to my left has halitosis and the one on my right thinks we're a lesbian couple." Please listen to me, girls, in five years' time you'll be glad you did.'

They can't, of course, so I go up to Fiona and plonk

down on her desk, with my feet up, the picture of boredom. She's on her BlackBerry, discreetly checking her emails under the desk, so no one can see.

'Hey, hon,' I say, patting her on the shoulder, although she doesn't feel it. Not even a shiver, nothing. 'Just thought of something funny. Remember the time you and me were in Italy on our InterRail hollier, and we were having a full conversation in our rubbishy, pidgin Irish about the general gorgeousness of this really Mediterranean-looking guy on the sun lounger beside us? And you were wondering whether or not he put sand down his Speedos just to impress women? Then he turned round and told us, in flawless Irish, that he was very flattered at our comments, but that he had a girlfriend, and, on a point of order, had never put sand up, down or anywhere near his swimming togs in his entire life. Turned out he came from Belmullet and just happened to be very, very tanned.'

No reaction. Which is kind of weird, after the way James nearly had a coronary every time he heard my voice this morning. In fact, it's funny to think I could stand up here in my nip and no one would as much as look twice at me. Ho hum.

Total silence in the classroom, apart from the furious scratching of pens on copybooks.

'Fiona? Fi? Oh, Fioooooona?'

Still nothing. Not that I expected there to be, I was

just trying to alleviate the tedium, that's all. Eventually, I decide to amuse myself by reading the screen on her phone over her shoulder.

'Sorry about this, love,' I say to her. 'I know I shouldn't, but the thing no one ever tells you about death is that there's not a huge amount there, in the line of entertainment. So . . . you don't mind if I read along with you, do you?'

She sneezes, which I take as a, 'Yes, no problem, Charlotte, work away, feel free.'

As it happens, she's checking her emails and . . . oh for God's sake. I do NOT believe this.

There's one waiting for her in her inbox.

From Mr Loves German Shepherds. Sent at 1 a.m. this morning.

Ooooooh, this had better be good.

From: lovesgermanshepherds@hotmail.com
To: lexiehart@yahoo.com
Subject: Grovelling apologies

Dear Lexie,
Firstly, I completely understand if you see my name coming up on your email and delete this message completely. After what happened last night, I wouldn't blame you. But there is an explanation and I'm cheeky enough to ask you, if you've read this far, to read on a little more.

'DELETE!' I say right into Fiona's face, but her eyes never leave the screen, not even for a second. 'Take my advice and delete it now, then run very far in the opposite direction from wherever this git is.'

But she reads on.

'Fiona,' I'm insisting at her now, 'wait till you see, he'll use the oldest tricks in the book to try and win you round. Mark my words: he'll tell you he had to take care of his sick granny who mislaid her glass eye at bingo, or else he was about to fly back from Belarus, where he's building an orphanage for sick kids, to come and meet you last night, when a sudden, freak thunderstorm meant his flight got rerouted to Swaziland, where he's emailing you from now. FIONA! Please listen to me!'

No joy.

Feck it, anyway. And on she reads.

I know that online it's de rigueur not to give out too many personal details, but after what's happened, I have no choice.

'Fiona, he just used the phrase de rigueur. If that doesn't scream gay at you, I don't know what will. Gay, gay, gay, gayer than the Christmas window at Brown Thomas, I'll lay odds on it. Would you please wake up and smell the KY?'

I'm a vet, and I work in a small practice in Carlow. Last night, as I was driving to Dublin to come and meet you, a local farmer rang my mobile to say one of his mares was foaling early. There was no one else at the practice free to help, so I had no choice but to go. The delivery took all night, far longer than usual, and I'd no reception at the farm, so I couldn't get in touch. I'm just home now and emailing you immediately, both to let you know what happened and, needless to say, apologize.

'OK, so maybe he's a gay vet,' I say right into her face, and believe me, it's beyond weird that she just keeps reading on, not an eyelid flicker, nothing. Weirder still, me talking about her love life in front of thirty adolescent girls.

'Fi, the fact remains, this is NOT the man for you, babes.' I'm doing my best to sound all Oprah-esque; you know, wise, yet concerned, but, as ever, nothing doing. Her eyes are racing greedily down through the email now, so, it's a case of, if you can't beat them, join them. I hop around to stand right behind her chair, so I can get a better view.

Believe me, I'm not the kind of person who would ever deliberately stand anyone up; this was a bona fide emergency. I know it's highly unlikely you'd ever agree to meet me again, but if you could see your way to giving me a second chance, I'd really love to hook up with you. Your online profile is one of the funniest I've ever read, you look stunning in your photo, and I'd love nothing more than an opportunity to apologize in person.

If you're not too busy with all your personal training in the gym, that is.

Right. Now Fiona's scarlet in the face remembering that she told him her alter ego Lexie Hart was a fitness instructor. And that bums, tums and thighs was her favourite class, if memory serves.

All the very best, and please feel free to contact me anytime.

By the way, the mare had a healthy foal, who we named Nelson. After Nelson Mandela.

Oh, the barefaced cheek of him, I think, furiously sitting back up on the desk again and kicking my legs off it. Using political correctness to win Fiona over. Times like this, there's nothing I wish for more than to be able to send her some kind of physical sign. I dunno; if I could only get my fingers to work properly and maybe type out a message for her on the keypad of her laptop? Or somehow, get her to turn on her car radio just as a song is playing which she'll magically know is a coded message from me. Dad does it with Mum all the time, I just wish I had the knack. Although, mind you, I'm not too sure if there even is a song called, 'Ignore That Stupid Bastard You Met Online, He Stood You Up and He's No Find.' Altogether now for the chorus:

> *He's no uuuuuuse,*
> *He's no uuuuuuse,*
> *He stood you up in town.*
> *Really let you down.*
> *Wouldn't buy you a cappuccino,*
> *He is such a mean-oh . . . etc., etc., repeat ad nauseam.*

The silence is broken as a bell rings in the far distance, next thing it's like there's a sudden thunderstorm, with the sound of chairs being scraped back and desks banging. The girls pack up and start tearing off in about twenty different directions, dumping their answer sheets on her desk as they trundle out, with grunts of, 'Thanks, Miss.' With the speed of light, the classroom empties, leaving Fiona all alone, looking wistful and forlorn, staring into space and drumming her biro off the desk.

Which means there's a good chance she believes that cock and bull story about Mr Loves German Shepherds going out last night and doing a James Herriot from *All Creatures Great and Small*.

Which, incidentally, was Fiona's favourite programme as a child.

Which clearly means it's time for me to intervene. And thank God for her that I'm here, that's all I can say. Honestly, I'm starting to wonder what she'd do if I *wasn't* around to guide her.

Later on, back in the staff room, Fiona's in her little cubby hole, face stuck into the computer, when she's interrupted by Mary Bell, one of the senior maths teachers. A kindly, round-faced, middle-aged woman who I remember Fiona telling me was widowed only last year.

'I don't want to interrupt,' she says, tentatively, as Fi expertly snaps her laptop shut, which means she was probably either on Facebook or else checking out her online horoscope.

'No, no, not at all, you're fine.'

'I just wondered how you were doing, I mean, after what happened to your poor friend Charlotte.'

'Emm, well, it's not been easy, that's for sure . . .'

'How are her family taking things?'

Oh God, I'm just not sure I'm ready to hear the answer to that one. Not yet. The thought of Mum and Kate being upset . . . no, you know what? I can't listen to this. It's just too painful. And somehow, the longer I spend on this side of the fence, the harder it's getting, even though I'm still seeing them all the time. Suddenly

I have to concentrate on breathing. So I leave them to it and drift over to the other side of the room, fingers stuck in my ears, waiting until kind old Mary Bell has moved off and Fi's back on her own again. Sorry, but even angels feel heartache, too.

There's a group of teachers, all the Marys, sitting around the coffee table and yakking, so I join them. Honest to God, one of the Marys is holding court about an article she read about how to read your cat's mind, another is giving out handy tips to keep your compost bin smelling nice and fresh, and the one nearest me is telling anyone who'll listen that she thinks she might be suffering from the early stages of gout. Gout? I'm thinking, isn't that all a bit, you know . . . Jane Austen? Poor old Fi, no wonder she spends so much of her free classes with her head stuck in her computer. Nothing against the Marys, they're all lovely, they're just so, so, SO much older than our Fi, that's all.

Anyway, I notice that she's back on her own again, so I muscle into the little cubicle space beside her and start reading over her shoulder.

She's typing out a list. Called 'Things I'd Really Like To Tell Charlotte.'

1. You won't believe item one on the agenda. Had the weirdest dream about, of all people, Tim Keating last night. Can't believe it, have scarcely thought of

him in years. Presume he's living the high life now with what's her name, Ayesha, and their twin girls, best of luck to them. Bizarre dream, too. You and me were at the church bit of his wedding, and I had the horrible jam-jar glasses on . . . why did you never tell me at the time how crap they looked on me? Anyway, you kept poking me and saying that Tim didn't look too happy to be taking his vows, and that you reckoned I was his one true love . . . hilarious. At least it would have been if it wasn't just a dream.

2. I saw your mum. I think it hasn't hit her yet, to be honest. She's numb, and in some ways, maybe that's not such a bad thing . . .

Sorry, but my eye just skims over this one. Mainly because I know if I start bawling crying, there'll be no shutting me up, and I've far too much else to be getting on with.

3. Match.com have just given me an extra six months' free membership as a consolation prize for not having met anyone yet. Now, lesser women than me would be mortally embarrassed by this, but I'm choosing to take it as a sign that I should stay on this path. For the time being, at least. Mind you, give or take a few protracted flings, the last proper, serious long-term boyfriend I had actually was Tim. That's

seven full years ram-packed with rejection. Puberty is a phase, seven years is a lifestyle.

4. If this losing streak keeps up, then I've spotted another online dating service, 'for the busy professional'. You would roar laughing, the web address is www.nevertoolatetomate.com. Their advertising slogan is what really impressed me: it actually says, 'We Delete Members Unfit To Date.' Guerrilla dating, clearly, is the new way forward.

5. Mr Loves German Shepherds apologized and actually sounds fairly normal. A vet, which, as you know, is one of the careers my fantasy boyfriend would have. That and New York firefighter. And US marine, and pilot with any airline at all, I'm not fussy. (I just have a thing about uniforms.) I like the sound of him, Charlotte. I shouldn't, but I do.

I'm back to almost yelling in her face and thank God no one can hear me.

'NO, Fi! After how he stood you up in public? And gave you that lame excuse? Why can't you just think of him, if you must . . . as an utter arsehole?'

6. The only other response from Match.com that I've had asking me for a date is from a Lufthansa steward called Günter. God help me. I don't like uniforms *that* much.

7. May give my vet another crack at the championship title. I know you'd go mental if you knew I was picking up fellas online, but . . .

8. Am not prepared to settle for myself. At home. Alone. With only a bottle of wine and the TV for company. I've my twilight years to look forward to all that in.

9. You know what really annoys me about the society we live in? If you're a battered wife, a heroin addict or a recovering alcoholic, you get sympathy, a government handout, sent on a methadone course, a charity ball is held to raise money for you, and you get a big round of applause when your support group go on the *Late Late Show*. If you're single, in spite of all the humiliation, misery and loneliness you suffer on a day-to-day basis . . . you get sweet shag all.

I read on, over her shoulder, shaking my head sadly.

OK, nothing for it, then. Time to implement part two of my cunning plan.

Just something else I need to check out first, that's all. But don't worry, I'll be right back.

Poor old Fi, by ten o'clock that night, she's fast asleep again, out for the count and snoring gently. She even lets out quite a girlie-sounding fart at one point.

I will *never* get over the things people do when they think they're alone.

Anyway, she's in her living room, stretched out on the sofa in front of the TV, which is still on, with a rerun of an old *Sex and the City* episode blaring away in the background. The one where Mr Big's marriage to the five-foot-ten modelly one breaks up, and he tells Carrie she's the real love of his life. Which is ironic, or at least it will be, when Fiona realizes where I'll be taking her later on tonight.

There's a pile of neatly corrected essays on the coffee table in front of her, and an empty tub of Ben & Jerry's Rocky Road ice cream, with the spoon still sticking out of it. Oh, and a lovely Diptyque lavender-scented candle burning away in the fireplace. I bought it for her last birthday, it cost a small fortune, and it's annoying me now that it's blazing away while she's sleeping and not getting the full benefit of it. That's the thing about dying young: all waste really gets to you. Even over-priced aromatherapy.

I try blowing it out, really try hard, till my cheeks are all puffed out and I'm sure I must be purple in the face. Nothing. I try again, blowing till I'm fit to burst a blood vessel, and . . . I'm not imagining it, it does . . . it actually *does* seem to flicker a tiny bit. Oh my God, this could be so amazing! If I could only just train myself to do physical things, then how much easier would it be

261

for me to give little signs to Mum and Kate and Fi? And batter James across the head with a hockey stick while I'm at it? Maybe it's a bit like training for a marathon: you start with little things like making candles flicker, then gradually work your way up to making butterflies land on people's shoulders and songs loaded with meaning play for them on the radio on cue. So, in no time at all, I'll end up being able to steer Kate and Fiona with all the precision and accuracy of a surface-to-air missile.

Then I look around the living room and realize.

She just went to sleep with the window open, and now the night breeze is fluttering in, making the candle flame flicker, that's all.

Shite.

Anyway, there's no more time to waste, so I wait till she's safely passed through that membrane between being awake and asleep, and in I go.

'Wakey wakey!'

She turns over on her side and keeps on sleeping. Jesus, it's like trying to wake the living dead.

'Fiona?' I say, gently at first, but then getting louder and louder, until her eyes gradually open and she sits sleepily up beside me.

'Hey, babes!' she says, hugging me warmly. 'It's so lovely to see you.'

'And you, hon.'

'Second dream in a row I've had about you.'

'I know.'

'How can you know?'

'Ehh, long story. Let's just say, I'm kind of on a bit of a mission here, and we need to get moving fast . . .'

'On a bit of a mission?'

'Yeeeeeeah, and it's important that you trust me. Now take my hand, there's something I need you to see.'

'Cool. Any clues as to what it is? The inside of the Brangelina mansion? One of the Wilson brothers in the nip? Luke or Owen, you know me, I'm not fussy.'

'Fiona! Shut up and grab my hand, will you? We've so little time before you wake up!'

'Or you know what would be *really* useful? If you could fix it for me to dream what comes up in this year's English and history Higher Level papers. Not that I'd cheat; let's say I'd just gently steer the girls towards what to focus on when they're doing their last-minute cramming, that's all.'

'Fiona! Just hold on to me and stop bloody yakking!'

'Or any chance we could beam into an RTE studio to get next Saturday's Lotto Plus numbers?'

'Last chance.'

'OK, OK, OK. Jeez, can I just point out that you're an awful lot bossier in my dreams than you ever were in real life?'

We lock hands and we're away.

★   ★   ★

263

Next thing, the two of us are standing in the front garden of a perfectly normal-looking suburban house, with a huge sycamore tree growing right at the gate. It's daytime, bright, warm and sunny, and there's a gang of kids going up and down the road on their bikes, screaming abuse at each other, like they're having a race.

Fiona looks at me, puzzled.

'I don't get it,' she eventually says. 'Where the fuck are we, Wisteria Lane? Or make that Hysteria Lane. So, what's going on, have you brought me here so I can dream about tomorrow night's episode of *Desperate Housewives*?'

'Shhhhhh.'

'I mean, I like the TV show all right, but not that much. Couldn't you have taken me somewhere with a bit more . . . pizazz? Like . . . I dunno . . . the Ivy in London, so we could celeb spot. Or the "reduced to clear" rack at some big discount store in New York, so I could see what I'm missing out on . . . or . . . well, pretty much anywhere except here, really.'

'Be patient, will you?'

'I just want to point out that right now, particularly after the last dream I had about you, I'm almost expecting a baby grand piano to fall down on my head, like in a Laurel and Hardy movie.'

'Fiona, just watch, listen and learn.'

'Good coming from you. When did you ever watch, listen *or* learn?'

'If you don't shut up, I'm taking you out of this dream and back to your sofa, and it'll serve you right for not trusting me. This is for your own good.'

'OK, OK.'

Just then, a black Range Rover jeep comes gliding smoothly down the road and pulls up right outside the house, only a few feet away from where we're standing. The door opens and out clamber two gorgeous little girls, very alike, same height, same long, swishy fair hair. It's like they've just come back from the matinee of a panto or something; one is dressed like Belle from *Beauty and the Beast* and the other one is in a Hermione from *Harry Potter* rig-out. They're both wearing tiaras, and are laden down with magic wands, popcorn, bags of chocolate and jellied eels from the sweet factory.

'That pair must be twins,' says Fiona, absent-mindedly. 'Aren't they little cuties? How old would you say they are? Four? Maybe five? I always find it hard to tell, speaking as a non-parent . . .'

She breaks off, as the penny slowly begins to drop.

'Hang on a second, Charlotte, they're twin girls of about five . . . and . . . if I'm not very much mistaken, we both know someone who, by an incredible coincidence, also has twin girls of about that same age, which begs the question, why did you bring me here to spy on them . . . ?'

She's interrupted by the driver's door opening, sees exactly who it is that emerges, then immediately ducks behind the tree, grabbing me with her.

'Merciful hour, what exactly are you trying to do to me? For Jaysus' sake, look! It's him! Tim Keating!'

'Shh, will you calm down, it's absolutely OK, he can't even see us . . .'

'I do not CARE, now get back behind this tree or I'll chain you to it. Why are you putting me through this, Charlotte? Is it punishment for borrowing your good Karen Millen black dress and getting vomit stains on it? Because I'll happily buy you another one, I'll do anything if you'll just beam us out of here, like . . . NOW.'

'Will you just stop rabbiting on and take a look at what's happening? Quick, you're missing the sideshow.'

Her back is to the tree, and she's slumped up against it, arms splayed, like an eco-warrior trying to prevent it from being chopped down.

'Don't suppose there's a chance I'm free to leave at any time, is there?' she hisses at me.

'Another two minutes, that's all I'm asking. For God's sake, you've spent longer on the phone trying to vote on *X Factor*.'

'Charlotte, PLEEEEEEASE!'

'Why won't you trust me? Just take a look behind you, one little peek, that's all I'm asking.'

'When I wake up on my lovely warm sofa, you are veh veh dead. Just so you know.'

I think nosiness eventually gets the better of her, though, because, a second or two later, she pokes the tip of her nose cautiously around the edge of the tree. And then she sees.

Sees Tim to be exact. Ex-love of her life. Except she sees him as he is now, slamming the jeep door shut with an expensive clunk, and striding in that lanky, long-legged way he always had towards the front door.

'Sweet Baby Jesus and the orphans,' says Fi in total shock, unable to take her eyes off him. 'It's Peter Pan with a bald patch. Look at him, he's taken a *coup de vieux*, as the French say.'

'Sometimes you're just too schoolteachery for me, hon; a *coupe de* what?'

'I just mean . . .' her voice breaks off a bit here, like she's starting to choke up. 'He looks so *grey*. Grey and washed-out and tired. That's not the Tim I knew. Not by the longest of long shots.'

It's a pretty good way of describing him, actually: he does look grey in the face. It's hard to imagine, but only a few short years ago, Tim was really something to look at, a head-turner, but in a couldn't-care-less kind of way. There wasn't an ounce of vanity in him: he only shaved because if he didn't, he'd end up looking like a caveman, and the only time he ever looked in a mirror was to put in his contacts. Tall and super-skinny with unruly black curls that nearly came to his shoulders, like a seventies footballer. Black eyes that danced at you as he made you nearly pee with laughter at one of his gags, or at some bit of messing and devilment he'd been up to. Back then, he always used to wear these mad T-shirts with slogans on them that said things like, 'My Mother Is a Travel Agent for Guilt Trips.' Or 'At My Age, I've Seen It All, Heard It All, Done It All. Just Can't Remember It All.' Then there was my personal favourite, and the one he wore to his twenty-first birthday party, 'I Just Do What the Voices Inside My Head Tell Me to Do'. Once, for Fiona's birthday, he even bought her one that said, 'Princess, Sufficient Experience With Princes, Seeks Frog.' Now a more high-maintenance woman would have told him to shove his T-shirt up his arse and go to the nearest jewellers to buy her a proper, decent, more boyfriendy type of present. But Fiona loved it so much, she even slept in it. Mind you, this is a couple whose song was 'Pretty Vacant' by the Sex Pistols. Not the most romantic, but there you go.

And now . . . now it's beyond weird to see him be-suited and bespectacled, looking so conservative and so worn-out and so, so *old*. Like *The Picture of Dorian Gray*, only in reverse.

'Jesus,' snaps Fiona, ducking back behind the tree again, 'he's rung the front doorbell. Suppose someone answers it and sees us?'

'Just look, will you? It's important.'

'Why? So I can describe it in court when I'm hauled up for stalking and harassment of an ex-boyfriend?'

'Hauled up by who, exactly, the dream police?'

'I'm too fragile for community service, I wouldn't last a wet day . . .'

'Watch, will you, you're missing all the action!'

This time, our two noses peek out from behind the tree, just in time to see the door opening and . . . drum roll for dramatic effect . . .

'Shite, shite, shite,' snaps Fiona. 'It's her, Ayesha, the wife!'

'Ex-wife, I'll think you'll find, love.'

Fiona looks at me, and for a second, I think she might actually throw up into the rose bush that's behind us.

'Are you telling me . . .'

'Separated since January. I sounded it all out for you. And there's more, take a look. See for yourself.'

Ayesha is standing on the doorstep now, in a Juicy Couture powder-pink tracksuit, still with her perma-tan, still stick thin, and with flashing nails that are far too long to be natural; no, those babies just have to be acrylic.

OK, I should bring you up to speed a bit.

Ever since Ayesha and Tim got married, her career has not exactly been the glittering, stellar success she had told everyone it was going to be. Turns out (I'm quoting Fiona here) that to fulfil her ultimate career goal and be a newsreader on Sky, it's a prerequisite that you have to actually be able to *read*, so that was the end of her. Then at around the same time they relocated back to Dublin, she got one of her mates in PR to do a huge, blanket-coverage media splash about how she was the 'hot' new thing to arrive in town, and would be taking RTE by storm any time soon.

'Ultimately, I'd like to host my own chat show,' I remember her announcing in some magazine interview. 'Everyone in London said I was a natural. I love, love loooooove meeting people, and you know? That TV show *Xpose* would be so perfect for my talents. I just feel I have so much I want to share with the Irish public. My role models in life are Oprah, Conan O'Brien and of course, Miriam O'Callaghan. For God's sake, my cat is even called Tubridy.'

Not long after that, Fiona and I started celebrating every day that she *wasn't* on telly. Because if she had ever ended up with her own TV show, I think Fiona would have ended up sitting in a darkened room taking tablets. Now, you can read Ayesha's hard-hitting showbiz column in the *Bray People* and, having exhausted her luck with TV, she's apparently trying to crack into radio.

'Well, that should suit her down to the ground,' Fiona said when she first heard that particular update. 'It's important that the ugly presenters should have somewhere to work.'

Ayesha, as you see, brings out a very bitchy side in our Fi.

'Please can we leave now?' she pleads with me. 'Can't you . . . throw water or something on my face to wake me up? An average night in hell couldn't be as bad as this.'

'One more little surprise for you before I'm letting you off the hook. Watch.'

Just then, from behind the hall door, a guy appears, wearing a Leinster rugby shirt and hovering proprietorially right behind Ayesha. Voices are wafting back to us across the lawn, Tim calmly handing the kids over and arranging to take them out to a movie night at the weekend. No one even asks him inside for a cuppa tea, nothing.

'I do NOT believe this,' hisses Fiona. 'It's like watching a real-life soap opera unfold . . .'

'This is no soap opera, it's as real as you or I.'

'Don't tell me . . . is Ayesha actually going out with that jockstrap behind her?'

I nod. 'What's more, he's moved himself in, lock,

stock and barrel. Into that house which Tim, by the way, is still paying the mortgage on. And your man had no problem doing it, either.'

She turns to face me, her face the colour of gazpacho.

'So . . . then, if all this is true . . . what about Tim?'

'Living in the International Financial Services Centre, in an apartment the approximate size of your average downstairs loo. All he can afford, now that he's forking out so much in maintenance for Fern Britton there.'

Fiona has her back slumped against the tree now, and honestly looks like she might need to breathe into a bag.

'OK,' she says, slowly, slowly, slowly. 'I'm starting to feel like someone just reached into my small intestine and pulled it out through my mouth. This is . . . this is . . . just so awful for Tim. What I mean is . . . he was always such a family-orientated person, to be a separated dad now must be *killing* him.'

Right then. I've waited long enough for this moment, might as well just go for it.

'Call him,' I say, eyeballing her. 'Don't think about it, or over-analyse it, like you always do with fellas, just do it.'

'What?'

'He's lonely, you're lonely, and I'll bet you there's not a single day goes by that he's not thinking about you.'

Now she looks confused.

'Oh, come off it, Charlotte, you have to be kidding me. After all these years? Suddenly for me to just contact him out of the blue? Wouldn't I look like a complete saddo? I mean, come on, even desperados like me have to draw the line somewhere.'

'And you have the nerve to wonder why you're still alone?'

'What have you turned into, anyway? The ghost of relationships past, present and future?'

Not quite, I think, keeping my mouth shut.

But if she doesn't do exactly what I tell her, she's given me a great idea for next time I visit her.

Chapter Thirteen
KATE

Aka, my single greatest angelic challenge. The one that has me bashing my head off the wall in sheer frustration. After I leave Fiona for the night, I pop in to see Mum, who's out for the count, hairnet and Ponds cold cream on, in the same fluffy peach dressing gown she's only been wearing for about the last twenty years or so. There's a novena printed out on a worn scrap of paper on her bedside locker, to Saint Clare, her desert island favourite saint, who she swears never lets her down. I know right well that she's doing the novena for me, and it's all I can do to fight back the tears and not give in to the wave of pain that comes over me every time I see her tired, worn-out face.

There's so much I'm bursting to talk to her about, and it's maddening not to be able to communicate with her properly, because I'm too upset to. I'm dying to tell her about James's disastrous meeting today, and how . . . dare I even think the thought . . . how, if I were a producer, I would have handled it so much differently. Like, ooh, I dunno, pitched Sir William Eames a half-decent idea for starters. In fact, after sitting in on their big meeting, now I find myself thinking . . . sure I could have done that. I could easily have followed my dream and been a producer myself, instead of constantly listening to James telling me I wasn't enough of a risk-taker, then letting him pinch half my ideas and pass them off as his own. Frustrating to think that I actually mightn't have been that bad at it, after all. And I would have *loved* it. The only thing that's stopping me now is that I'm dead. Which kind of puts the kibosh on things.

Then there's the news about Tim Keating being newly separated, and how I'm trying to cleverly engineer him and Fi back into each other's arms. Times like this, I almost wish Mum wasn't so religious, because then maybe I could chat to her when she's dreaming some night, and maybe even convince her it would be a great idea to go to a seance. And I wouldn't be one of those wishy-washy spirits, either, the ones who short-change you by only giving one knock for yes and two for no; none of that crap. In fact, the medium wouldn't be able to shut me up. I'd tell Mum how much I love her and miss her and watch over her every day and how every time I see her, it breaks my heart all over again. And how sorry I am that I never even got to say a proper goodbye to her. And most of all, how I would have lived my life so differently if I'd known it was all going to be snatched away from me, aged twenty-eight.

She's put a photo of Dad and me on her bedside table, one that was never there before. It was taken after our school Christmas play, when I was about ten or so; we did Cinderella and I was an ugly sister. Typecast, Kate had said at the time, leading to much whingeing on my part, and much accusing her in later years of effectively squishing any latent vocation as an actress I might have had. But then, that's sisters for you.

I stay with Mum for the whole night. Just watching over her, that's all.

Early the next morning, the phone on the bedside table wakes her, and I know before she even picks it up that it's Kate. Let's face it, only a relative or a telesales caller would dare ring at this hour.

'Yes, oh hello, love.' God, even hearing her voice makes me realize how much I've been missing her. Even though I can only hear this side of the chat, I gather that Kate's having a good old giving-out rant about Perfect Paul. At least judging by the amount of times Mum keeps saying things like, 'But sure, he has to work, love. And it's not his fault his band is always playing in the west, now is it?' Then, just as I'm racking my brains wondering what in hell I can do for Kate, the break-through comes.

Mum is in the middle of giving her a shopping list for stuff she wants back from Lidl, and is just wondering whether to get rashers and white pudding, her favourite, or if she should try to be healthy and go with the wholegrain bread instead, when out of nowhere she says, 'Kate, you don't have to do this, you know. No, not the shopping, I need you to do that, love, and you know what a great help it is to me. Although if you bring that disgusting low-fat spread again, I'll send you straight back with it. Full-fat butter or nothing, thanks. No, I meant, you don't have to stay with me today. Not if you'd rather go down to Galway to be with Paul.'

Bingo, I think, looking at her, amazed. Exactly what Kate needs. Quality time with her fella, away from all of the stress and worry and grieving. I'm willing her to say yes, thanks a million, wait till I just pack the sexy La Perla underwear, and I'll be in the car in five minutes, but she must put up a bit of a fight because Mum has to keep reiterating, 'Yes, of course I mean it,' over and over again, getting firmer and firmer each time. Eventually she insists, telling Kate that it's not like there's anything that she can do by being here, and that she'll only be on the other end of a phone should Mum need her urgently. After all, Kate will only be going for an overnighter and, most importantly of all, Mum's pal Nuala is staying with her for the entire day, so she won't be all alone, if she gets upset and needs someone.

Which makes me choke up all over again. Just at the thought of what poor Mum must be going through. I can't even bring myself to think of how unbearably painful it must be for her, so I do what I always do when confronted with this nightmarish thought. Tune out, tune out, tune out. Focus on all the miracles I can work for everyone from this side of the fence. Stay blinkered, eye on the ball.

Sorry, but I really am that much of an emotional coward.

'It's been a terrible time for all of us,' Mum finally says to Kate in her best, firmest, 'I'm hanging up now' voice. 'And you need the break, love, so take it while you can, and I'll see you when you're back tomorrow.'

Ooh, this is working out far, far better than I ever could have hoped. An hour later, we're on the road west, with me sitting beside Kate in her nippy little Mazda convertible, which was, I'm not joking, a thirtieth-birthday present from Perfect Paul. Honest to God, if I didn't love her so much, the jealousy would finish me off entirely, especially seeing as how James, who is rubbish with important dates, forgot my last birthday, then remembered at the last minute and ended up running to the garage across the road to buy me air freshener for the car, a family-sized tub of Cadbury's Miniature Heroes, and a packet of condoms. Three items on every girl's wish list, har di har, is probably what went through his warped, deluded brain. He made up for it afterwards, giving me a beautiful, guilt-purchased necklace, but the sting remained. Bear in mind, this is a man whose idea of a perfect romantic Valentine's Day gift is a tin of Roses without a dent in it. Then, the birthday before that, he actually managed to remember it, but only because I had a party in the house, and he presented me with . . . two goldfish called Little James and Little Charlotte. Which he subsequently forgot to feed when I went away on a girlie holiday with Kate, and when I came back, they had mysteriously disappeared. Flushed down the loo, Fiona and I reckoned. Romance, thy name is James Kane.

Anyway, time to talk about Kate, not me. The journey to Galway takes just over three and a half hours, and it's all very Thelma and Louise, minus any kind of conversation or interaction with each other, or the cops chasing us. Oh, or the sexy hitchhiker they pick up in the back, who wouldn't have lasted a wet day with Kate, anyhow; she has a thing about gum chewers. I spend most of the journey willing her to turn on Love FM, a local station that plays romantic smoochy songs back-to-back, anything to get her into the mood. At one point, about an hour into the journey, she does click on to it, and I think Hallelujah, God be praised, but they're playing the Carpenters' 'Goodbye to Love', which she immediately snaps off. We do the rest of the journey in silence.

When we do eventually arrive, mid-afternoon, Kate heads straight for her brother-in-law Robbie's big, sprawling neo-Georgian house in Salthill, on the outskirts of the city, where Perfect Paul always stays whenever he's in town. I should fill you in a bit. Of all the brothers, Robbie is the one closest to Paul, in age as well as everything else. There's only a year between them, and they even look alike, right down to the chunky neck and big, beefy, man-size presence, which Mum always says reminds her a bit of Desperate Dan in the comics she used to read as a kid. I'm not messing, they're the type of fellas that you almost expect to walk into a restaurant and order a large helping of cow pie. In fact Mum and I often joke that Paul's breakfast consists of a full packet of cornflakes, a pound of sugar and a pint of milk, all served up in a giant salad bowl. Which, when you consider that Kate's the type to pick at a bag of lettuce from Marks & Spencer, then make jokes about how her target weight is two pounds above kidney failure, you're left shaking your head in wonderment at just how opposites can attract.

Anyway, Robbie is pretty much Paul's number two, his *consigliere*; if this was *The Godfather*, then Robbie would play Tom Hagen to Paul's Vito Corleone. He's married to Rose, who Kate refers to behind her back as Briar Rose on account of how prickly she is. More anon.

So anyway, one deep, nerve-calming gulp of air later, Kate scrunches her car through the gates and on to the gravelled driveway, then whips out her mobile and calls Paul. It goes straight through to his voicemail, though, so she leaves a short message telling him that surprise, surprise, she's here, and can he please ring her as soon as he picks up the message? My heart goes out to her as I see her drumming her fingers nervously off the steering wheel. Knowing that, now Paul's not around, she'll have to face into meeting Briar Rose and her brood all on her own. Next thing, before she's even had a chance to get psyched up, she's spotted by one of the nephews, a kid of about six or seven. (Don't ask me which one, there's so many of them at family gatherings you'd almost wish they all wore individual sticky name-tags.) Anyway, said kid comes running round to the car door, thumps on it and demands to know if she brought him any sweets.

'Oh, hi there!' says Kate a bit over-brightly, rolling down the car window. 'Eh, sorry, but I'm afraid I didn't stop off to buy anything . . . emmm . . . Sean . . .'

'I'm not Sean, I'm Jack,' says the kid, looking at her disgustedly. Next thing, Briar Rose herself appears at the front door, tea towel in hand, to see for herself who the flashy Dublin reg car in her driveway belongs to.

'It's Auntie Kate come from Dublin,' Jack shouts

back to her. 'And she didn't bring anything, either. Not even crisps.'

Jaysus, poor Kate. Five minutes later she's in the kitchen, surrounded by about eight of the nieces and nephews, plus all three sisters-in-law, one of whom is breastfeeding, while another one, who's about eight months pregnant, keeps screeching out the window at some kid called Tommy to stop tormenting his twin brother with the water hose. Kate looks totally out of her depth, and although I can tell by her that she's doing her best to fit in and be a good sport, the sisters-in-law are having none of it. As if they've long ago made up their minds that Kate is some snooty, superior cow from Dublin who occasionally graces them with her presence purely to lord it over them all. That's the label they've chosen for her, and she's stuck with it. Whether she likes it or not.

Which is just so unfair it's starting to make my blood boil.

OK. Here's how the conversation *should* have gone.

Kate: 'Hi, Rose, great to see you, you're looking well. Hi, Melissa, hi, Sue, my how your kids have all grown since I last saw them!'
Rose: 'Lovely to see you too, Kate, and thanks so much for popping in. How well you look, is that a new coat?'

Kate: 'Oh, this old thing? M & S, cheap as chips, just threw it on ... etc., etc. ...'

Rose: 'We're just having a little snack, the kids are starving after school, will you have tea and a ham sandwich?'

Kate: 'Lovely, you're very kind. Please allow me to help you. Also, can I assist with removing the mashed-in banana from that child's hair?'

Rose: 'Wonderful. If you could also unhook the satellite dish so as to finish the row that's currently blazing in the TV room, I would be most grateful, ha ha ha.'

Kate: 'Ha, ha ha. Don't suppose there's any sign of my husband, by any chance?'

Rose: 'Out touting for work with my husband, and generally slaving away to keep we ladies in the manner to which we are accustomed, hee hee.'

Kate: 'Yes, proper order, hee hee. Isn't it terrific that we can sit cosily around the kitchen table, just a gang of sisters-in-law, and all get along so famously?'

Rose: 'Too bloody true. I'm sure I speak on behalf of all the family when I say what a delight it is to see you, Kate, and how much we all wish you lived here permanently. My, the sisterly fun we would all have ... etc., etc. ...'

But, sadly, this is how the conversation actually goes.

Kate (*Nervously.*): 'Emm . . . hi, everyone!'

Rose, Melissa and Sue (*Barely looking up from their screeching brood.*): 'Howaya?'

Rose (*Eyeing her up and down.*): 'That a new coat?'

Kate (*Embarrassed.*): 'Oh, this? Eh, yeah, I got it at a designer discount warehouse sale . . .'

The breastfeeding sister–in–law *(Insincerely.)*: 'Very swish.'

Kate (*Overeager.*): 'Oh, do you like it? Because if you do, I could easily get you one in your . . . emm . . . size.'

(*Cue a disgusted look from the breastfeeding sister–in–law, who is, shall we say, still battling with her baby weight.*)

Rose (*Yelling out the window at some unfortunate child.*): 'Rory! You do NOT charge your cousins admission into that tree house. You know right well it's for you all to share. Now hand back that two euro! (*Then back to Kate.*) Do you want tea and a sandwich?'

Kate (*Who is coeliac.*): 'Emm . . . would it be OK if I just had tea?'

The pregnant sister–in–law (*Deeply suspicious.*): 'Are you not hungry after the drive? God, I'd be starving after nearly four hours in the car.'

Kate: 'No, I just can't eat bread, that's all.'

(*Cue much hilarity around the table, with Kate getting more and more mortified by the second.*)

The sister–in–law who's breastfeeding (*Gleeful.*): 'Sure

that's the most mental thing I've ever heard in my whole life. If one of my kids said that to me, I'd clatter them. Not eat bread? Sure what are you supposed to live off? Thin air?'

Kate (*In a brave attempt to get off the subject.*): 'Don't suppose anyone knows where Paul is, by any chance?'

Rose: 'He left here with Robbie early. Gone looking at a site above in Gort. Poor man was still knackered this morning, after doing that awful drive down here yesterday.'

Heavily pregnant sister-in-law: 'At least if he was based here in Galway, he wouldn't have to sit in a car for three and a half hours every time there's a bit of cheap land for sale. Ridiculous carry-on, if you ask me.'

Rose (*Hammering the point home.*): 'But sure, I suppose when you've no kids, it doesn't really matter so much. Take it from me, though, Kate, the pair of you won't be able to flit around the country so much when you have a baby. Not a chance in hell. Poor aul Paul, every time I see him kicking a football around the back with one of mine, my heart goes out to him. I'd say he's only dying to become a father. Sure he's a born dad, so he is. And he was starving when he got here, too. Ate a massive dinner yesterday, then he had a full fry-up for breakfast this

285

morning, and was still looking for second helpings. I don't know, Kate, do you feed the man at all?'

OK, I can't stay silent any longer. And it's not like anyone can hear me, either, so I can say what I like.

'Hmmm, let me see now,' I say, as I plonk down at the kitchen table, wedged right in between Rose and Kate. 'It can't be National Bitch Day, because all the banks are still open . . . so you're clearly only needling Kate like this because, let me think now . . . oh yeah, because you're an unutterable bloody cow, that's why. Tell me this, Rose, was your mother by any chance a jackal?'

Wasting my fragrant sweetness on the desert air, as usual, but it sure as hell makes me feel better. Just then, the door opens, and in bursts Robbie with Connor, the youngest brother, and they, at least, are both marginally politer to Kate than the wives all were. Robbie even asks after Mum and sympathizes with Kate about me, which is far more than any of the others did. There's chaos and mayhem and kids running around screaming, demanding to be taken either to the movies or else McDonald's, or basically anything other than knuckle down to doing actual homework.

'Eh, don't suppose you know where Paul got to?' Kate has to shout, to make herself heard over the racket.

'Ehh . . . band practice,' says Robbie, shoving a ham

sanger into his gob. 'Down in Sheehan's pub. Julie and
the others wanted to try out a few new numbers before
the fortieth-birthday party tonight.'

Even the mention of Julie's name brightens the
collective mood of the sisters-in-law, all of whom, it
seems, know Julie from schooldays, are best buddies with
her, and think she's well on her way to being the next
Christina Aguilera. Only playing pub gigs in Galway
temporarily until she gets her big break, either from
going on *X Factor*, or from Louis Walsh discovering her,
or from suddenly becoming a huge overnight YouTube
sensation.

The way you do.

'I must get her to sing "Beautiful" for me tonight,' says
Rose fondly. 'Because that's my song, isn't it, girlies?'

Kate eventually says fine, that she'll go down to
Sheehan's to find her husband, but no one either hears
or answers her. In all the commotion, she slips out,
and I don't think any of them even bother to say goodbye. Then, I don't know why, but some latent sixth
sense makes me stay on after she's left. The minute
she's left the room, they all start talking about her. *All*
of them.

'Always a joy!' Rose says sarcastically to the closed
kitchen door. 'Seeing you leave, that is.'

'Oh, I don't eat wheat,' the breastfeeding sister-in-law
says, doing a lousy impression of Kate's clipped tones.

'I got my coat at a designer sale,' chimes in the pregnant one.

'And did you hear her telling me she'd try to get me the same coat . . . in my size. Cheek of her. I've lost three full pounds since I had the baby, you know.'

'Oh, and you can totally tell!' the other two chime obediently.

'And did you see the way she was looking me up and down, like I'm some kind of beached whale that wouldn't fit into one of her bloody designer coats? God, I hate the superior way skinny women go on sometimes. Would you say she even feeds Paul? With her, "Oh, I don't eat bread."'

'Oh, look at me, afraid to put too much dip on a cracker just in case I might sprain my wrist,' says Rose, doing by far the worst impression of the lot of them.

'Definitely not,' says the pregnant one. 'At least not judging by the huge clatter of sausages and mash he ate the minute he got down here.'

'How do you think I feel, girls?' says Rose. 'She'll expect to stay the night here with Paul this evening and wait till you see: nothing will be good enough for her. Well, if madam thinks she's getting the red-carpet treatment in this house, she's another think coming.'

Much clicking of tongues and umming and dark nodding of heads at this. Particularly unfair, as I happen to know that Kate is a really good house guest. I mean, OK, she may be a little high-maintenance, but her heart's in the right place. In fact, I remember one famous occasion when she and Paul were staying with Mum while the builders were in their house, and Kate donned a pair of Marigolds and started scrubbing down the bathtub, much to Mum's disgust. ('Where does she think she is, anyway, the house that hygiene forgot?' I remember Mum snarling at me, like I'd anything to do with it.) Anyway, the point is that Kate means well, but try telling that to this shower.

'Wouldn't even sit for more than five minutes with us, the uppity aul cow,' Rose goes on, shaking her head sadly. 'Poor aul Paul. You'd really have to feel sorry for him.'

By the time I rejoin Kate, she's back in the car, on her way to town, almost trembling at the coolness of her reception.

'Bitches,' I say to her, but of course, she just stares straight ahead. 'That's all they are, Kate, so there's no point in letting them get to you. They've made up their mind that you're an outsider, and that they're not going to like you, and there's no turning them. Best you can do is have as few dealings with them as possible. I mean, everyone has in-laws they don't like, don't they?'

She tries calling Paul on the mobile again, but still no answer. So, a few minutes later, she pulls up into the car park of Sheehan's pub, which isn't too far from Rose's house, and heads inside. Paul's car is there, too, thank God. I follow her in, but it's packed with a coach party on their way to see the Spanish Steps, and there's no one serving behind the bar. Eventually, she stops a lounge girl laden down with a trayload of soup and sandwiches, with hair extensions so long they're almost swishing into the consommé, and asks her if she knows where the band for tonight are practising.

'Function room upstairs,' says hair-extension girl, without even looking at her. So up the back stairs Kate goes, with me hot on her heels, dying to see the look on Paul's face when he sees her. That she's driven all this way just to be with him. That she's here to make up for the humdinger of a row they had early yesterday morning. That she loves him and knows just how lucky she is to have such an ideal husband, to rob from Oscar Wilde. That it's not his fault that his brothers all married such harridans: Kate and Paul have each other, and that's all that matters.

From down the corridor outside, you can hear a guitar playing 'Yesterday' by the Beatles, and a deep, mezzo-soprano woman's voice crooning along. The fabulous, about-to-be-discovered Julie, I assume, plus the rest of the band rehearsing for tonight.

Kate bursts in, all smiles, with a big, 'Hi, love, it's me!'

But it's not the full band at all.

Just Paul and Julie on their own.

And they don't even look all that pleased to see her.

Later on that evening, I'm still with Kate as she wanders aimlessly around the Brown Thomas branch off Eglinton Square, having spent the last few hours guilt-buying gifts for all the horrors-in-law. She's shaken, I know she is, and I just couldn't bring myself to leave her. There you go, that's just the kind of 24/7 angel I am. By now, she's laden down with all kinds of presents: scented candles for the pregnant sister-in-law, perfume for the breastfeeding one and a huge chocolate cake for Rose. Not including the bags and bags of colouredy pick and mix stuff from the Sweet Factory for the kids, to make up for arriving empty-handed earlier.

Paul was perfectly polite to her earlier, in Sheehan's, but stood firm, telling her that he and Julie needed to rehearse before tonight, and that he'd see her back at the house for dinner later. Which left Kate with the choice of facing back into making small talk with his awful family till he arrived, or else skiving off for a few hours to fill the time with shopping. And really, would you blame her?

Come sixish though, and it's not like she can absent herself for much longer without it seeming rude. And believe me, you wouldn't want to give this shower any ammunition to use against you. She calls Paul, yet again gets his voicemail and tells him she'll see him back at Rose's house. My heart goes out to her as she faces back into the kitchen of horrors, where, apart from there being about a dozen or so kids sprawled out in front of the telly, no one seems to have budged all afternoon. But then, that's just the way this family are, I have to remind myself; they just seem to really enjoy living in each other's pockets all day long. I dunno, maybe because it's all the easier to bitch about outsiders like Kate when they intrude on their poisonous little web of hating the entire world outside of their four walls.

Timidly for her, Kate distributes the gifts, then excuses herself to go upstairs and freshen up for dinner. Paul still isn't back from rehearsing yet, so I figure she'd rather be alone in the spare bedroom than having to deal with this shower. I stay behind, though, and sure enough, no sooner is she out the door than the backbiting starts. Honest to God, Kate trying to be nice to them is such a big mistake. A huge mistake, in fact. With cellulite and love handles and thunder thighs. Put it this way: this is one family tableau that I doubt Norman Rockwell would want to paint.

'She bought me a shaggin' cake?' is Rose's opener. 'When everyone knows I was a county finalist at this year's bake-fest above in Oranmore? Bloody cheek of her.'

'She left the price on the scented candle she got me,'

mutters the pregnant one. 'Forty-two euro! Scandalous. Imagine forking out that amount of cash for a candle? She'll have poor Paul ruined in no time.'

'And buying bag-loads of sweets full of E-numbers for the kids,' snipes the third witch in the coven, who's at the sink draining spuds. 'They'll all be so full of sugar they haven't a chance of sleeping tonight, and wait till you see, they'll give the babysitter hell. My one night out, too. Thoughtless cow.'

Jesus Christ, I think, going straight back to where Kate is changing upstairs. She can't bloody win with these people. Damned if she does and damned if she doesn't.

Nor do things improve when Paul eventually does get back. By my reckoning, he's in and out the door in about thirty minutes flat, only stopping for a lightning-quick shower, to change clothes and wolf down the roast chicken and spuds dinner that's plonked in front of him. He's like a whirlwind, in and gone before you'd even know it.

Leaving Kate alone. Yet again.

I stay with her as she politely offers to drive anyone who wants a lift to Sheehan's for the fortieth party, but the horrors-in-law all elect to travel in Rose's big people-carrier mammy wagon. Together. Without Kate. Connor, the youngest brother, must feel a bit sorry for her, though, as he hops in beside her, just so she's not totally alone. It's the nicest thing any of the family has done for her all day.

The party is beyond awful. Kate doesn't even get two seconds alone with Paul, as he's playing non-stop for the night, and on the rare occasion when the band do take a breather, they just chat among themselves about the playlist for the next set. And apart from Paul's family, she knows no one, nor do any of the in-laws bother introducing her around. When the beers kick in, things start getting a bit raucous, and in no time, everyone's up on their feet dancing to some Chuck Berry number, arms in the air, having great crack.

Everyone except Kate, that is. She's sitting all alone at the family table, while the in-laws are dancing around their handbags, knocking back the Bacardi Breezers, laughing their half-pissed heads off. Honestly, poor Kate might as well have a sign over her head saying, 'Do not engage the social leper in conversation, she doesn't fit in. In case anyone hadn't noticed.' Another break in the music and this time the famous Julie is over to Paul, all wiggling hips and deep-voiced and doe-eyed. She's young, about twenty-three, with the head so bleached off her that if you look at her sideways, she kind of has a look of Eva Braun.

So yet again, Kate sits at the edge of the family table, the picture of isolation and loneliness, while her husband blatantly ignores her. Doesn't even come near her once all evening. Doesn't even look over in her direction to see whether she's OK. Doesn't offer her a drink, nothing. After a few hours of this appalling treatment, Kate looks utterly miserable, so unhappy that she's only about a heartbeat away from recording a Country and Western album. In her defence, she sticks it out till about midnight, then makes her excuses and leaves, pleading exhaustion after a long day. No one says goodbye to her. No one looks sorry to see her go.

In fact, I don't think anyone even notices.

I don't stick around for the bitch-fest which usually erupts the minute Kate leaves her sisters-in-law, I go straight back to Briar Rose's house where Kate relieves the babysitter, pays her (not that she'll get any thanks for it), then slopes forlornly off to bed. Hours and hours later, there's a commotion in the driveway as the rest of the family land back, and from the sound of it, head straight for the kitchen where Rose sticks on a late-night fry-up. Kate's lying awake, staring at the ceiling with the smell of rashers and toast wafting upstairs to her, and I have a horrible feeling that I know exactly what's coming next.

'Don't do it, Kate,' I say out loud. 'Don't pick a fight with Paul. Not in this house, where Briar Rose probably has a CCTV camera here so she can watch the whole thing live, then play back the edited highlights to the other pair of witches tomorrow. Trust me, don't do it.

At least wait till you're home, in your own space, where you have some privacy.'

No such luck, though. Not long after, Paul falls in beside her, pissed as a fart, and off Kate goes. As marital rows go, it's a particularly ugly one, with Kate coolly dissecting how completely ignored she felt for the whole day and night, and by the husband she'd made such an effort to come and see. A fair point, but Paul's way too slaughtered drunk to even come back at her; he just grunts at her to leave him alone so he can sleep off his bellyful of beer.

'Paul, I'm talking to you,' she says, wobbly voiced, all the upset, anger and frustration of the whole crappy day and night coming back to her.

Kate, please don't do this, not here and not now. I wouldn't put it past Rose to be outside the door with an empty jam-jar pressed against it so she can hear every word you're saying. Sorry, shouting.

'Ah leave off your nagging and go to sleep, woman,' growls Paul from somewhere under the duvet.

Which only starts her off on a fresh bout of rowing, the theme this time being, 'On what planet do you think this is an acceptable way to treat your wife?' On and on they go, with Paul eventually sitting up on one elbow, wide awake now, realizing that he won't get a wink of sleep till the row has run its course. He gives as good as he gets, and at one point even drunkenly tells Kate to shut up, cop on to herself, and that all his brothers reckon he's married to a heart scald. Horrible phrase, and if he had said it to me, I'd probably have clocked him one. Then, as if the atmosphere wasn't hostile enough, he adds insult to injury by accusing her of making no effort with his family, none at all, because she reckons she's too good for them. Which is both untrue *and* unfair. The *pièce de résistance*, though, is when he slurs from the side of his mouth that behind her back, the bitches-in-law all refer to Kate as Hatchet Face.

Ouch, ouch ouch.

As for me, as I watch, a horrible little doubt is beginning to ferment at the back of my mind.

Could it be possible?

Or maybe, just maybe, is Perfect Paul not quite as perfect as we all thought?

Chapter Fourteen

JAMES

Like I said, Dad's a great man for inspirational quotes, and I always remember a particular one from *Hamlet* that he was for ever trying to hammer home to me and Kate. When sorrows come, they come not single spies but in battalions. Which might sound a bit Elizabethan, but when you hear what's lying ahead for James, believe me, it'll all start to make sense. I think after the awfulness of Kate's miserable night with Paul, I need cheering up, and what better way to do it than by calling in on someone who's a helluva lot worse off than any of us, including me.

And, like, I'm the *dead* girl.

Screechy Sophie appears to have just moved herself in, and when I get to the house bright and early the following morning is actually standing in the converted loft upstairs wearing my dressing gown and ironing one of her flowery summery dresses, *humming a song*, the bare-faced bloody cheek of her. What next? Is she going to start wearing the rest of my clothes and dancing around on my grave singing the 'Hallelujah Chorus'? Meanwhile, bastard-face James is in our bedroom . . . get this . . . clearing my stuff out of the wardrobe. And dressing table. And bathroom. Everything. My books, including a first-edition John McGahern that Fiona gave me one Christmas. Signed by the author, no less. My CDs, even the ones that he himself bought me. All my make-up and cleansers and out-of-date magazines. Jesus, he even grabs the photo of me and Kate on her wedding day off the dressing table and flings it into a plastic bag.

OK, now I'm getting *really* angry.

I remember when Dad died, I couldn't bring myself to throw out any of his old clothes or even donate them to a charity shop, nothing. All I wanted to do was smell his jumpers and coats, and be in some weird way comforted by just how much his lingering scent brought him back to me. But here's cackhead James actually flinging my stuff into Tesco's bags. Not even pausing for the briefest whiff of my perfume, nothing. I'm rooted to the spot staring at this latest war crime in total and utter shock, just as the doorbell clangs and brings me back to my senses.

'You unimaginable . . . fecking . . . fecker,' is all I can barely spit at him as he legs it past me and races to the bottom of the stairs leading up to the loft, where Screechy is ironing. Not my best piece of oratory, but, trembling with rage and blind fury, sorry, it's about the best I can come up with. He's in such a mad rush, though, he's not even listening to me.

At least, not yet he isn't.

'That'll be her, now,' he shouts up the stairs to Miss Screechy. 'I'll get it, and remember to stay well out of sight!'

'As if I want to have to make small talk with some interfering aul bag,' she squeals back down. 'Get rid of her quick, though, I've an audition this morning and I can't be late.'

'James Kane, did you HEAR what I just said to you?' I stammer at him, afraid now that maybe he can't, and that therefore I won't fully be able to torture him and get him back for this latest outrage. In a long line of outrages. But I think he's too flummoxed to hear me as he races downstairs. So I follow, hot on his heels. He flings the door open and there's two people standing there. One is the postman who makes him sign for a registered letter.

The other one is my mum.

'Mum!' I almost sob, my mood immediately switching from seething, boiling anger to waves of relief that she's here. An ally. Who might even, metaphorically, kick James's arse on my behalf.

'I've so much to tell you,' I say tearily, immediately going to hug her. 'I was with Kate last night, and all of Paul's family, including Paul, were horrible to her . . .' it takes me a minute to fully trail off, realizing that, of course, she's completely deaf to me. And even when I do hug her, my arms go right through her, like in some kind of weird 3D movie. And I just want to talk to her so much right now that it's breaking my heart. She's stood on the doorstep, wearing her good, brown 'important occasions' suit and her least comfortable pair of shoes, handbag clutched rigidly over one arm, glaring at James, almost daring him to ask her in.

Astonishing, though, just how quickly his personality switches to 'arse-licking sycophant'.

'Mrs Grey,' he smarms, holding the door open for her. 'How lovely to see you. Won't you come in and have some tea?'

'Do NOT fall for the charm, Mum,' I howl at her. 'His new girlfriend is stashed away upstairs like Anne Frank in the attic, and if you'd seen the bastard flinging all my stuff into plastic bags . . .'

I break off, realizing that James is doing that thing of looking around him, wondering where my voice is coming from. Finally. Then I see Mum wavering for a second, weighing up her innate dislike of James with the fact that he's being nice to her.

'Say no, Mum! Say no and tell him to feck off!'

James starts rubbing his temples like his head is splitting him, but Mum doesn't seem to notice.

Or care.

'No, thank you,' she eventually says to him, primly. 'If I can just get some of Charlotte's things, I'll be on my way. Kate is anxious to get all her books and music back particularly.'

OK, so now this visit is starting to make sense.

'The upstairs loft, Mum. Tell him that you happen to know most of my stuff is in the upstairs loft.'

Oh shite, shite, shite, why can't she hear me?

'Not a problem, Mrs Grey, but no, there's nothing at all belonging to Charlotte in the upstairs loft,' says James, more unctuous than a greasy paparazzo. 'Please, won't you come in?'

'I never said anything about upstairs lofts,' says Mum, gingerly stepping inside the door, but no further.

'Oh, right, yes, yes, of course,' says James, covering. 'So . . . emm . . . how have you been, Mrs Grey?' he says, flinging yet more of my stuff into . . . dear Jaysus . . . a binliner.

Mum looks suitably disapproving, but stops short of calling him an unfeeling, insensitive arsehole, my preferred outcome.

'As well as can be expected, under the circumstances.'

'She thinks you're a total gobshite, you know,' I say right into James's face. Totally worth it, just seeing the blood drain away, while he's simultaneously trying to suck Mum into the vortex of his charm. 'So you're wasting your time with the pleasantries. She knows about your legendary moodiness . . .'

'You know, Mrs Grey,' he says, interrupting me, and for a second, I'm almost impressed at how good he's getting at blanking out my voice. 'As you're here, there's something I'd really like to say.'

'Mum also knows about the time you did a line of coke in her downstairs loo. 'Cos I told her.'

'If that's OK with you, that is. I know what an awful time this is for you, and I'd be the last person on earth to add to that,' he smiles at her, the eyes black as soot, still ignoring me, the bastard.

'Oh and James, dearest? I forgot to tell you. Mum is also fully aware that we had sex on her new sofa, right after her sixtieth-birthday party, when she was gone up to bed.'

A total lie on my part, but soooooo well worth it, just to see him starting to stammer.

'. . . That's not true . . . at all . . . never violated your new sofa like that, and the line of coke was a once-off . . .'

'James?' says Mum, putting on her imperious face. 'Are you quite well? What are you talking about sofas and lines of coke for? Everyone knows Coca-Cola comes in bottles, not lines.'

'I'm so sorry, Mrs Grey,' he mumbles. 'It's just . . . just . . .'

'Tell her,' I snarl at him. 'Go on. Tell her that by some freak of nature, you can hear me loud and clear. And that your new girlfriend has already shacked up with you and is now cowering upstairs in *my* dressing gown. Tell her and I'll consider calling a halt to my campaign of harassment against you. Take my advice, James Kane, this could be your one and only chance at redemption.'

'It's just what?' Mum says, looking at him funnily.

But I'd underestimated the actor that he is.

'Just . . . oh, Mrs Grey. I wish I could make you understand how hard this is for me, too,' he eventually says.

'Go on,' I say to him, 'confess to her just how much of a bastard you've been. Tell her all about Miss Screechy Voice, and in return I promise to leave you in peace. I'm throwing you a lifeline here, James Kane. You do that for me and I hereby promise to leave you alone.'

'. . . it's just . . .'

'What?' snaps Mum, rudely for her.

'The thing is . . . well, I suppose the most diplomatic way of putting it is to say that, of course I realize that . . . in the past, you and I never really saw eye to eye. I'm sure there were plenty of occasions when you felt Charlotte could have done an awful lot better than me. God knows, you'd enough reason to.'

Mum hears him out, though, and for a horrible second I think she might be buying into his act.

'But I just want to tell you, Mrs Grey, that I'm actually broken-hearted without Charlotte. It's just devastating for me coming home every night, when she's not here.'

'NO, MUM!' I yell right into her ear, even though I know how useless and futile it is. 'Tell him to shag off, tell him anything, but do NOT fall for the devastated boyfriend routine . . . it's nothing more than one, big fucking act!'

It's just killing me that she can't hear me. (Although, I know if she could, she'd clatter me for all the bad language.) Killing me, even though I'm already dead.

And his swansong is yet to come.

'There's just so much . . . that . . . I never got to say to her.' I swear to God, he actually turns his face upwards to catch the light as he says this, like a silent movie star. Then the faint, distant sound of footsteps coming from the attic above makes him look momentarily furtive, but in a nanosecond, he's readjusted his face back to looking like a holy picture on a Mass card. Daniel Day-Lewis himself wouldn't have turned in such a sterling performance.

The bollocks.

Fair play to her, though, Mum remains pretty much unmoved, takes the binliner that's proffered to her, turns on her heel and gets the hell out of there.

'I have to go, my friend Nuala is waiting for me,' she calls back over her shoulder, not even saying goodbye to him. Proper order.

'Is she gone?' says Screechy, coming downstairs from the loft.

'Give it a minute till she's well out of sight,' he shouts back upstairs before disappearing off into the kitchen in search for his fags.

'Goodbye, you interfering, patronizing, self-righteous old boot!' Screechy yells at the front door, when Mum is back in her car and well out of earshot.

Meanwhile, I'm sitting on the sofa, mute. Dumbstruck at just how much of a hypocrite James can be. And of course, wishing hellfire and damnation on him.

'Please, please, please dearest, nicest God,' I find myself praying, 'if you exist and even though I might have had my doubts, there's a pretty good chance you do or else, let's face it, angels like me would be redundant, please can this unutterable . . . emm . . . so and so, get his comeuppance . . .' I trail off, managing to stop short of using really foul language to describe James to a higher power.

'It's just the two-facedness of him that I can't take, God: him weeping and wailing and gnashing his teeth to Mum's face, like he's going to hurl himself into the grave on top of me because his life is so worthless without me around. Acting the part of the distraught boyfriend in

public, when all along, he had that . . . floozie moved
in the minute no one was watching. Sure you can see
for yourself at the way he just upgrades women like cars.
Rod Stewart doesn't even go on like that. Ah, go on, God,
I'm not telling you how to do your job or anything,
but you're always visiting hurricanes and tsunamis on
innocent victims, how about wreaking a bit of desolation
and disaster on someone who actually has it coming to
them, for a change? We're not exactly talking about John
Paul the Second here: this is a horrible, hateful, cruel,
malevolent member of society, who probably should have
been drowned at birth to prevent him from spreading his
unique brand of misery on everyone he comes in contact
with. Please, it's only fair. I mean, if you think about
it, God, everyone wins. And I'll never hit you for any
favours again, swear, swear, swear.'

Just then, James remembers something and comes
back from the kitchen, fag in hand, and saunters over to
the coffee table right in front of where I'm sitting.

The registered letter.

He plonks right down beside me and rips it open,
with me, of course, reading it over his shoulder.

It's from the bank.

I scan down it, and can't believe what I'm seeing. The
words are swimming on the page in front of my eyes,
but I'm just about able to take in the gist of it.

'Dear Mr Kane . . . repeated failed attempts to contact

you . . . mortgage repayments on the property at Strand Road now three months in arrears . . . neglected to present yourself at our scheduled meeting last week . . . very unfortunate . . . amount outstanding on your account . . . please call and arrange an appointment for interview at your earliest possible convenience . . . regret to inform . . .'

My eyes scroll down to the final, magical word.

'. . . repossession.'

James looks at the letter in complete shock while I turn my eyes upwards to heaven, like I'm having a road-to-Damascus vision.

At this exact moment, I've just officially, totally, one hundred per cent started believing in God.

'Thank you so, so much,' I say in awe. 'Bloody hell, you are *good*.'

Carlsberg don't do days from hell, but if they did, this is how it would be. *Exactly* how it would pan out, in fact. Initially, I'm every bit as shocked as James is: I mean, how could he have let this happen? The deal he and I always had was that he took care of the mortgage while I took care of household stuff, shopping, groceries, dealing with plumbers/electricians/handymen whenever there was a leaky loo/central heating on the blink/broadband out of order, etc., etc. Like a fifties housewife. In fact, all I needed to complete the image was a white picket fence, a prom dress and a Liz Taylor hairdo.

Fiona used to give me a desperate time about this, and would regularly beg me to either buy a shoebox apartment somewhere and rent it out so I'd at least have something to show for myself, or else pay James rent so it was a more equal economic relationship and I wouldn't be under any obligation to him. But did I listen to her? Like hell. With my bowels withering with embarrassment, I can even recall primly telling her that quite apart from the fact that I couldn't afford to buy anywhere, not on a lowly assistant's salary, and although technically it *might have been* James's house, with his name on the deeds etc., we loved and trusted each other so much that it was only a matter of time before we got married and it would end up being half mine anyway.

I'd say God must have had a great laugh at that particular episode in the twenty-eight-year long-running sitcom of my life. In fact that clip would have made it into 'Charlotte Grey: Classic Comedy Moments', in the DVD extras of my short, rubbishy little life.

James is still beside me, still staring uselessly into space, shell-shocked, when Screechy bounds in, wearing a flowery dress Carmen Miranda would have baulked at, and demanding to know how she looks for her audition.

'Jamie, tell me the truth, do I still look young enough to play the part of a giggling ingénue to a T? Or rather, a tee hee?' Then she goes off into a peal of screechy laughter at her own gag.

'Unless the show is *South Pacific*,' I cut in over her, 'tell her she looks like a fiesta *del* failure.'

James shakes his head at the sound of me, wincing, like he's just been stung by a wasp. But, unbelievably for someone who's insensitive enough to move into a dead girl's bedroom with her ex-boyfriend, then parade around in her dressing gown, Screechy looks at him askance, and seems to pick up on his dark mood.

'What's up, Jamie honey? What's in that letter? It looks like . . . something official. Parking fine? Jury duty?'

He doesn't answer her at first, just slowly palms his eyes, then hops up, stubs out the cigarette, grabs his car keys, and in a single bound is over to the hall door, suddenly in a mad, tearing rush to get out of there. Then he turns around, like this is the first time he's even noticed she's in the room.

'This? This is nothing, babe,' he grins, shoving the letter from the bank into his jeans pocket. 'Hey, you know what? I once had to shoot an adaptation of *Little Women* where three out of the four lead actresses all pulled out the week before principal photography. This, believe you me, is nothing.'

Minutes later, we're in his car, he's on the phone, and I'm listening in to every word, like a radio play.

'We understand how regrettable this situation is, Mr Kane,' the bank manager is saying, over the car's Bluetooth sound system. A nasally, thin, weedy voice which immediately gives me a mental picture of some kind of rodent. 'But sadly, we feel we've extended every courtesy to you, and now we're left with no choice but to proceed with the course of action outlined to you by registered mail.'

Clearly uncomfortable with the word 'repossession', then.

'Yes, but you have to understand that in my business things are in a perpetual state of highs and lows,' says James, brimming over with misguided confidence, while I'm beside him, shrivelling up with mortification, glad I never owned a home in my whole life, so I never, ever, *ever* had to have a conversation like this. 'I need for you to bear with me, that's all. I can guarantee that in three months' time, when finance is in place for my next TV project, all arrears will be paid in full. With interest. With penalties. With anything you want. Come on, you've been dealing with me for a long time, you know I'm good for it. Can't you just be patient? Is that too much to ask for?'

'From our viewpoint, Mr Kane, sadly the answer is yes. It is too much to ask for. We don't make exceptions when mortgages are almost eleven months in arrears. Plus we feel that our patience has already been stretched to breaking point. It's regrettable, but there you have it. I would strongly suggest that you call into the branch as a matter of urgency . . .'

The irony is, there's me feeling like I could throw up at the thought of the house being repossessed, even though I never technically owned it, and am already dead, so it's not like they can throw me into debtor's prison or anything, but Mr Cool Hand James actually interrupts his bank manager to tell him that he's another call coming through, and that he'll call him back. I mean, I've heard of being overly self-assured but this is really taking the piss.

'Just so you know?' I say to him. 'If you honestly think that treating the man who has the power to make you homeless, like someone you can just brush off the phone is a good idea, then . . . then . . .'

'Jesus,' he says, swerving the car at the sound of my voice. Just then the oh-so-urgent other call comes through on the speakers, and once again, I'm tuning into a radio play.

'Ehh . . . hello? Is that James Kane?' says a deep, baritone voice, putting me in mind of an opera singer who weighs in at about twenty stone.

'Speaking. Is that . . . ?'

'Thaddeus Byrne here. I hope this call isn't interrupting you?'

Thaddeus Byrne . . . I immediately start racking my

brains to drum up where I know that name from. Then it hits me. The ex-priest. Author of *Let He Without Sin*. The book which James paid through the nose to option, for his famous more-boring-than-watching-back-to-back-reruns-of-*Big-Brother*, non-existent, practically unfinanceable TV series.

'Hey, Thaddeus, man, great to hear from you!' smarms cackhead. 'All good with you?'

'Well . . . actually . . .' comes the booming baritone, and call it angel's intuition but I know, just know in my waters, that there's trouble ahead. 'I've just had a call from Declan at Meridius Movies,' Thaddeus eventually says, or rather bellows. 'About your meeting with Sir William Eames?'

'Yeah, yeah?' says James, and it's only a measure of how important to the company Thaddeus is that he doesn't come out with his usual, unbelievably rude catchphrase: 'Whatever it is, gimme the last sentence first.'

'Declan said that finance for bringing my book to the screen has effectively fallen through.'

A snorty, disparaging laugh from James. 'Complete nonsense, Thaddeus, and you have my word as a gentleman on that.'

'Your word as a *what*?' I spit out, almost making him crash the car. Shite. I better shut up if I want to find out what this call is all about.

'That's not what your colleague at Meridius is saying.

Also, he's suggesting that we now look at a possible co-production to get this off the ground.'

'That's one hundred per cent right,' says James with such conviction I'm almost forgetting that he's the one who normally baulks at the very mention of a co-production. 'Yeah, we're actively looking into possibly putting something together with the BBC, and I'm confident that I'll have news for you asap.'

'James,' says Thaddeus gently, but then as an ex-priest, I suppose he's no stranger to treating people with extreme sensitivity. 'I've just told your colleague, and I feel it's only fair to tell you, too, that I'm deeply unhappy with this latest twist in, may I say, a catalogue of one delay and setback after another. It's amateurish to say the least. Also, from where I'm standing, it's starting to reek of unprofessional, unacceptable behaviour.'

OK, maybe not so hot on sensitivity, then.

'Yes, but, Thaddeus, this is the way that the TV business works, delays are par for the course . . .'

'You've had the rights to my book for almost two years now, and nothing's happened. I could have sold them to a dozen other production companies, but I gave them to you because you faithfully promised that the project would be fast-tracked and hitting the screens while the book was still on the bestseller lists. You're an experienced producer, James, so you hardly need me to point out to you that that hasn't happened. You sat on the rights and did nothing.'

James is sweating now, actually sweating, which *never* happens.

'Yes, but in our business, this is par for the course. We're currently sounding out the *right* TV company to co-produce this astonishing project, and let me tell you something, you have no idea the money that will be injected into this. The production values I'm planning will be through the roof. Think shooting in sepia, think intercutting with Pathe newsreel footage from the fifties, think jangly piano music . . .'

Typical James Kane dazzle-them-with-shite talk.

But, by the sounds of it, he picked the wrong person to schmooze.

'James,' thunders the voice over the speakers, sounding more and more like James Earl Jones. 'You don't understand. I've been listening to this from you for two full years. Your time's up.'

'I'm sorry, Thaddeus,' says James, nearly hitting a cyclist that's meandered out in front of us. '*What* did you just say?'

'That, as you're well aware, my contract with you runs out at the end of this month. And I thought it only right that I should let you know I won't be renewing it.'

Strike three takes place all of half an hour later. In the upstairs office at Meridius Movies, where poor, unknowing Declan is at his desk on the phone, when James bursts in, flames practically shooting out of his nostrils.

'What the fuck did you think you were doing, telling Thaddeus Byrne that we couldn't get finance for his TV series?'

'I'll ring you back,' says Dec, tactfully ending his call, then hanging up.

'I asked you a question.'

'I heard you,' says Dec, cooler, still in control. 'The answer is, I dunno, maybe telling the truth? Affording one of the elder statesmen of literature in this country the courtesy of letting him know exactly where we stand on this project? Have you any problem with that?'

'Emm . . . why don't I go out and get us all some . . . emm . . . lattes?' says Hannah from her corner desk. I'm so engrossed in the row that's brewing that I never even noticed her quietly sitting there. James ignores her as she grabs her bag and slips out. Not even flirting, not even eyeing her up. He *must* be annoyed.

Good.

'He's withdrawn the rights, because of what you just said to him, Dec. Which, in case you hadn't noticed, leaves us with precisely nothing. No product. *Nothing* on the table. Nothing in the pipeline. I don't get you, why couldn't you have kept your fucking mouth shut? I'd have strung Thaddeus along and probably had a co-production in place by the end of the week.'

'Well, I don't happen to think that it's OK to string people along, as you put it,' Declan bats back, keeping his voice steady and letting James do all the roaring. Bloody hell, Dec is certainly good in a row. Tough and firm. In fact, if it wasn't for the still-living-with-his-mammy thing, I'd nearly start to find him attractive.

'You're nothing but a big-mouthed arsehole,' James roars at him, 'and I hold you personally responsible for us losing those rights. *Now* what are we going to do?'

'James, you need to listen to me, because I'll only say this once. Are you aware that I've been here all morning, in fact, pretty much all week, trying, pleading, begging anyone to come in and co-produce with us? And you want to know the answers I'm getting? No. Because no one in the town wants to work with you. That's why. And to be brutally honest, I can see exactly where they're coming from. You're boorish, you're difficult, you wouldn't know a schedule if it walked up and introduced itself to you . . .'

'That is such horseshit . . .'

'. . . you lie so much, I sometimes wonder if it's something pathological in you . . .'

'. . . oh, piss off with yourself . . .'

'. . . you seem to think scruples is a hairdresser's on Leeson Street . . .'

317

'. . . bollocks . . .'

'. . . you don't pay people properly, me included. You spend money you don't even have . . .'

'. . . complete crap . . .'

'. . . you think you can manipulate everyone around you just by charming your way around them . . .'

'. . . can I get a word in here, please?'

'. . . you mistreat actors and actresses, bar the ones you want to shag . . .'

'Don't fucking talk to me like that, do you realize the day I'm having? And now I have to take this shit from you?'

'Well,' says Declan, drawing himself up to his full height with great, unyielding dignity. 'Let me tell you something. Your day is about to get a whole lot worse.'

'Jesus, what now?'

'I quit.'

Chapter Fifteen
FIONA

. . . has started making faux calls. I know because I catch her at it, back at her house later on that evening, when school's out for the day. You know, picking up her mobile, blocking her number (clearly, she's not new to this lark), then ringing a certain other number, then hanging up after the phone's rung only once or twice. Next thing, she's putting the kettle on, then parading up and down the rug in front of her fireplace, rehearsing a speech out loud and doing the dance of the faux call.

It goes a bit like this.

Three paces to the right, then three to the left, then she grabs the fireplace with both hands and shouts out loud, 'For Jaysus sake, he's only a fella! With a receding hairline!' This is then followed by four paces across the room to where her mobile is perched on the sofa, picking it up, clutching it to her bosom like a prop dagger in a

Shakespeare play, then hurling it back on to the sofa and striding towards the kitchen to check and see if the kettle's boiled in the meantime. She repeats this about three times, all the while saying, then self-editing, then abusing her speech.

'"Emm . . . Tim! Hi! Long time no hear!" Shite. Too casual. Too bright and breezy for a guy whose marriage has just broken up. Also, why the hell am I sucking my stomach in? It's the *phone* for God's sake, it's not like he can see me. OK, take two. Try telling the truth.'

She clears her throat then puts on this sexier, breathier voice.

'"Ahem, ehem. Tim, Fiona here. Wilson, you roaring eejit. Before you pick yourself up off the ground in shock at my calling you after all this time, let me tell you the chain of events that led to this. You see, I had the most mental dream that you and Ayesha broke up and I just wanted to get in touch to commiserate . . ." (*Then back to her normal voice, thank God.*) NO!! Total crap *AND* a barefaced lie. I did a jig for pure joy when I heard that the beautiful rumour was true, that you'd finally seen the light about Miss Ayesha, she of the amber, tangerine and burnt-orange false-tan palette. OK, scrap that, take three.

'"Ahem, ahem. Tim, you won't believe this, but for absolutely no reason at all you were on my mind, so out of the blue, I decided to get in touch. But of course I only had your UK number. Then I called your mum to get your new Irish mobile number, just so you and I could have a long overdue catch-up chat. For no other reason, no ulterior motives whatsoever, cross my heart. Imagine my astonishment when she said you and Ayesha had split up . . ." (*The normal voice again.*) SHITE!! A Leaving Cert English student would phrase that better. And an amateur actress would make it sound more convincing. Right then, take four.'

Then, in sympathetic tones of condolence I haven't heard since Dad's funeral, off she goes again.

'"Tim, Fiona here. I heard the news. About you and Ayesha, that is. And I just want to say . . . say . . ." (*Normal voice.*) Oh, for God's sake, say what? "Now that you're back on the market again, how about we hook up?"'

She pours herself a cuppa, with hands trembling so much that it's a minor miracle she doesn't scald herself. She takes a sip, burns her mouth, curses, then goes back to where the mobile is looking at her accusingly from the sofa.

Cue take five.

'"Look, Tim, I know you'll think it's a bit odd hearing from me after all these years, but the fact is, you're newly single and the last guy I dated might as well have had three sixes carved into the back of his scalp. So . . . so . . ."' Then she breaks off, and dives into a pack of chocolate digestives on the coffee table in front of her, then starts yelling at the telly.

'THIS,' she says, stuffing her face, 'is all your bloody doing, Madam Charlotte. Putting these thoughts into my head. I was perfectly happy until you started messing round with my psyche.'

I sit beside her and put my feet up on the table.

'But you have to admit I was right, though. Didn't Tim's mother confirm what I told you? He's single, and if it wasn't for me, you'd never have known. No need to thank me, love, that's what we guardian angels are for. All in a day's work.'

But she's on her feet again, about to make one last faux call. She picks up the mobile, punches in all but the last digit of his number, then holds the phone against her mouth and starts muttering to herself again.

'What is wrong with me? Why can't I just go through with this? He has a bald patch, for God's sake. And an ex-wife and two kids, baggage you'd need a container-load for; he should be down on his knees, thanking his lucky stars, *thrilled* to hear from me . . .' She lets out a shuddery sigh so deep it practically comes from her shoes, then clicks off the phone.

'Oh, make a bloody choice, Hamlet.' I'm pleading to deaf ears, but just at that second, her mobile beep-beeps suddenly and sharply as a message comes through.

'Jesus Christ!' we both say together, clutching our

chests in unison with the fright, like a pair of panto-
mime dames minus the garish costumes.

It's an email which the two of us read together, side
by side.

From: lovesgermanshepherds@hotmail.com
To: lexiehart@yahoo.com
Subject: Dinner this weekend?

Dear Lexie,
I feel it's the very least I can do, to make up for so rudely
leaving you high and dry earlier this week. Please let me
take you to dinner; it just so happens my brother-in-law
owns the best Chinese restaurant this side of Beijing, so
if you were free at all, it would be a pleasure to take you. I
absolutely promise, the beef in oyster sauce is something
that's reduced grown men to salivating morons.

If you don't have a weekend packed full of aerobics and
spinning classes, that is.

All the best for now,

Blah, blah, blah.

She smiles, then wavers a bit as she's reading it, and
I can practically see her wondering whether she should
give him a whirl or not.

Which clearly means it's time for me to step in.

Honestly, these mortals haven't the first clue what's good for them. I don't know what they'd do without me, I really don't.

Three-quarters of an hour later, Fiona's tucked up in bed and sound asleep, so in I go.

'Hey, sleeping beauty, wake up, I've something to show you.' OK, so maybe I neglected to tell her that it's not necessarily something she'll like, but like a parent with a bold child, I'm only doing this for her own good. After much tossing and turning, she eventually notices me sitting on the edge of her bed.

'Charlotte! Oh my God, I've so much to tell you.'

'You don't need to, I already know.'

'Know what?'

'About your twenty-five failed attempts to call Tim, you big wussbag.'

'Oh . . . emm . . . that.'

'Have I let you down once? Ever since you started dreaming about me, have I fed you one single false bit of info?'

'Emm . . . well . . . no . . . but . . .'

'So what's with all the faux calls? Honestly, you spend half your time moaning and whingeing about being single, then when I present you with a golden opportunity like this, you start acting like a twelve-year-old girl.'

'Is that why you've come back to haunt me? Are my

dreams going to be like some kind of war room till I agree to call him?'

'Ehh . . . pretty much, yeah.'

'Because I'm almost getting afraid to go asleep. This is like *Nightmare on Elm Street*.'

'It's for your own good, you know.'

'You should have seen me trying to ring his mother last night. I had to have two full glasses of wine before I could even bring myself to do that.'

'I'm actually raging I missed it. I could have done with seeing the look on your face when you found out what I'd been trying to drum into you all along was true, and that Tim is a free man again. But I was with Kate last night and haven't figured out the art of bi-location yet.'

'Besides,' says Fi insistently, 'the best I can ever hope for with Tim is that we become friends again. I mean, it's years since we dated. So aren't we jumping to con-clusions to think that he'll say, "Oh, great to hear from you out of the blue like this, Fi, what a daft mistake I made marrying Tangerine Head, please come back into my life, and let's live happily ever after?"'

'How will you know unless you call him? What are you, psychic?'

But she's gone off on a tangent, acting out Tim's dialogue in the phone-call-to-be.

'"Oh, Fiona Wilson?"' she says sarcastically, doing

Tim. Or rather, trying to. '"Yeah, I remember you, ex-love of my life. And now that the word's got out that I'm separated, you're straight on to my mum to try and track me down . . . say, tell me this, Fi, are things really that tough for single women in Dublin that exes from years ago are back on the menu again? Who in the name of Jaysus do you think you and I are, anyway? Prince Charles and Camilla?"'

'I understand you're apprehensive,' I say soothingly, 'but to let him slip through your fingers once is a misfortune. Twice is just carelessness.'

'Oh, that's not fair, what about the vet guy? He asked me out to dinner, you know.'

'The man who stood you up? And who would probably have no difficulty whatsoever doing it again? If you arrange to meet him, you're a worse eejit than I took you for. Mark my words, he'll leave you sitting pretty in a restaurant all over again because a kitten farted somewhere in Carlow and he just *has* to be there.'

'What is this . . . do you get some kind of kick out of bullying me?'

'No, that was an unexpected bonus. Now take my hand, we've work to do.'

She's used to me by this stage, because she does as I ask without my having to arm-wrestle her, and away we go.

★　　★　　★

She opens her eyes . . . and discovers that we're right back where we started, in her house, this time in the living room, though. Except that it's changed completely. Instead of looking fresh and new and all Ikea'd the way it usually does, now it's tired and mangy with damp patches on the walls. Not a touch I'm particularly proud of, but needs must. In the corner beside the fireplace, there's the saddest-looking Christmas tree you ever saw, covered in faded tinsel, with the tinfoil starting to peel off the edges. The TV's on in the corner, some Christmas Day compilation show, while Fiona sits on the sofa, with an opened selection box in front of her.

Then she notices what she's wearing.

OK, OK, so I may have overdone it just the teeeeeeniest bit here, but you know, sometimes we angels just have to lay things on with a trowel. Fiona's wearing a granny cardigan that looks like it should only ever be worn either for jam-making at the Irish Country Women's Association or else saying novenas in, a sensible tweed skirt, and flat, comfy brogues, the kind you only get in Marks & Spencer.

'What is this, national dress-up-as-your-granny day? Or am I on my way to a fancy-dress party, by any chance, and I decided to come as Barbara Bush Senior?' Fi asks, hopping up to the mirror above the fireplace to get a better look at herself. 'Oh sweet Baby Jesus and the orphans, what have you done to me? You've just turned

327

me into the poster girl for liver spots. I do love you, Charlotte, but just so you know? Right now I'm loving you like a cold sore.'

She's actually aged well, but at seventy-odd years of age is showing signs of wear and tear. Her hair is in a neat Marcel wave and she's wearing those massive bifocal glasses that cover most of her face.

'I look like my granny,' she stammers. 'Christ, I even smell like her,' she says, sniffing at her wrists. 'Yardley's Lily of the Valley. The choice of pensioners. Charlotte, not to put it too mildly, HATING this! Can you just, like, beam us out of here, please? Or at least splash some cold water on my face to wake me out of this night-mare?'

'Not just yet,' I say, firmly. 'Look, look around you.'

Suddenly the TV catches her eye. The King's Christmas Day speech is just coming on.

'The . . . King?' she mutters, staring at it.

'We now go live to Sandringham,' says the announcer, 'where King William will address the nation.'

'King William?' she splutters in disbelief, then grabs the remote and starts flicking channels. The news is on Channel Four, with a feature about President Clinton's Christmas visit to the victims of global warming in Alaska.

President Chelsea Clinton.

'What . . . ? What the fuck is going on . . . ?' says Fiona. Then she notices a Christmas card on top of the TV, which she grabs. The outside greeting screams, 'Happy Holidays and Have a Great 2050!'

'Twenty bloody fifty?' stutters poor, bewildered Fi, before she rips the card open.

'Dear Miss Wilson, have a terrific Christmas and a magical New Year. We miss you so much here at Loreto, things really aren't the same without you! But we hope you're having a long and happy retirement, and that you'll call in to see us very soon.'

'So, I'm like . . . seventy?'

'Yes, you are. Ahead of all of us, you know.' Well, except me.

'But . . .' she hesitates, looking all around her as the horrible reality starts to dawn on her. 'Charlotte . . . hang on a sec . . . it's Christmas Day, right?'

'December twenty-fifth.'

'And . . . I'm here, still living in the same house . . .'

'Correct.'

'Still single . . . because that card calls me Miss Wilson . . .'

'Yes, love, you never married.'

'And . . . I'm alone. *ALONE*. On Christmas Day.'

'Well, what did you expect? This is the life you've chosen, Fi. Doesn't exactly look like a barrel of laughs, now, does it?'

'You're right,' she says, slowly slumping on to the sofa, moving like an old, old lady.

'Charlotte, just look at me. I'm pathetic and sad and lonely and I HATE this so much I can't tell you. I know it's only a dream, and in case you're wondering why I've this constipated look on my face, it's because I'm actively willing myself to wake up and snap out of this torture. For God's sake, who have you turned into anyway? The ghost of relationships future?'

For a second, the eyes start to tear up, but then she quickly pulls herself right back together again.

'Anyway,' she snaps primly. 'I would never be alone on Christmas Day. Sure, I'd be with my parents for starters.'

'I'm sorry to tell you, but your parents have long since passed on, hon. And your brother and his family are all off skiing.'

'What about my other friends?'

'All with their own kids and grandkids today, I'm afraid. They've invited you over for Boxing Day, but let's face it, Christmas is a time for family, and you chose not to have one, remember? Believe me, I don't like being the bearer of bad news, but this is the life that you've chosen for yourself.'

God, there's times I hate being an angel. The tough love you're expected to dole out would nearly finish you off entirely. I sit down beside poor, shaken Fi and take her hand.

'All that went wrong in your life is that you met your soulmate *young*. That's all. And now he's alone, and you're alone, and you won't even pick up the phone to call him. Yes, he made a mistake marrying Ayesha, but aren't we all allowed mistakes? Jeez, you only have to look at the gobshite I spent five years with for proof of that. Don't let pride lead you to this,' I say, waving around me.

She looks up at me with red, swollen eyes.

'Fiona Wilson, we all have a road not taken. Here's a rare chance to do something about yours.'

Next thing, she's wide awake, sitting bolt upright on the bed and sweating, actually sweating. She can't see me now, but I'm right beside her, willing her to call Tim. There's a radio on her bedside table, still switched on quietly in the background, and the ten o'clock news is just coming on. It's early still.

'Come on, come on, girl, you can do it,' I whisper encouragingly. 'Everything will be fine, I faithfully promise you. If it's one thing I've learned, it's that life is not to be taken in baby steps.'

She gets out of bed, throws on a cardigan, then does a bit of pacing. The will-I-won't-I-call-him two-step.

She picks up the mobile, then puts it down at least three times before she starts muttering under her breath.

'OK. If the phone rings out and he doesn't answer,

331

then this was a mental idea. Tim and I were never to be, and that's the final proof. If it goes to his voicemail, then there's a tiny chink of hope for us. But then if he actually answers . . . oh shite . . .'

She slumps back on to the bed, her resolve weakening, and I just know the one thing she needs more than anything else.

A sign.

I'm concentrating harder than I ever did in my whole life, sorry, I mean death, and then it happens.

The news finishes and the DJ on the radio butts in. He sounds young and nerdy, and I'd guess is about twelve.

'OK, we've a very special request here for an oldie but a goldie, this is going out to all you kids at Loreto College, youse have mad taste so you do, but you asked for it, so here ya go . . . it's Sid Vicious and the Sex Pistols with "Pretty Vacant".'

Dear Jesus. That was their song. Fiona and Tim's song. Not the most romantic or smoochiest, but it was definitely their song. I dunno how it happened, I'm not even sure whether I was the one who made it happen, but by God it does the trick. She doesn't miss a beat, just picks up the phone and calls.

It rings once . . . twice . . . three times . . .

'Hello? Tim? Hi! Emm . . . you won't believe who this is!'

And it's that easy. Not that I'm eavesdropping or

anything, but they chat for a good hour, laughing and messing and picking up exactly where they left off, like you can only do with people from the past that you really, really loved. I'm not sure what he says, but just before Fi hangs up, she says that yes, of course he can call her tomorrow, and no, that she hasn't eaten in that particular restaurant, but would really love to this weekend.

Waves of euphoria wash over me as she clambers back into her bed and snuggles under. Worth dying just to see the look of pure bliss on her face. She's just nodding off when her phone beeps as a message comes through. It's another email from Mr Loves German Shepherds, saying that if she doesn't like Chinese food, they could always eat somewhere else this weekend.

She doesn't even bother scrolling down to the bottom of the email, just deletes it, switches off the light and drifts off to sleep.

The girl is learning. Finally.

Chapter Sixteen

KATE

Six months hence. And she's back sitting at Briar Rose's kitchen table in Galway, which, as ever, resembles Grand Central Station with all the comings and goings. There's hordes of kids running in and out, fighting with each other over who had the remote control last/one of them calling another one gay/that particular pre-teen saying their accuser doesn't even know what gay means/ the first kid then subsequently changing their insult to, 'Well, what would you know, anyway, sure you're only an arsehole'. . . etc., etc. All three of her horrors-in-law are present and correct, so much so that you'd almost swear they were all part of some religious cult that are required to live under the same roof as each other, co-parent each other's kids and all eat together at the same table.

Like Moonies. Or that weird religion that Tom Cruise is in.

But, this time, there's one big difference. Briar Rose is prattling on about how her eldest, Robbie Junior, just got two As and a B plus in his last school report and how he's clearly destined for academic greatness, while the other two horrors-in-law are drinking mugs of tea, buttering hot, fruity scones straight from the oven, and bragging about how gifted their kids are at rugby/breaking into cars/pilfering from supermarkets, whatever their respective talents are. Nothing unusual there, then. Except that, instead of squirming in her chair and making half-hearted attempts to contribute to the conversation, all the while wondering how the hell she can get out of there, Kate sits serenely in the middle of them, nodding politely at their competitive bragging and admirably restraining herself from throwing in the odd cutting comment, such as, 'Oh, but Melissa, I always knew your Tommy was highly skilled at tackling other kids and hurling them to the ground in a rugby scrum, I think he must get it from you, ha ha ha.'

Then, just as Rose goes to the window to yell at some kid who's whingeing that her sister won't let her have a go on the Barbie bike, Kate looks down, and gently pats her tummy.

There it is, no mistake. A tiny little bulge, neat and perfect.

'So, emmm . . . where are you having it, then?' one

of the horrors-in-law demands, mouth full of buttery scone.

'Mount Carmel in Dublin,' Kate smiles.

'Never heard of it. Is that a proper hospital?'

'Not really, it's a nursing home.'

This, of course, then leads on to a heated and lengthy debate about the merits of the maternity hospital where the whole lot of them had all of their kids versus the newest addition to the family being born in some fancy nursing home up in Dublin. But Kate doesn't seem to care or even look in the least stressed about it. She just nods, smiles graciously and keeps on rubbing her little bump, miles away, floating on a little cloud of bliss.

'And what about names for the baby?' demands Rose suspiciously. 'Have you thought about that?' Honest to God, the woman is probably the only person alive who can make such an innocuous question sound like an interrogation.

Kate beams at her, and I'm almost willing her to say something like, 'Oh, for a boy we thought something distinctive like Plantagenet Winston Raphael, and for a girl, we're going with my three all-time favourite recording artists, Britney Whitney Madonna.' Just to shut them up. Just to put manners on them and see the looks on their faces. But, of course, this being Kate the ultra-conservative, she doesn't.

'Paul for a boy, after his dad, of course,' she smiles, 'and I think Charlotte for a little girl, after . . .'

Shite, now I'm tearing up. Oh my God, that's so thoughtful, naming a new little niece after me!

Just then, the kitchen door bursts open and in comes Perfect Paul, all six feet two of hulking manhood, with one of his nephews sitting up on his shoulders and another one swinging out of his arm begging for pocket money. He makes a big deal of fishing in his pockets, letting on he's broke, then producing ten euro each for the two of them to buy sweets with, leading to much crowing of, 'Ah, Paul, you shouldn't have, you're far too good,' from all the horrors-in-law. Then he's straight over to Kate, kissing her and asking the others if they've taken good care of her while he's been out.

'Why don't you have a lie-down, love,' he says to her tenderly. 'And I'll bring you up a nice cuppa in bed?' The others look a bit enviously at her, and Rose snipes something about how you're treated like a goddess for your first pregnancy, but by your second, third and fourth, you're expected to carry heavy groceries in from the car with a toddler screaming at you and a three-month-old strapped to your back.

'Not my missus,' says Paul proudly, helping her out of her chair and guiding her to the door, as if she's lost the use of her limbs. 'If she fancies me playing soothing whale noises to her while she's having her bubble bath, then that's what I'll do. Now come on, Kate, bed rest for you and Junior. Then later on, when you're up and about, I want to talk to you about exactly how you'd like the nursery decorated and what colour schemes you want. So I can get started on it as soon as we get home.'

There's a collective, 'Oh, that's so loooooovely,' from the others as Kate beams serenely.

'Suppose you'll pay for a nanny, too?' says one of them, on to her third scone by now.

'Interviews start Monday. We've gone through three different agencies, just to be on the safe side.'

'Jaysus,' mutters Rose. 'If I was getting a nanny, as long as they didn't have a police record, I'd hire them on the spot.'

Just then the phone rings loudly, and suddenly Kate's sitting bolt upright, wide awake. She looks disorientated for a minute, but then it's not really surprising, she's not a great one for crashing out on the sofa with the telly on.

No, Kate, ignore the phone, stay with the dream! You've no idea how important it is!

She doesn't, though. Shit. And I wouldn't mind but I was making great progress with this particular one. Ho hum, back to reality, then.

'Hello? Paul?' she says, sleepily answering the phone on the end table beside her.

But it's not Paul. It's Mum, to thank her for coming back from Galway early so she could be with her all day today.

'Oh. Right. Emm . . . yeah . . . that's OK,' says Kate.

Am I imagining it, or does she sound disappointed that it's not Paul calling her? Mum must ask her where he is, because Kate flicks the TV over to *Sky News*, realizes that it's just gone eleven at night, and that he's still not home. Then she clicks Mum on to speakerphone and starts tidying up her already spotless living room. Sorry, I mean drawing room. (She's the one who insists we all call it by that grand title, not me.)

'Shit, Mum, I must have nodded off. I thought he'd be well home by now.'

'No need for the corner-boy language, love.' Mum's voice is filling the whole room now, bouncing off the walls nearly.

'Oh, ehh, sorry. Can I call him, and then call you back?'

'Of course, love. I was only ringing to say that Nuala's only just rung me now, very late I know, but it wasn't her fault, she was waiting in to hear back about the arrangements for the Mass . . .'

I'll spare you all the nitty gritty details, as Mum's a great one for giving you the preamble to a story, dated from about twelve hours ago. E.g., Question: 'Hi, Mum, how did you get on at your book club tonight?' Answer: 'Well. I got up at eight this morning, then I had a quick shower, oh no, hang on, I'm telling it all wrong, I meant to say, then I *went* to have a quick shower but the immersion wasn't on, so then, of course, I had to wait a good twenty minutes for the water to heat up . . .' Then there usually follows a whole spiel about the minutiae of her day, and then, approximately three-quarters of an hour later, you finally get to the part where the Merry Widows all debated the merits of *The Kite Runner* versus the latest Maeve Binchy. In other words, you'd be well advised to allow a minimum of an hour and a half for even a lightning quick chat with her.

I think living alone must make you go a bit like that.

Anyway, to condense Mum's speech: it seems that her pal Nuala, who has a brother home from the missions, has organized a Mass the last Sunday of the month for . . . well, for me, as it happens. Which sets me off thinking: a whole month? Have I really been dead that *long*?

'Yes, of course I'll tell Paul, but look, Mum, I really have to go now . . .'

'So, don't forget, now, it'll be twelve o'clock Mass in Blackrock church . . .'

'Yes, you said, so I'll just go and ring Paul now . . .'

'Yes, do, and tell him all his family are invited, too. Although they'll hardly drive all the way from Galway, but, all the same, I'd like them to know that they are welcome.'

'Fine, fine,' Kate says curtly, plumping up cushions.

'And then, maybe we should treat everyone to lunch afterwards?'

'Whatever you say . . .'

'Or else maybe have a brunch beforehand?'

'Yeah, yeah, that's better by far, so look, I'll head off now . . .'

'You just keep agreeing with me, so which option will we go with? Brunch before or lunch after?'

'Emm, after, then,' Kate almost shouts at the speaker-phone from the other side of the room, where she's blowing out scented candles.

'Oh yes, and I didn't invite James Kane to the Mass, by the way. I never told you, love, but when I went to the house to collect some of Charlotte's things, he was acting most peculiarly. Of course, maybe I'm rushing to judge the lad, and he's completely distraught about what happened, he certainly insisted to me that he was, but then, as you know, I never really had much time for him . . .'

'I know, Mum, I know, look I really have to go . . .'

'Oh. Rightie-oh. Did you want to get off the phone, then, love?'

'Mum! I'll ring you back, OK?'

It takes another few minutes to sign off on the chat,

and then Kate immediately hits the speed dial and rings Paul's number.

She's left the speakerphone on, so I can hear both sides of it.

And I wish I hadn't.

'Kate, hi,' he answers the phone flatly. It's noisy in the background, like he's out and about.

'Paul, where are you? It's eleven at night! I've been worried sick about you.'

'Yeah, yeah, sorry about that, I meant to ring you. I'm still with Robbie and the developers. I've been with them all day, and I just didn't have time to call. We went for a business dinner and I couldn't get out of it. Sorry, but it's been well worth it. Times are tough and they just wanted us to have a meal together to try and thrash out a few more ideas.'

'And you never thought to ring me and let me know? I've been out of my mind here.'

'It's work, Kate. WORK.'

'I'm just saying, would it have killed you to even text me to say you wouldn't be home tonight? I cooked dinner for you, you know. Your favourite, too, fillet steak and chips. I wanted to . . . well, I wanted to make it up to you for the awful row last night. I'm sorry for acting the way I did, Paul, I really am. It's hard for me to be around your family, and I just could have done with a bit of moral support from you, that's all.'

I look at her, delighted. She's making such an effort. I'm not saying it's all thanks to me and the subliminal mind-games I've been playing with her, but . . . well, let's be honest, it is *mostly* down to me.

There's a pause filled with laughing and chatting and busy, buzzy restaurant noises. I think Kate must be waiting for Paul to tell her that he's sorry, too, for not going near her all night last night, and for abandoning her to the horrors-in-law.

But he doesn't.

Instead he just says that Mike, the senior partner in the development company, has just ordered another bottle of Château Margaux, and that he'll stay down in Galway tonight, but will call her first thing in the morning. The phone clicks as he hangs up, and Kate slumps down on the sofa, looking seriously pissed off.

She stays there for a minute or two then mumbles under her breath, 'Oh shit, the Mass.' So she redials Paul's mobile number, but this time he doesn't answer. Probably can't hear it ringing, with all the restaurant noise in the background. So she leaves a voicemail message, thinks for a minute, then whips out her mobile, scrolls down through her address book until she finds the number she wants. I'm reading it over her shoulder, and I nearly pass out when I see who she's about to call.

Briar Rose herself.

You see? I think smugly. The power of suggestion. Not that Kate will ever be bosom buddies with any of her horrors-in-law, but they are family and . . . won't things be so much better when they can all get along? Particularly when a certain happy event takes place, it'll be lovely for Kate to have the love and support of her sisters-in-law, who are all mums, and who've all been there before.

OK, so maybe love and support is a bit of an exaggeration, but you see what I'm getting at. I mean, everyone knows that Jackie Kennedy didn't really see eye to eye with all the rah rah rah Kennedys whenever she had to go and visit them at Cape Cod, but she still managed to make it work with her usual grace and elegance, didn't she? Same thing.

Kate punches in the number and it rings through.

'Hello?' A little girl's voice. Which is odd, to say the least.

'Ehh . . . that's not Rose, is it?' says Kate, puzzled.

'No, it's Kirsten. Is that you, Auntie Kate?'

'Yes, it is, pet. What are you doing up so late?'

'I'm not supposed to be, so don't tell my mammy, will you? The babysitter is on her mobile to her boyfriend, and she said we could watch DVDs if we kept our mouths shut while she's on the phone.'

'Oh, right.'

'But, Auntie Kate?'

'Yes, love?'

'I think she's having a fight with her boyfriend. I heard her saying bold words.'

'And where's your mummy tonight?'

'She said fecker about four times, and that the boyfriend was a total pisshead.'

'They're very naughty words, Kirsten, and you shouldn't repeat them.'

'I couldn't help hearing, the babysitter was screaming down the phone at him. My cousin Tommy was roaring laughing at her, but I wasn't, honestly. I don't like bad words.'

'Good girl, I'm glad to hear it. Now, where's your mum?'

'Like when you were here last night? I heard Auntie Melissa and Auntie Sue say bold words about you, and I didn't like that, either. Not after the bag of jellied eels from the Sweet Factory you gave me. That was really nice. I don't care what anyone else says, Auntie Kate, I think you're lovely.'

Kate gives a deep, painful sigh.

'Kirsten, pet, is your mum out for the night? It's just that I need to leave a message for her.'

'Oh, yeah. Mum and Dad are gone to some party down in Sheehan's pub.'

'OK, love, would you ask her to call me in the morning?'

345

'Uncle Paul is with them, too. Did you want to talk to him?'

'What did you say, love?'

'Uncle Paul was here earlier with that girl from the band, the one with the yellowy hair, and they were laughing and messing in the kitchen. They were here all evening, the four of them, and Uncle Paul gave me money. Then they took mammy and daddy down to the pub with them. She's nice, the lady with the yellowy hair, but I forget her name.'

Kate looks completely shell-shocked.

'Her name is Julie, love.'

I stay with her for the night, not having the first clue what to do now. I can't even plant a happy dream in her head, because she spends the entire night tossing and turning and not even sleeping a wink.

Chapter Seventeen

JAMES

. . . is scribbling out a list. I should know, I'm reading it over his shoulder. Five names, five contacts, five people who he's now trying to ask for help in digging him out of the black hole he's found himself in. All scrawled across a tatty bit of Meridius headed notepaper in his sloping, scary-looking, serial-killer handwriting. My thoughts are still with poor old Kate, but very early this morning she finally did nod off, and I figured it best to leave her and give the girl a bit of peace, for the moment at least. I'm dumbfounded, gutted, and still not able to quite believe that Paul, Perfect Paul, would lie so blatantly to Kate. It just can't be true . . . can it? I so want to believe that maybe it's all a big misunderstanding, that Kirsten, who innocently ratted him out on the phone, somehow got it all wrong. She's only about eight after all . . . but until Kate actually gets to speak to Paul to clear this up, I'll just have to wait and see.

No other option. For now, at least.

So, in a blind temper, I look in on James, and I'm glad I did: he's like living, walking proof that sometimes bad things do occasionally happen to complete and utter bastards, and it goes a long way towards making me feel that there is actually some sort of justice in this world.

His begging list reads as follows:

1. Simon Webb.

   (Another independent producer, but unlike James, one who behaves like a gentleman, treats everyone who works for him fairly, and most importantly of all, actually gets stuff made.)

2. Alex Mackey.

   (Wealthy socialite, divorced from a billionaire, and rarely out of the papers, where she's never photographed in the same designer outfit twice. Kind of pally with James in that they air-kiss whenever they meet, call each other darling, and she gives good red carpet at any premieres he's having: i.e., will always turn up in her glad rags, look suitably glam, and garner many miles of column inches in the press.)

3. Shane Ferguson.

   (President of the Irish Film Board. Dug James out of a hole years ago by investing in a documentary he made. Probably worth a try.)

4. Joe McKinney.
   (A real long shot. Multi-millionaire who made his money by buying a radio station, then building it up to become one of the biggest in the country. I'm classifying him as a long shot, however, as he's well known to hate James's guts, and has on more than one occasion rubbished projects he's been attached to, and encouraged his DJs to do so as well. Live, on air, that is.)
5. James's brother, Matthew.
   Oh, sweet Jesus. That's a measure of just how desperately bad things have become. In fact, throw in four horsemen and you've pretty much got the apocalypse on your hands.

He's sitting on the couch at home, looking rough, dishevelled, red-eyed and hungover as a dog. There's a half-empty bottle of Jack Daniel's beside him, which he keeps topping up his glass with. At nine in the morning. With a slightly shaky hand he picks up the phone and hits his first call. I want to shout something at him, but I can't think what. Something suitably cutting . . . like, 'This, James Kane, is the law of karma in action.' Or maybe, 'You see? Your downfall stemmed from treating everyone around you like a piece of shite, and look at you now. Poorer than Michael Jackson.' Then again, on the other hand, maybe I'll just limit myself to sitting on the sidelines like Madame Defarge, cackling at the proceedings while waving a pair of knitting needles in his face.

But, bloody soft eejit that I am, I take one look at his trembling hands and his ashen, wasted face and it stops me in my tracks. Then I look around the house and think, he's this close, inches away, from losing it altogether. After everything that I've done to it, all my hard work and effort and energy and money and . . . OK, you know what? I have to stop myself right here, because in the mood I'm in right now, there's a good chance I might just start pitying him, and I'm not allowed.

So, quite apart from the fact that he's about to lose his business, not to mention Declan, the best thing that ever happened to Meridius Movies, where the hell is he going to go and live? This is a man who doesn't do friends like the rest of us, so crashing out on some sympathetic mate's sofa for the duration isn't a runner. And I doubt very much that there's any kind of plan B. Unless he's planning to call his brother, to see if he can stay with him for the time being. Even thinking that sentence, I can hear the sound of barrels being scraped. To put it mildly, they never really got on, and anyway, the pair of them haven't actually spoken since about three Christmases ago, and then it was only because they were having a row.

Bloody hell.

He calls Simon Webb first, is told by an assistant that he's not available, so James, in his politest, humblest phone voice leaves a message then hangs up. He puts a '?' beside his name on the list, and moves on to his next target. Alex Mackey, or Her Ladyship as he jokingly refers to her. Well, half-joking, half-meaning it. Amazingly, considering it's this early in the morning, she answers. I only get one side of the call, but it goes like this.

'Alex? James here, glad I caught you, honey . . . oh you're on your way to the gym? You're kidding me, babe, with a body like yours? Women go to the gym so they can end up looking like you . . .'

He chats on, while I pause to gag. God knows why, this is the way he communicates with all women. I just forgot how nauseatingly, revoltingly sick-making all the forced flirtation is, that's all. And that he can effortlessly switch into it in his half-pissed state just goes to show his level of desperation.

'. . . is it really that long since I've seen you? The film festival in Belfast? You're kidding me . . . my God, is it really three months since then? Yeah . . . yeah, I really enjoyed that night too, babe. We must hook up soon and do it again sometime . . .'

OK, now I'm starting to sniff something in the air, and I'm not even sure what it is.

'. . . but I did call you afterwards, Alex, I did. You

were in such a rush to get out of my room the next morning before anyone saw you, I didn't know what to think . . . of course no one saw us . . . I'm positive . . . because, Alex, remember? On the last day of the festival, the hotel was crawling with journalists, and if they'd copped on that something happened between us, we'd have been tabloid fodder for weeks. Charlotte would have got wind of it, made my life hell till she cooled down . . .'

'I KNEW it!' I yell out loud. Can't help myself. All of a sudden, I feel like this Berlin Wall of white-hot fury has just been torn down, and now there's no stopping me. I remember him going to that film festival like it was yesterday: he called me from the hotel so many times I lost count, to tell me how boring it all was, how, apart from the screenings, there was bugger all to do, 'no one to go out and play with' as he put it. Even on the last day of it, he rang to say how much he missed me, wished I'd been there, and couldn't wait to get back home.

While, all along, he'd spent the previous night with Alex.

'You slept with her?' I snarl into his face. 'You actually slept with her? You know, I didn't think that it was possible for you to slip any lower in my estimation, but congratulations, you just did. You lying, cheating, two-faced, hypocritical . . .'

He covers his ear with his hand, as if I'm just a

background noise that he can block out, and keeps on talking.

Big, big mistake.

'James, hang up the phone.' I'm deliberately keeping my tone loud, clear and steady, like the way trained hostage-negotiators talk to kidnappers. He winces a bit, looks around, decides he's imagining things, then goes right back to the full-on flirt-fest with Alex.

'So listen, honey,' he says, huskily, reaching for a Marlboro and lighting it up with his free hand, 'I'm glad I caught you, because there's something I wanted to run by you. An investment opportunity . . . no, not a movie, a TV series . . . ooh, it's A list all the way, baby . . . guarantee you'd triple your money in next to no time . . . well, thing is, they're queueing up and down the street to invest in this, but I thought I'd give you first refusal on account of us going back a long way . . . entry-level investment would be in the region of fifty thousand, but obviously, the more you put in, the more you'll get back . . . oh. OK. Right then. Fine. Yeah, 'course I understand. Well, it's your decision, Alex, but I have to tell you, you're passing up a golden opportunity. Right, say no more. If you're not interested, you're not interested. Not a problem, babe. Just a shame that you're passing up on this. A shame for you, I mean. Yeah, lunch on me next time I see you. I'll get Hannah at the office to set it up. OK, take care.'

Then he slams down the phone and starts talking scarily slowly, as he does whenever he's dangerously angry.

'You dooozy, tight-fisted biiitch, Alex Mackey, what's fiiifty poxy graaand to you, anyway?'

I'm standing right in front of him now, shaking with uncontrollable anger.

'James, I know you can hear me, and for your own sake, you'd be well advised to listen to what I have to say.'

He's about to dial another number, then freezes, listens, checks the amount of Jack Daniel's he's actually drunk, then decides he's still a bit pissed, and that's all that's wrong with him. That's why he's hearing things. So he pulls on his cigarette and starts rubbing his temples. Ignoring me. He looks around for a bit, is satisfied that it *was* all in his head, then keeps on dialling.

Take more than that to shut me up, though.

'Call me the voice of your conscience if you like, James, but can't you see what's going on here? You've spent your entire life treating not just women but everyone around you like complete and utter shite, and now it's come back to haunt you. Chickens coming home to roost, and all that. For God's sake, will you put the phone down, and for once in your life just listen to what I have to say? Or do I have to bitch-slap some sense into you?'

He's still rubbing his temples, like I'm some irritating, whiskey-fuelled internal, semi-drunken monologue that won't go away, when someone answers the phone.

'Hey, Shane, man, how are you? James Kane here . . . long time, no see . . . look, can you talk for a sec? There's something I need to run by you, an investment opportunity . . . yeah . . . come on, man, we go back a long way and you were the first person I thought of calling . . . no, no, just hear me out . . . but, Shane . . . you were paid back every penny last time you invested with Meridius . . . well, it's hardly my fault if you didn't make back as much as you thought . . . come on, all investment is a risk, you know that . . . so, you've no interest in what I have to say to you, is that what you're telling me? Fine, Shane. Absolutely. Your loss, mate, not mine.'

'Another one turned their back on you,' I almost sneer at him.

I know, I know, I'm a horrible person, but right now I feel elated, vindicated, completely over the moon that this sad excuse for a human being, who ruined my life, is now, finally, getting his comeuppance.

'Don't you see, James,' I say, standing over him and trying to steady my voice, 'what's happening here? The universe is trying to teach you a valuable lesson: treat people badly, shaft them, lie to them, cheat on them, and it can only come back to bite you in the arse. Surely even someone as insensitive and plain buck-stupid as you can realize what's happening? It's your punishment for treating me the way you did. Call it divine retribution, call it what you like, but you're finally getting your just desserts, and here I am, with a front-row seat, cheering on your downfall. My God, if there was a gold medal for pure evil, I'd be the one handing it out to you. Maybe that's why you can hear me, and no one else can. So I can act as Greek chorus to your final ruination. And believe me, I intend to make a full three-act opera with intervals and all out of this. Because it couldn't happen to a more deserving person.'

He's still blocking me out, hand over one ear, and is on to the next call, though. Joe McKinney. He doesn't get him, though: Joe's assistant answers, takes a message, then hangs up. Meanwhile, I've worked myself up into a right state, so I'm now railing at him, like all the combined furies of hell, all rolled into one.

'What really gets me,' I splutter and spit, 'is that after all the time we spent together, after everything I did for you: always putting your interests first, never for one second doubting that you loved me, and that we'd be together for the rest of our lives . . . all the while you were just stringing me along. And I couldn't even see it. Everyone around me could, except me. But I paid the highest price possible for being such a blind gobshite, and now you're doing the same. And it's what you deserve. Dear Jesus, if hell ever needs an ambassador, you'd be it.'

'For fuck's sake, who is saying that?' he witters, looking a bit scared now.

'Who do you think?'

A long pause as he looks at the whiskey bottle, then does a three-hundred-and-sixty-degree scan of the living room, checking, looking, panicking.

'Charlotte?'

'Who else?'

'I've had too much to drink, that's all that's wrong here,' he mutters.

'Oh, you arsehole, don't you understand? You NEED to listen to me! Why do you think I'm even bothering to be here, when I've far better things I could be getting on with?'

But just then, another call is answered. This time, it's his older brother Matthew. Hedge-fund manager and filthy rich with all the trappings. The five-bedroomed house on millionaires' row in Malahide (close to the sea, close to the airport, dontcha know), the trophy wife and the two perfect, gifted kids, and the holiday home close to a golf course in the fashionable part of the Algarve. Although he's not as much of a charmer as James, he's a far, far more honourable, decent, gentlemanly character.

Which, let's face it, wouldn't be too difficult.

James does his pitch, somehow managing to make it sound like he's actually doing Matthew a favour, by bringing him in on this mega-deal that will propel Matthew to even greater riches. But like a two-bit conman, he seriously underestimates his mark. Matthew didn't get to where he is in life without asking tough questions, and pretty soon, whether it's through exhaustion or semi-drunkenness, James is confessing everything. Bit by bit, Matthew somehow manages to prise it all out of him. That the real reason for the first phone call he's graced his brother with in years is that he's having cash-flow problems. That the lease is up on Meridius's office in a few weeks, and he doesn't have the money to renew, and then, the *pièce de résistance*, that his house is about to be repossessed.

I can't hear what exactly Matthew says, but judging from James's curt response, I'm guessing it goes along the lines of, 'Who exactly do you think you are, calling me up looking for handouts when I haven't heard from you in over two years? What do you take me for, anyway, some kind of ATM machine . . . etc., etc., etc.'

Then comes the killer blow. I press my ear right up close to the phone, so I can hear it for myself, so it's muffled, but there's no mistake. The normally cool Matthew is raising his voice at James now, making it all the easier for me to tune in.

'Fine, bro,' James snaps. 'I ask you for a bit of short-term help, and you can't even see fit to dig out your own brother in his goddamned hour of need.'

'I am trying to do you a favour,' Matthew explains patiently. 'You're at rock bottom now. This is the best thing that could happen to you, because your hand's forced. You're hungry and you're going under. Isn't that when you artistic types do all your best work? When the wolf is at the door?'

'Matthew, ten grand would see me out of this, come on, it's not like you're even going to miss it, now, is it?'

'My company has already given to all our designated charities this year. Which, considering we're in recession, we feel is more than generous.'

'Hear me out, will you?' James wails, sounding close to real hysteria now. 'I mean, come on, we're brothers, aren't we? If you don't help me, what am I going to do?'

A long pause.

'You say you've a few weeks before the lease on the Meridius office expires?'

'Yeah, yeah,' says James, gratefully grabbing at this lifeline. 'Even if you could sort me out for the cash to cover that . . .'

'I was about to do no such thing. All I was suggesting is that, when your house is repossessed, at least you can crash out on your office floor.'

Chapter Eighteen
FIONA

Well, thank God for one angelic success story, is all I can say. Though, I suppose in a way I can count what's happening to James as a success of sorts. He asked for it, and yeah, he got what was coming to him, although you wouldn't wish it on your worst enemy. I then remind myself that James Kane *is*, in fact, my worst enemy. I hope for his sake that he'll somehow unearth the life lesson that's to be learned in there, and who knows? With me hissing in his ear every opportunity I get, there's a chance that even a hopeless moron such as he is might, just might, make the correlation between how he's behaved and how his whole world has turned upside down. As for Kate, poor, strung-out Kate, I haven't decided how best I can help her now, and until she has a showdown with Paul, there's damn all I can do for her. So I go to see Fiona, my golden project, if I do say so myself.

It's a gorgeous, balmy, summery Friday evening and when I join her, she's strutting down Wicklow Street in the heart of the city, checking out her reflection in just about every shop window she passes. She does this a fair bit, and it's not out of vanity, more like insecurity. No need for that tonight, though, she's really pulled out all the stops, and is looking jaw-droppingly amazing in a gorgeous, fuchsia-pink dress, cut to show off her neat, trim little figure. I've never seen it on her before, which means she must have gone shopping especially for tonight, when my back was turned.

Which is such a good sign. Balm to my wounds, in fact.

Her neck is craned checking, checking, checking out the name of every dinky little restaurant she passes, then eventually she lights on the one she's looking for, Trentuno. It's small, but cosy and romantic, with the doors thrown open to let in the cool evening air, and a gorgeous smell of garlicky sauces drifting out from the kitchen.

It's packed full with Friday-evening revellers, but good old reliable Tim is there ahead of her, patiently waiting at a discreet table for two at the back, and I swear I think my heart is racing just as much as hers must be, at the sight of the two of them greeting each other. Not knowing whether to hug or not, then going for it, but a bit awkwardly, then accidentally banging their heads off each other, and both laughing nervously. They talk over each other, overlapping sentences at the same time, and it's just so endearingly cute to see how red-faced and teenagery they are around each other.

It's not that I *want* to earwig, it's just that, given my own disastrous relationship history, it's so refreshingly good to see actual soulmates come together. After what I've been through, there's nothing more heartening than the sight of a good woman and the man who's held a candle for her all along, and who adores the ground she walks on, getting it together. Finally, after all these years. I look on at the two of them proudly, delighted that at least here is a little bit of earthly happiness that I can take total credit for.

The conversation begins awkwardly.

'You haven't changed a day.' Tim smiles at her as the waiter delivers the wine list.

'Except I got rid of the jam-jar glasses.'

'I *liked* the jam-jar glasses. They made you look cute.'

'Come off it, they made me look like Deirdre from *Coronation Street*.'

He smiles again, as the waiter drops off the wine list.

'What would you like to drink? Red or white?'

'Wet and alcoholic will do me grand, thanks,' says Fi.

'No, you *definitely* haven't changed. That was always your standard answer to that question.'

'Emm, neither have you,' says Fi politely, but she's actually lying through her teeth, as Tim now looks so completely different from the mad messer we knew all those years ago, that you'd pretty much be hard-pressed to pick him out of a police line-up.

A long pause, while they both take stock of each other.

Go on, get some alcohol into you, guys, that'll jump-start things a bit!

Tim takes the cue, thankfully orders a bottle of Chianti, and they both ease back into their chairs.

Another bleeding long-drawn-out pause.

'So,' Fi eventually says tentatively. 'Emm . . . how are things since, emm . . . well, you know, since . . .'

'Since Ayesha and I split up, you mean?' he finishes the sentence for her.

'Emm, well, yeah.'

'Fiona, all I can say is that I hope neither you nor anyone else I know ever has to go through what I'm going through right now.'

'I'm really sorry, it must be awful. But you know I'm here for you.'

Good. This is good stuff. Now he'll open up to her about the miserable years he spent with Ayesha, and then, who knows? After the Chianti kicks in, maybe that will lead to him musing about how different his life would have been had he and Fi stayed together, which in turn might lead to them getting back together again, etc., etc.

If I say so myself, this is one angelic project I can be *seriously* proud of.

'I think I'm still completely raw about the whole thing,' Tim says, just as the wine arrives. 'The hardest part is not being able to see the kids every day.'

'That must be terrible. I can't begin to imagine what you're going through,' says Fi, sitting forward in her chair, with me willing her to take his hand.

Companionably, of course.

'So, how are things with you?' he asks politely, but I'm guessing that he can't get off the subject quick enough.

Fi does what we all do on dates: lies stoutly about her life, over-exaggerating the fabulousness of it by about eighty per cent.

'Seeing anyone?' says Tim casually.

No she's not, no she's not, no she's not . . .

'Oh, you know, I'm out there, dating, but no one special,' she says, airily.

Perfect answer. Makes it sound like she's hordes of fellas after her, and that it's just a matter of picking the most eligible one, nothing more.

'Mind you, these days I use the word "boyfriend" to be synonymous with "it'll all end in tears".'

But then she had to go and blow it.

Fi, stop using comedy to hide heartache, that's my department!

'Fair play to you,' he smiles. 'I really admire anyone who can brave the whole dating, clubbing, pubbing scene. Would you like to settle down, though? Be married, have a family, I mean?'

'One day,' she answers, doing a great Mona Lisa smile.

Oh, this couldn't be going better!

'Fiona, can I ask you something?'

'Of course. Anything.'

'Did you ever take a good, long, third-person audit of your life and wonder exactly how you got to where you are now?'

'How do you mean?'

'I suppose what I'm trying to say is . . . did you ever stop and say to yourself, hang on a sec, my life was supposed to turn out completely differently?'

Oh, yes, here we go, and far sooner than I would have predicted! Cue Tim confessing the horrible mistake he made by marrying Ayesha, queen of the spray-tan, when his true soulmate was under his nose the whole time. I'm sitting right in between them, hands cupped around my chin, like I'm watching the most romantic soap opera unfold right before my very eyes.

'Go on,' says Fi, the eyes full of . . . I'm not quite sure what. Apprehension? Hope?

Yeah, go on, you've a wider audience than you might be aware of, sitting here with bated breath, waiting to see what you're going to say!

He takes a long sip of wine and looks into the middle distance, carefully formulating the next sentence in his head.

'I'm nearly thirty,' he eventually says. 'And I'm supposed to be happily married, living with my beautiful wife and two gorgeous daughters in our family home that we paid a fortune for. And instead, I'm stuck in a shoebox apartment down in the IFSC, with a bedroom so tiny that if I sit up I can actually touch all four walls. I'm paying rent I can't afford on top of a huge mortgage on the home that I *should* be living in, which Ayesha's new man just ups and moves himself into, without a second thought. Did I tell you that she's seeing someone? And the other day, Sorcha, that's my youngest, actually called him Dad. I felt like someone had ripped my heart out through my gut. I wanted to kill him, actually kill him. I'm not messing, Fiona, I'd do time for the bastard, and no jury in the land would convict me, either.'

OK, so maybe not what I was hoping he'd come out with, but, hey, the night is young.

'He's called Rick, so I've christened him Rick the Prick.'

And . . . clearly, on top of that, Tim has a lot of anger issues to resolve, but then, isn't that perfectly natural, given what he's been through?

'He calls himself a golfing coach, which as far as I can see involves him sitting around on my sofa all day watching DVDs of the Ryder Cup, then arsing off at weekends to play with his mates. Wanker. Doesn't pay a bean towards bills, so basically I'm supporting him. I mean, what kind of a guy does that? Just walks into another man's shoes and expects his lifestyle to be completely subsidized by him? I could strangle him, I really could.'

'That's just terrible,' says Fi, nodding her head sympathetically.

'She was having an affair with him for about a year before we broke up, you know,' Tim goes on, white-faced with bitterness now. 'But of course, the husband is always the last to know. I don't know how, but I kind of smelled something was up for a while, and you know how I finally found out?'

'Emm . . . no.'

'Last October bank-holiday weekend, she told me she was going to the K Club with the girls for a hen weekend, so I said fine. Then I was in our bedroom and I noticed her packing all this new underwear she'd bought. Really sexy stuff, basques and thongs, all kinds of things that she never wears. At least, not for me. At least, not any more. I got suspicious, but, eejit that I was, I trusted her and gave her the benefit of the doubt. Next day, Heather, my oldest, got a really bad tummy bug, high fever, the works, so I called Ayesha's mobile I don't know how many times, but it was always switched off, which in itself was odd. Then I tried ringing the hotel to let her know what was going on, and that I was taking Heather to the hospital. There was a "Do Not Disturb" on her bedroom phone, so I figured she left it on by accident, and I asked to talk to her best friend, who I'd been told was on the hen weekend, too. 'Course, the receptionist had no such person staying there, which really got me suspicious. Eventually, hours later, I finally managed to get through to Ayesha's room, and Rick the Prick answers the phone, cool as you like. And that's how I found out that my marriage was over. Pathetic, isn't it? I'm in Temple Street Children's Hospital trying to take care of a sick little child who just wants her mum, while she's off shagging someone else in a five-star hotel.'

'Tim, that's the worst thing I've ever heard.'

Poor Fiona looks devastated for him.

'It's nothing compared to what happened next. When we separated, I thought the best thing for the kids was to stay on in the family home, so I moved out and let her have the house.'

'Which was really decent of you . . . well, considering.'

'The kids come first, in the middle of all of this hell, that's the one thing I kept coming back to. So I move into the shoebox flat – where, by the way, I can actually hear conversations in full swing from the couple living next door, not raised voices, mind you, just normal, ordinary conversations – and I figured, at least my girls are OK and I can see them whenever I like. I thought, OK, I may be at rock bottom, with my whole life in shreds, but I do have something to live for. My kids. Who are still at home, so if nothing else, at least the disruption to their little lives is minimal.'

Fiona's nodding away approvingly.

'Then I get a solicitor's letter summoning me to the family courts.'

'You're kidding.'

'Do you think I'd joke about something like this?'

'Oh, sorry, no, no, of course not.'

'I almost threw up when I got the letter. She was actually taking me to court, so the times that I got to see my own kids could be laid down by some bloody eighty-year-old judge who hasn't a clue what I've been put through.'

'So what was the outcome? What did the judge say?'

'That I can see them one evening a week and for, big swinging deal, a full day at weekends. We have to go back to court regularly for progress reports, and get this, it'll take about another two years before I'll actually be able to take them for overnight access. When I'd been used to seeing them all the time, the way any normal dad does. Now I'm reduced to picking them up and dropping them back at court-appointed times, while Rick the Prick gets to see them every night of the week. I'm lying awake in my shoebox apartment, staring at the ceiling, wondering how much more of this hell I can take, while that freeloader is tucking my kids into bed in my home, with my wife beside him. I can't tell you how that feels, Fiona, but I'll say this. If ever I was close to suicide, these last few months were it.'

The waiter interrupts to take their order, and they both regroup a bit. Me included.

OK, so maybe Tim has a long way to go to heal and maybe get his head around seeing someone new, but at least we're kind of, sort of, on the right track here. Aren't we?

Fiona tops up their wine glasses.

'Tim, I really don't know what to say. What you're going through is . . . painful beyond words, but . . . well, if there's anything I can do to help . . .'

He looks at her, and for a minute I think he might actually start getting teary.

'You were always such a good friend,' he says. 'I know we haven't been as close in recent years, since I got married, but you know . . . kids and all.'

'I know, I know.'

'I mean, all your priorities shift when you have a family, and it's easy to lose touch with people from your past . . .'

'Sure, I understand . . .'

'You'll have kids of your own one day, and you'll know exactly what I'm talking about.'

She blushes a bit before answering him.

'All I'm saying, Tim, is that I'm here if you need me.'

'That's good to hear.'

I'm on the edge of my chair now, holding my breath, waiting on him, *willing* him to tell her how seeing her has made him realize just how huge a mistake he made in marrying the wrong woman. How much he's pined for her all this time, how incredible it is that she's come back into his life right now, when he's at his lowest ebb and needs her most.

'I mean it,' she adds sincerely.

'I know you do. And I also know that you're one of the few people who I can rely on to help me through this.'

'Of course.'

'You know, I couldn't believe it when you called me out of the blue like that. You were like some kind of angel being sent to me in my hour of need.'

OK, here it comes. Here's the part where he gently introduces the idea that, in time, down the road, when

371

he's a little less raw, that maybe, just maybe, she'll consider taking things to another whole new, wonderful level. Suddenly all the background noise in the restaurant, the chatter, the clinking of glasses and the laughter is really starting to annoy me. I just want to yell at everyone to shut up so I can focus on what's coming next.

'Hey, I'm here for you. Anytime you need me, just pick up the phone,' Fi says, blushing like a forest fire.

'You know what, Fiona? Seeing you has really made me realize something.'

'What's that?'

I hold my breath. The waiter at the table behind us is going through today's specials so loudly that I want to clock him one for shattering the mood here.

'I look at you and there you are, single, out there, dating . . .'

'Yes? And?'

'And I think, I can't go back to living that life. I don't even want that life any more.'

'So, you said that seeing me made you realize something. Em . . . *what*, exactly?'

'Well, what do you think?'

'Emm . . . you tell me.'

'That I want to be married, of course.'

'Ehh . . . to . . . ehh . . . who?'

'Well, to Ayesha, of course. Who else?'

Chapter Nineteen
KATE

I'm worried sick about Kate, so as soon as Fiona's date ends, I go straight to see her. It's still earlyish, and she's in the living, sorry I mean drawing room, with the TV on, flicking through the channels but not really taking anything in. I know by the glazed look on her face and the way she keeps glancing at her watch every thirty seconds. She looks washed-out and exhausted, tense and strained, and, I'm not joking, you can practically feel the nerves ricocheting off her.

Which can only mean one thing.

I run over to the living-room window, look out and . . . confirmation in bold capitals, if I even needed it. Even though it's pitch dark, I can see that there's only one car parked in the driveway . . . Kate's. Which means Paul never came home. Not in the last twenty-four hours. After everything: the awful row they had back in Galway, Kate finding out that he lied to her about meeting all his developer contacts, when the whole time he was out drinking with Robbie, Briar Rose . . . and Julie. And because I was with Fiona all evening, I've no idea what's been going on in the meantime, if he's phoned her to explain, or even if he's on his way home to her now.

But judging by how fraught and strung-out Kate looks, I'd hazard a wild guess that the answer's no.

Just then, she suddenly springs up, strides to the window and squints out, up and down the avenue where they live. She's standing right beside me now, and, instinctively, I put my arm around her shoulders. No reaction, which you'd think I'd be kind of used to by now, but I'm not. She just looks so edgy and over-wrought, and it's killing me that I'm not here for her. Really here, I mean. In the physical sense. Here's my big sister, really needing me, and all I can do is look on.

Being dead would drive you mental, it really would. Times like this I find myself thinking, what did I have to go and die for, anyway?

Kate goes over to her mobile and hits the redial button. Paul's mobile I'm guessing. She listens, waits for a bit, then clicks her tongue as it goes straight through to voicemail.

'Paul, it's me. Again. This is about the tenth time I've tried calling you, and I can't believe you haven't got back to me. It's past ten at night, I'm worried out of my mind here, you have GOT to call and let me know where you are and what's going on.'

She sounds wobbly and strained and then comes the time-honoured phrase which might as well come with subtitles saying, 'You're in big trouble.'

'We have to talk.'

She clicks off the phone, and goes back to channel-hopping on the TV, with me slumped down beside her, desperately trying to get my head around all this. That he hasn't come home, and hasn't even bothered to pick up the phone to his wife. Perfect Paul. The guy I used to hold up as an example of how gentlemanly and adoring some fellas could be. All the years I spent looking at Kate's life from the outside, and envying her flawless marriage. I'll tell you something, whoever said that before you judge someone walk a mile in their shoes wasn't messing.

But then, I find myself reasoning, whatever's going on with Paul, there is at least one tiny granule of hope that I can cling to: maybe this is just a blip, nothing more. I mean, don't all marriages go through rocky patches? Isn't it possible, just possible that that's all that's going on here? Then I look across at Kate's stressed face, and it kills me all over again that I can't be here for her. One hundred per cent here, I mean.

She channel-surfs to the *Late Late Show* where the chat is all about a luxury holiday for two they're giving away to the Maldives for some lucky competition winners. Suddenly, I get an instant brainwave: oh my

God, sure, this is so obvious! Sure, that's all that Kate and Paul need, a bit of time away together, away from grieving and work and all of her horrors-in-law, and Paul's obsession with his bloody band! I can't believe I didn't think of it before.

I wait till she eventually switches off the telly, locks up and hauls herself wearily upstairs to bed. Alone. I'm seeing it all so clearly in my mind's eye: I'll plant a seed in her head so she dreams about her and Paul on a secluded five-star beach resort, the kind that you only ever read about in the *über*-posh travel supplements. Her with a cocktail in one hand and a trashy novel in the other, him in very tight Speedos looking divinely sexy. Throw in hot sun, a Jacuzzi for two, room service and champagne and you've a recipe for the most wonderful setting where they can, I dunno, reconnect with each other and remember why they fell in love in the first place. I haven't the first clue what's going on with him, and why he's behaving the way he is towards Kate, but wouldn't a second honeymoon set their marriage straight again? That's all they need, you know, I'd put money on it.

And then I swing back to feeling helpless and useless and utterly frustrated all over again. I mean, why can't I send her a proper, decent sign? Something that would gently guide her towards, in no particular order, a travel agency, a lingerie shop and somewhere she can get her legs waxed? No joy, though. In fact, poor Kate spends so much of the night tossing and turning I don't think she gets a wink of sleep at all. I stay with her, watching over her.

Watching and worrying. Eventually, very early the next morning, she does manage to drift off a bit, so I hastily jump in.

Right then, here goes.

Next thing, she opens her eyes and finds herself on a sunlounger, looking out towards a crystal blue sea. It's baking hot, and she's wearing big face-covering Posh Spice shades, with a pretty white linen sundress, sipping a cocktail that starts off green at the bottom and changes to peach at the top. She's also wearing a floppy straw hat, why, I don't know, because the jammy cow can actually take the sun and doesn't end up looking like a burnt, gingery, freckly, Duchess of York lookalike, as I do after about four seconds on a beach.

That aside, this is a good start.

Looking bored, she tosses her book aside, sits back and starts looking around her. Then, in that surreal way that dreams have, she starts to hear music. She listens for a bit, then realizes that it's Paul singing 'Something' by the Beatles, her all-time favourite song, the one they had as their first dance at their wedding.

Better still.

She gets up and strolls back to the hotel, which is

huge, so she wanders down marble corridor after marble corridor, trying to find him, looking into room after room, calling out his name. The corridor she's on now suddenly stretches out to about five times its length, with door after door on either side. She's breaking into a run now, starting to get panicky, flinging each door open, calling out his name, but, somehow, every room she sticks her head into is completely empty. So she goes on running, sprinting, getting faster and faster. The only sound is Paul's singing getting louder, and the flip, flop of her sandals on the marble floor, racing still more rapidly. But now the marble floor has changed, so it looks like that brown, swirly carpet in the horror film *The Shining* . . .

Shite, no, this is turning into a nightmare!

On and on she runs, and now all sorts of unlikely people are walking towards her and leering at her creepily: Simon Cowell and Nicole Kidman wheeling a buggy. Still the singing is getting louder and louder, till eventually she comes to a door facing her, right at the very end of the corridor. It has a 'Do Not Disturb' sign on it, but she hammers on it and bursts in anyway.

Paul is there all right, sitting up in a king-size bed strumming on his guitar.

With Julie in the bed beside him.

I don't even have to snap Kate out of it, as just at that exact moment, a key turns in the hall door downstairs.

Phew.

Suddenly she's wide awake, with beads of sweat covering her pale, drawn face.

'Paul? Is that you?' Like a bullet, she's out of the bed and racing downstairs to where he's dumping an overnight bag on the hall table.

They look at each other, but neither one speaks. Then he goes back to taking off his jacket and flicking through a pile of mail. Blanking her.

'Mind the good cream rug, your shoes are filthy,' she says, out of habit more than anything else. Then she looks mortified at having come out with something so utterly nagging and stupid and completely daft at a time like this. Paul just turns to look at her, kicks the shoes off, sending them flying against the bottom stair, and now it's like a 'who'll blink first' contest. Like he knows right well there's a row coming, and is content to sit back and let her strike the first blow.

Which she does.

'Why didn't you return my calls?'

'Battery on my phone went dead.'

'You couldn't have called the landline? I've been worried sick, you know.'

'Does it matter? Sure, I'm here now, aren't I?'

'Of course it matters.'

He continues to stare stonily at her, and there's another long pause.

Oh God, it's like I can't watch, and yet feel compelled

379

to. Because I just have a slow, sickening feeling that hell is about to be unleashed.

'Do you want some breakfast?' Kate eventually asks, but then she's a great one for skating over surface tensions.

'No, just a shower. I've been in the car since seven this morning.'

He brushes past her to go upstairs, and I'm standing there thinking, is that it? No mention of the row the other night? Or of the fact that he spun her a yarn about being with property developers when he was out on the piss with his family and bloody Julie?

Kate lets him get half-way up the stairs before stopping him.

'You know, I think, Paul,' she says in an unsteady voice, 'that you at least owe me an explanation.'

'Oh, here we go,' he answers coldly, turning to face her defiantly, arms folded, like he's waiting for a full-on verbal onslaught.

'You told me the other night that you were having a business dinner . . .'

'That's because I was.'

'So how come when I called Rose's, her youngest told me you were all gone down to Sheehan's pub for the night?'

'Because that's where we went after dinner. Jesus, Kate, what is your problem? What are you trying to do anyway, spy on me?'

Right, that's done it. Gloves off, barriers down, as Kate really lets him have it.

'Don't dare speak to me like that, after all the worry I've been through . . .'

'Well, you asked for it, have you any idea how embarrassed I was in front of my whole family after you picked a fight with me back at the house, the night of the party for the fortieth?'

'After you ignored me for the entire night, you mean?'

'I was playing with the band, in case you hadn't noticed. Christ Alive, Kate, do you ever listen to yourself? Do you ever stop to think about anyone other than yourself?'

'I went all the way down there to be with you, and you didn't exactly look over the moon to see me, to put it mildly.'

'I was just surprised, that's all . . .'

'Then you leave me all alone with your family . . .'

'I was practising for the birthday do! Anyway, what's wrong with my family? Is this what this is really about, Kate?'

'I think it's no secret that Rose and Melissa and Sue don't really like me, and yet I sat with them for most of that awful night just to be there, just so I could support you . . .'

'Maybe they don't like you because you don't make any effort with them . . .'

381

'That is so bloody UNFAIR! I make every effort with them . . .'

'Not what they all say . . .'

'And what about Julie? How do you think I feel when I see the two of you all cosied up, you playing and her singing together?'

'You've really done it now,' he says coldly. 'She happens to be a good friend of mine. If you're insinuating something, why not come right out and say it?'

Kate stops, as if she's realizing that she's beginning to sound irrationally jealous, and that maybe she went a bit too far. So she regroups.

'All I'm trying to say is that, on top of everything else that I'm dealing with at the moment, I wouldn't have minded a bit of support from my husband. Is that too much to ask?'

He gives a shrug and doesn't answer her. As if he's finally realizing that he's acting like a complete tosser.

'It was a stressful time for me,' he eventually says, but a bit more gently. A bit more like the Paul I know. 'And I didn't expect to see you down there.'

Good, thank you, God, thank you, God. This is an improvement.

'But . . .' he goes on and I'm not liking that but . . .

'Seriously, Kate, what exactly is it you want? That I hold your hand every time you're with my family? On the rare occasions that you actually condescend to visit them, that is.'

Oh shit, shit, shit, nonononononono.

That's really done it now.

'Have you any idea how hurtful that is?' she screams back at him, hand clenched tightly on to the banister rail, with him still half-way up the stairs, coolly looking back down at her. I'm sitting in on a stair between the two of them, covering my ears with my hands, feeling hollow and empty and helpless, like a kid whose parents are bickering and not caring about the emotional fallout of the accusations they're hurling at each other.

Stop this, stop this, please stop this now, before one of you says something you can't take back . . .

'I made huge efforts with Rose, and with your other sisters-in-law, but they've made up their minds that I'm not one of them, and that's all there is to it.'

'Well, maybe you just need to spend more time with them. Take the trouble to get to know them. They're family after all, and family comes first.'

'I know. Of course I know.'

I look up, suddenly heartened that they actually seem to be agreeing on something.

'I'm glad you feel that way, Kate. Because given that any bit of construction work going seems to be in the west these days, I think it's time we looked into getting a place down there. Close to my family, close to work, save me doing this ridiculous drive every time there's a sniff of a job . . .'

'Hang on, hang on,' she says disbelievingly. 'What about my family, in Dublin? How am I supposed to see Mum for starters, if we're living three hours' drive away? How's she supposed to cope without me?'

'So maybe I get a flat in Galway, and stay there on my own.'

He was way too quick to say that, which makes me suspect that he's been thinking about this for a long time.

'Why would you want to do that when your home is here? With me?'

'I dunno, Kate, maybe because I hate the colour cream. Maybe I'm sick and tired of feeling like I'm dirtying up your spotless mansion. Maybe I'm fed up with how every single conversation I seem to have with you these days somehow turns into a screaming match. Maybe I just want some shagging peace.'

Kate just looks at him, like she's been punched with a knockout blow.

'But . . . but Paul, if you get an apartment in Galway, and I'm here in Dublin, then . . .' She gulps, as if she's somehow trying to find the courage to finish her sentence.

'. . . then, what's the point in being married?'

'I honestly don't think I know any more, Kate. You tell me.'

Chapter Twenty

FIONA

I just had to get out of there. Away from Kate and Paul ripping each other apart, away from the rows and accusations and bitterness. It's eating me up just watching them, and all I can think is . . . where will it all end? I'm such an emotional coward, I need to get as far away as possible from the pair of them and be around someone happy and positive and whose life is turning a corner for her . . . so that'd be Fi, then.

I should fill you in. Her date with Tim wound up earlyish, with him dropping her back home in a cab and promising that he'd call her. And yes, OK, I admit he did do a fair bit of talking about Ayesha and a possible reconciliation, but I'm putting that down to him being male and therefore an eejit in all matters of the heart, and therefore needing signs flagged in neon waved under his nose saying, 'But your wife treated you appallingly! And now Fiona is back in your life! You loved her once and will learn to do so again, moron!'

Mortals. It scares me to think how they'd manage without angels like me watching over, guiding, steering, manipulating, etc. And do you think I'll get as much as a word of thanks?

Saturday mornings, Fiona usually makes out all these 'to do' lists for herself, along the lines of:

7 a.m.: rise, breakfast on a slither of Ryvita covered with a thin glaze of low fat spread and some hot water with a tiny squeeze of lemon juice. Read papers from cover to cover, including the boring financial bits.
8 a.m.: spinning class at the gym.

You get the picture, virtue on a monument. Her *actual* morning, however, tends to be a bit more along the lines of:

10.30 a.m.: roll over for second sleep.
11.45 a.m.: eventually haul ass out of bed.
12 noon, stick on frying pan and stuff face with rashers, sausages, eggs, white pudding etc., etc., then maybe start to think about leaving the house.

So by the time I get to her, just after midday, she's sitting at her desk, I guessed right, still in her dressing gown, putting away the last of a breakfast fit for a builder, eyes glued to the computer, reading her online horoscope for the day ahead.

'I wish you could hear me, Fi,' I say morosely, parking my bum on the desk beside her. 'I'm sick with worry about Kate, and I'd so love to pick your brains about it.'

I'm now starting to *seriously* resent not being able to even have a proper chat with her. Funny the things you really miss about being alive: it's a cliché to say it, but it really is the little things. Nattering to Fi on a lazy Saturday morning being one. *EastEnders* being another. Oh and Hob Nobs. Being able to talk to my mother whenever I feel like it.

Oh well. Whether I like it or not, I'm stuck in this dimension now, so I might as well just get on with things. Made my bed, have to lie in it, and all that.

Lazily, Fi stretches, burps, then hops up, and, bringing her empty plate with her, heads into her tiny kitchen, where she dumps the plate on the table and pours herself out a fresh mug of tea. Then she's straight back to her computer, with me at her shoulder, checking into her emails.

Another one from that vet fella. Jaysus, I'll say this for him, he might not be the guy for Fiona, but if nothing else, he's persistent.

From: lovesgermanshepherds@hotmail.com
To: lexiehart@yahoo.com
Subject: Tomorrow, Sunday . . . ?

Dear Lexie,

OK, OK, I get the hint. So a Chinese meal doesn't do it for you. Not a problem. Thing is, I still feel like such a heel for letting you down the other night, and I'm worried now that I'll never get a chance to apologize to you in person. So here it comes, my final game plan. If, by a miracle, the sight of my profile picture doesn't make you want to be physically sick, and if you think you could put up with me for a few hours, then I'd like to invite you to my local annual summer fair tomorrow afternoon, down here in Carlow. I'd be really happy to come and collect you wherever you're based (I'm guessing Dublin?) and then, of course, drop you back whenever you'd like. A mad invite I know, but I promise you one thing: it's always hilarious, one of the funniest days out of the year, in fact. I'm judging the under-twelves 'best pet' contest, so I can promise you VIP access to all the tents. Of course, this basically means you get to stand in your wellies in the front row for all the events, surrounded by kids carrying parrots in cages, fighting over whose has the best-groomed plumage. I kid you not, think Glastonbury, only with bands that aren't on drugs, more mud and animals everywhere. If you're reading this and wavering . . .

I look over to Fi, who's taking a slurp of tea out of her mug.

She is wavering, the eejit!

'OK, Fi, you know what? That's quite enough of this shite. Honestly, who does he think you are? Felicity Kendal from *The Good Life*? The kind of woman who'll conveniently forget about being left all alone in a restaurant, throw on a pair of wellies and then go haring off down to Carlow?'

She keeps reading on, though, so I do, too.

... then let me tell you a bit more about myself, so you'll know you're not about to sign up for an afternoon with a psychopath or an escaped convict.

1. I do have a sense of humour, honestly. OK, so everyone says that on their profile, but my mates really do tell me that I'm funny. And just while we're on the subject, I think it's a complete myth that women find men who can make them laugh sexy, because I'm always making girls laugh, and can't get a date for the life of me. (You see? If nothing else, I'm honest about it!) Also, if it was true about women loving funny men, then Woody Allen wouldn't have had to marry his adopted daughter, would he?

Fiona snorts aloud at this.

'Stop right there,' I say bossily to her. 'All this from the gobshite who stood you up? If you agree to meet this tosser, then you're only sending him a message that it's absolutely OK for him to treat you like that. Come on, what about Tim? Remember? Lovely gorgeous Tim who's now miraculously back in your life and newly single?'

She scrolls down, though, totally engrossed.

2. Once upon a time, men set great store by a woman who could cook. Me? I'd be over the moon just to meet a girl who can eat. My last date was with a non-fish-eating, wheat-intolerant vegetarian who was 'off carbs' for a year. Oh, and who didn't drink alcohol, either.

'I love my food,' Fi mutters, so keenly interested that it's starting to worry me. 'Plus, show me a bottle of Pinot Grigio and I'm in heaven.'

'Switch off the shagging computer, and put this thundering eejit out of your head!' I'm yelling at her, now, pointlessly of course, she just keeps on reading. 'Oh and, on a point of order, I should tell you there is no alcohol in heaven *at all*. Like permanent Good Friday up there.'

3. A lot of the guys I hang around with talk about their perfect woman. One mate is looking for a combination

of Catherine Zeta Jones, Germaine Greer and Abi Titmuss. And he thinks he'll meet her in Carlow by the way, where men outnumber women by about four to one. Another pal says his ideal mate is a half-Swedish, half-Japanese permanently twenty-five-year-old, five foot eight bisexual gymnast, with a penchant for wearing tastefully slutty cocktail dresses. Lexie, there are times when I despair. Particularly when I can sum up what I'm looking for in a life partner thus.

I'd like to find a Linda McCartney and not a Heather Mills.

'So sweet!' Fiona mumbles, impressed.

'Oh stop being so gooey-eyed, this is probably a standard round robin email that he sends to every girl he stands up. Why he bothers I don't know, but then they say serial killers can be exceptionally charming when you first meet them, too.'

Just then there's a loud thumping on the front door. Fi jumps up, looking puzzled, like she's not expecting anyone, then pads barefoot down the tiny hallway to the front door.

'Who is it?' she calls out, cautiously waiting for a reply before unlocking all the deadbolts and chain locks.

'Ehh . . . hi . . . Fiona? I hope I'm not disturbing you, but do you think I could come in for a sec? It's me, Tim.'

Oh thank God, thank God, thank God. This is so

amazing! Perfect timing, too. He'll bring her back to her senses and stop her from fantasizing over Vet Man and his bloody welly-fest in Carlow.

She unlocks the door, which I'm not joking, takes almost another ten minutes, then lets him in. Poor old Tim, he's looking even greyer and more washed-out than he did last night, and that's really saying something.

'Sorry for barging in like this,' he apologizes, following her into the kitchen, where she sticks on the kettle.

'No, it's no problem, none at all!' she says over-brightly, pulling her dressing gown tightly round her, like she's suddenly mortified to be found half-dressed and not wearing her contact lenses. 'Coffee?'

'Love one. Look, if I said I just happened to be in the area, you know I'd be lying,' he says, standing behind her as she pulls down mugs and a jar of Nescafé from the cupboard above her head.

Good, good stuff, Tim, now come on, this is no time for shyness or game-playing. Tell her, I dunno, that you've been thinking about her all night, that you couldn't wait to see her again . . . you're a guy! Go to it . . . romance her!

'You're welcome to call anytime,' Fiona smiles, spooning coffee into the mugs.

'It's just that . . . oh Christ, you mightn't be able to get your head around what I have to tell you. Do you mind if I sit down?'

'No, go ahead.'

He plonks himself down at her little table, with the remains of her big greasy fry-up still sitting on a plate in front of him.

'Can I get you some brekkie?' says Fi, whipping the plate away, embarrassed.

'It's good of you to ask, but I think food might just make me sick.'

Ooh, nerves, this can only be good.

'Why's that?' Fi asks, concerned.

'You won't believe this. I can scarcely believe it myself,' he says shakily, and I just know that there's something coming. Some big declaration. Something that'll change the whole course of Fi's life. Call it angel's intuition, but if you ask me, it's nothing less than fate that he called here this morning. It's destiny, in fact. I'd stake my life on it.

Sorry, I keep forgetting.

A long, Pinteresque pause. The only background noise is the kettle boiling and then the clink clank of Fi stirring coffee round the mugs.

Hmm . . . wonder if he'll ask her to get back together right here and right now? Which leads me to wonder whether he'll pounce on her right here, right now . . . which leads me to wonder if Fi's had a leg wax, and whether or not she has the good sheets on the bed upstairs . . . which leads me to wonder what I'll do with myself if things start getting hot and heavy round here, I mean, I can hardly hang around, can I? Too voyeuristic by far, no thanks . . . oh, I know what I'll do, I'll go and see Mum, it's been a while . . .

'So, what's up?' says Fi, gingerly sitting down opposite him, and passing him over the hot mug of coffee. She keeps fidgeting with her glasses, whipping them off, then wiping them off on her dressing gown, which is a nervous habit with her. She must sense that there's something coming, she *must*.

He runs his hands through his hair. Antsy body language of his which, bizarrely, I remember with astonishing clarity from all those years ago.

Another long pause, the longest this side of a Samuel Beckett play.

Oh, for God's sake, come on, Tim, faint heart never won fair lady!

'Look,' Tim says after what feels like about half an hour. 'It's easier if I just say it straight out.'

'Go on.'

Yes, go on, the suspense is driving me mental!

A long sigh. 'The thing is . . . and I'm not proud of this . . . I just had a huge fight with Ayesha's jockstrap of a boyfriend, Rick the Prick, and now the bastard is threatening me with assault charges,' he manages to get out, twisting and turning in his chair, ejector-seat jumpy.

'What the *fuck*?' Fiona and I say at exactly the same time.

'OK, OK, let me put it into context for you. This morning, I went around to Ayesha's house, that's MY house, to pick up the twins, as arranged. So, OK, I was maybe half an hour early, no big deal, right?'

'No, no, 'course not,' Fi and I say, again, together.

'So jockstrap opens the door, MY hall door, in his bloody Leinster rugby shirt, and coolly tells me that I'm early and the kids have gone to the supermarket with Ayesha. Fine by me, I said, I'll just come in and wait for them. Not a good idea, the smarmy git smirks at me. Seeing as how you don't live here any more, he says. I swear, he was nearly goading me, just to see how far he could push his luck.'

'So what happened?' Fi asks, her eyes like saucers.

'I lost it, I totally lost it. Honestly, I frightened myself with the blind rage I went into. Told him this was my home, which I'm paying the mortgage on, and who the hell did he think he was anyway, barring me from going inside?'

'So then what?'

'So then the arsehole starts getting all technical, saying that Ayesha's dad actually helped out with the down-payment on the house, so therefore it's only half mine. I'm roaring into the git's face at this stage, and I'm aware that I'm making a show of myself in front of the neighbours, but I'm so far gone with fury that I don't even care. So I shout at him and ask how he can call himself a man, yet live in a house that I pay the mortgage on as well as all the bills. How do you live with yourself knowing another man is supporting you, is the point I was trying to make, but the bastard twisted it and said . . . and said . . .'

'Go on.'

'. . . said that if Ayesha had been happy and satisfied with me, then she wouldn't have needed to look outside of her marriage. So that's when I really lost it. I shouted at him to step outside so we could settle it once and for all, but he wouldn't. I went at him, from where he was standing in the doorway, and landed him one clean, hard punch right square in the gob.'

Fiona looks like she doesn't know what to do or say, so she goes back to putting the glasses back on, then whipping them off again.

'Gave him a right shiner. I was thrilled. But here's where the git is so clever. I couldn't figure out why he wasn't hitting me back, because I'd have killed him, I swear I would have. He just stood there with a smirk across his ugly face. Then I saw why: without me realizing, Ayesha and the kids had already pulled up on the road outside and witnessed the whole bloody thing. Of course, then she wouldn't let me take the kids, said they were too upset by what they'd seen. So then git-face starts saying that his brother is some hotshot lawyer and that he'll make sure they apply for a barring order against me. Oh, and that he'll press assault charges, which shouldn't be a problem as now he has witnesses. A barring order, Fiona? From going into my own home? I'm at my wits' end here; I'm at rock bottom. Just when I thought things couldn't get worse, they do.'

'Oh, Tim, that's just terrible,' says Fi, full of sympathy. 'I don't know what to say.'

'All I want is to win her back. And I can't do it alone. Help me, Fiona, please, for the love of God, help me. I know it's hard to believe, and I know I mightn't exactly have been husband of the year, but in spite of everything, I love the ground that woman walks on. She's the other half of my soul, and I'm only sorry I had to go through all of this crap to realize it.'

Another silence as he takes a gulp of coffee, scalds his mouth, curses, then dumps the mug back down again. Fi just looks on with an expression on her face that I can't make out.

She's not liking this any more than I am, though, and that's for sure.

'So,' Tim continues, 'now you see why I had to come round here. I just needed to talk to a friend.'

'A friend,' she repeats dully.

It's like he's not even hearing her, though.

'Right, then,' he goes on, thinking aloud, 'here's what

I think the best thing to do is. I need to take some time, but when I've calmed down a bit, and when she'll agree to see me again, I need to go round there on bended knee and try to get to see her alone. And then I'll beg, like I've never begged before in my life, for her to take me back. No matter what she asks of me, I'll do it, if I can just get rid of Rick the Prick and get her back. I've no pride left, Fiona, and I don't even care any more. You're the only person I could come to for help, so for old times' sake, I'm asking you now. Will you help me, Fi? To win my wife back?'

They continue talking for a bit, or rather, Tim continues talking while she just listens. Silently, non-judgementally. Then after a while, she excuses herself and says she's slipping upstairs to get dressed. On her way up, though, she stops at her computer, where Vet Man's email is still flickering away on the screen, unanswered.

Discreetly, she clicks on the reply button.

From: lexiehart@yahoo.com
To: lovesgermanshepherds@hotmail.com
Subject: Tomorrow . . . Sunday?

Hi there.
It's a date.
And by the way, my real name is Fiona.

Chapter Twenty-One
JAMES

Everything's going wrong. Everything. Kate and Paul are ripping each other apart, while Fiona and Tim, who I had such high hopes for, are a total disaster. All he can live, eat, drink, sleep or talk about is Ayesha, Ayesha, bloody Ayesha: how much he loves her and how he'll do anything to get her back.

The guilt is suffocating me. It's all my fault. I mean, I'm the one who engineered them back into each other's lives, and what good has it done? In total despair, I leave them to it, and go back home. Sorry, back to James's house, I mean. Don't even know why I'm drawn there, all I can put it down to is that it does my heart good to witness James down on his luck and at rock bottom. Where he belongs.

Next thing, I'm in our, sorry, his, living room and . . . oh, for Jaysus' sake. Screechy Sophie is here, mid-screech. Another row in full flight. Dear Jaysus, how many more of them am I supposed to witness? Everyone is suffering. Everyone is miserable. And all I can do is look on, powerless.

I'm starting to think that the life of an angel sucks, it really does.

'So, that's it, then? You've nothing else to say to me?' Sophie is yelling at him, and it's only then that I notice two packed suitcases sitting neatly at the front door.

James is lying stretched out on the sofa looking like death on a plate. The nesty hair, the same manky jeans and jumper he had on last time I saw him, looking like he hasn't bothered to haul himself up off the sofa since then, either. To complete the hobo look, he has a blanket pulled around him, and, because I'm close by, he shivers, pulling it closer to him. Right beside him are two bottles of Jack Daniel's, one empty and one half-empty. He looks like he hasn't stopped drinking since I last saw him, and, what's more, that he doesn't even give a shite.

'I'm doing this because I do still care about you, you know,' howls Sophie, standing over him. He's not even reacting to her, just staring ahead, glazed. Glazed and pissed, that is. 'But if you think I'm staying another minute under this roof just to watch you drink yourself to death, James Kane, you've another think coming.'

No response.

'I've had it with you. I've given you every chance, and you're just behaving like a complete boor.'

Still no reaction.

'Everyone goes through tough times with work, you know. It's not like you're the first person this has ever happened to. I mean, look at me. I went for that musical audition the other day and I never even got a recall. But do you see me wallowing in misery, refusing to even get up off the sofa? No, because I'm a survivor, that's why. I deal with the knocks and I move on. Just like Liz Taylor.'

Oh yeah? I'm thinking, looking at her big, stupid poodley head. Because what happened to you, and what happened to James is the exact same. Not getting a callback for some dopey musical, and what he's dealing with: i.e., losing his home, company, career and right-hand man, all within the same few miserable days.

'James?' Sophie's nearly on top of him, now, and I'm starting to worry that her decibel level will actually dislodge plaster from the ceiling. 'Are you even listening to me?'

No reaction. In fact I wish I could figure out how he's managing to tune her out, because, God knows, it'd come in very handy.

'This is it, you know. Because once I walk out that door, there's no turning back. You can beg and plead all you like for me to give you another chance, but you've had your final warning. I won't take your calls, I won't ever see you again, and God help me, but if you even dare to come near me in public, I'll throw a drink over you. Do you understand?'

James just does that thing of rubbing his eye sockets with his palms, but otherwise stays silent.

'Right, then,' she says, the penny eventually dropping that he's not exactly putting up a fight to get her to stay.

Hee hee hee.

'Well, James, this is it, then. If I can give you one piece of advice before I go . . .'

It's the first time he's actually turned to look at her.

'. . . it's that you get help. Look at yourself. You're a complete mess. Drag yourself down all you want, but don't for a second think you can drag me down with you. Right then. I'm off. Don't try to contact me, there's no point.' With that, she swishes the stupid poodley curls, picks up her cases and opens the hall door.

'Sophie?' he calls after her in a gravelly voice, just as she's about to leave.

'Yes?' She's straight back in, and I get the feeling that all it would take from him is a minor bit of grovelling for her to do an about-turn and agree to stay. And maybe agree to throw a Hoover around the place as well; it's so filthy, it's driving me mental.

'Just before you go . . .'

'Yes?'

'Throw me over my cigarettes, will you? They're on the hall table right beside you.'

She doesn't, though. The only thing she throws is a filthy look, and with a deafening, 'to hell with you' door slam, she's out of there.

I manage to find a tiny bit of the coffee table that isn't covered in ash or discarded scripts or empty glasses, and sit down beside him, just taking in the whole scene. I'm so close to him, I can smell him, and it ain't pretty. Hasn't washed in days by the whiff off him.

'So,' is all I can manage to say.

He looks up sharply.

'This is what it's come to, James.'

'Oh, for fuck's sake,' he says, leaning over and pouring himself out another glass of JD. 'Now that she's gone, at least I have the voices in my head to keep me company,' he says, clinking his glass off the bottle, then taking a huge gulp. 'Thank you for that unexpected bonus, Mr Jack Daniel's. Thanks a bunch.'

I'm watching him, numb. I said I'd be here for the final act in his demise and here I am, front-row stalls. Exactly as I'd wished for. Just a shame I can't feel anything. Not pity or sympathy or anything.

'James, you know, none of what you're going through means anything unless you can learn from your mistakes.'

'Voices in my head moralizing at me now, lovely. Nice touch.'

'For once in your life, you've got to listen. You shafted everyone you came into contact with, me included. You lied, you were horrible to people who were in your corner the whole time, like Declan, you manipulated all around you . . .'

'Yeah. It's called being a producer. Get used to it.'

What's weird is that, right then, he starts laughing. A loud guffawing cackle. Real gallows humour.

For some reason, I'm starting to get frightened, and I don't know why. Something's going to happen, I'm just not sure what. All I know is that I'm beginning to be afraid.

I don't have long to wait.

Another gulp of whiskey later, and he's up on his feet, unsteady. He knocks over a table lamp and sends it flying on to the floor. Then he kicks it savagely.

Now I'm holding my breath.

Staggering, he somehow makes it to the downstairs bathroom, and suddenly I can breathe again. It's OK. Panic over. He's just going to the loo, that's all.

But he's not.

There's a crashing noise, and I follow to see what's going on. He's at the bathroom cabinet, but is so plastered drunk, he's sent the entire contents of it flying. Boxes of Tampax, a few bottles of foundation

I'd completely forgotten I even had, vitamin C tablets, Berocca, lavender oil, all go clattering across the tiled floor. Now he's rooting around, like he's searching for something.

Oh holy shite.

At the very back of the cabinet, there's a box of pills belonging to me, from ages ago.

Sleeping pills.

I got a prescription for them about a year ago, after a trip to New York with Kate, to help me get over the jet lag, and I forgot all about them. James clearly hadn't though: he knew exactly where they were and where to look. He seizes on them, almost goes flying when he trips on the jar of lavender oil, steadies himself, then somehow makes it back to the sofa.

Oh, please, don't let this be happening . . .

He opens the jar and there's about a dozen pills left. So he grabs the bottle of whiskey, pops one of the pills into his mouth and slugs it down, with a gulp of Jack Daniel's.

'OK, James, stop it, stop it right there. This is a crazy carry-on, what do you want to go and take sleeping pills for? On top of the amount that you've drunk? Don't you realize that's lethal? You've had one, that's enough, now stop, please STOP.'

He doesn't, though. He takes another and another and another. Now I'm shouting at him, begging, pleading with him to stop, but it's like he's gone to another place where I can't reach him.

Down and down he swallows more and more, and now I'm hysterical. I'm tearing my hair out, screaming, shrieking, terrified of what's going to happen, what he's trying to do to himself . . .

'Don't, James! Please stop this! Oh for the love of God, is there somebody who can help me? HELP ME! For God's sake . . . PLEASE HELP!!'

And, suddenly, like that, I'm yanked out of there.

Chapter Twenty-Two

I don't know what's going on. All I know is that I'm frightened. Terrified.

Slowly, uncertainly, I open my eyes and . . . find myself sitting all alone in what looks a bit like a bank-manager's office. Oversized oak desk, swively chairs, the works. Honestly, the only things missing are a pile of mortgage application forms, a Bank of Ireland calendar, and bars on the windows. I blink and look all around me, desperately trying my best to take it in. My heart's still walloping against my ribcage after the fright I got with James, and now I'm starting to get even more panicky. And yet, there's something about this place that's giving me the strangest sense of déjà vu.

Then the door bursts open, and the minute I see who's standing there, suddenly it all clicks into place.

It's Regina. Marshmallow lady, in a pink suit, with her pudgy pink roundy cheeks and pink-rimmed glasses. Who sent me to angelic training school, and who got me

Claudia Carroll

the gig looking after James in the first place. I remember thinking how pleasant and lovely and friendly she was when I first met her. Kind of like a cross between Angela Lansbury and an Aer Lingus hostess. Except she doesn't look a bit warm and stewardess-like right now. Her face is thunderous as she strides up to the chair opposite me, dumping a pile of papers down on to the desk with a dull wallop.

'Well, Charlotte Grey, I hope you're proud of your-self.'

'What? I'm sorry . . . but *what* did you say?' I ask, my mind completely baffled. She doesn't answer me, though, just clips on one of those telephonist headsets, like the one Madonna wore on her *Blonde Ambition* tour, then starts a conversation with . . . well, with thin air.

'Gabriel? Regina, back here again with an update. Yes, we've sent in a replacement angel who got on the case immediately. All taken care of. The cavalry has arrived, so to speak. The charge will get a nasty shock, and certainly won't feel particularly well for the next few days, but otherwise should pull through, thank God.'

Then she turns to hiss at me. 'No thanks to you.'

'I'm sorry, what did you say?'

'. . . I beg your pardon, Gabriel, what was that? Oh no, I have her here in front of me. And madam has some serious questions to answer as soon as I'm off this call, I can tell you. Righty-oh. Well then, over and out, and I'll brief you again shortly.'

She clicks her headset off her, stands up and walks over to a big bookcase covered in files that's right behind her desk, with her back to me. A long silence, and now I'm feeling just like I used to in school whenever I'd be hauled up in front of the headmistress for some bit of messing in class. I'm almost expecting her to turn around and tell me she's 'spoken to my unhappy parents'. (Our head nun's one-size-fits-all phrase reserved for when you'd seriously acted the eejit.) And that they're now on their way in to drag me back home.

But she doesn't. Instead she looks at me for a long, long time. A disappointed look, which somehow is far, far worse than if she'd started roaring and flinging furniture at me.

'I told your father this wouldn't work out, you know. I warned him.'

'Regina, I'm sure you're furious with me, and I'm sure I managed to make a complete pig's ear of everything. Just like I usually do. But can I just ask one thing? Is James going to be OK? I'm so worried. I couldn't believe it when he started popping pills, and on top of the amount of booze he'd drunk, as well . . . I was watching him, so completely helpless and powerless, it was terrifying . . .'

'To light and guard, to rule and guide. Does that phrase ring any kind of bell with you?'

Her voice is stern now, icy cold and cutting.

'Yes, Regina.'

God, it's exactly like being called to the carpet back in school. The rhetorical questions. The grinding embarrassment. I'm hating this, and I just want to get out of here, like, NOW.

'So enlighten me, Charlotte. Where exactly was it that you stumbled on that phrase before?'

'Umm . . . at angel school. We were told that . . . was our . . . emmmm . . . job.'

'Oh good. So your memory *is* working, then. And you're not entirely stone deaf.'

Another thing that reminds me of school. Dry sarcasm. God almighty, throw in train-track braces and pimples, and I'm right back to being fifteen years old again.

'Anything else you learned? That you'd like to share?'

'Emm . . . something about not interfering with free will?'

'I see. Nice to know that you were actually paying attention. But what's puzzling me about you, Charlotte, is why you heard one thing, then took it upon yourself to go and do the exact, polar opposite. Maybe you'd care to enlighten me?'

'Look, Regina . . . I'm sure what you're getting at is

that I messed up. But, please, I just want to know how James is . . .'

Regina pulls her swivelly chair out, sits down and reads out a line from what looks like a fax in front of her.

'As I speak, the emergency services are on their way to Strand Road, Dublin, to collect James Kane, where he'll be rushed to the A & E department at Saint Vincent's hospital. He'll undergo an extremely unpleasant stomach-pumping procedure, and will certainly be in pain for a few days, but otherwise, yes, he'll pull through.'

A wave of pure relief washes over me.

'Well, if nothing else, that is good to hear. You've no idea the fright I got when he started throwing back the sleeping pills, I was yelling at him like a demented lunatic to stop, honestly I really was, but it was like he'd made his mind up that this was what he was going to do, and there was absolutely nothing I could do about it . . . I've never felt so completely powerless . . .'

'You don't need to tell me, Charlotte, I saw the whole thing.'

'Emm . . . you did? How?'

She doesn't answer me, just swivels her desktop computer around to my side of the desk, so I can see the image on it, clear as crystal. Just like watching telly.

It's James. Lying on the sofa, exactly where I left him, except now he's choking and spluttering. I can't hear

Claudia Carroll

him, but by the look of him, I'd guess he's calling out for a bucket to be sick into.

'I don't get it,' I stammer, 'how are you able to see this? Is it like some kind of live CCTV feed or something?'

'Well, what did you expect, dear? My department is the centre of all ground operations, you know. The only reason it's made to look like a conventional, more earthly office is so as not to confuse rookies like yourself. Who, frankly, have caused me quite enough trouble as it is.'

'But . . . I don't get it. James was falling down drunk when I left him . . . how did he manage to call an ambulance?'

'He didn't.'

Just then, as I look back to the computer screen, I see Sophie coming in from the kitchen, with a wet face-towel which she then gingerly applies to James's forehead, like a cold compress.

'Screechy . . . sorry, I mean, Sophie came back?'

'Sophie came back. Took a lot of fast work on her angel's behalf, of course, but we got her there just in the nick of time. It seems she'd forgotten her phone, so her angel prompted her to remember it just when she'd got to the bottom of the road. She turned her car back, let herself back into the house, then found him, with an empty jar of sleeping pills lying beside him. Knowing right well that he'd been drinking steadily for days on end, she thought on her feet, rang emergency services immediately, and now they're on the way. In the nick of time, too.'

I sit back, and suddenly I can breathe again.

'So, he's going to be OK then?'

'As I said, no thanks to you, Missy.'

'Oh come on, that's a bit unfair. It's hardly my fault that everything in his whole life went pear-shaped, now, is it?'

'To light and guard, to rule and guide, means just that, Charlotte. Whereas somehow you took that to mean, to wreak havoc, sabotage, lecture and then round it off by having a good old laugh at him.'

'I never did!'

She rifles through the mound of papers in front of her, picks one, then starts quoting from it.

'Oh really? Incident one. When you first realized your charge had the ability to hear you, you then proceeded to taunt and terrify him, at one point telling him that you were the voice of his conscience and that his life was doomed. Correct?'

'Emm, well . . . OK, so I might have started to have a little bit of fun with him, but, in my defence, it was pretty incredible that he could hear me in the first place. No one warned me about that, no one even said that it might be a possibility . . .'

'Your father's idea.'

'Dad?'

413

'Yes. When you first came here, you were in such a raw emotional state about your break-up, he thought it would help the healing process. If you could somehow communicate with the man you loved and lost, maybe in time, you'd be able to feel pity for him rather than the blind fury, which, if I may remind you, was eating you up when you first arrived here.'

'Oh my God, that was *Dad's* idea?'

I can't think of anything else to say, my mind's gone into total meltdown. The funny thing is though . . . in a roundabout sort of way . . . it worked. What Regina's saying is actually true. I'd just forgotten. How fraught and angry and white-hot with rage I was with James when I came here initially, but now . . . now . . . I just feel sorry for him. Somehow along the way, without even noticing, I've detached emotionally. And, what's doubly weird is that, as I've witnessed James's carry-on from this side of the fence, I suppose it's finally beginning to hit me just how unhappy I was with him, even when I thought things were going well with us. We were so fundamentally unsuited. We're two very different human beings, and it's only now that I can see it with any kind of clarity. I spent my entire time with him trying to bash a square peg into a round hole, constantly forgiving all his bad behaviour and convincing myself that I could turn things around for me and him. But the simple fact is, it never would have worked. If Sophie hadn't come along, if my accident hadn't happened, and if we'd stayed together, now I'm asking myself . . . then what? What would the rest of my life have been like? Even a thicko like me would sooner or later have realized that James just wasn't my soulmate and that he was pretty much treading water with me until the big love of his life came along. Either that or else he'd just have had a string of affairs, one after the other, until eventually it would have driven me away. A life of misery was all that awaited me either way, that's for sure.

Not that any of this matters, now that I'm dead. It's just nice to have that clarity that you only get from stepping back from things a bit, that's all.

Regina's far from finished with me, though.

'Incident two. When your charge went to a very important meeting at an investor's country house to try to raise funds for a television project.'

'Oh . . . yeah, I remember,' I say, snapping out of my reverie and focusing on her again. 'Sir William Eames.'

'And what did you decide to do, madam?'

I think back. Shit. Now I remember.

In fact, how could I have forgotten?

'Well, now . . . can I just say in my defence . . . that was totally, one hundred per cent not my fault. You see, there were Dobermanns there, two of them, and I have this terrible phobia about dogs, but you know what animals are like, they completely sensed that I was there and started having a go at me . . .'

'That is *not* what I was referring to.'

'I only meant to say that what happened wasn't my fault. Well, that is to say, it wasn't *entirely* my fault.'

'Did you or did you not begin to goad your charge, telling him that his pitch was rubbish? In the full knowledge that he could hear you, and that you'd ruin any chance he might have had of winning over a would-be investor? Your exact words were, I believe, that a cat could have coughed a better script out of its rear end.'

OK, I've kind of had enough of the lecturing, and now I'm starting to get defensive. Which, with me, is usually only a prelude to full-scale bawling my eyes out.

'Regina, this is the man who ruined my life. And let's be honest, he's not exactly a likeable man. But I loved him. I loved him to distraction . . .'

'And he lied and cheated on you. Yes, yes, yes, heard it all before. Do you honestly mean to tell me that you think you're the first woman in history to have been disappointed in love? You know, the strength of a person's character, Charlotte, comes from adversity. Or as I'm fond of saying to all my angels that pass through here: a woman is a little bit like a tea bag. You don't know how strong she is till she's put in hot water. I'm not denying that you went through a hard time with this man, all I'm saying is that we offered you the chance to watch over James, and to prove that you were the bigger person by safeguarding him from this plane. By protecting him and gently guiding. Like you were supposed to. You could have shown him forgiveness and compassion. But no, you decided to wreak havoc instead. Very mature, Charlotte. Nicely done.'

This shuts me up. But then tough love tends to have that effect on me.

She's not finished with me, though.

'Incident three.'

I groan inwardly, thinking, oh Jaysus, is there more? Can't I go now?

Not a bloody hope.

'When James had reached rock bottom, as you call it, how did you decide to help? When he was at his lowest ebb, with his company in trouble, and on the verge of losing his home, what did you do? Took the high moral ground and gave him a good lecture about how his behaviour in the past had led him to this.'

OK, I have to stick up for myself here.

'But, Regina, I was only pointing out the truth! He shafted people all around him, and that's why he ended up losing his company. No one, not even his business partner, wanted to work with him any more. His own brother wouldn't help him out financially. It was like he was being hit by a boulder of karma. All I was trying to do was point out to him that if he'd treated people a bit better, then maybe things wouldn't have gone pear-shaped on him. That's all. Honestly.'

'You mean you decided to judge him, like you've any right to do that. To play God.'

'Well, if you put it like that . . .'

'Charlotte, there's only one person around here who gets to play God.'

I'm gobsmacked into silence. But there's still more to come. Regina shifts through yet more mounds of files, then opens another one.

'Anyway. Leaving that fiasco for the moment, and moving on from there,' she says, seizing out a piece of paper and reading from it. 'Yes, here we are. Your friend Fiona.'

For the first time since this earbashing started, I'm actually able to look her in the eye. Confident that I did good work there in bringing Tim back into Fiona's lonely life again. OK, so it might take a bit of time, given what poor old Tim is going through with his marriage break-up, and OK, so maybe he *thinks* he wants to get back with Ayesha, but that just goes to show you what mortals know. The fact is, I reintroduced soulmates and surely I can't get into too much trouble there. Can I?

'In the first place . . .' Regina starts off, with me staring right back at her, defiantly. Feeling on steadier ground here.

'. . . what made you think you had the right to begin tampering with her life?'

'Well . . . I wanted to help her, of course. She was fed up being on her own and looking for someone to share her life with, looking in all the wrong places, if you ask me.'

'There you go, judging others again. Who are you to say she was looking in all the wrong places?'

'Because . . . she was spending all her time with her face stuck in her computer, and everyone knows that really only gay men are any good at finding love online, so . . .'

'So you decided you'd interfere and cause all sorts of mischief there, too?'

'No! I knew she and Tim were perfect for each other, and all I tried to do was . . .'

'Mess around with her head, plant all sorts of thoughts and dreams about how she'd die alone unless she got back in contact with an ex-boyfriend who she'd long since moved on from? You threatened her. Your best friend.'

'That's not true, at least, that wasn't my intention . . .'

'But the worst damage you did, by far, was in trying to steer her away from someone else. Someone far more suited to her.'

'What?' My head is actually swimming now; I haven't the first clue what she's on about.

'This is classified, naturally,' says Regina, reading from yet another file. 'But Fiona Wilson is not destined to live her days alone, as in that delightful Charles Dickensesque tableau you chose to paint for the poor girl.'

'So . . . there's someone out there for her? That's . . . not Tim?'

'Does the name Gerry Reynolds mean anything to you? No,' she says, seeing the blank look on my bewildered face. 'I don't suppose it would. You're more likely to know him by his computer username. Loves German Shepherds.'

'Oh my God, the vet guy?'

'Is her actual, true soulmate, as you'd put it. But not only did you do just about everything in your power to keep them apart, you brought Tim Keating back into her life. Who is destined to get back with his wife Ayesha in, ohh, let's see now . . . yes, here it is, in about six months' time, if I'm correct.'

'Tim is meant to *stay* with Ayesha? You have to be kidding me! She's not for him, sure, she wasn't even faithful to him!'

'There you go again. Playing God. Becoming a bit of a habit with you, isn't it, dear? As it happens, Tim loves his wife and family and will do anything to win them back. Which he will, in good time. He'll forgive his wife, and they'll all be as before. Not that you even stopped to think about that.'

I'm too stunned to even answer her back. Fi's going to end up with Mr Loves German Shepherds? And Tim's going to get back with fake-tan queen?

I got it all wrong. Completely arseways. And I've never, ever felt so humbled.

'Sorry, Regina,' I manage to mutter. 'I didn't know.'

'Ignorance didn't stop you from interfering, though, did it, dear? Moving on from there . . . where did I put that folder, oh yes, here we are . . .'

I don't believe it. Now she's reading from a file with Kate's name on it.

Well, I'm OK here, aren't I? I mean, I couldn't have messed up too badly with Kate and Paul, could I? Yes, OK, they seem to be going through a rocky patch in their marriage, but all I'm guilty of is trying to make Kate remember why she fell for Paul in the first place. That's all.

Regina whips off her pinky glasses and eyeballs me.

'This may come as an unpleasant shock to you, but Kate is not destined to be married for very much longer. In fact, she and her husband Paul are to separate by mutual consent, in . . . emm . . . where did I write it, oh yes, here we are . . . this November, as it happens. Just before Christmas.'

'*What* did you say?' For a second I think I'm hearing things. That can't be true, I don't believe it. OK, so they might be at each other's throats, but it's just a blip, isn't it? Just temporary not-getting-on and nothing permanent?

'Hard for you to hear, I appreciate that, dear. Remember they married in a terrible rush altogether, and you know what they say: marry in haste, repent at leisure.'

'But, Kate will be devastated! She loves him, and OK, so he's been acting like a bit of a prick . . . sorry, I mean, he's been acting the eejit lately, but . . .'

'But what? Surely you saw for yourself that he wasn't exactly behaving like husband of the year towards her? And remember everything she's going through right now, with what happened to you, and with all the worry over your poor mum, too. Again, I suppose you thought you were helping by planting all those dreams in her head about how in love they were when they first met. But yet again, you interfered where you shouldn't have, and, surprise, surprise, managed to get everything wrong. Again.'

Once more, I'm silenced. Like I've just been punched in the solar plexus. Kate and Paul? Splitting up? Paul, the man I used to hold up as an image of earthly perfection in a male?

'But . . . will Kate be OK?'

Then, out of nowhere, the tears start to fall, and once I start, there's not a chance of stopping me. Somehow, this is worse, far worse even than seeing James trying to top himself, and God knows that was traumatic enough to have to witness. All Kate's hopes and dreams about having a baby, completely gone out the window.

'The simple answer to your question is, no. It's going to be a horrible Christmas for Kate, her worst ever. Particularly as Paul, her ex-husband, moves on very quickly. A bit too quickly, in fact.'

'Oh holy shite, don't tell me with Julie? The singer one who looks like Eva Braun?'

'Yes, sadly for Kate. And I'll thank you to watch your language round here.'

'Sorry,' I manage to say, sobbing uncontrollably now. Can't help it.

'And you accuse me of playing God?' I bawl. 'This is just crap, Kate doesn't deserve it, none of it! All she wanted was to be a mum, and she'd be a brilliant mother . . .'

'Oh, she will be, in time.'

'What?'

'Let's see now . . . yes, here we go. Not for a while, of course, healing takes a long time. But by February 2011, she'll have met someone else, and they'll adopt. Beautiful little girl, too, a gorgeous soul from China. Then, about a year later, she'll become pregnant naturally. A boy, a lovely spirit. He'll bring great joy into all of their lives.'

I heave another sob, half-relieved that things will work out for Kate, and yet still devastated at what lies ahead for her, in the short-term. So Paul ends up with that cow Julie? Jaysus, they deserve each other. And, OK, so there might be someone new for Kate coming down the pipeline, but I get all teary again just imagining what she'll have to go through in the interim.

What's weird is that Regina seems to read my mind like it's a website, and she's a search engine.

'Short-term will be a very tough time for Kate, yes,' she says, studying her files. 'But remember, in the long run things will work out so much better for her and her ex-husband. They'll both be far, far happier with their new partners than they ever were with each other, you know.'

The funny thing is, I *do* know. For a second I get a flash back to Paul's horrible family, and how vicious they were and always have been to Kate, all the while oohing and ahhing every time Julie's name was as much as mentioned. It'll suit them down to the ground anyway, and that's for sure. And at least poor Kate won't ever have to see that shower of horrors-in-law ever again, which is small consolation for a marriage break-up, but it is something.

F*ck, I really hate not being there for her. And really I hate being dead. But more than anything, I hate sitting here in this office listening to how much I messed up all around me when I had the chance to go back as an angel.

Useless in life and a failure in the afterlife, too.

'So . . . what'll I do now? Where should I go?'

'Well, where do you think?'

Back to the old folks' home, I suppose. Sorry, I mean the assessment area, or whatever it was Dad called it. Back to daytime telly and bingo and bridge. Stair lifts and the Queen Mother and sherry in the afternoon. For God knows how long. Maybe even for all eternity. I mean, when I was alive, I used to think it was a long wait for my pay cheque to arrive from month to month, but that's nothing compared with actual *eternity*.

Oh well. Maybe I'll take up bridge. And get to enjoy it. Or else just raid the drinks cabinet and spend all day every day pissed out of my head on sweet sherry. But at least I'll get to see Dad again, which is something. Mind you, when he hears how I managed to bugger up my life as an angel, he'll probably have a few stiff words to say to me . . .

Regina interrupts my thoughts, though.

'You, Madam Charlotte, are going back down to earth. Just as soon as I have all this paperwork done.'

'WHAT? You're sending me back?'

'That's right.'

'After I made such a pig's ear of everything?'

'Absolutely correct. We have no room for quitters up here, you know.'

'But . . . but I was a useless angel, completely rubbish and . . .'

'So you can consider this your yellow-card caution. Oh, and by the way? Don't even think about coming back here till you've managed to repair at least some of the damage you've done. Now close the door on your way out, dear.'

Chapter Twenty-Three
FIONA

I am a horrible, horrible person. And a crap, crap friend. There was me, steering poor old Fi away from the man she's destined to spend the rest of her life with, and all the while shoving her into the arms of Tim. Who still loves Fake Tan Queen and is about to get back with her. Thinking I was doing the right thing by both of them, but still managing to get the whole thing completely arseways.

You couldn't make it up, you just couldn't.

No sooner has Regina dismissed me out of her office than I find myself back in Fiona's living room again. I've no idea what time of day or what day of the week it is, or how long has passed since I was last here. None. And there she is, tweaking the curtains back and peering out the window on to the street outside.

'Fi? Fi, it's me.'

No reaction, not that I expected one.

'I know you can't see or hear me, hon, but if you could, I owe you such an apology. I've been a complete gobshite, which isn't anything unusual, but . . .'

Oh forget it, it's just too hard to explain properly. I mean, how am I supposed to get her to give Mr Loves German Shepherds a decent whirl, and at the same time, completely extricate Tim from her life? After badgering her to invite him back there in the first place? No, all I can do is wait till she's sleeping and then have a proper chat with her . . .

Shit. No, no, NO. Except I can't, can I? Because then I'll only end up back in Regina's office getting an earbashing about interfering with free will. Light, guard, rule and guide, that's all I'm allowed to do. That's *it*.

Bugger it, anyway.

Next thing, Fiona's at the mirror over the fireplace, double-checking her make-up and doing that thing of checking what she'd look like with a facelift. She's in jeans and a warm woolly jumper with big comfy, flat-heeled boots, dressed casually as though she's about to go hiking up a mountain, but yet with her hair freshly washed and blow-dried and wearing flawless 'barely there' make-up. The kind that takes far longer to apply than normal 'just lash it on' make-up.

Which makes me wonder where the hell she's going. She's too dressed-down for school and yet, if she's only kitted out for goofing around the place, why the perfect grooming? Next thing, she plonks down on the sofa, struggles to yank one of her boots off, then slips on a high-heeled wedgie instead. She stands up again, hobbles over to the full-length mirror in her hall, then checks to see which works best, by alternately standing on one leg, then the other.

Flat-heeled boot, or else wedgie that makes her taller . . .

Then two things happen simultaneously. From upstairs, there's the sound of the loo flushing, just as the doorbell rings, causing Fi to clutch her chest like the Widow Twankey in a panto. All in a millisecond, she manages to whip off the wedgie, shove it under the hall table, grab the matching boot from the living-room floor, shoehorn herself into it, leg it out to the front door, fling it open . . . and gasp in astonishment.

Standing there is one of the handsomest men I have ever seen. Tall, with a chunky build like a rugby player, fairish hair and lovely deep-blue-lagoon eyes. Carrying a bunch of tulips tied together in a pink ribbon, and somehow managing to make it look un-gay. Fiona's eyes bulge out of her head in shock, and knowing that she can't rave about his beauteous beauty to his face, I save her the hassle and do it for her.

'Sweet Mother of the Divine, who rang for the Hugo Boss model?' I gasp, wondering what he looks

429

like bare-chested. Like Jonathan Rhys Meyers, I'll bet, in *The Tudors*.

'You must be Fiona,' he smiles, a bit nervously, thrusting the tulips at her. 'It's really lovely to finally meet you. These are just to say sorry for last week, and thanks for being so understanding about it. Not many women would be.'

Soft-spoken, gentle, hangs his head a bit, either to compensate for being tall or else shy. Overall effect: devastatingly sexy.

'Emm, not at all, and thanks, they're lovely,' she somehow manages to say, still gazing at him. As am I.

'It's Gerry, by the way.'

'Hi, Gerry,' she and I say together.

A lovely, warm moment where the two of us just stare adoringly at him. Then I cop on.

'Jaysus, this is him, the vet! Oh, Fi, you are one lucky bitch, that's all I'll say. Go on, tell him his online profile picture doesn't even begin to do him justice. He's given you non-garage flowers, he's divine-looking, throw in that he comes from money, and I'll come back from the dead to haunt you if you don't wear the face off him before this day is out.'

'Emm, thanks for coming all the way from Carlow to pick me up,' she smiles, looking all pretty and feminine, and even managing to blush.

'My pleasure. Least I could do. You're a sport to agree

to come to the fair today, but I think you'll enjoy it. At least I hope you will. Hey! And ten out of ten for wearing boots; you'd be amazed the amount of girls who come to this festival in high heels and end up looking like eejits traipsing through fields of mud.'

Fiona does a tinkly, girlie little laugh, while kicking the discarded wedgie surreptitiously under the hall table.

Oh, I could watch this all day. Their first date. First of many, hopefully. Today must be Sunday, then, the day of the summer fair he invited her to in the last email I read from him. My God, she even trusted him enough to give him her home address? This is amazing!

And then I remember my last horrible conversation with Regina. I'm not allowed to interfere, meddle or mess with Fiona's head in any way. This has to evolve naturally, if the two of them are to make a go of it. No, I'll just be like an impartial observer on the sidelines. Besides, so far so good. Off to a flying start. My work here is done. Not that I did anything, exactly, but you know what I mean.

Then a man's voice from upstairs.

'Fiona? Is there any hot water? I wanted to have a shower.'

Oh, for f*ck's sake.

Tim. He mustn't have left. He must have just crashed out here yesterday, after his fist-fight with Rick the Prick.

'Sorry, Gerry,' Fi says, flustered now, the mood shattered. 'That's . . . emm . . . a friend of mine who stayed over last night.'

Now, I'm fully certain that Tim stayed the night in the spare room, of *course* he did, but just then he appears at the top of the stairs, with only a towel wrapped around him, and nothing else. Which, from Gerry's point of view, doesn't really look so good.

Fiona must be thinking along the same lines, because she immediately starts over-compensating.

'Oh, emm . . . Gerry, meet Tim, who's a friend, who emm . . . who stayed over last night,' she manages to stammer, mortified.

'Hi, there,' Gerry smiles politely up at the semi-naked stranger standing at the top of the stairs.

'Hi,' Tim calls back down, watching them both, taking it all in, in no hurry whatsoever to move off.

Fi, just go, leave now. You and Gerry. Just get in the car and go. This first date is too, too important. So GO. Choose the future and not the past!

An awkward moment, while the three of them just look at each other. Now ordinarily, I enjoy tense moments, God knows I've witnessed enough of them lately, but not this.

'So how do you two guys know each other, then?' Gerry asks pleasantly.

'College,' says Fi, a bit too fast, dumping the tulips

on the hall table and not even stopping to put them in water. That's how awkward it is. 'So, will we head off then? Tim, just bang the door behind you when you're ready to leave.'

Good girl, now off you go!

'We dated in college, actually,' says Tim as he comes down the stairs, and I swear I could thump him. I mean, come on, was there any need for that completely useless bit of extraneous information? What is it about guys that they have to get all competitive over women, even the ones they aren't particularly interested in?

'Oh, but that was years and years ago,' Fi chips in, over-brightly. 'Tim's married now.'

'No, I'm not.'

Oh, for Christ's sake, Tim, just turn around, go back upstairs, get into the shower and leave them alone! At least give her a chance with this fella, will you?

It's as if he can hear me, because just then he turns on his heel and heads back upstairs.

Good.

Fi grabs her bag, and is just on her way out the door when he calls after her again.

Not good.

'What about the alarm?'

'Ah, sure there's no need to bother, nothing here worth robbing!' She's on the doorstep outside now, dying to get out of there and start the date, as you would be if you saw the sublime gorgeousness of Vet Man.

'Right, then,' Tim calls back, looking all forlorn, and fidgeting with the towel. 'Well . . . I suppose I'll talk to you later on, then?'

She's gone, though. Thank Jaysus.

Let the date begin.

My God, Gerry even holds the door of his jeep open for her to clamber up into. Nice touch. Like it.

11.30 a.m.

Absolutely, one hundred per cent could not be going better. They've chatted away non-stop in Gerry's big jeep, the whole way to Carlow, and have so far traded the following information about each other. Fiona has confessed that:

1) she can't sleep in bed without her electric blanket on, even in summer, and that she always takes it with her whenever she's away, as otherwise she has to ask housekeeping at whatever hotel she's staying in for half a dozen extra blankets, and they look at her like she's deranged.

2) Whenever she confiscates either chewing gum or crisps from her students, she keeps them, then eats them later on herself.

3) Her deepest, darkest secret is that, at aged fourteen,

she shoplifted a hair scrunchy from Boots, was never caught, but the guilt was worse than in that Edgar Allan Poe story, *The Tell-Tale Heart*, and now, to this day, she still can't cross the threshold of Boots without breaking into a sweat.

Gerry, for his part, has fully entered into the spirit of the conversation and has owned up to the following:

1) He only became a vet because there was a girl he fancied in his school who said she thought vets were the sexiest men around. He never got it together with her, and loves his job now, but when people talk about it being a job you need a 'vocation' for, he just snorts laughing.

2) His sister bet him two hundred euro that he couldn't quit smoking, and he told her he's fully off them, but has the occasional sneaky one while on Facebook.

3) His deepest, darkest secret is that he hates *Top Gear* and can't see what all the fuss is about, but has to pretend to like it when in the pub with his mates, all of whom think Jeremy Clarkson is the ultimate lad–god.

'But, I'm warning you,' he grins across at her, 'that information does not leave this car.'

So all is going swimmingly, with me perched on the back seat behind them like some kind of invisible, angelic chaperone. They even stop off at a garage for petrol, and end up buying a toasted cheese baguette each to munch at in the car. I can't help noticing Gerry look admiringly at Fi when he sees just exactly how much she enjoys her food.

And then her mobile rings.

She answers it, and I'm guessing that it's Tim from the amount of times she goes, 'Oh no, that's terrible. You mean you never got to see the twins at all today? And Rick the Pr . . . ehh . . . sorry, I mean Rick is absolutely insisting on pressing charges?' She makes an apologetic face across at Gerry and tries to wind up the call but it's like he just won't let her off the phone.

Hang up, Fi, come on, positive selfishness, today is about YOU, not Tim!

Eventually, after about twenty minutes more of her making soothing noises and saying things like, 'But look, Tim, I promise you, there's no problem that can't be fixed,' we finally arrive in Carlow, at the country fete. Which is basically in a big field outside the town all dotted with tents, with music playing loudly and a load of kids tearing around, having great crack altogether. Then, a bit more firmly, she tells him she has to go and hangs up, thank God.

'I don't mean to be nosy,' Gerry says politely, 'but is everything OK with your ex-boyfriend?'

Fiona dutifully fills him in, and Gerry says all the right things: how terrible the whole situation is and how a friend of his went through something similar recently, but without the added annoyance of a Rick the Prick in the background.

'What's really weird, though,' Fi adds, 'is that I've barely seen Tim at all since he got married. One of those people that you just lose contact with, you know? In fact, up until last week, he just wasn't in my life at all. So strange.'

From the back seat of the car, the guilt feels like heartburn.

2.00 p.m.

The fete is in full swing and things couldn't be going better. Gerry and Fiona are by now chatting away like old pals, getting on so well that I really do feel there's nothing more for me to do here, except step back and let nature take its course. They're in a huge marquee, where Gerry is just about to read out the names of the winners in the under-twelves' 'best pet' contest. The place is jam-packed with kids, all with either kittens in cat-boxes or dogs on leads. There's even one little girl carrying a parrot in a cage, which keeps squawking at inopportune moments, much to everyone's amusement.

'OK, everyone,' says Gerry into a very echoey sound-ing mike, standing right in the middle of the tent. 'A very high standard this year, so big congratulations all round.'

A polite round of applause.

'So,' he goes on, 'cutting to the chase, I'll now an-nounce the winners, in reverse order. In third place, with Ollie and Charlie, the bichon frise lapdogs, is . . .'

And then a mobile rings, to much exasperated click-ing of tongues from all the mums and dads. It's Fiona's. She blushes scarlet red and clicks it off. And then it rings again, so, mortified, she slips outside the tent.

Tim. Again.

I don't even know why he's calling her this time, but cue a worrying amount of, 'Oh no, that's just awful!' from Fi. Then she says something about how he should most definitely try to see Ayesha today, outside of the house and away from Rick the Prick . . . maybe he could ask her if she fancied going for a coffee somewhere? Her suggestion must do the trick, as he lets her off the phone and she heads back inside the marquee.

4.30 p.m.

Keogh's pub in Carlow town, packed to the gills. Fi and Gerry are sitting cosily in a corner, laughing and messing, both finishing off a big pub-grub feed of roast beef, Yorkshire pudding and all the Sunday-lunch trimmings. Fi is so relaxed with him, I'm half-surprised she doesn't belch. For his part, Gerry seems to be having a ball with her, regaling her with great stories about all the politics that goes on behind the scenes in judging a pet contest. More backstabbing and rivalry than a Republican convention, according to him.

'Seriously,' he insists, to much giggling from Fi, 'during the judging, I asked an eleven-year-old girl how she kept her puppy's coat so shiny and clean, and she told me she used her mother's dust-buster. Then the mother tried to bribe me with a twenty-euro note so the kid could at least go home with a highly commended certificate. Didn't respond well at all when I told her this was one judge who couldn't be bought, dust-buster or no dust-buster.'

Fi guffaws.

'That was nothing to a boy of about ten who told me that, for luck, he'd tried to baptize his kitten.' They both throw their heads back, helpless with titters, when Fi's mobile rings.

Yet again.

Surprise, surprise, it's Tim.

I haven't a clue what's up with him now, but once more, he doesn't have the slightest problem taking up about twenty minutes of Fi's time, knowing right well that she's on a date. She's way too soft-hearted a person to mind all the constant calls, but I mind for her. Mainly because it's my fault. She is now officially his crutch, his support person, his rock, which is all very well and good, but dear Jaysus, did it have to be today, of all days? And worst of all, there's nothing I can do about it except hiss at her to get off the phone NOW. Uselessly, of course.

Gerry, in fairness to him, seems perfectly easy and affable about the whole thing, leaving her to her call, and getting another round of drinks in for both of them. Well, a fizzy water for him and a glass of Pinot Grigio for Fi, along with a bag of her favourites: Tayto cheese and onion crisps. Honest to God, one date and it's like he's already known her for years. He stays at the bar, politely chatting to some people he knows, and doesn't come back to join her till she's snapped her phone shut, so as to give her a bit of privacy. Like a perfect gentleman.

'Everything OK?' he asks, plonking the drinks in front of them and handing her the crisps.

She looks up at him, worried.

'Well . . . no, not really.'

'When a beautiful woman says that, there's only two possible things a guy can reply. What is your problem, and how can I help?'

Fi and I both look at him gratefully. And then yet another wave of humiliation hits me when I think about all the years I spent lecturing and haranguing Fi to get off the internet and start looking for a fella in the real world. 'No one can download love', I believe was the exact phrase I used, and boy, am I swallowing my words now.

Lesson: if you're ever forced to listen to the crap advice Charlotte Grey comes out with, the exact, polar opposite is the correct course of action to be taken.

'Look, Gerry, I really am so sorry about this,' Fi begins. 'This must look like I'm trying to get away from you, and I'm not, I'm really not. I've had a lovely day with you, but the thing is . . .'

'. . . You need to leave.' He smiles kindly.

'Yeah. Believe me, I don't want to, but it's just that . . .'

'Something to do with your ex-boyfriend?'

Oh no, no, no, please, Fi, please don't do this, please don't leave because of Tim. He's a big boy and he can take care of himself; please, just this one time, put yourself first!

'I'm afraid so. He's just having such a miserable time right now, and doesn't seem to have anyone other than me who he can turn to. He went round to his ex-wife's house this afternoon to try to get her to talk to him, but he couldn't get past her new boyfriend, who he had a bust-up with yesterday, so the poor guy is just desolate. Plus, now a whole weekend has gone by and he hasn't even been able to see his daughters.'

'Say no more,' says Gerry thoughtfully, looking straight ahead. 'He's going through a rotten time, and you need to be there for him. I understand, honestly.'

'He was just telling me that he went back to this tiny little apartment he's renting just now, but couldn't hack being there alone, so he's asked if he could stay in my house again tonight. If I wouldn't mind, that is. So what could I say? I said of course he could. It's not right that he's alone at a time like this.'

'Drink up so,' Gerry smiles, getting up, 'and let me drive you home.'

'Are you sure?'

'Of course. Hey, I'll even buy you another bag of crisps to eat on the drive.'

6 p.m.

Back at Fiona's house, where Tim is parked outside, waiting on her to come home, just as Gerry pulls up outside. An awkward moment where I can physically see Fi weighing up whether or not to ask him in or not. After all, he did do all the driving, and she was the one to cut the date short. Also, I can't help but notice that there's no mention of a second date. Or as Fi always refers to it, the date where you can let out your tummy.

However, Gerry saves her all the bother and embarrassment by making a decision for her.

'So, it's Sunday evening . . .'

'Yes?' she looks up at him, hopefully.

'It's still early . . .'

'Yeah . . . ?'

'So . . .'

'So . . . ?'

'. . . Do you have any decent DVDs that I can come in and watch?'

6.20 p.m.

The only movie in Fi's limited DVD collection that they could all agree on was *The Godfather*. Which Fiona, Gerry and Tim are now clustered together on her tiny, two-seater sofa watching.

All three of them.

Chapter Twenty-Four
KATE

Fecking dire. Everything. Things are so disastrously awful that it takes every ounce of strength I can draw on to bring myself to look in on Kate. Mainly because I'm way too terrified of what I'll find.

Turns out, I've good reason to be frightened.

Sunday evening and she's just opening her hall door to . . . I can hardly believe what I'm seeing . . . Robbie, Paul's brother, Briar Rose, their eldest daughter Kirsten, who has a day off school tomorrow and who wanted to come on the road trip and . . . wait for it . . . Julie. Bloody Julie with the head bleached off her. Who, according to Regina, will have shacked up with Paul within a disgracefully short length of time, after he and Kate eventually separate.

I'm shaking like a leaf, I'm nauseous and I honestly think there's a good chance I'll barf.

What makes it so much worse is how lovely and nice

and welcoming Kate is being to all of them. It's as if she's fully aware that she and Paul are going through a rough patch and is now making a heroic effort with his God-awful family. All to please him. The man who won't even be in her life in a few months' time. Yes, I know that ultimately things will work out for her, but it's killing me to think of what has to happen first. Why does life have to be so bleeding hard, anyway? Tears are springing to my eyes just thinking about what's ahead for poor Kate. And I'm not even here for her. All I can do is look on, hopelessly and uselessly.

Anyway, it turns out the reason for this unexpected visit is that, at the last minute, Robbie got his hands on tickets for tonight's Bruce Springsteen concert in the RDS Arena. Four tickets to be precise. For him, Briar Rose, Julie and . . . there's an unhung question mark over who'll take the spare ticket, but Kate jumps in.

'Paul, darling,' she says stoutly, 'you take the ticket. You love Bruce Springsteen, and besides, then I can stay here and take care of Kirsten.'

'That would be really cool, Auntie Kate,' beams the child, throwing her up a grateful little smile with about five teeth missing.

'How come you've no school tomorrow, sweet-heart?'

'Teachers' meeting. Or as my daddy says, bloody teachers' meeting.'

No one even thanks Kate for offering to babysit, it's as if they just expected it of her all along. Nor does Paul as much as show the tiniest bit of gratitude for her letting him take the spare concert ticket; again, it's as if the decision was made ages ago, and actually had very little to do with Kate.

What really gets me is just how much she's bending over backwards to please all of them. Pouring out drinks for them, asking whether they'd like a bite to eat now or after the show, at one point even offering bleach-headed Julie a tour of the new house. I'm trembling with anger and frustration as I watch Kate get down her best wedding china, then rustle up some goat's cheese and roasted red pepper crostini in her pristine kitchen, which she politely passes around to all her guests. Who, by the way, have just dumped their bags on her drawing room floor, so much baggage you'd think they'd come to crash here for a full week.

And, by the way, I don't remember hearing a single one of them ask whether or not it was OK for them to come and stay, not even for form's sake. Robbie even puts his feet up on the good glass coffee table, rips the tab off a tin of Bud Light and switches on the TV, like he lives here. It's a measure of just how gargantuan an effort poor, good-hearted Kate is making with these people that she lets him, doesn't say a word, doesn't even put a coaster under the tin of beer, nothing. Meanwhile, Paul is behaving like a complete arsehole, so much so that I start formulating an evil plan at the back of my mind to start haunting him at every available opportunity, like I did with James. When he's on the loo, or in the shower, or at some huge important contractors' meeting, or flirting with Julie, or basically doing anything that upsets Kate.

Except I'm not bleeding allowed, am I?

The only one out of the whole miserable, rude, boorish, shagging lot of them that's even half-way polite to Kate is little Kirsten. She even offers to go into the kitchen with Kate to help her make more antipasti to offer around.

I linger back after the two of them leave, to hear exactly what the others have to say about her behind her back. Given that these people's favourite hobby is talking about whoever's just left the room.

Robbie starts off first.

'You could have at least offered to help her, Rose,' he says, eyes glued to the Sunderland match that's blaring away on the sports channel.

'Piss off, you,' says Rose. 'Sure, I wait on that one hand and foot whenever she comes to stay with us in Galway, don't I?'

Then she realizes Paul's still in the room, but out of earshot. He's over by the bay window chatting away to bleach-headed Julie, on the pretext of giving her a tour of the house.

'Sorry, Paul,' Rose calls over, but he doesn't even hear her. Or else he's not listening.

'What the feck are these yokes anyway?' says Robbie, peeling the skin off the goat's cheese and dangling it in front of him.

'Ah, some fancy thing of Kate's. Sure, you know what she's like.'

'Tastes like feet.'

'Don't talk to me. Sure, what's wrong with just giving us a few sandwiches, I'd like to know? Poor aul Paul, imagine having to live off this shite. No wonder he's losing weight.'

'That was offside, ya bloody eejit of a ref!' Robbie yells at the telly, only half-listening to her.

Take more than that to stop Briar Rose from a good bitch-fest though.

'Come back here to me, Julie,' she calls over, 'and tell us what you think of the house.'

'Ehh . . . it's very nice,' is all Bleach Head can say, she's so engrossed in her chat with Paul, way over in the bay window of the dining room.

'Wouldn't be my taste at all, now,' mutters Rose. 'What is it with that woman and the colour cream? You'd know a mile off this was a kid-free zone. Sure, mine would have the walls destroyed with crayons and markers inside of two minutes. And good luck to her trying to keep cream carpets clean. But then I suppose madam has a housekeeper to do all her dirty work for her. Too up herself to get her own hands dirty. And then, of course, that leaves her free to spend her time having lunch with the girls, or out spending Paul's money, or whatever the hell it is she *does* do all day.'

Kate comes back into the drawing room, carrying a fresh tray of drinks, just in time to hear that last sentence.

Rose realizes she's been rumbled, but doesn't bother apologizing or covering her tracks, just looks at Kate, shrugs and says, 'No offence.' Like that's her ultimate get-out-of-jail-free card.

Kate wavers for a minute. A knife-edge moment. I'm right beside her, shouting in her ear, 'How DARE that bitch speak about you like that in your own home? Go on, Kate, fling the tray of drinks at her and order her out of here, go on, go ON!'

Kate, though, is far more of a lady than I ever was. Coolly, calmly, she gives Rose an icy smile, and gently slides the tray on to the coffee table in front of her. I'm standing right over Briar Rose, willing Kate to take the bottle of gin from the tray and pour it over her hypocritical head, but no. Instead Kate holds the silence, mixes the drinks, plops in a cube of ice with a tongs and politely hands Rose a gin and tonic so big you could wash your hair in it.

Rose shifts uncomfortably, aware of the mood, but

then focuses on the TV, the cowardly bitch. Doesn't even have the guts to look Kate in the face. Robbie must be aware of the tension, too, because his hand freezes around his tin of Bud, mid-gulp, and he looks like he'd love nothing more than to be airlifted out of there.

'Just to enlighten you, Rose, purely on a point of order,' Kate eventually says, in a calm, clear voice, still smiling and drawing herself up tall. 'I do NOT spend my days having lunch with the girls, or spending Paul's money, as you put it. As a matter of fact, I've been spending all my time recently taking care of my mum. My family are going through a very trying time right now, in case you hadn't noticed, and comments like yours certainly don't help matters.'

Rose turns to face her, but doesn't interrupt.

'So I suggest you finish your drink, go to your concert, and when you do come back here later on tonight, I'll thank you to remember your manners. I'll also remind you that you're a guest in my home. Got it? Good.'

Good woman, Kate! That put the pole-axed old cow in her place, although you were a bit restrained for my liking, and could have perhaps littered your little speech with well-chosen phrases such as, 'Up yours, you two-faced bitch.' However, it's a good start.

Rose doesn't touch the drink in front of her. Just stands up and announces to the room that they'd better get going or they'll miss the start of the concert. And all the while, Paul, the man I had looked up to as an image of manly perfection on earth, was so focused on Julie that he never even noticed what was going on. Doesn't notice that his wife is shaking, doesn't ask if she's OK, doesn't notice the cut-throat atmosphere, and doesn't even care, by the look of him.

Hours later, Kate and Kirsten are snuggled up on the sofa watching the Disney channel and eating popcorn. Kirsten, very advanced for an eight year old, is expounding on her little philosophy of life.

'I have two rules,' she says to Kate, munching on the popcorn and doing her best to look all wise and grown-up. 'One is, when Mammy's mad at Daddy, *never* let her brush my hair. The other one is, when someone hits me, don't hit back. They always, always catch the second person. How about you, Auntie Kate? What rules do you have?'

Kate looks ahead, and thinks for a bit.

'That sometimes there's no pleasing some people, pet. So you might as well not bother.'

'You know, I really, really like you, Auntie Kate. You're the only adult I know who never shouts at me. Can we always be friends?'

'Of course we can.'

'Special friends?'

'I think that's a great idea, love. Because sometimes, in this life, we all need a special friend.'

The others don't come back until well after 3 a.m., pissed as farts, the whole lot of them. Paul brings them into the kitchen, and they all stay up even later, drinking and talking, not seeming to care about the racket they're making.

I stay with Kate the whole time, just watching over her, and when she starts sobbing, I do too.

Chapter Twenty-Five
JAMES

Next morning, out of guilt more than anything else, I manage to pull myself away from the slumbering Kate and go to look in on James. I do what I normally would: i.e., focus on him, and then expect to just appear at his side, at his house, more than likely. But no, this time it's different. Because when I open my eyes, I find myself in hospital. In a public ward, with six beds in it, packed full with visitors, doctors doing their rounds, nurses bustling in and out of the little cubicles. It's noisy and frenetic, with a TV on in the background, trolleys clattering, phones ringing, and what sounds like about twenty different conversations going on at once.

And then I see James. In a bed right by the door, hooked up to a very frightening-looking monitor. He's pale, washed-out and weak as a kitten. The only patient in the ward who's all alone, with no visitors. His is the only quiet, dark corner in the whole busy ward.

'Hi,' I say softly, terrified I'll give him a heart attack to add to his woes. His eyes open. 'Don't worry, I'm not here to lecture you,' I half-smile, sitting on the edge of the bed. 'At least, not this time.'

Now his eyes dart around. The spark, I can't help noticing, has completely gone out of them. He looks like a shadow of the man I once knew and loved. He looks broken.

'Drugs,' he murmurs in a voice so low and faint, I have to sit up just to hear him. 'They must have me on some serious drugs. Class A. Only explanation for your voice in my head, Charlotte. Can't be the booze this time, gotta be drugs.'

'How are you feeling?'

'Worried that if the medics see me talking to myself, they'll put me into a psychiatric unit.'

'Stop messing.'

'I've just had my stomach pumped. You really want the details? When the doc told me what exactly was involved, my reaction was, "So do I have to be there?"'

'You went for a gag. A lame one, but still, a good sign. You must be on the mend.'

He slumps back on to the pillow, looking drained and exhausted.

'When are they letting you go home?'

'Later today, I hope.'

'Are you kidding me? You're far too weak to leave here! Sure, look at the state of you!'

'It's OK. Sophie's coming to pick me up. And stay for a bit, keep an eye on me. Make sure I don't try anything like that again.'

Guilt washes all over me. Sophie. Who I was so horrible about, so bitchy. I mean, yeah, she did steal my boyfriend, but she also saved his life. She was more of a guardian angel to him than I ever was. Light, guard, rule and guide was my remit, and I completely buggered it up, the way I completely bugger everything up, and if it wasn't for Sophie . . .

I can't even bear to finish that sentence.

So I say what I've come to say instead.

'James . . .' I look around while I'm trying to work out how to phrase this right. No, there's nothing else but just to come right out with it.

'I owe you an apology.'

'The voice in my head is apologizing to me? Please don't ask me to answer you. They'll put me in a strait-jacket, then a padded cell, then throw away the key.'

'Look, just don't interrupt or I'll never be able to get this out. When I first realized you could hear me, I went out of my way to make your life hell, and I shouldn't have. As far as I was concerned, you were responsible for my accident, and I was so . . .' I break off, and then Regina's phrase comes back to haunt me '. . . so full of

Claudia Carroll

blind fury, that I wanted you to suffer too. I felt this was the perfect way to give you your just desserts. To put it mildly, you weren't exactly boyfriend of the year, and this was my chance to get back at you. To get even. To make you pay.'

'Charlotte . . .'

'No, let me finish. Then there was your big meeting with William Eames.'

'Did you have to remind me about that? I might just need a second stomach pump.'

'And I ruined it for you. I mean, OK, your idea was brutal . . . sorry, there I go, judging you again. OK, reboot. Here we go. So, I may not have liked your pitch, but I didn't have to make a holy show of you. I didn't have to reduce you to a gibbering wreck.'

'Was I a gibbering wreck?'

'Worse. Far, far worse. And then, to cap it all, there was the other night. You were at your lowest ebb, and what did I do? I played God. I told you that this was all your own doing, and that you'd brought it on yourself.'

'In a way, I suppose I did, really.'

'But it wasn't my place to hound you into the ground about it. To drive you almost to . . . suici . . .' I can't even bring myself to say the word. So I change tack. 'The thing is, James, I've realized so much recently. OK, so you didn't exactly treat me very well, but I've learned that the only person who can take the rap for staying

456

in a such a bad relationship is me. I was a woman who loved too much, and I just couldn't see what everyone around me could. All the time . . . I . . . I thought you were like a couture fit for me, and the whole time, you thought I was . . . Topshop. I loved you warts and all, but to you, I was only ever . . . like a Lidl version of your ideal woman.'

'Tortured metaphors, love it.'

'Anyway, I suppose in a roundabout way, what I'm trying to say is that, for my part in reducing you to this . . .' I look around the tiny cubicle, at all the machines that he's wired up to, at the general, miserable, rock-bottom state of him. 'I'm sorry.'

'Doctor Walsh says you can have tea now and a piece of dry toast,' says a nurse, crisply whipping back the curtains around the bed and letting in a shaft of light. 'Did I hear you talking to yourself just now?'

'First sign of madness.' James half-grins at her. For the first time I notice that his flirt gene is still working. Which is a sign that he's on the mend. And what's even better, it doesn't bother me the way it used to. A sign that I'm finally over him. OK, so it took a lot to get here, but better late than never.

The nurse disappears off, and James flops back on to the pillow, still ghostly white.

'The single greatest eye-opener in the world,' he whispers, 'is to find yourself at your lowest ebb and realize that you have no one to help you back up. No one. It's the loneliest place to find yourself in, and then lying here . . .' He breaks off, indicating the general horribleness of the cubicle we're in. '. . . Really hammers it home. I know an awful lot of people, and not a single one would lift a finger to help me. Not a pleasant thing to have to face up to at my age. In fact, I've been lying here wondering which lever to pull to get crushed by a safe.'

'Well, you don't get wake-up calls any louder or clearer than this. Maybe it's time for you to start building bridges with people. You know what? You should do out a karma list.'

'A what?'

'You know, a karma list. You write down the name of anyone you may have wronged, or in your case, shafted, then you figure out how you can make it up to them. Think of all those people you called looking for money that turned their backs on you. Then figure out how you can make amends to them.'

'Are you kidding me? That shower of bastards?'

'No. *Wrong* attitude. For instance, you called your brother, Matthew, and he wouldn't help you. So you need to ask yourself why, then pay your karma forward. Make it up to him. He's the only brother you have, after all. No row is worth falling out with family over. Why did you argue with him, anyway?'

'Over you, as it happens.'

For a split second, my heart stops.

'One Christmas. He had a go at me for the way I was treating you. We'd just had a row at my parents' house about . . .'

'Don't.' I stop him, shuddering at the memory of what I used to put up with. I remember that particular row too: it was Christmas Eve, and he never came home, even though I'd a dinner all prepared for him, me, Mum, Kate and Paul. The plan was, we were all to eat, and then go to midnight Mass together. Not only did James stand us all up, but then he added insult to injury by spinning me a yarn about how he'd crashed out on some pal's sofa, had no batteries on his phone to call, etc., etc., etc. The row continued right up till New Year's Eve, if I remember, and it was horrible, ugly and awful. But bless Matthew for sticking up for me.

It's just a shame I didn't have the guts to do it myself when I was alive, that's all.

'No, I guess I wasn't exactly boyfriend of the year, was I?' he says, accurately reading my thoughts.

'It's not too late. You can pay all this forward. Be good to Matthew, and remember blood is thicker than water. And then there's Declan. Kind-hearted, hard-working Declan who did nothing only slave away for Meridius Movies, and got rewarded with a kick in the teeth. And all for what? For telling the truth about the book option to that ex-priest guy? Can you blame the poor guy for quitting?'

'Don't remind me,' he groans. 'I was a complete shit to him, wasn't I?'

I nod, then remember that he can't see me.

'You can apologize, James. Remember, it's never too late to start over. It's too late for me, but not for you.'

'What did you just say?'

'I don't know what you'll go on to do with your life, but I do know this much. You will never again be at rock bottom if you just treat people a little better. Trust me on the karma list.'

'No, I mean what did you mean by saying it was too late for you?'

'. . . Which brings me to Sophie,' I barrel over him. 'Now she may not be my favourite person, but she did save your life. Treat her well, James. Better than you did me. You can do it, I know you can.'

Then I glow a bit here, reflecting on just how far I've come. When I first heard about him and Sophie, I wanted to machine-gun the pair of them down in a hail of bullets, but now . . . now I'm cool with it. Better than cool.

I'm OK.

I've healed.

'You can be such a charmer when you choose to be,' I go on pontificating. 'When you turn on the full megawatt force of that natural magnetism you have, you're incredible. You've been so gifted in life, and you've everything going for you. Just stop using all that charisma to further your career, or else trying to cajole some girl to go to bed with you . . .'

Funny, I could even say that, and it didn't hurt a bit. Amazing.

'. . . be kind for no reason. Be kind even when there's nothing in it for you. And you'll never hit that rock bottom again.'

'I . . . I will try.'

'Promise?'

'Promise.'

'Worth dying just to hear you say that. And, from my point of view, if you can start treating the people around you a bit better, then maybe I won't be such a useless failure of an angel, after all.'

He sits propped up on both elbows, and the weird thing is, even though he can't see me, he's looking right at me.

'Charlotte?'

'Yes?'

'What the fuck are you talking about?'

'Well, it's a long story, but we angels aren't entirely unsupervised, you know. There's, like this boss who we all have to report to, and I'm telling you, you SO don't want to get on her wrong side . . .'

'Did you just use the word *angel*? Did you say it was worth dying to hear me promise to try and be a bit nicer to people for a change?'

'What's wrong with me saying that?'

'Well, nothing, apart from the fact that you're not dead.'

I look at him in shock.

'WHAT did you just say?'

'Charlotte, you're still in the coma. You never came out of it. At this moment, you're lying in an intensive-care unit. In this very hospital, if I'm not mistaken.'

Chapter Twenty-Six

It's total crap. James is wrong and that's all there is to it. He *has* to be. I can't even answer him. I'm reeling with shock. Stunned and numb, I leave him and desperately try to focus on someone else. Mum or Fiona or Kate, anyone. But it doesn't work. The old charm of thinking about someone one minute, then magically being beside them the next, is gone. No matter how hard I try. So I run from James and walk, sorry, make that *stagger* down the hospital corridor. No one looks twice at me, even though I can see all of them clear as day. An angel's passing by, and no one knows. I somehow make it to the reception desk and ask if there's a Charlotte Grey registered, but of course, the receptionist can't hear me, and just keeps on typing. Then I see the hospital layout written out behind her, with signs and arrows pointing in about a dozen different directions.

There it is, intensive-care unit. Level three, ward two.

So I somehow stumble to the lifts, which have reflective doors, but I can't see myself in them, even though I'm standing right in front of them.

You see? James got it arseways, that's all. He'd just had his stomach pumped, and he wasn't thinking straight. Out of his head on sedatives, more than likely. Of course I'm dead. Of *course* I am. I'm an angel, for Jaysus' sake, aren't I? The lift doors trundle open and in I go. It's packed, but no one makes eye contact with me.

'Excuse me, but can anyone here see me?' I shout at decibel level, to total silence. The only time they all react is when an elderly lady's mobile goes off, and she starts having a full-blown conversation right into the phone, at the top of her voice, causing everyone around her to wince. Even a guy with an iPod on, at its highest volume.

'HELLO? YES, LOVE, I GOT PARKING, OK. WHAT? CAN YOU SPEAK UP? I'M IN THE LIFT. I'M ON THE WAY. I SAID I'M OOOOOON MY WAAAAAAY.'

The doors open and we're on the third floor. And there it is, a sign directly above me.

INTENSIVE-CARE UNIT.

Except there's a door, which, of course, I can't open. So I wait for an orderly wheeling an empty trolley to come out, and slip in. Down the long corridor I go, racing into any ward with an open door, looking for . . .

Oh, this is ridiculous. Looking for what, myself? If I wasn't so traumatized, I'd laugh. I know that James is drugged out of his head and got everything wrong, and I just want confirmation, that's all.

I pause for a minute at the nurse's station, and that's when I see them coming towards me.

Mum and Kate.

Kate's carrying a pile of CDs and Mum's balancing two take-out cups of tea, one in each hand.

OK, I think I'm going to faint.

I stand right in front of them, and call out to them, but they stride right past me, not even interrupting their chat, not for a second.

'You look very tired this morning, love,' Mum is saying. 'You should have had a lie-in. Sure, I could have come here myself. I'm well used to it by now.'

'No, you're fine,' Kate sighs, exhaustedly. 'I don't like you visiting her on your own. You should have someone with you.'

'So how did you get on with Paul's family last night? Did you tell them about the Mass for Charlotte?'

'Em . . . no, I didn't get around to it. They all went off to a concert, and I ended up babysitting.'

'Are you all right, love?'

'Fine,' Kate says crisply, in that slightly narky tone she gets when she doesn't want to be drawn into talking about something. 'Last night was . . . oh look, it doesn't matter. Come on, let's go in.'

Numbly, I follow them.

They open the door of room 201 and go inside. And there I am. For real. Lying on the bed with a ventilator covering my face, my leg in plaster and my head completely covered in bandages. I'm cut and bruised all over, with stitches on every visible piece of skin. There's even a bolt on the side of my head.

I look like Frankenstein's monster.

Mum and Kate don't bat an eyelid, though, like they're just used to me, from God knows how many visits. Instead Kate puts on a CD, the soundtrack to the *Sex and the City* movie. And Mum starts talking to me and massaging my hands, quite normally. And I just stand at the foot of my own bed, flabbergasted. Knocked for six.

All this time, when I'd overhear people talking about me in the present tense . . . I put it down to them not being able to accept that I was dead and gone. While I was here the whole time. And when they'd all say how upset they were, I assumed it was because they were grieving . . . whereas it was because I was still in a coma.

I am such a moron.

'So, love, how are you today?' Mum asks cheerily. 'Fiona rang, by the way, to say that she'll be in after school this afternoon. Says she's loads of boy news for you. And that she's been having the oddest dreams about you all week.'

'That's funny,' Kate says, clicking on the CD player. 'So have I.'

Then, just as 'How Can You Mend a Broken Heart' by Al Green and Joss Stone comes on, I pass out.

Chapter Twenty-Seven

'Charlotte? Charlotte, can you hear me? It's OK, pet, you're safe.'

It's the word pet that brings me round. Because there's only one person in the world who ever calls me that.

And when I open my eyes, it turns out I'm right.

Dad is right beside me, holding my hand tight and looking at me, the picture of concern.

'I don't get it, I just don't get it,' I keep saying over and over. 'I'm alive? All this time, I never actually died?'

'Shhhh, shhhh, pet. Everything's fine. You've had a bit of a shock, that's all.'

'No offence, but I'd have had less of a shock if I'd just gone and stuck two fingers into a plug socket. What's going on, Dad? I don't mean to be over-inquisitive or anything, but would you please mind telling me whether I'm dead or alive? If it's not too much bother, that is.'

He takes a moment before answering, which gives me a chance to look around and see where exactly I am.

Oh, for Jaysus' sake.

Back in the old folks' home. In what looks like the day-care room. Except we're alone, sitting on a brown corduroy sofa in front of the TV, which thankfully is switched off, so there's no daytime racing on. At least.

'Let me try to explain,' Dad begins, slowly and calmly. 'At this moment, your poor little body is lying in what I believe is called a medically induced coma. The swelling to your poor brain after the accident was so huge that your doctors felt this was your only chance.'

'Dad, how do you know?'

'Because I was there.'

I look at him, in complete and utter bewilderment.

'But . . . but you never told me. That all along I was alive, the whole time.'

'Oh, pet, I know this is hard for you to hear, but let me try to explain where I was coming from. After the accident, when you first came here, remember how I told you this was an assessment area? And how worried you were about it?'

'Yeah, but . . .'

'. . . and I told you that your assessment would happen in good time?'

'Yes, of course . . .'

'Well, you've just completed it, pet. And now, a final decision has been made.'

Now I don't feel faint any more, I feel nauseous.

Panicky. Dreading what's going to happen next. Worse than waiting on *X Factor* results.

'Tell me,' I manage to stammer, weak as a kitten. 'Please, just tell me.'

A long pause. All I'm aware of is my heart battering against my ribcage.

'It's been decided that you'll go back.'

'Back to . . . my old life?'

'Pet, hear me out. You came to us here when you were still in a coma, and that's why you had to be assessed. So it could be decided whether or not you were *ready* for death. Ready to join us on this plane, that is. Ready to be a wise angelic presence. What we thought was that, by revisiting your life and all of the people you'd left behind, you would in time, come to see that, actually, you'd so much to live for. And what better way to do that than as an angel? That's why I sent you to Regina. That's why you went on the AWE programme. It was important that you could see for yourself what a wonderful life you really had all along.'

'So being an angel . . . *was* my assessment?' There was me thinking it was just something to do to pass the time and get me out of the old folks' home.

'That's right, pet.'

'But I was completely useless, wasn't I? A big, rubbishy, useless failure. I failed my assessment, like I failed every other assessment I ever sat in my life.'

470

'No, not useless, and certainly not a failure.' He smiles in that slow, gentle way he has. 'Never that. It's been decided that it's just not your time, that's all. That you still have your whole life's purpose ahead of you to fulfil. But look how far you've come, pet. When you first came here, you felt you had nothing to live for any more, remember? Now . . . well, you can see for yourself just how loved you are down there, can't you? Yes, so maybe a relationship didn't work out, but there are so many other reasons why it's wonderful news that now you get to go back and start all over again. Why this is absolutely the right thing for you. Do you see now?'

The funny thing is that I do. Shell-shocked and all as I am right now, I can see what Dad is saying makes total sense. I know, just know in my heart and soul, that my going back is . . . as it should be. I remember back to how raw and emotional I was when I first came here, when all I could eat, drink, sleep or think about was James and how ill-used I'd been. But now, when I think about him, I feel nothing. No, that's not true, I feel . . . pity. And hopeful that he'll try to behave a bit better from now on. But nothing else.

Which, given the state I was in when I first came here, is kind of a minor miracle.

'So, do you see, pet? I couldn't tell you that you were still alive, because if your assessment had gone the other way . . .'

471

He doesn't even need to finish that sentence. We're both thinking it. If I'd been any use as an angel, then I'd have got to stay. Really die, this time, that is.

Jaysus.

'But . . . but . . .' I stammer. 'What about Regina? I mean . . . the last time I saw her, when I was . . . hauled back up here, she was . . .' I stop short of saying what I really want to, which is, 'she was completely vicious to me', and trail off with, 'she was . . . well, let's just say she gave me a right earful about making such a mess of things.'

Dad smiles. 'Yes, pet, she mentioned that she might have been a little hard on you, all right.'

'A *little*?'

'From the very start, though, she felt that you weren't ready to join us here. That it just wasn't your time. After she'd spoken to you, she even sent you back to Earth again, to give you a second chance. Just to be absolutely certain. And . . .'

'And she was right,' I finish the sentence for him, my mind still reeling. 'So . . . I wasn't actually being assessed for heaven or hell at all, was I? The whole time, I was being assessed for . . . for . . . life or death.'

Good Jesus. I'm starting to tremble all over again. Completely shocked at just how close I came.

'But, Dad . . .' I eventually manage to croak.

'Yes, pet?'

'There's something I don't get. When Regina sent me back that second time, I . . . well, I really did try my hardest. Honestly, I didn't interfere or play God. I even managed to be nice to James.'

'I know you did, Charlotte. Try to understand though: in spite of all your best efforts, it's just been decided that you have more, so much more, to live for than to die for. The world is a better place with you in it, and not over on this side. At least not yet. Not till it really *is* your time to join us here.'

Then Dad looks at me, keenly. 'What are you thinking, pet? I hope you're not unhappy about this?'

'No, not at all.' I manage to smile at him. 'I was thinking about Kate and Fiona and Mum and how . . . how, over the last while, all I've wished for is that I could be there for them. I felt so heartsore and useless that all I could do was look on at them and do nothing. So many times in the last while, I've wished for this; wished I was still alive, that is.'

'Well, your prayers were heard. Now you know that the door is open, pet. You can go back anytime you like. Just say the word.'

I have never felt such a conflict of feelings in my whole life, death, whatever you call this no-man's-land I'm in now. I'm . . . thrilled that I get a second chance at life, because how many people in this world get to say that? But . . . there's something else. Something so painful that I don't know if I can even say it aloud. Without bawling crying, that is.

'Dad . . . I know that I messed up really badly when I was meant to be lighting, guarding, ruling and guiding. I failed my assessment, but now . . . the worst part is . . . now . . . now I have to say goodbye to you.'

'Oh, my little Charlotte. Don't you remember me telling you? I could never leave you, and I never will.'

And that's when the tears start rolling.

I heave and gulp back a fresh load of tears. I think about Mum, and how much I miss her. How overjoyed I know she'll be to see me open my eyes in that hospital bed and come back to her. Then I think about Kate, and this time the tears turn to full-on sobbing.

Dad's read my mind.

'Kate will be just fine, you know, pet. Her heart will heal, just as yours did. She'll make such a wonderful mother, and has great happiness ahead of her. Few people on the mortal plane are ever lucky enough to know the great happiness that Kate will. But in the meantime, I know she could certainly use having her little sister around.'

I take a minute to wipe my eyes.

'And while you're back there, maybe it's time to think about following your dream,' Dad says encouragingly. 'Be a producer. You've always wanted to do it, and I know you can. It would work, you know.'

He's gripping my hand now, and what's weird is that some of his confidence is somehow slowly starting to seep into me.

'It would? For real?'

'Within five years, pet, you will be one of the most successful producers in town. And I'll be watching over you. Every single step of the way.'

A surge of excitement comes over me. It might just work. I might just be able to achieve my dream. No more Miss Useless Failure going nowhere in a dead-end job. I could go into partnership with Declan, could start pitching to TV studios . . . I could do something I love. And best of all, I could be with my loved ones while I'm at it.

'This is the right thing, I know. It's just that . . .' I say, welling up all over again. 'Well, when I go back, Dad, I won't see you again, will I?'

Call me unmitigatingly selfish, but I'm a great one for wanting to have my cake and eat it. Plus, what'll I ever do without him?

'But I'll see *you*, pet. Every single day.'

Suddenly, out of nowhere, our surroundings start to fade, as the light begins to get brighter and brighter, warmer and whiter. Pretty soon, I can't see the old folks' home any more, everything is just a big, blinding glare. No more brown corduroy sofas, or TV or stair lifts.

Just whiteness. Blinding whiteness.

'It's time, pet. Time for you to go.'

I hug him so tight I think I'll never let him go.

'Oh, Dad. What will I do without you? What did I ever do without you?'

'Remember what I told you, pet. I never could leave you, and I never will.'

'I love you so so much. I'll never meet a man who can hold a candle to you.'

'Oh yes, you will, my little pet. And an awful lot sooner than you think.'

'Goodbye, my darling Dad,' I sob, actually able to feel my heart breaking.

'It's never, ever goodbye, pet. Because I'll be right here.'

Next thing I'm aware of, I'm lying on my hospital bed, still gulping back the tears from saying goodbye to Dad.

Mum is here, and Kate is here, and I can feel them holding on to one of my hands each.

Somehow, I manage to open my eyes.

And, just like that, I'm back.

Acknowledgements

Huge thanks, as ever, to Marianne Gunn O'Connor, amazing agent, amazing friend and an amazing human being. Oh, and, by the way, she's *officially* the hardest-working woman in the Northern hemisphere. I'm also lucky enough to have THE most wonderful editor in Francesca Liversidge, whose brilliance and kindness are legendary among all her Irish 'family'. Visit soon, please!

Thanks to the incredible team at Transworld, especially Larry Finlay, Joanne Williamson, Madeline Toy, Sarah Roscoe, Jessica Broughton, Gary Harley, Martin Higgins, Kate Tolley and Vivien Garrett. I am so grateful to you for your hard work and support. Thanks also to Eoin McHugh and Lauren Hadden at Transworld Ireland; it's such a pleasure to work with you all.

Huge thanks to all the team at Gill Hess: Declan Heeney, Simon Hess and Gill – the man himself. And, of course, to my friend Helen Gleed O'Connor; going on book signings with you somehow never feels like work!

A very special hi to Pat Lynch; what would any of us do without you? And to the fabulous Vicki Satlow, who's always so positive and encouraging when I tell her my half-baked ideas and who does such an incredible job. And who knows? Maybe Morag Prunty and I will be allowed back to Italy very soon . . . hee, hee . . .

A huge thank you to Wendy Finerman in the US, an incredibly gifted and visionary lady who it's my absolute pleasure to work with. And to Robin Swicord and Liza Zupan for all their tireless hard work in getting *I Never Fancied Him Anyway* to the screen. You are all so talented and inspirational and I'm deeply indebted to you.

Special thanks to all at HarperCollins in New York, especially Carrie Ferron, Claire Wachtel, Julia Novitch and Tessa Woodward. See you all very soon, I hope. Thanks also to Karen Glass and a special hi to Drew Reed at Fox . . . hope you'll come to Ireland very soon!

On a personal note, thanks as always to Mum and Dad, Richard, Patrick, Sam, Clelia Murphy, Clara Belle Murphy, Susan McHugh, Sean Murphy (and Luke too!), Karen Nolan, Larry Finnegan, Isabelle and Miss Caroline, Marion O'Dwyer, Alison McKenna, Frank Mackey, Fiona Lalor, Sharon Hogan, Sharon Smurfit, Cathy Belton, Karen Hastings, Kevin Reynolds, Derick Mulvey, Rory Cowen, Weldon Costelloe, and all the Gunn family.

A very special thank you to four amazing ladies: Patricia Scanlan, Anita Notaro, Amanda Brunker and

Morag Prunty. Always on the other end of the phone and always available for fry-up brekkies and massive brain-storming sessions.

And . . . drum roll for dramatic effect . . . thanks to my wonderful friend, Pat Kinevane. If you ever decide to write a novel, Pat, you'll put us all out of business!

Finally, to all the readers out there who have supported me from day one and who've sent such gorgeous, encouraging letters and messages; in these troubled times, I'm deeply humbled whenever anyone forks out their hard-earned cash to buy something I've written, so a very sincere and heartfelt thanks to you all.

I'm so blessed to have you and am praying you'll enjoy this one too . . . xxxxxxxx

DO YOU WANT TO KNOW A SECRET?
by Claudia Carroll

Vicky Harper is still hopelessly single and having to face up to the unpalatable fact that the last time she had a relationship with that highly elusive species, the decent single man, was *well* before *Phantom of the Opera* hit Broadway.

So, having discovered an ancient book which says you can have anything you want from the Universe . . . and that all you need do is ask, she decides to give it a whirl. Turns out all she has to do is focus on *thinking* her wildest fantasies into reality. Kind of like Pollyanna, except with a Magic 8 Ball, a mortgage and a *lot* of vodka.

So, along with her two beyond-fabulous best friends, Vicky decides to put 'The Law of Attraction' into action. Trouble is, 'The Law of Attraction' doesn't come with an instruction manual and Vicky soon realizes that you have to be very, very careful what you wish for . . .

9781848270244